The Ki

CW00501719

For G

Rosemary Hayes

with best wishes,

Rosemary Hayes

Nov. 23

Cover: This painting by the 19th century artist, Jan Antoon Neuhuys, is an imagined scene of Huguenots fleeing France long before the time of this story. However, it perfectly illustrates the anguish of a family forced to choose between their God and their country.

This book is dedicated to the memory of the author's Huguenot
ancestors
Lidie and Samuel de la Fargue

THE KING'S COMMAND

La Tremblade, Spring 1691

The smudge on the horizon. Surely it was only a low cloud or the top of a distant wave? Lidie rubbed her eyes.

I am overwrought and bone weary. My mind is so confused that I am imagining things.

But when she looked again, it was taking shape.

The fisherman was fully engaged in keeping the boat on course, fighting with the wind and the waves. Lidie moved over to him and tugged on his arm, shouting a warning, but the wind snatched away her words, so she pointed.

He turned his head.

'Merciful Christ,' he muttered and immediately altered course, going about so abruptly that the party was pitched from one side of the boat to the other.

Lidie's mother had not heard the man's words but she raised her eyes to the horizon. What had been a mere smudge only minutes ago was now clearly defined as a ship and it was heading in their direction.

'What vessel is it?'

The fisherman didn't answer so Lidie once again tugged on his arm.

He yelled over his shoulder. 'It is one of His Majesty's frigates. Hide yourselves, for pity's sake. Cover yourselves with the old sails in the bulkhead. Hurry or we shall all be taken.'

The two women looked at one another and Lidie muttered a quick prayer. She glanced back to the English vessel, still anchored in the lee of the island, becoming smaller now as they sailed away from it.

So close! We had nearly reached it.

But now the fisherman was heading his craft in the direction of La Rochelle.

'Hide!' he shouted.

Lidie and her mother crawled around in the bottom of the boat, pulling some old sails out of the bulkhead. The children watched them, Esther awake now and whimpering and little Jean shaking with fever. Only Elias was still, his eyes wide and his fists clenched.

'We shall all lie under the sails and see how quiet we can be,' said Lidie trying to keep her voice steady as she and her mother pulled the children down and started to cover them, but Esther immediately shrieked in protest and fought to free herself.

Then, as her screams grew in intensity, Elias grabbed her arm and shook her.

'Be quiet,' he hissed. 'Stop your noise!'

The child was so taken aback that she ceased her screaming and sobbed quietly, her thumb wedged in her mouth.

When they were all covered by the sails, Lidie spread her arms so that each of her three children could feel her touch.

'Lie as still as stones, children,' she said. 'Make no sound, I beg you. If you cry out we shall be discovered.'

There was no chance that they could outpace the oncoming frigate. The fisherman knew this and took no avoiding action, indeed he sailed deliberately towards it. The minutes passed while the frigate drew ever closer and the little party lay still at the bottom of the boat. Then, as their teeth chattered with the cold and sea water swirled around their bodies, they heard the frigate hailing them.

'Whence are you bound?' came the shout over the water.

The fisherman glanced down at his firearm.

THE KING'S COMMAND

Chapter One

Castillon sur Dordogne Summer 1680

Lydia Brunier's underskirt swirled around her legs as she bounded down the wooden stairs, holding her upper gown and train with one hand, until she landed on the stone floor of the vestibule. She crossed the floor and reached for the handle of the thick studded door which led to the street outside but then she hesitated and turned back to look in the mirror.

Mama didn't encourage vain preening, but Lidie's heart beat a little faster as she smiled back at her reflected image, distorted slightly in the uneven glass.

She glanced quickly round but there was no one to observe her so she tilted her head to one side. She could see more of her image now and of the womanly curves accentuated by the close-fitting bodice.

I look so grown up in these silks. All the company are sure to remark. I wish I did

not blush so readily.

She and her mama had chosen the material when the Master Silk Weaver visited the house last year and left the pattern book with them. Strangely it had been the pastor, Pierre Gabriac, who had made up their minds for them. He had bent down and slowly turned over the pages, frowning as he scrutinized each one in turn. Then he'd pointed.

'There. That one is perfect for her complexion. And that other one there, perhaps, for the underskirt.'

Mama had laughed. 'My dear Minister,' she had said. 'I would never have taken you for a man of fashion!'

Pierre Gabriac had smiled. 'Ah Madame, you forget that I studied in Saumur; impossible not to acquire an eye for colour in that city of master tailors.'

Later, when he had taken his leave, Mama had said. 'Do you know, Lidie, I think he is right.' Then, under her breath, 'I wonder he can have time for such frivolities when he has so many other worries.'

The dressmaker's work had been exquisite and the silks looked even better than Lidie could have hoped, with the low waisted underskirt of the palest water satin and the sleeves and bodice of the upper gown of green trimmed with fashionable ribbons and lace.

Her first silks, to be treated with the utmost care and only to be brought out on special occasions. She had never before worn such finery.

'Bonne anniversaire, mam'selle!'

Lidie whipped round and squinted into the gloom at the far end of the room.

'Annette, you startled me!'

Carefully, the woman set down the pitcher of water she was carrying then crossed the floor to stand in front of Lidie. Her lined face under her white cap split into a grin.

'Sixteen,' she said. 'How is it possible? How did you become a lady in fine silks?

How did you grow up so quickly? Why, I remember when you were born, a sickly, pale little creature, and we feared you'd not survive and we prayed day and night that you'd not go the way of the others before you, God rest their little souls, and then the good Lord heard our prayers and…'

Lidie stopped listening. She leant forward and touched the ornate pattern at the edge of the mirror. She remembered the day her father had brought it back with him and how her mama had been secretly thrilled. despite protesting that he was fostering vanity. He had just laughed and embraced her, saying that the mirror was a thing of beauty, like her, and they should both be cherished.

They had been so happy then, only two years ago. When her father was away on his frequent trips. the house had settled into routine quietness, waiting for his return and then, when he came back, his boots clanging across the stone floor, the house expanded again and burst into life to accommodate his physical presence and his warmth and enthusiasm.

But everything was changed now. His noisy cheerful presence was gone for ever and the house had lost its sense of expectancy and become a place of uninterrupted order and serenity.

He had died just over a year ago, from the Viennese plague, in a foreign city away from his family.

Papa should be here with us for my birthday celebrations. He should be at the centre of them, laughing and rubbing his hands, teasing me and my cousins, welcoming all his friends and making sure that no one felt left out.

And no doubt embarrassing me, too!

'Miss Lydia! Mam'selle!'

'Annette, I'm sorry. I …'

Annette rolled her eyes. 'Not listened to a word,' she muttered, then, louder, 'I said to come into the kitchen and see what is prepared. It is all ready to take over to the big house.'

'It will be wonderful, Annette, but I'm already late. I promised cousin Cécile that she would be the first to see my new silks. I'll tell them the food is ready.'

Lidie headed for the door to the street and it was only then that she noticed the figure of a young girl lurking in the shadows in the far corner of the room. She frowned, not recognising her.

'Who is this?'

Annette glanced in the direction of the child. 'Your new maid,' she said.

'What! Mama told me nothing of this.'

Annette looked discomforted. 'Ah … it's a sorry story …'

Lidie sighed. 'Well I have no time to listen to it now,' she said firmly. She reached the outside door, flinging it open and letting the strong afternoon sun flood in briefly, lighting up the grey stone slabs on the floor, before slamming it shut behind her. Outside, one of the male servants stood ready to accompany her the short way down the street to the big house.

Annette addressed the closed door. 'Huh! She gets more like her father every day!' But she was smiling as she turned away to close the shutters against the heat of the afternoon, then she picked up the pitcher of water and went through the far door into the kitchen.

The young maid scuttled after her.

5

Lidie paused briefly on the steps, her eyes adjusting to the harsh light. She was very conscious of her new finery as carts rumbled by and a group of women stopped their gossiping for a moment to stare at her. She smiled at them and as she did so she felt the colour rising in her cheeks. Carefully, she made her way down the steps and into the street, picking her way across. Here in the pleasant faubourg, the streets were wider and cleaner than those in the town centre. Even so, she kept her eyes on the ground to be sure to avoid horse droppings or other muck which might stain her new slippers.

The male servant walked behind her.

Her cousin Cécile lived in a much bigger house only a little way further down the street, closer to the river, and as Lidie reached it and waited to be let in, she gazed at the great river Dordogne in the distance and had a sudden sharp memory.

She saw herself, with Mama, on the bank of the river, bidding Papa goodbye and wishing him God speed before he stepped onto a sailboat to take him downriver to Bordeaux from where he would set off on one of his long business journeys.

Then her thoughts were interrupted as the great door before her swung open and she was immediately being hugged by her cousin.

'Let me look at you!' said Cécile, drawing away from Lidie.

'My little cousin,' she said. 'You look beautiful! So grown up.' She fingered the lace at Lidie's sleeves and bosom. 'Is this the lace you spoke of?' And when Lidie nodded, Cécile went on. 'Oh it is so light and pretty. And without it,' she said, pointing at Lidie's chest, your bosom would be …' Then she started to giggle.

'It's not too immodest is it?' asked Lidie. Cécile took her hand and started to pull her towards the great staircase. 'Of course not,' she said. 'It is perfect. Very feminine.

Lidie was still blushing as they mounted the staircase and entered the main reception room of the house where she immediately found herself in the midst of a crowd of chattering relations. She looked around the room and spotted her mother. Sara Brunier was still erect and graceful, striking in a dress of darker silk which suited her well and although the underskirt was plain and low waisted, the overskirt was beautifully embroidered and trimmed with lace as were the cuffs of her elbow length sleeves and the neckline of her bodice. Her dark hair fell in ringlets down to her shoulders and was anchored at the front with a thin band of pearls.

She beckoned Lidie over. 'Is the food ready?'

Lidie nodded. 'Annette said to fetch it directly.'

'Excellent,' said Sara. 'I think everything is prepared here. It will all be set out in the library.' She pointed through the far door to the room beyond. 'The men have put two great tables in there and they have cleared furniture from this room for the dancing.'

Dancing! Lidie was still surprised that her mother and Aunt Louise and Uncle Jacob had agreed to allow dancing, although it would be of the most dignified kind. There would be no close dancing, no clasping of partners.

'Are you pleased with your silks, Lidie? They look well on you,' said Sara.

Lidie nodded and looked round the room. Great tapestries hung on the two main walls, woven in pale blues and browns. The elegant chairs which were set against the walls, clustered round little marble topped tables, were also covered in woven tapestry, all worked by a fine hand. On every one of the tables stood a candelabra filled with tall candles waiting to be lit when darkness came. The waxed wooden floor was bare, stripped of its rugs and chalked to prevent dancers slipping.

Although it was warm in the room, it was sweet smelling, for scattered around on every available surface and on the mantelpiece and within the great fireplace, were pretty pots full of a fragrant mixture of dried herbs and flowers which would help to hide the smell of human body odours.

Lidie sighed. 'You and Aunt Louise have thought of everything.'

'It has been a welcome distraction.' Sara turned to make an adjustment on one of the tables. 'Oh, and Louise tells me that they have also invited some of their friends from outside our town, and their sons and daughters.'

'I thought it was just …' Lidie frowned. 'I did not realise that there would be strangers.'

'That was my understanding, too, but your aunt has a generous nature. She loves an occasion, a chance to gather people round her.'

Lidie continued to look worried so Sara reached out and took her hand.

'I can see why they want to include others,' she said. 'Your anniversary is a good excuse for a gathering, not just to see our relations and friends but to hear news of the Reformists further afield. Some families from Montauban will be here I believe.'

Sara's face clouded for a moment at the mention of Montauban, once one of the main fortified centres of the Reformists, but now, like so many similar towns, indeed like Castillon itself, with its city walls destroyed on the orders of the King's father.

She released Lidie's hand and raised her voice to be heard above the chatter.

'Cécile, gather up your brothers and come and help bring the food over. Annette sent to tell us that it is all ready and we shall need many pairs of hands.'

There was much laughter and teasing as the cousins trooped back and forth between the houses, helping the servants bring food from Lidie's house to the kitchen in Cécile's house. The light was dim in the kitchen but it was a little cooler there now that the main baking had been done. The cook took the dishes from the young people and set them down on the great scrubbed wooden kitchen table then shooed everyone away, but Lidie and Cécile lingered and when Lidie glimpsed some of the sweet pastries and compotes she clapped her hands.

'They look so delicate,' she exclaimed. And, indeed, beside the fare that had come from her own house – the bread, cheeses, nuts and platters of viande – the pastries looked quite exotic.

'Cook has been trying out some new recipes,' said Cécile stretching out a hand to grab one but the cook glared at her. 'You'll have plenty of time to taste them later,' she said sharply. 'There's to be no thieving before the party. There's just enough to go round and none to spare; you know very well the cost of sugar and how hard it is to get supplies.'

8

Cécile grinned and licked her sugary fingers before fetching more muslin to cover the food on the table to keep the flies away.

Lidie smiled at the cook. 'It looks wonderful.'

'You can have a taste of the fruit drink if you wish,' said the cook and she took a ladle and poured a little of the drink from a tall pitcher into an earthenware mug for her. Lidie took it in both hands and sipped.

'What about me?' said Cécile, and although the cook sighed and clicked her tongue, she poured out a draught for Cécile as well.

'Not bad,' she said.

The cook flapped the cloth she was holding. 'Now be off with you, both of you. Take your drinks and get out of my way.'

Lidie and Cécile wandered out of the kitchen. Visitors were starting to arrive now and there was a crowd of chattering folk coming in from the street.

'All here to see you, Lidie,' said Cécile. 'You'll be the centre of attention.'

Lidie frowned and moved closer. 'I feel … I don't think I'm ready.'

Cécile smiled. 'Don't be shy, little cousin.' But when she saw the flush on Lidie's cheeks, she said, more gently. 'We'll go to the library for a while and you can finish your drink and compose yourself.'

Careful not to spill any of the fruit drinks and holding their over skirts free of the floor, they hurried up the main staircase, crept round the edge of the reception room and slipped into the library. No one else was there and the two large tables were bare, waiting to be covered in food and napery.

Lidie loved the library with its huge, intricately carved wooden bookshelves that rose up and met the ceiling, every shelf full of leather-bound books. When they were younger, while the boy cousins had attended the school attached to the temple, she and Cécile had learnt their letters here.

Cécile sat down on the edge of the great table and swallowed the rest of her fruit drink. She put her head on one side and looked at Lidie.

'You look very thoughtful.'

9

Lidie smiled and picked at the lace on her sleeves. 'It's just when everyone's happy and there's lots of noise and laughter…'

'Your papa?'

Lidie nodded. 'He always enjoyed a gathering.'

'He would have been at the street door to greet everyone,' said Cécile, 'and that loud laugh of his would have been heard right up here.' Then she got up and, pulling on Lidie's arm, guided her over to the long plain mirror which hung behind the wall sconce.

She took Lidie's face in her hands. 'Look at yourself,' she said. 'See how pretty you are in your silks. Your papa would have been so proud of you.'

Lidie turned away from the mirror. 'This is the second time today I have admired my image. Mama would not approve!'

Cécile giggled. 'I think we are the only Reformist families in the town to have mirrors and I warrant that your papa would rejoice that you take care with your appearance.'

Lidie bit her lip. 'You have all worked so hard to make preparations.'

'Then hold up your head and let's go and greet the guests!'

Lidie smoothed down her silks and straightened her shoulders then she and Cécile went back into the reception room where they were immediately surrounded by a crowd of relations and friends.

'Lidie, so grown up. See, we have a little gift for you!'

'Over here, Lidie. It's too long since we've seen you. What pretty silks. Such a delicate pattern.'

Everyone wanted to see her, embrace her, comment on her clothes, press little gifts into her hands. This was her first birthday celebration without her papa, her first birthday celebration wearing grown up silks and just for a moment she felt his absence so keenly that she could hardly breathe but then she saw her mother looking at her from across the room and she forced herself to smile.

Suddenly there was a noise at the door as some late arrivals entered the room. Aunt Louise and Uncle Jacob immediately went to greet them. Lidie looked to see who it was and frowned. She didn't recognize them.

10

'Ah, my dear Doctor Verdier,' she heard her Aunt say. 'How good it is to see you. And Samuel, too!'

'Apologies for our late arrival,' said Dr Verdier. 'Samuel's journey from Puylaurens was not without incident. He only arrived at the house half an hour since.'

'My goodness Samuel,' said Aunt Louise. A long journey for you indeed. But you are back here in Castillon for a while now?'

'Just for a month, Madame. Then I resume my studies.'

'Remind me what you are studying, Samuel,' said Uncle Jacob. 'The law, Sir.'

Aunt Louise frowned. 'Were you not destined to study in Montauban, Samuel?'

'Er, no Madame, I was always to go to the Academy in Puylaurens.'

Uncle Jacob smiled indulgently at his wife. 'You forget, Louise, the Montauban Academy was closed some years' ago.'

'Oh, how foolish of me, of course it was. It became …'

She didn't finish her sentence but Dr Verdier helped her out. 'You are right,' he said. 'It became impossible for students to study there. The atmosphere was hardly conducive to calm learning.'

'We are too wrapped up in the goings on in our own little town,' said Aunt Louise, quietly. 'We should be more alert to what is happening further afield.'

There was a beat of silence between them and then Uncle Jacob smiled. 'Let us not speak of such things now,' he said.

'No, indeed,' replied Dr Verdier. 'You are celebrating an anniversary, are you not?'

Yes, a sixteenth birthday,' said Uncle Jacob. He spotted Lidie and beckoned her over.

Shyly, Lidie walked over to her uncle.

'Lidie,' said Uncle Jacob, 'I don't think you have met my good friend Doctor Verdier and his son, Samuel?'

Lidie bobbed a brief ourtsey.

'My niece, Lydia,' said Uncle Jacob. 'The only child of my wife's widowed sister.'

Doctor Verdier smiled at her.

As was her habit when she met someone new, Lidie's eyes immediately went to their clothes. The good doctor was wearing a long well fitted coat of a sober dark blue, but the brocaded cloth was of a fine quality and there was a touch of frothy lace at his neck and wrists. His stockings were dark and he wore fitted shoes with a slight heel and although he wore a wig, it was not extravagant and suited his cheerful countenance. His costume met with Lidie's approval.

Samuel was less formally dressed than his father. He had a plain white cravat at his neck with a simple dark coat over a waistcoat with wide buttonholes. His breeches and stockings were also in a dark colour. He wore short boots on his feet and he was unwigged, his brown hair neatly tied back.

What a serious looking young man! I can see him as a lawyer, studying dusty tomes in some library.'

At last the food was served and Lidie found herself standing among her cousins while Uncle Jacob said grace, thanking God for the abundance of good food before them. Then he paused for a moment and quoted from the psalms.

I will sing praises unto my God while I have any being. Put not your trust in princes nor in the son of man in whom there is no help.

For a moment there continued to be a thoughtful silence and then Jacob invited everyone to sit down. Chair legs scraped across the wooden floor and the noisy chatter began again.

Annette's crusty newly baked bread with cheeses, viands and fruit sent up from the Brunier farm, were followed by the delicate pastries made by Louise and Jacob's cook and washed down with wines from their small vineyard on the Southern plains. Lidie had drunk wine from an early age, watered down liberally, as was the custom, but tonight there was to be no watering down and Uncle Jacob poured a measure of the sweet golden liquid into a glass for her. Then he clapped his hands.

'A toast to Lidie. Happy birthday, pretty niece, and may God protect you and may your life be joyous and pleasing to the Lord and continue to be full of friends and laughter.'

Lidie smiled and blushed as all eyes turned on her and the whole company raised their glasses and repeated. 'To Lidie.'

Lidie looked around her at all the familiar faces and felt secure in their love for her. Her Mama was in deep conversation with Dr Verdier and they seemed to be enjoying each other's company for Mama was smiling and, as Lidie watched, she saw her throw back her head and laugh at something the good doctor had said.

She looks a little more as she did when Papa was alive.

They lingered a long time over the meal and the shadows outside began to lengthen. Already they could hear the musicians tuning up their instruments next door in the reception room but still the older folk seemed reluctant to move. It wasn't until Aunt Louise got up from her place and went to whisper in her husband's ear, that anything happened. Jacob was looking very serious and talking earnestly with Pierre Gabriac, the pastor, and a friend of his from Montauban. He dragged his attention away from his conversation and focused on his wife. Then he smiled at her and stood up.

'We are so engrossed in our talk here that I had forgotten to urge you move next door,' he said. 'The musicians are already there, as you can hear, so let the dancing begin.'

In the reception room, the windows had been flung wide open and the candles lit. It was a pretty sight, with the last of the sun making liquid gold of the river in the distance and the soft candles glowing all around the room, their flames fluttering in the light breeze coming in from outside. The room was still full of the scent of the herbs and flowers and as the guests came through the doors from the library, the musicians struck up a lively gavotte to welcome them.

Cécile whispered to Lidie as they entered the room. 'Is it to your liking, Lidie?'

Lidie's eyes were shining. 'It's perfect,' she breathed, hugging her cousin. And then the musicians called for everyone to arrange themselves for the dance and once the lines had been organized, they struck up again, sedately at first, watching to see that the company knew the quick and coordinated steps incorporating the little hop on the upbeat which was such a feature of the dance.

Lidie and the others flung themselves into it with enthusiasm as the dancing pairs switched places. Once the musicians saw that the company understood the pattern of the dance, they increased the tempo; ladies' silks whirled and the gentlemen's feet stamped on the wooden floor and the flames of the candles trembled.

Sara Brunier was not dancing. She and Dr Verdier were sitting at one of the little tables at the edge of the room observing.

'It is a pretty dance, is it not?' she remarked.

Dr Verdier nodded. 'Very pretty and well executed, Madame.' He sighed. 'I am cheered that your families have not forbidden dancing as some of our brethren have, but how much longer will our children be able to enjoy these happy frivolities, I wonder?'

'I know. I worry so keenly for the future. There's not a month goes past without our people being subjected to yet more restrictions.'

The doctor turned in his seat and met her eyes. 'I always swore that I would never forsake our faith,' he said quietly. 'It would be a denial of all that I hold dear.'

'Nor shall I,' replied Sara. 'It would be a betrayal of my ancestors and all the freedoms they fought for in the wars of religion.'

Isaac Verdier nodded. 'My family have always been faithful to the Reformed cause and many of them lost their lives defending it, yet now...' He did not finish his sentence.

'And your son, Samuel, how does he feel?'

'He is of the same view. He assures me he will never abjure.'

Sara looked over at Lidie. 'I feel sure that Lidie will remain a true Reformist.' She turned back to the doctor. 'She is still very young but she has a sensible head on her shoulders and she has been well taught. I try not to burden her with my own fears but she will soon see for herself how things are changing for us.'

'Indeed, it would be a shame to dampen that charm and enthusiasm. She's a credit to you, Madame.'

They sat there in companionable silence watching the dancers weave in and out and skip and twirl across the room. When at last the musicians played the final bars of the gavotte, there was much laughter as the dancers dispersed to talk in groups or to fetch refreshment.

More lively dances followed, including the Farandole, where there was a skip and a hop in every other step, but the young people never seemed to tire and begged the musicians for more.

The sky outside had darkened and the town buildings leading down to the river were indistinguishable when at last the fiddle player held up his arm. 'You have worn us out,' he said, smiling. 'This shall be the last dance.'

There were cries of disappointment from the company but when they heard the unmistakable notes and rhythm of the minuet, a much slower dance, they came together again, this time reforming in couples.

'Come now,' said Isaac Verdier, scraping back his chair and holding his hand out to Sara. 'This is a stately dance, Madame. Will you do me the honour?'

At first Sara hesitated. 'It has been a long time, sir,' she began, but when Isaac continued to hold out his hand, smiling, she rose to her feet and took it. He led her forward and with the others, they formed a figure of eight on the floor.

And as they did so, she caught sight of Lidie, partnered for this most elegant of dances, with young Samuel Verdier.

After the minuet, the musicians put away their instruments and all the visitors, young and older, with all the household, assembled together to sing, quietly and unaccompanied, psalm 20, translated into the French language by the scholar Marot. The pastor, Pierre Gabriac, led them with his fine tenor voice muted so that they could not be heard from the street outside.

May the Lord answer you when you are in distress; may the name of the God of Jacob protect you. May He send you help from the sanctuary and grant you support from Zion. May He give you the desire of your heart and make all your plans succeed.

'Amen,' they all said.

'Amen indeed,' muttered Isaac Verdier, looking across at his son.

Chapter Two

It was no distance, but Jacob insisted on seeing Lidie and her mother back to their house after the party. The summer night was still warm, though the breeze coming up from the river had strengthened. Jacob held the lantern high so that they could see where they were walking. At the door of their own house, Jacob embraced them then went on his way.

Sara sighed and stretched. 'What an evening!'

'Umm,' replied Lidie, yawning. 'A birthday to remember.' She smiled. 'Did

you enjoy the company of Doctor Verdier, Mama?'

I did,' said Sara as she headed towards the stairs. 'He is a wise and compassionate man.'

She hesitated and seemed about to say more, but instead reached for one of the candlesticks on the chest at the bottom of the stairs and struck the tinder box to light the candle, then she started to climb up to her bedchamber, calling for her maid who emerged from the shadows, stifling her yawns.

'Do not linger, Lidie,' Sara called over her shoulder.

Lidie took another candle and went into the kitchen. It was dark except for the glow of the fire in the hearth. She poured herself a drink of water from a pitcher and sat down at the table, the candle throwing just enough light to give shape to the great dresser and reflect the shine of the large copper cooking vessels which hung on the wall.

She sat there for some time, re-living the evening - the food, the drink, the dancing and the company.

The company. Nearly all intimate acquaintances, nearly all people she had known all her life, people she felt easy with, though there were some new acquaintances, too, including Dr Verdier and his son. At first she had thought Samuel Verdier rather dull; he wasn't loud and lively like most of her boy cousins and she had dismissed him as being a dreary scholar, too attached to his books to be diverting. She'd not been surprised when he'd asked her to dance the minuet. After all, the party was in her honour and she supposed he was only being polite and doing his duty.

But she *was* surprised at how well he danced - and then he'd not excused himself afterwards but had stayed by her side talking to her while the company was beginning to break up. He'd asked her about herself, about what she enjoyed doing, and she'd been flattered. Even her beloved Papa had not bothered to discuss anything of more weight with her than childish things.

Lidie stayed in the kitchen for a while, occasionally fiddling with the melting wax at the top of the candle and then, yawning, she rose from her chair and left the kitchen. The young maid who she had seen earlier was curled up at the foot of the stairs, fast asleep.

Lidie frowned. Had Annette told her the girl's name? If so, she could not remember it. And why was this new girl to help her? Why was Annette not here?

Then she chided herself. Annette was no longer young and the celebrations had given her much extra work. She was no doubt exhausted. Lidie bent down to look at the maid, who could not be more than twelve or thirteen, and shook her shoulder.

The child awoke with a start and jumped to her feet. She attempted a clumsy curtsey while rubbing her eyes.

'Beg pardon mam'selle,' she muttered. 'I did not mean …'

Lidie cut her short. 'I'm sorry I have kept you so late,' she said. Then she added. 'Annette did not tell me your name.'

'Susanne,' said the girl, scrambling after Lidie as she mounted the stairs. 'Was it a good party, mam'selle?'

Lidie was surprised by the forwardness of the child and by her unfamiliar accent. She frowned: 'An excellent party Susanne, but now I am ready to retire.'

As Susanne helped her undress in the candlelit chamber, clumsily unlacing the silks and hanging them in the armoire, Lidie remembered Cécile's comments about her figure. She turned quickly to put on the shift which Susanne was holding out to her, discomforted by the girl's appraising stare.

When she had dismissed Susanne, Lidie climbed up onto the mattress on the four-poster bed, the bed ropes beneath her protesting even at her slight weight. She blew out her candle and lay back on the pillows, pulling the linen sheet up to her chin. A feather, loosed from the mattress stuffing, drifted down onto her face and made her sneeze. As always, before settling, she addressed her dead father.

'God bless you, Papa.'

It was late now and there wouldn't be many people still abroad, only one of the night watchmen passing by from time to time, keeping the townsfolk safe and alert to any whiff of smoke which might signal a fire breaking out among the wooden houses.

Lidie's head was full of thoughts of the evening and she lay awake for a long time before eventually falling into a deep and dreamless sleep.

But Susanne did not sleep. She stayed alert, curled up on the crude truckle bed set up for her on the landing outside, chewing at her fingernails.

When at last the house was still, she rose from her bed, wrapped a blanket round her shoulders and quiet as a mouse, crept down the stairs, her heart jumping in her chest when she stepped on a creaking board. She froze, listening for any movement, but nothing stirred and she continued to the bottom of the stairs and then tiptoed across the floor and into the kitchen.

At the back door she hesitated, listening again, then unlocked the door, the noise of the bolts drawing back exaggerated in the silence. The door creaked when she opened it and she stood rigid for a few more moments before slipping outside into the lane. The night was warm but she was shivering, and she wrapped the blanket tighter round her thin frame as her eyes adjusted to the darkness.

The back entrances of the grand houses here in the faubourg were not so impressive. Outside the door was a vat full of urine from the emptied chamber pots, ready for collection by men from the tannery, and the acrid smell hung in the air and made her eyes smart. She leant forward, turning her head to catch the slightest sound and straining to detect any movement.

He's not waited.

Then as she turned to re-enter the house, there was a sudden movement behind her and she gasped and whipped round as a figure emerged from the shadows, but when she recognised the man, her shoulders dropped and she relaxed.

'You startled me. I did not think you would wait.'

'Took your time, wench!'

She held the blanket even more tightly about her. 'There was a party,' she whispered. 'They were late to bed. I …'

He was right beside her now, leaning over her. She flinched, turning her head away from the smell of alcohol on his breath.

'How is it, child? Tell me how you find the household. Do they treat you well?'

***

Lidie had slept soundly until she was woken by Annette shaking her shoulder.

'Stir yourself, lazy bones. Your cousin is here and waiting for you.'

Lidie yawned and stretched.

Annette put a pitcher of water on the table under the window, beside a bowl. 'I hear your party was much enjoyed,' she said.

Lidie yawned again and then slipped out of bed. 'It was wonderful Annette. You should have seen all the fancy pastries and the pretty napery and the little bowls of herbs and flowers.'

'I heard about those pastries,' muttered Annette. 'Too fancy by half, I warrant. I don't doubt your digestion will suffer. Now hurry yourself and get washed and dressed. Shall I send young Susanne up?'

'No,' said Lidie.

She had not meant to sound so abrupt and Annette raised an eyebrow. 'I admit her manners are a little rough,' she said, 'But she will learn our ways soon enough.'

'You should have told me she had been hired, Annette. Where does she come from? What do we know of her?'

Annette frowned but she did not reply, turning quickly and leaving the bed chamber.

Lidie splashed water on her face and neck and put on a plain day dress of a light material, low waisted but with a much higher neckline than her finery of last evening and with short puffed and slashed sleeves. Over it she slipped a clean apron to protect the dress and then quickly brushed her hair and pinned it up, then slid her feet into her slippers and ran downstairs.

'Good morning sleepy head,' Cécile said, rising from a chair. 'All our servants are busy putting the house to rights, so Mama has asked me to get provisions from the market and I'm looking for company.'

Annette heard them talking and tugged at Lidie's arm. 'You are to go nowhere without breaking your fast, Mam'selle,' she said firmly. 'And then I suppose I'm expected to go with you to the market,' she muttered as she drew them both into the kitchen, where she had laid out freshly baked bread with honey.

'You missed morning prayers, Mam'selle' she went on, her face stern, 'So make sure you thank God for your food at least.'

Lidie bowed her head and said a quick grace and then gobbled down the honey soaked bread, eager to be outside. She licked her sticky fingers when she'd finished. Annette glared at her.

'What do you think that bowl is for?'

Lidie grinned and dipped her fingers in the small bowl of water on the table and then dried her hands on the cloth Annette held out for her.

'What would I do without you to chide me about my manners, Annette?' said Lidie, giving her a brief hug before running out of the kitchen.

Annette sniffed but then she smiled.

Cécile followed Lidie, snatching up her basket as they headed for the front door.

Sighing and clicking her tongue, Annette caught them up. 'Make sure you watch out for any Catholic procession! If they see us not bending the knee when they pass, we'll be in trouble.'

They made their way through the streets of the faubourg and up the hill towards the centre of the town. Here the streets were crowded and for a while they were kept back and had to wait in the sunshine while two carriages tried to pass one another in a narrow space, the drivers cursing and trying to manoeuvre their horses through to continue their journeys.

All around them was bustle and noise. There were street hawkers, men of business in earnest conversation and servants on errands for their masters, everyone taking care to avoid the evil smelling river of human and animal waste in the middle of the street which flowed sluggishly down the hill.

Lidie, Cécile and Annette joined a group of people heading up to the marketplace.

The market was full of noise and odours. Dogs were running this way and that between the stalls which had cloths strung above them to keep the goods in the shade. On one side of the square was the meat and poultry market, the butcher slicing from sides of pork and beef strung up behind him and the poultry sellers offering ducks and hens, either alive in wooden dome shaped cages or freshly killed, ready for the table. There were hawkers with trays of baked goods approaching likely buyers and on the other side of the market were stalls selling fresh herbs, fruit and vegetables brought over the river from the farms in the plains.

'I'm surprised Aunt Louise is in need of any victuals,' said Lidie, at the same time as shaking her head at a persistent hawker, 'You must have much left over from last night's feast.'

Cécile turned, raising her voice above the clamour. 'She sent the viandes back to your house,' she said. 'But she only needs a fowl for today – and a few more herbs and vegetables. Then we'll get some fish from that place near the river.'

Cécile chose a plump duck from one of the stalls, handed over some coins and stuffed the dead bird into her basket, its neck hanging limply over the edge. They walked past the butcher's stall where flies were swarming all over the carcasses hanging there, and went in search of vegetables.

Several times they saw people they knew and stopped to exchange a brief greeting but the day was heating up and they didn't linger. Once they were away from the market, the noise and smells lessened and they slowed their pace as they made their way down towards the river. Annette stopped and caught her breath for a moment while the young women walked on.

'Papa is in an ill humour,' said Cécile. 'He heard this that one of his business associates, Monsieur Boucher, has abjured. The news has truly unsettled him.'

Lidie stopped to mop her brow with a lace handkerchief. 'But your papa would never deny his faith?'

Cécile shrugged. 'Papa has much to lose if he does not abjure,' she said slowly, 'His land, his property, his business.' She looked down and absently stroked the feathers of the dead fowl in her basket, 'I suppose it may be safer to abjure than to face penury.'

'How can you say that! I know that Mama would never deny her faith.'

'But then she has not so much to lose, has she?' Cécile's voice was sharp.

Lidie did not answer and Cécile took her arm. 'We all have to live together, Lidie, Catholics and Protestants.'

As they walked on, Cécile leant in closer, smiling. 'I saw you deep in conversation with Samuel Verdier last night, little cousin. What was it that you were discussing?'

'I … we. He was asking me …' stammered Lidie.

Cécile laughed and drew away from her. 'You like him, do you not?'

'I like him well enough,' muttered Lidie.

'He seems a serious fellow. The family have land close to our farm and we see them sometimes at harvest time. My parents are very fond of his father.'

'What of his mother?'

'She died giving birth to Samuel; he is the only boy. His older sister is married and has a family of her own now.'

Lidie didn't reply but then Cécile voiced her thoughts.

'So, you have that in common. You have both lost a parent, though I think he's a bit serious for a gay young thing like you.'

'Cécile!'

But Lidie thought again of how she had been so easy with Samuel and the way he had smiled at her when they parted.

When they reached the banks of the great river Dordogne, all was noise and busy-ness once more. The Dordogne connected all the settlements up and down river and trade was brisk. The gabares, the large wooden flat bottomed boats transporting wood and slate, salt, wine and other goods were loading and unloading. Those going downstream to the great sea port of Bordeaux would complete the journey with all speed. It was work, though, for those going back upstream; men or beasts had to haul them, against the current, by ropes from the river banks.

There was a crowd of folk going hither and thither on the wide flat expanse of the river bank. There were wooden carts pulled by oxen and laden with casks, men on horseback riding in both directions, fishermen and sailors shouting and laughing, men and women selling their wares; fish and some of the goods unloaded from the gabares, as well as harness for animals and tackle for boats.

Lidie, Cécile and Annette headed to a stall at the far end of all this activity. They were greeted by the stallholder, a cheerful woman dressed in plain dark clothes with a white cap on her head and a white apron over her dress which was already soiled from her work, her hands red raw from gutting fish. She was familiar to them, being part of the Reformist congregation.

'Bonjour demoiselles,' she said. 'What can I get you today? We have shad and zander and a good many grayling and trout - and even some catfish. All fresh and newly caught.'

Lidie couldn't help drawing back as the woman picked up a huge catfish to show them, with its ugly great mouth and menacing whiskers.

Cécile chose a fat grayling and handed over a large piece of muslin and some coins.

The woman took the muslin and coins and as she was carefully wrapping the fish she asked 'How is your family, mam'selle?' And then, as Cécile was replying, she interrupted, saying quietly. 'And are we to meet again to pray this week?'

Cécile nodded. 'Of course, Madame.'

'In the same place?'

Cécile nodded again. 'As far as I know.

The woman sighed. 'I cannot believe that our blessed Lord would wish us to be so secretive. Surely He rejoiced when we sang psalms and praised His name so happily and openly. But now...' She looked about her and then leant forward and whispered. 'They say that our temple will be destroyed soon. That beautiful building

23

built with such loving hands. It makes me weep to think it may be pulled down.'

'Indeed, Madame,' said Cécile.

In the distance, they heard the sound of a bell ringing, signalling the passing of a Catholic procession. The girls looked at each other.

'Do not worry, demoiselles,' said the fish seller quietly. 'They will not pass this way.'

The woman's other customers were getting impatient and she turned to serve them.

'Is that true about the temple?' asked Lidie as they wandered away from the fish stall.

Cécile shrugged. 'Papa says that many in our region have already gone.'

'How can they …' Lidie began, but Cécile interrupted her.

'What do I know! There is no sense in any of it. Come on Lidie. Let's take the short way back.'

Lidie looked round. 'Where's Annette?'

Cécile pointed to one of the other stalls where Annette was gossiping with one of her acquaintances. 'She'll soon follow.'

As they walked along beside the river Lidie said. 'She's right, the lady at the fish stall. It was a happy time when we could all gather in the temple. Our pastor must feel sad.'

Aye. He's harassed by the Catholics all the time, and then there's his poor wife.'

'What is wrong with her? She is never seen abroad these days.'

Cécile pulled Lidie to one side to avoid stepping in some animal turds. 'They say that losing all those babies has affected her mind.'

'She's still young,' said Lidie. 'Maybe she will bring one to term yet.'

'Maybe,' said Cécile.

As they turned to walk up from the river towards the remains of the city ramparts, Cécile stopped and looked around her.

'It is all so familiar, is it not?'

Lidie frowned. 'Of course, it is our home.'

'Yet so many of our faith have gone to seek their fortunes in other countries.'

Lidie frowned. 'We would never leave!'

Cécile put down her basket and stretched her arms above her head. 'Aye, we Gascons are a stubborn breed, but this King vows to stamp out our faith.'

'But surely, down here in the South …'

Cécile rolled her eyes. 'Wake up girl! It was the King's man, the Intendant of the region who forbade our people to worship in public. Don't you recall the time when the curé and that Catholic mob came and forced us from the temple?'

Lidie did not reply though she remembered the incident well even though she had been so young. She remembered how the mob had burst in on them at prayer and how the congregation had had to flee from the violence of the pursuing Catholic crowd. She remembered, too, how her papa had picked her up and run with her in his arms towards the safety of their house in the faubourg.

They walked on, passing the stables where many of the richer townsfolk kept their horses.

Suddenly there was a loud shout just behind them and they looked round, startled.

Two men were chasing a third out of the stables, pushing him and shouting at him. The third man stumbled as one of the others drew his dagger yelling 'Bloody heretic,' and rushed at him trying to stop him getting free.

'I demand you give me back my money! That mare you sold me is slow as a donkey!'

The man being pursued staggered to his feet and broke away, then tried to reason with his attackers. 'Sirs,' he protested, 'The mare goes well. She is sound and healthy….'

'Blasphemer, unbeliever,' said his attacker, picking up a stone, 'You shall pay for this.'

The man started to run towards the river, but he staggered again as the stone hit the side of his head with a furious force and precision and even from a distance, Cécile and Lidie could see the blood spurting from his wound.

The two men began to laugh. 'Huguenot filth,' they shouted.

The girls looked on in horror. 'He is one of our brethren,' said Lidie. 'We should go and help him,' and she started to run to him, but Cécile grabbed her arm.

'Don't be a fool,' she hissed. 'See, he's on his feet again. He'll find his way home.'

'How can you be so heartless,' said Lidie, tugging her arm away. But then she glanced behind and saw the two men looking at them, leering.

'Friend of yours, is he?' said one, approaching them, swaying slightly.

The girls didn't answer and began to walk faster towards the ruins of the town ramparts where they knew they could squeeze through, but now the second man had joined his friend and they ran in front of the girls blocking their way.

'Where's Annette!' whispered Lidie, glancing behind her. Then she saw her, hurrying, as much as she was able, up from the river, but she was still some distance away.

'Little Huguenot maids,' said the first man. 'Ripe for the picking I warrant.'

'We could have some fun with them,' replied the other. 'They look to have pretty figures underneath those dresses.'

One of the men reached out and grabbed Lidie's breasts. She screamed and jumped back.

'Run,' said Cécile pulling Lidie after her. 'They're drunk.'

But the men continued to pursue them, shouting insults.

'Tight arsed little Huguenot bitches! Wait 'til we catch you. We'll have those undergarments off and fuck you senseless.'

The girls had never run so fast, gathering up their skirts and sprinting towards the main town, gasping for breath. They scrambled over the remains of the city wall and at last came upon a throng of people. Their pursuers finally gave up and staggered off, laughing and continuing to mutter obscenities. Lidie was in tears when at last they stopped to catch their breath outside a merchant's house. When Annette finally caught up with them she was red in the face and breathing heavily.

'You should have waited for me, mam'selles, I saw those men. If I had been with you …'

Lidie's dress was soiled and she was trembling.

Cécile took her hand. 'They were not from our town, Lidie. I warrant they were strangers passing through, but …'

'But what?'

'It will happen again,' she said. 'It's as if His Majesty himself is giving Catholics permission to torment us. Come, let us go home where we are safe.'

The three of them headed for the little bridge over the moat that led to the spacious streets of the faubourg then Cécile and Lidie went to their separate houses, Annette fussing behind Lidie as they climbed up the steps to the front door. To Lidie the day which had begun in such a carefree manner, suddenly seemed full of threat and she felt as if all the joy and happiness of the celebrations of the evening before had been squeezed out of her.

They entered the house and Annette, still muttering, headed to the kitchen but Lidie heard the sound of talking coming from one of the rooms downstairs and she recognized the voice of Pierre Gabriac. Feeling an urgent need for her mother's company, she walked into the panelled room with its great oak table in the centre and the family portraits hung on the walls.

Pierre Gabriac and Sara stopped speaking when Lidie entered. Pierre rose to his feet.

'Lidie, how good to see you,' he said. 'I was calling to thank your mama for last night's entertainment and to ask her if we may hold a service here in your house.'

Lidie swallowed, trying to compose herself, aware of her red face and dishevelled appearance.

'I hope you didn't feel it was too frivolous, Monsieur Gabriac?' she stuttered. 'I know that there are some of our faith who frown upon too much feasting and dancing.'

Pierre smiled. 'In these difficult times we all need a little distraction, Lidie. And that dancing master of yours has taught you well. It was a pretty sight to watch you all complementing the music in such an excellent manner.'

Sara interrupted. 'It is stifling hot today; I warrant the market was very crowded was it not?

Lidie nodded and changed the subject.

'How is your wife, Monsieur Gabriac? We were sorry she was not able to be with us last night.'

Pierre hesitated and frowned. 'She is not in good health at the moment, Lidie, but we pray that God will soon restore her strength.' Then he turned to Sara.

'I have taken up enough of your time, Madame. I must go about my business.' Then he made his farewells.

When he had left, Sara sighed. 'He's so young. It is hard for him to have such a sickly wife.'

They were both quiet for a moment and then Sara clapped her hands.

'What do you say to a visit to the farm?' she said. 'The wheat harvest will be under way and I should see how it is faring – and Louise tells me that they are all to spend a few days on their estate. It is so hot at the moment that it would be good to be in the countryside for a while, do you not think, Lidie?'

Lidie nodded. 'I should like that,' she said.

Away from the insults of men like those outside the stables.

'Good, then I'll tell Louise that we shall join them there when I've completed my business at our farm. They'll take their carriage, of course, but ours is being repaired so I'll see if we can hire one.'

Lidie's head jerked up. 'Don't go down to the stables yourself, Mama.'

'No, of course not. I'll send one of the servants.' Then Sara frowned.

'Why do you say that, Lidie? Has there been some trouble?'

'Nothing. It is of no matter.'

'Did you come back that way just now?'

Lidie stayed silent.

'What happened? Did someone insult you?'

Lidie nodded. 'Some drunk Catholics at the stables.'

Sara rose slowly to her feet and walked over to the wall to gaze up at the portrait of her husband. She stared at it for a few moments and then she turned back to Lidie.

'Since the end of the wars of religion our people have prospered and been loyal subjects of the Crown,' she said, 'But now…

Lidie looked down at her dress. It had snagged on the stonework when she had scrambled over the ramparts.

Will Annette be able to mend the damage?

Sara raised her voice. 'Your forebears lost their lives to protect their faith. It is well you remember that.'

'But all that was so long ago …'

Sara's eyes were hard. 'Not that long ago, Lidie. The horror of war stays long in the memory and both sides were guilty of atrocities.'

Lidie looked at the floor, remembering the taunts of the drunkards outside the stables and felt again those groping hands.

'I would not wish you to be ignorant, Lidie,' Sara continued, more gently. 'You may think that we are protected in our town where there are so many of our faith but   edicts are being announced all the time in the marketplace or by the curé at the Catholic mass and each one restricts our lives further. And your uncle tells me it is likely that Huguenot lawyers and doctors may soon find it hard to practise.'

Sara went on to speak about the power of their local Intendant, the instrument of the King in their region and of the many injustices at their local parliament.

Lidie had ceased listening, though one thing did register with her. The Verdiers, father and son, a doctor of medicine and a student lawyer. What might this mean for them?

Chapter Three

Isaac Verdier jerked awake as his carriage stopped outside his infirmary. He'd been up for most of the night, called to visit a woman in one of the nearby villages.

Protestant midwives had that very year been banned from practising their profession and it was unusual for a Catholic midwife to ask for Isaac's assistance.

It was the woman's eighth confinement and she'd been labouring for hours when he'd arrived. At first he feared that neither mother nor child would survive but she was at last delivered of a baby boy. Only two of her children had lived past infancy, but Isaac was hopeful that this one would survive longer, though the circumstances of the family were dire, as were so many of the peasants in the region.

He and the midwife had worked well together, in quiet understanding, but midwives were authorised to baptize children into the Catholic faith at birth and it saddened Isaac to know that she would do this as soon as he had left, whatever the mother's wishes.

He got down from the coach, stiff and tired, clutching his medicine chest, and looked up at the coachman, who had driven him out the night before and waited for him in the village.

'Thank you my friend. It was a long night for you.'

'Glad to be of service, doctor,' said the coachman, then he flicked the reins on the horse's back and headed off.

Isaac stood for a moment looking after him then he turned to go into the infirmary. It was a simple building, placed a good distance outside the town, and he was well pleased with it. He had worked hard to raise funds from the Huguenot community for its construction and gain permission from the authorities to undertake the work, patiently putting his case to them for a place where ordinary folk could be treated, those who could not afford a visit from a doctor to their homes, where he could train up local peasant women to help nurse the sick and to see to it that standards of cleanliness were upheld. Isaac had observed and noted how his patients responded to certain treatments. He had begun to correspond and exchange ideas with colleagues both in the realm and beyond, though these 'foreign' advances and ideas were slow to be accepted, being thought by many to be heretical.

There was little enough relief for the sick. The hospitals set up by the King were only situated in large cities and they were largely for beggars and prostitutes cleared off the streets. These folk were then usually confined there for the rest of their lives and given constant religious instruction. However, the mission of St Vincent de Paul's 'Daughters of Charity' a lay foundation, was spreading through the realm and running some of the Hotel Dieus for the sick. But many of these could no longer cope with the demand for their services and the sick were frequently accommodated two or three to a bed.

Which is why Isaac had seen the urgent need for setting up his own independent infirmary; he had approached some of the wealthy Reformists in the municipality and they had responded magnificently. Minor nobles, merchants, professionals, they had all dug deep into their pockets and as a result his little infirmary was soon built and well equipped, though it already struggled to treat all those who came through its doors.

He sighed as he spotted a carriage approaching the entrance to the infirmary. No doubt it was another patron wanting to see how their money was being spent and they would insist on being shown round, distracting him from giving his time to the sick in his care.

If only they would leave me alone to get on with my work.

His work! Who knew how long he would be able to continue with it? Already Protestant membership of the Physicians' Guild in Bordeaux was being restricted and the new guild soon to be founded in La Rochelle was only to accept Catholics. For the moment, small towns like Castillon were outside the control of these guilds, but Isaac knew that he could not be complacent. It would only be a matter of time before the Catholic authorities put obstacles in his way.

However, he reflected, as he continued to watch the progress of the carriage, the medical corporation in Bordeaux would not accept young graduates unless they had had some practical experience and this is something he could still offer.

He watched as the carriage came to a halt and an elegant woman stepped out. Immediately his irritation turned to relief as he saw that it was his friend, Louise.

He smiled. 'Welcome dear madame,' he said. 'Have you come to see that your money is being put to good use?'

Louise took his hand and stepped down. 'My dear Isaac, no indeed I have not. I know how precious your time is. I came merely to say that we shall be spending a few days at our farm and to ask if there is anything we can bring back for you. We should have some early grapes and there are figs and plenty of eggs – and herbs of course. And some of our melons may be ready.'

Isaac smiled. 'Do not overwhelm us with your generosity, Louise. As you know, the infirmary is very small. However a little of any of those would be well received by our cook here. But we have no need of herbs. We have a good supply in our garden here.'

'I'll see to it,' said Louise. 'And now I'll leave you to your work.' She made to get back into the carriage but the doctor put a hand on her arm.

'I have not thanked you for the entertainment the other evening. It was most diverting.'

'I'm very glad you could tear yourself away from your work for a while. And it was good to see Samuel, too. He has become a fine young man.'

'He enjoyed seeing the other young people. I fear it is dull for him at home with me.'

'And how fares your daughter?'

'Well, I believe, but I seldom see her.'

'And how long will it be before Samuel finishes his studies?'

Isaac sighed. 'Another year, if he is allowed.'

Louise frowned. 'Allowed? But surely …'

'I pray that his studies won't be interrupted but the times are so uncertain.'

'You look tired,' said Louise. 'Could you not spend a little time on your farm, too? Surely that would revive you?'

He nodded. 'You are right. I must visit my farm soon,' he said, 'But just now there is so much to do here.' He stifled a yawn and then continued. 'I might ask Samuel to go on my behalf.'

Louise hesitated. 'If we are there when he visits, I hope he will call on us.'

'I'm sure he will.'

He raised his hand to her in farewell as the wheels made a great circle and the carriage went back the way it had come. As it left he saw another approaching, so he hurried inside the infirmary.

'Good morning doctor.'

He smiled as he greeted one of the two local women who helped nurse the patients. Though he was grateful for the patronage of the bourgeoisie, he preferred to train up peasant women from the villages to help him. He found that they were hard working and practical and quite used to dealing with bodily fluids and seeing raw wounds.

However, some of his wealthy patrons had been very insistent and he had occasionally let some of the women help him in his work but it had always ended badly. Their sensitivities were too fine and they swooned at the sight of blood and gore. Their creed told them to help the poor and the sick but in truth they were nothing but a nuisance. They liked the idea of giving succour to those in need but they would rather not see them at close quarters. Usually they lasted less than a day and only hindered his work.

His patrons were much more use to him raising money to buy more supplies and equipment.

'Better disappear, doctor!'

He dragged his attention back to the woman in front of him and saw that she was pointing at the carriage coming down the hill towards them.

'Looks like another of your patrons coming to visit.'

'It is good of them to take an interest,' he said flatly.

'Huh! They waste our time!'

He couldn't suppress a smile. 'See them off for me would you? Tell them I'm too busy.'

'With pleasure,' said the woman, heading for the door.

'But mind your manners!'

33

She turned back, grinning. 'I'll bob a curtsy and simper and grovel, doctor, don't you worry.' Then she observed him more closely. 'You look exhausted. Will you not take a little refreshment before you see your patients?'

She's right. How often do I tell others to feed themselves properly?

He wanted to get to work but he knew he needed sustenance to get through the day and he couldn't remember when he had last eaten. He hurried through to the kitchen at the back of the infirmary, disappearing just before the other carriage drew up at the entrance.

He was surprised to see that the young girl, Marie, had been left in charge of the kitchen, but the cook had told him how capable she was. She was a skinny youngster of no more than sixteen years and although the doors of the kitchen were open to the garden at the back of the infirmary, letting in some fresh air, she was still sweating from the heat as she bent over the range, stirring a pan of pottage with a long spoon, a large apron covering her kirtle and chemise. Her sleeves were rolled up above the elbow and her hair was severely drawn back under her coif.

When she saw Isaac come in, she took the pan off the heat and bobbed a quick curtsey.

'What can I get you, sir?'

'I don't want to take you from your work, Marie, but I need a little sustenance before I see my patients.'

Marie bustled around and soon she had assembled soup, bread, butter, fruit and cheese and a beaker of water.

As he ate, he looked round the kitchen with satisfaction. Marie was a hard worker and he knew she would do anything to please him since he'd saved her family from certain starvation by employing them here at the infirmary. Her mother had died and her father could no longer work on the land as he was so twisted and bent and racked with disease. Marie and her brother were just skin and bones last year when he'd gone to visit their sick father but if they owed him anything they had more than repaid their debt. Her father tended the herb garden and saw to the horses and her brother helped with all the heavy work and maintenance around the place and, with some guidance, Marie had mastered the skills of making simple, nourishing meals for the very sick patients who had to stay in the infirmary and of preserving fruit and vegetables during the times of glut in the summer months. The shelves in the kitchen were already filling up with jars of preserves.

'This is excellent broth, Marie,' said Isaac.

Marie blushed and looked down at the floor. 'Thank you sir.'

'It is for me to thank you, Marie. I feel able to face the day now.'

He patted her gently on the back and turned to leave and then, for some reason, his thoughts turned to young Lidie Brunier. What a contrast between the two young women, both the same age, but coming from such different backgrounds. He doubted that Lidie would be able to cook and preserve with such skill.

Then he chided himself. It was not a fair comparison for Lidie had many other attributes – but he wondered how Marie might have flourished given all the advantages that Lidie had in life? He thought back to the feast laid out for Lidie's sixteenth birthday and compared it to what was available to the peasants in the region. After a day's back breaking work on their master's land, they ate only black bread, thin gruel and a little preserved meat and, if they were fortunate, some fruit and vegetables in season. There was common land in the town where peasants could forage for firewood and fruits and nuts, but not enough to provide for a family – and there was little enough money left after they had paid their taxes.

His tour round his infirmary pleased him. His instructions had been well heeded and the two rooms, one for women and one for men, each containing three beds, were light and airy, the bed linen clean and the patients washed. How different from some of the places for the sick that he had seen, where the importance of cleanliness was not recognized.

As he went from bed to bed, he listened carefully to what the nurse told him of the patients' symptoms. During his lifetime there had been some new thought and advances in his profession, not so much in France, where they were largely viewed with suspicion, but in the wider world. The old accepted theories of medicine, the four humours in the body, were becoming discredited in some countries and there was so much more knowledge and understanding and exchange of ideas. These were exciting times. Now that printing presses were common, there were new manuals being published on surgery and anatomy. He read everything he could of the advances in the study of human anatomy and new medical techniques. There was now much emphasis on observation and the importance of cleanliness, and he was excited, too, about the new thinking on how the blood circulated around the body and how blood could be observed under the microscope, and of the properties of opium tincture for the relief of pain and a range of other medical conditions. But it was largely through his communication with physicians overseas that he had expanded his knowledge and ideas. The Paris medical faculty did not accept many of these new theories and there was still the belief that sickness was a punishment from God.

The constant wars, too, had brought advances in the treatment of wounds from firearms and now there were trained surgeons assigned to battlefields, and although he could always detect high fever in his patients, he had on occasion used the thermoscope, a sealed glass tube filled with alcohol to measure a patient's temperature, but he found it not very accurate and preferred to rely on his own observation.

He made his rounds, prescribing bleeding with leeches, mixtures of herbs, a different diet, purgatives and other remedies, taking the time to speak to each patient, even if it was only for a moment, and always observing, so that, afterwards, he could make notes.

When he had finished his rounds, he and the nurse washed their hands in a basin of fresh water, then he thanked her and she went away to put his instructions into practice.

Isaac set to writing up meticulous notes from all he had seen that morning and comparing them to what he'd observed previously, so that he could monitor progress or otherwise, in his patients. Then he wrote up prescriptions to be made up by the apothecary in the town, ordering more oil of cloves, liquorice root, tincture of opium, camphor, potassium nitrate, mercury and fresh leeches to treat the various ailments.

He had just finished when Marie entered, bringing him a drink. He smiled at her.

'Thank you Marie. I have my day's prescriptions here. Could you ask your brother to take them to the apothecary's shop for me.'

Marie nodded, took the list and slipped away.

Just after she'd left, there was a commotion at the main entrance. Isaac took little notice of it. People were always coming, bringing their sick friends and relations. They would be seen by one of his two nurses, attended to and sent on their way, unless they were very sick and it was felt they needed to be given a bed, in which case they would send for him.

He rubbed his eyes and stretched, then rose from his seat and walked outside to inspect the herb garden. It was shady here and Marie's father was carefully watering the plants. He was younger than Isaac yet looked years older. Unrelenting harsh work in the fields had taken their toll and he was still frail and stooped but the disease which had nearly killed him had finally left him and although he would always be breathless and tire easily, he had filled out since he'd been working at the infirmary and the light work of tending the herb garden suited him. He stopped when he saw Isaac and stood leaning on his hoe, his head bowed.

'Good morning Adam. What an excellent job you are doing here. The plants thrive under your care.'

Adam's solemn face broke into a smile. 'Thank you, sir,' he muttered.

Isaac leant down to inspect the neat rows of herbs. 'Some have been freshly picked I see. Has the apothecary's lad been down here already?'

'Yes sir, he was here early.'

'Good. Good,' he said, then he frowned. There was still noise coming from the entrance to the infirmary, with angry, raised voices.

'Do you know what's going on there?' he asked Adam.

Adam shook his head.

'Would you find out for me?'

Adam put down his hoe and limped off. While he was gone, Isaac sat down on the garden wall, turned his face to the sun and closed his eyes, trying to shut out the angry shouting which continued unabated.

Adam came back at last, hurrying, crablike, towards him.

'Sir, there are two men, one bleeding everywhere, but he won't let the nurse treat him. He was brought here by his friend,' he added.

'Umm,' said the doctor. 'My guess is that he is a Catholic suspicious of us Huguenots?'

'I think so.'

Isaac sighed. 'I'll go and see if I can calm him.'

It was a gory sight that greeted Isaac when he'd walked round the building. There was blood everywhere and it was clear that one of the two men there was severely wounded but he was yelling at the nurse trying to treat him and lashing out at her. His companion was trying to reason with him.

'You'll die, man. You must let them help you.'

The wounded man was beginning to lose consciousness but he was still flailing about, lashing out with his arms and muttering.

'Bloody Huguenots. They'll poison me. Let me go, I say.'

The nurse looked up with relief when she saw Isaac.

'Give me the tourniquet,' he said, rolling up his sleeves. 'If we don't stop the bleeding, the man will die.'

The injured man was still objecting but he was getting weaker. Isaac bent forward.

'Keep still, man,' he said gently.

The man tried to resist but then suddenly his head slumped forward.

'He's fainted,' said Isaac, taking the tourniquet from the nurse, 'we must hurry if we are to save him. He has lost so much blood.'

Within a matter of minutes the flow of blood was stemmed and Isaac was able to examine the wound. He turned to the man's companion who was standing awkwardly to one side.

'Will you tell me what happened,' he asked.

'It was a fight,' he muttered. 'I was taking him to the Hotel Dieu but …'

'You did right. He would not have survived the journey.'

Isaac ordered the man to be put on a stretcher and carried into the room set aside for minor surgery. The man's companion tried to push into the room but the doctor waved him away.

'It is important, sir, that this room remains free from any contagion,' he said firmly. 'For your friend's sake, I beg you stay outside. He is in good hands.'

The man looked uncertain but eventually he stepped back.

It was a deep wound and although Isaac was not a surgeon, he had, through his reading, developed some surgical skills. He worked fast, cleaning the wound while the nurse forced a little opium between the lips of the unconscious man, then, in partnership, they stitched and bound up the wound and when they had finished, the man was taken to lie in the only vacant bed.

Isaac washed his face and hands, left the nurse to clean up the room, and went to speak to the patient's companion who he found pacing up and down outside the entrance.

'Good day sir.'

The man spun round. 'How is he? Will he live?'

'With God's help,' said Isaac. 'It was a deep wound and he is very weak from loss of blood and there is always a risk of infection.'

Their eyes met, the Catholic and the Protestant and for the moment they were simply two men concerned about another.

'We shall do our best to help him recover,' said Isaac.

The man nodded. 'Thank you, doctor,' he said. 'I appreciate your help.' He hesitated and then added. 'I hope he will not be a difficult patient. He has strong views.'

Isaac smiled. 'My job is to tend the sick, whatever their background or beliefs.'

The man nodded and seemed about to say more but stopped himself and instead thrust out his hand.

Isaac took it. 'Will you come back tomorrow to see how he fares?' he asked.

'I will doctor, you may depend on it.'

Then the man turned and went over to his horse and cart which he'd left in the shade under a tree by the side of the building. As he heaved himself into the driving seat and took up the reins, he raised his hand in farewell.

Isaac watched him drive the cart away.

A conflicted man.

Later that day, before he left to go to his own house, Isaac visited his patients in the company of his nurse. Some in his care, he knew, were unlikely to get well and, in low tones, he discussed with the nurse the best way of making their last days comfortable.

'We have plentiful supplies of opium,' said the nurse quietly.

Isaac nodded. 'It is a blessing, that drug,' he said, 'It certainly eases the passing of their poor souls.'

'As does the comfort from our Elders,' said the nurse.

'Indeed,' said Isaac. 'And from our pastor, too. We are lucky to have Pierre Gabriac amongst us.'

Since the infirmary had opened its doors, Isaac had treated many ailments. There had been broken bones to set, infections of the mouth, infections from old wounds, and scrofula, an infection of the neck glands known as the King's evil. The superstition remained that scrofula could be cured by the touch of royalty. The King would touch numerous coins to be purchased and distributed to sufferers for them to string around their necks. Although Isaac knew this would have no effect on the course of the disease, he did not try and dissuade patients from this habit. If it eased their minds then it probably had some value.

He came to his most recent patient, the man with the deep wound who had resisted his help so violently. He stood looking down at him for a few moments. A young man of about Samuel's age, twenty perhaps, he guessed, in good physical condition, possibly a soldier. If he was a soldier he would be in the King's army where soldiers were conditioned to hate all Huguenots.

As Isaac watched him, the young man groaned as he tried to turn over. He was still drugged but his eyes opened slowly and he stared up at Isaac.

'How goes it with you, young man?' asked Isaac gently. 'That was a vicious wound you sustained.'

The young man looked confused as he took in his surroundings, then he frowned and his eyes became wild. He tried to sit up but cried out with pain and fell back onto the bed.

'Where are the sisters?' he whispered.

Isaac smiled. 'We have no sisters of charity here my friend but there are those here to care for you. You are in good hands.'

'I told him to take me to the Hotel Dieu.'

'Your friend did the right thing. If you had travelled any further, you would have died.'

'This is a Huguenot place?'

Isaac didn't answer the question. Instead he said, bending down to lift the man's arm, remove the dressings and inspect the wound. 'This is a place where we heal, young man. And we take no heed of the beliefs of our patients.'

'But ...'

Isaac eventually released the man's arm and replaced it on the sheet. He stood up straight.

'You need to rest, my boy,' he said. 'If you are to recover, you must rest and let my nurse care for you.'

The young man's eyes were less wild now but still fearful.

'No one will harm you here,' said Isaac. 'I promise you. You are in no danger.'

At last he seemed to relax. His fists unclenched and he lay back, and as Isaac moved away, he thought he heard a whispered 'thank you, sir.'

It had been a long day and wearily Isaac walked back past the herb garden to where his horse was stabled. Adam was there waiting for him and had already put saddle and bridle on the solid bay cob.

'I could have saddled him myself, Adam. No need for you to test those sore limbs of yours.'

'I take pleasure in being near the beast, sir,' said Adam. 'It is no hardship.'

'Yes, I understand your feelings. I, too, find the company of animals more relaxing than the company of some humans.'

Adam grinned as he held the horse's head and Isaac swung himself into the saddle. He raised his hand in thanks, then, taking the reins up, he trotted down the track which led to his home.

Unlike most of his friends, Isaac had elected to live in one of the villages which lay some way outside the town. The air was fresher here and he'd felt it a healthier place to bring up his family, though it meant that he was not protected by the watch as were those living in the town or the faubourg.

As his house came into view, his shoulders untensed. This place held so many happy memories for him. It was where he and his wife had lived since their marriage. It was where their children had been born. Momentarily his mind went back to that dreadful night when Samuel had made his entrance into the world and he'd been unable to save the life of his beloved wife. He had learnt so much since that time. Now, he probably could have saved her as he had saved the life of the peasant mother and her baby last night.

Once through the iron gates set in an ancient wall which surrounded the house, the cob pricked up his ears and trotted more briskly sensing home and food, but Isaac

reined him in briefly and sat looking at the house, too big for him now, but always welcoming, with its soft stone walls and wooden shutters, tranquil in the evening light and flanked by trees on either side. It was a simple grange, once a farmhouse and still with a little land. Isaac grew enough vegetables and fruit for the household but the land he owned in the plains was much more productive.

Although it was a large house, Isaac was seldom alone. Apart from the servants who had mostly been with him for years, friends and colleagues came and went and there was plenty of room to accommodate those travelling from further afield. And now he had the pleasure of Samuel's company for a few weeks before he left again to continue his studies.

He sighed, loosened the reins and let the cob head round to the stables, then dismounted and had a quick word with his groom before going inside the house. After the hustle and bustle of the infirmary, he loved the peace of this place and he always took a moment, when he entered, to look round and take in the solid rooms furnished comfortably put plainly. Unlike the homes of some of the rich Huguenot merchants in town, Isaac had never felt comfortable surrounded by the trappings of wealth. He wanted for nothing but he was not interested in acquiring baubles or fancy goods to display. His wife had felt the same and she had kept a simple but happy home here when their daughter was growing up. Then she had fallen pregnant again and carried the child to term and they had both been excited about the impending birth of a late baby, perhaps a boy this time, to succeed Isaac one day.

'Father!'

Isaac's thoughts were interrupted and he saw Samuel striding across the hall to greet him.

Isaac smiled widely and he put an arm round his son's shoulders. 'What have you been doing today?'

Samuel stretched and rubbed his eyes. 'Reading, mostly,' he said. 'Reading and more reading until I feel my head must burst.'

Isaac laughed. 'It is the lot of a student of law – or of medicine for that matter. So much to learn, so many facts to absorb. But I hope that you will leave your studies for the rest of the day at least and let me enjoy your company.'

Samuel nodded. 'With pleasure. And what of your day, father?'

'Much the same as usual. Avoiding the offered help of my patrons, watching the progress of disease, trying to keep the infirmary free from infection, patching up wounds. Oh, and treating a young Catholic soldier somewhat against his will.'

'How so?'

Isaac told him of the incident and Samuel frowned. 'If he is a soldier then he'll not change his views of us. He will have been trained to think of us as enemies.'

Isaac nodded. 'Of course. But I am trained to think of every patient as a human being.'

'His Majesty has much to answer for,' muttered Samuel.

'Indeed,' said Isaac, 'Though I suspect he may not understand the deep hatred which will be rekindled through his actions. I feel that his advisers are more to blame.'

Samuel frowned. 'The court is far removed from what goes on in the rest of our country. Down here in Gascony we have always been a people of independent mind.'

'Indeed', said Isaac, smiling. 'We are a strong and stubborn breed, are we not? But come, I have a good appetite and am looking forward to dining with you.'

They dined well but simply, on one of their chickens, fresh bread and fruit, washed down with one of the wines from a local vineyard.

'I am glad to see that you take no notice of the Catholic days of fasting, Father,' said Samuel, spearing a piece of chicken breast and devouring it with relish.

'Huh! I intend to eat meat whenever I wish,' said Isaac. 'The Bible says nothing of abstaining from meat. I refuse to take notice of these papist inventions.'

Samuel looked serious for a moment. 'Our defiance may count against us.'

'Defying foolish laws is admirable,' said Isaac. 'And here in the Bordelaise we have always been a strong in ignoring unreasonable edicts.' He laughed. 'I love the Gascon people,! Why, here in the town we are still holding marriages in Advent and Lent and I see few people bending the knee and crossing themselves when the priests pass by, holding the Holy Sacrament aloft.'

They went on then to speak about the management of their farm in the plains and then Samuel was able to advise his father about the constant legal fights to protect the rights of Protestants.

'Will any of these succeed?'

Samuel shook his head. 'It is doubtful. Since there are only Catholic judges in local parliaments these days, no ruling is likely to be passed in our favour.'

They were silent for a while and then Isaac turned the subject to his interest in the new thinking abroad about the practice of medicine.

'His Majesty is encouraging the study of anatomy and certainly improvements in surgery have been made, but our thinking here in France is behind that of some other countries. Then Isaac went on to speak of what he was learning in his exchanges with other medical men abroad, and Samuel listened attentively, frowning with concentration, trying to follow his father's words.

At length, Isaac stopped. 'I'm sorry, Samuel, forgive me for lecturing you; it is so seldom I am able to voice my opinions on this for I fear that many of my colleagues here would find my thoughts heretical.'

He stretched and yawned. 'I'm for my bed. It has been a long day.' He scraped back his chair and stood up. 'It would be useful if you could spare the time from your studies to visit our farm and see what needs attention. I have so much to do at the infirmary that I find it hard to get away.'

'I'd enjoy that,' said Samuel. 'But you should go too. It would benefit you to get away from your work, surely?'

'Not just now,' said Isaac. 'Later in the month perhaps.' He turned but then stopped and looked back at Samuel. 'And make sure to pay a call on Louise and Jacob. They are leaving for their own farm tomorrow I believe.'

He headed for the stairs, pausing for a moment, as he did every night, to hold up his candle and look at the portrait of his wife which hung on the wall.

Chapter Four

A few days later, Lidie, her mother and Annette set off to visit their farm in the plains just below the village of Pujols. Though it was only a few miles from Castillon, Pujols lay to the South and they had first to cross the great river Dordogne.

They left in the early morning and it was another cloudless day. The hired carriage took them through the faubourg and up into the town and then down towards the great River Gate, the Porte de Fer. As the carriage swayed along Annette stared silently from the window.

'Catholics,' she muttered.

Sara sighed impatiently. 'What now, Annette?'

'They are saying in the market that our temple will be pulled down.'

'You should not believe all the gossip you hear, Annette,' said Sara sharply. 'Our faith has been dominant here in Castillon for many years and the King has only decreed that the newer temples be destroyed. I warrant that it will continue to stand for many years to come.'

'Aye,' replied Annette. 'But we'll not worship in it again.'

Sara had no answer to that, but she went on. 'We are lucky here that is so close to the town. Our brethren in other towns were forced to build their temples a good deal further out.'

'Aye, too close. It is a bitter reminder of happier times,' muttered Annette.

Lidie cleared her throat. 'We were so occupied in getting ready to leave that I have not had a chance to ask you about the new maid,' she said, addressing her mother, 'And when I question her, all she will say is that she is come from Bordeaux.'

Sara looked at Annette who shuffled in her seat.

Lidie frowned. 'What is it?'

'Your mama was kind enough to agree to employ Susanne,' she said.

'A kindness which I hope I shall not come to regret,' said Sara, still looking at Annette.

46

Annette turned to Lidie. 'She arrived at the house a week ago, Mam'selle. She is the daughter of my niece who is …'

'Who is?'

Annette licked her lips. 'Susanne has left an unhappy household,' she said quietly. 'God alone knows how she managed to travel here by herself from Bordeaux but He must have been looking over her. She sought me out and begged me to find her employment.'

Lidie frowned and Annette continued. 'Pray be patient with her Mam'selle. She has rough manners I know, but she will learn.'

Lidie regarded Annette sitting across from her in the coach, so familiar in her coif and simple rough dress with her stout legs protruding beneath its hem. Annette who had been with the family as long as Lidie had lived.

Yet what do I know of her? I know she had a husband who died young and that she has no children but beyond that I have never asked.

'Your niece, you say?'

'Aye. My sister's child. Susanne is her daughter.'

Annette, who was usually so eager to talk, seemed reluctant to say more. Lidie glanced across at her mother but Sara continued to look out of the window of the carriage.

Lidie was tempted to enquire further but Annette was looking down at the floor, her cheeks flushed, so she kept her counsel.

At last the coach reached the Porte de Fer and they dismounted, the coachman helping to deposit their luggage on the wooden jetty at the river's edge where boats were lined up ready to ferry people across. It was not long before they were settled in one of these boats but there was little wind and although the ferryman tacked from side to side, skilfully catching in the sails any wind he could, it was a slow journey.

They had sent word ahead that they were coming and when they finally reached the other side of the river, the farm cart was already there, a solid cob between the shafts, the farm's stable lad holding its head,.

Although it was not far from the town, it was a different world out here in the plains and Lidie's spirits lifted as the first of the orchards and fields came into view. The wheat harvest was in full swing and the cart bumped down the earthen tracks and rattled past groups of peasants in the fields, the men scything and the women binding up the sheaves and loading them onto the ox-drawn carts.

Lidie looked about her.

Papa loved it over here. He was so proud of the farm. I can still see him striding around his land, inspecting the trees and vines with the workers, making plans. Always bursting with new ideas.

Sara frowned as she observed all the activity.

'I worry about our harvest,' she said to Lidie. 'Your father was so knowledgeable and he always took care of the farm business. I fear I still have much to learn.'

'Can you not ask Uncle Jacob for advice.'

Sara nodded. 'I will. Indeed I have, but if only I had taken more heed when your father was alive ...' She cleared her throat. 'Yes, you are right, Lidie,' she said more strongly, 'I shall continue to seek advice and I shall learn. Then maybe next year I will be better informed.'

'Abel and Martha would help you ma'am,' said Annette, mentioning the couple who lived in the farmhouse. 'They know the land as well as any.'

Sara nodded. 'Of course, I shall seek their advice, too.'

Abel and Martha were a peasant couple who had once had their own small farm but the royal taxes and several bad harvests had ruined them. They'd taken loans they couldn't repay and at last had to leave their little piece of land. Now they were employed by the Brunier family to keep house and to oversee the day to day running of the farm.

Many of the peasants grew a few crops on small parcels of land but others owned no land and just kept a few animals in or around their dwelling places. Their only way of living was to barter their labour for food or clothing. If disease swept through a village, they were often underfed and had no resistance.

Before long their own land came into view and Sara asked the lad driving to go slowly so that she could observe it. To her untutored eye, it all seemed in order, the wheat harvest, as elsewhere, had just begun and the vines and orchards looked well tended. When they drew up at the modest farmhouse and climbed down from the cart, they were greeted by Abel and Martha and Abel carried their luggage inside. While Sara and Lidie settled themselves, Annette followed Martha to the kitchen at the back of the house and sat down heavily in a chair while she watched Martha prepare some refreshments. They had only exchanged brief pleasantries before Annette burst out.

'My niece's child has come to serve in the household!'

Martha whipped round to face her, a ladle held aloft.

'Not that family from Bordeaux?!'

Annette nodded. 'The very same,' she said.

'Oh Annette, that family are trouble.'

Annette stretched back in the chair to ease her aching limbs. 'Aye,' she said, 'And I had hoped to have no more truck with them, but what could I do? The child threw herself on my mercy and begged me to find her employment.'

'She had travelled from Bordeaux – by herself?'

Annette shrugged. 'As far as I know. She has said nothing of her journey and in truth I am nervous to enquire.'

'Have you told the mistress of what went on in that household?'

Annette shook her head. 'If I did, I fear she would throw the girl out of the house.'

Martha turned back and continued with her work. 'I will say nothing. You can count on my silence.' She bent to pick up a large wooden tray and set it on the table. 'After all, it is not the child's fault.'

'My thoughts exactly. But I pray she'll not disgrace me.'

'Aye, and we must pray that she'll not …'

'Not say anything of her background to young mistress Lidie? You cannot wish that more fervently than I, Martha.'

Annette heaved herself out of the chair and started to help Martha. A few minutes later they made their way into the front room carrying the refreshments.

Lidie and Sara were sitting down and Abel was standing, twisting his cap in his hands.

'How goes the harvest?' asked Sara.

'The weather's not been on our side, Madame,' said Abel. 'There's been precious little rain during the season so the crops won't be as good as last year.'

They went on to discuss yields and irrigation and rotation of crops. Although Sara had said she was ignorant of farm matters, Lidie was surprised at how much her mother seemed to know and she listened for a while but once she had sampled Martha's refreshments, her attention began to wander and she excused herself and went up to the little bedroom which was set aside for her on their visits.

There were no servants here to unpack for her and, in truth, she had brought very little with her, only those things required for her toilette and a few plain dresses and shifts. They would only stay here for a day or two, to give Mama time to inspect the farm, and then they would go over to see Cécile and her family who had a larger farmhouse and a much bigger estate.

Lidie drew up a chair and stood on tiptoe to look out of the small slanted window set high in the eaves and stared across the land. Uncle Jacob's estate lay to the west of their farm and she gazed in that direction. She wondered where the Verdier farm might be – Cécile had said it was close to theirs – and whether Samuel and his father might visit it. Most landowners came during harvest time to check that all was in order.

Suddenly restless, she jumped down from the chair and clattered down the stairs and outside. It was mid-morning and the sun was not too intense as she wandered round the farm. She had loved doing this with her papa and when she watched the chickens pecking at the ground in the farmyard, she was sharply reminded of him. She could see him so clearly in her mind's eye, gently picking up a chicken to inspect it, checking on the oxen in the barn, patting their great flanks or taking harvested grain and rubbing it thoughtfully between his thumb and finger. And, when she was a child, leading her round the yard astride one of the farm horses.

She smiled to herself.

Mama never approved of that! She would pretend to be shocked that he let me ride astride.

THE KING'S COMMAND

Although Lidie enjoyed her life in the town with all its activity and socialising, the air was sweeter here and the smells of the farmyard were of the earth and blended with the air unlike the filthy stench of human and animal excrement that flowed in the town, trapped between houses in the narrow streets. She was thankful they lived in the faubourg.

First she inspected the largest barn. The harvest had only just begun so there weren't many sheaves of wheat inside it as yet. Soon it would fill up and once the sheaves dried they would be threshed with a flail to separate the grain from the straw. One of the smaller barns was set aside for the pair of oxen. That, too, was empty, waiting for the beasts to return from the fields dragging the cart behind them. Lidie pulled a piece of straw from one of the sheaves and looked at it. In town she gave little thought to how the grain became milled and milled flour was made into the bread they ate nor yet of the labour involved. During the summer and autumn months the peasants worked from dawn to dusk harvesting the grain and fruits for the wealthy town folk to enjoy. Her own life was idle by comparison.

She walked on past the barns and into the orchards where the apples were ripening, ready to be picked later, after the summer was over. There was some shade here and Lidie took her time, strolling between the neatly planted rows of fruit trees. At the edge of the orchard she stopped and shaded her eyes to look over the fields of vines beyond where a few labourers were picking some of the early varieties of grape.

After a while, she sat down on the ground, chewing a blade of grass and listening to the sounds of summer, the occasional cry of a bird, observing the flash of a butterfly on the wing and hearing the buzzing of bees.

Inside the house, Sara was still speaking to Abel and Martha trying to learn everything she could about the management of the land.

'I am so grateful to you both,' she said. 'Since my husband died I have relied on you more than I should, but it seems that you are doing an excellent job here.'

Abel and Martha exchanged a glance but they said nothing.

'Is there anything amiss?' asked Sara. 'Is there something I have failed to do?'

Abel shook his head. 'No Madame, your husband took a great interest in the place and made many improvements. It is in a good state.'

'You would tell me if you need anything, would you not. Money for repairs and suchlike.'

'Of course,' said Abel. He looked down at the floor.

'So, what is it that worries you?' asked Sara, leaning forward.

Abel scowled.

Martha sighed. 'Abel feels you should not be troubled, Madame, but I think you should be told.'

'Told what?'

Martha twisted the material of her dress between her fingers.

'There are rumours, Madame.'

'Martha!'

'No, Abel, do not chide me. She should know.'

Sara frowned. 'I would know. Whatever these rumours, I would rather know.'

Abel, who was still looking at his feet, said. 'There have been strangers here,' he said. 'Men enquiring in the village. Asking who owns the land.'

'Who are these strangers?'

'It is said that they are sent by the Intendant of the Généralité, Madame.'

Sara looked puzzled. 'Why should the Intendant send men to our land?

'To spy,' said Martha. 'To spy for the King, I warrant.'

'Why should you think that, Martha? Surely no one has business to inspect the land we own except us?'

'This King does what he pleases,' said Abel, 'and the Intendant is the King's man here in the region. It seems all Reformist landowners are being pestered by him and his agents.'

Sara chose her words carefully. Unlike in town, where the majority of folk were Protestants, many of the peasant folk had no special loyalty. The Catholic priests handed out charity from time to time and summoned them to Mass in the church in the village, but most of the peasants still clung to their long held superstitions, mixing their allegiance to formal religion with their belief in witchcraft and magic and signs in the sky and the wearing of amulets to ward off evil spirits.

'Abel,' said Sara gently, 'we Reformists do not hate the King; on the contrary, we are completely loyal to him and it is only on the matter of religion where we differ.'

'But what of the taxes the King levies on the peasants? Are they fair?'

She frowned. 'The taxes are high,' she said. 'I grant you that. But the King has waged these expensive wars and his treasury is much depleted.'

'Huh!' said Martha. 'What have foreign wars to do with us? What does he want from us now, Madame? Why are his agents sniffing around? Does he plan to punish the landowners who are not Catholic? Will he drive them off their land?'

'I understand that you are worried, Martha. It is unsettling when strangers come asking questions.' She paused. 'Have they been here, to our farm?'

'Not to the house,' said Abel, 'But some of the workers reported seeing them riding on your land.'

'If anyone made to approach them they rode off,' said Martha.' They stayed well away from where there were workers. They kept to the edge of the land.'

Sara continued to try and placate the couple, though she was much alarmed by what they told her. A little later, however, the subject was changed and the talk moved on to the ailments and troubles of some of the labourers.

'Should I visit them?' asked Sara.

Martha shrugged. 'If it pleases you, Madame.'

'Did… did my husband visit them?'

'Sometimes,' muttered Abel. 'But …'

Sara held up her hand. 'Then I shall, too,' she said.

Once, again, Abel and Martha exchanged glances. Abel cleared his throat.

'If that is what you wish Madame, I'll take you in the morning.'

When Lidie came in from her walk, Sara rose from her seat.

'Abel and Martha have been telling me about some of the peasants who are suffering from disease or privation. I have resolved to go and visit them tomorrow when I go round the farm. Would you come with me?'

Lidie hesitated, not relishing the prospect, but then she thought of all the peasants in the fields working for their benefit, scything, bending, tying up the sheaves, day after day with little respite.

'Of course, Mama.'

The next morning, Abel was at the door with the farm cart, ready to take Sara and Lidie round the estate. Lidie stroked the cob's nose while she was waiting for Sara. He was old now and she'd known him most of her life and always looked forward to seeing him when they visited.

'He's still working then, Abel?'

Abel held the reins loosely in his hands. 'Not heavy work, Mam'selle. He's past pulling heavy loads, but he's fit enough for his age and he's good and steady.'

Lidie climbed up into the cart where Abel had placed some rough cloth across the wooden planks to shield their dresses from the dirt. After a few minutes, Sara appeared and they set off.

It was a wearisome business, with Abel stopping at every field, or so it seemed to Lidie, explaining what was planted, how it was developing, when it would be harvested and where it would be sold, but Sara took note of everything and asked many questions.

The sun had crept much higher in the sky by the time they left the fields and the cob drew them up the hill to the village of Pujols. At the edge of the village stood a magnificent stone church, built centuries earlier, but Abel drove the cart passed this and drew rein at a collection of mean hovels where children were gathered, playing in the dirt among the animals that wandered freely. The children were painfully thin, some with sores on their faces and limbs and all of them were dirty. They stopped their game and stood staring at the horse and cart, fingers in mouths or hiding behind one another.

Hearing the cart arrive, a woman came out of one of the hovels. Lidie felt her mama tense up beside her as the woman observed them. Her clothes were not much better than rags.

Sara cleared her throat. 'Abel,' she said quietly. 'I didn't know …'

'These are some of the most deprived,' said Abel. 'The families where there has been death and disease and now there are no workers to hire themselves out to help with the harvest.'

He gestured towards the few animals wandering in and out of the buildings, picking at scraps. They, too, looked thin and undernourished.

'These are all they have to sustain them,' he said, getting down from the cart and offering his hand to Sara.

'Come and see for yourself, Madame.'

For a moment, Sara hesitated, then she took Abel's hand and climbed down to the ground. She turned. 'Come Lidie,' she said, and Lidie followed her, holding up her skirts clear of the dust and dirt.

Abel beckoned to the ragged woman who came forward and bobbed a curtsy, but said nothing.

They all stood there awkwardly for a moment and Lidie could sense that her mama was trying to find the right words. At last she moved towards the woman and took her hand.

'What is it that you need most?' she asked.

The woman raised her head and looked at Abel who nodded at her.

'Will you come inside?' she asked.

The children were mostly toddlers but Abel found a slightly older boy who was deformed in the leg and asked him to hold the horse's head then, once the woman had shooed out some skinny chickens and a pig which had wandered inside in search of scraps Sara, Lidie and Abel followed her into the tiny hovel.

Lidie stared around her. She had never been inside such a house before, though you could hardly call this a house. It was just a rude shelter with holes in the roof and a single room with a mud floor. There was hardly any furniture, just a low stool beside a small brick fireplace with a few cooking implements on the ground beside it and over which was suspended an iron kettle. In the corner of the room there was a bundle of rags where, she guessed, the whole family slept.

The woman drew the stool forward and gestured to it.

'Will you sit, Madame,' she said. Her accent was harsh and guttural.

Not wanting to offend, Sara lowered herself onto the stool and the rest of them stood.

It was Abel who spoke first. He said to the woman. 'Would you tell Madame what befell you?'

There was something in the way she stood that spoke of a past life where she had some dignity and Lidie observed her closely. She might have been a good looking girl once but her face was lined and old before her time.

'We had a little land when we first married, she began. 'We were never rich but we managed. We traded what we grew for anything else we needed, we preserved our fruits and salted down our meat against the winter.' She started coughing then, a hacking sound that shook her whole frail body.

'What befell you?' asked Sara.

The woman finally stopped coughing and swallowed. Even in the gloom of the room, they could see the anger in her face.

'First it was the taxes,' she said. 'Higher and higher taxes levied upon us.'

'The salt tax was hard to bear,' said Abel.

Sara nodded. 'We have all suffered from that,' she said, then immediately regretted her insensitivity and blushed.

'Indeed,' said Abel, drily.

Lidie felt embarrassed for her mother. The taxes were an inconvenience for them, no more than that.

'We had a bad harvest and had to borrow,' the woman continued. 'Then one of our children got very sick with a fever and we borrowed again to pay for medicines for him.' She looked down and muttered. 'They never cured him.'

She fell silent then and Abel went on. 'You had to sell the land then, like us.'

She nodded. 'Then my husband and another son died, so I was left with the youngest children to feed and little work to be had.'

She started coughing again and Lidie wondered if she, herself, would survive. They all waited until the cough had subsided and Abel took up her story.

'She minds the babes for her neighbours so they can work in the fields and they give her what they can.'

The woman looked up. 'They are kind. They do what they can for me – and the priest helps me.'

At the mention of the Catholic priest, Lidie glanced at her mother.

Sara nodded. 'Did my husband help you?' she asked.

The woman nodded and, for the first time she smiled and Lidie could see, even in the poor light, that she was missing several teeth.

'Then we shall continue to do that,' said Sara. 'If you tell Abel what you need, I shall make sure you have it.'

'Thank you Madame,' she said.

When they got into the cart, Sara turned to Lidie. 'I feel ashamed,' she said. 'Papa has been gone for over a year and I have been little concerned about the fate of these people. I didn't know that he was helping them.'

As they were trundling back towards the farmhouse, Lidie was quiet. How little *she* knew of their lives, or of the beggars they sometimes saw in the town. She felt admiration for the woman they'd seen. She had fallen on hard times but she didn't grovel when she'd been offered help. She accepted it with dignity.

Her thoughts were interrupted when Abel suddenly drew rein and stopped the cart.

'Look,' he said, pointing ahead.

In the distance, there were two riders coming towards them on horseback.

'Do you know who they are, Abel?' asked Sara.

He shook his head. 'They're coming this way, so we'll find out soon enough,' he said and urged the old cob onwards up the track.

'Strangers,' muttered Abel as they drew closer. 'I'll wager these are more of the Intendant's spies.'

As they reached the two riders, one of them called out, 'Out of the way, man, let us pass.'

There was a ditch on either side of the track and it would have been impossible for the horse and cart to make way for the two men on horseback. Abel drew rein and the cart creaked to a halt.

'Make way, man!' shouted the rider again.

Sara rose to her feet, her fists clenched.

'Sir, you trespass on my land. What is your business?'

Lidie shrank down, trying to make herself as small as possible.

'Ha!' said the rider, standing up in his stirrups and staring at Sara. 'So you're one of those rich Huguenot landowners!' He laughed and turned to address his companion. 'See how these damn traitors and blasphemers feather their nests!'

Sara met his eyes. 'You trespass, sir, I would ask you to leave my land at once. You are not welcome.'

'We'll leave when you move your nag and cart.'

Sara spoke again keeping her voice level.

'There is a ditch either side, sir, as you can very well see. It is not possible for us to make way for you. Please leave my land or …'

'Or what?' laughed the man. 'You Protestant folk don't have so much power now, do you?'

His companion interrupted. 'Come on, man, we're done here. We've seen enough.' Then he urged his horse down into the ditch and up the other side and past the cart. But the other man drove his horse forward, squeezing past so that their cob sidled in fright and Sara lost her balance and fell over. As the man passed, her face was so close that she was brushed by his horse's bridle as he leaned over and spat, a gobbet of phlegm landing on Sara's dress.

'How much longer d'you think you'll be able to hang onto your land, Huguenot bitch?'

Chapter Five

Abel leapt down from the cart and shouted after the men as they rode off, shaking his fist at their retreating backs.

Lidie helped Sara up from the floor of the cart. 'Are you hurt, Mama?'

'A little shaken. It is nothing.'

'I'm so sorry Madame,' said Abel. 'That fellow treated you vilely.'

Sara smoothed down her dress. 'I confess I was shocked, Abel. But let us forget the whole sorry episode and go back to the farmhouse. I refuse to be discomforted by their rudeness.'

Abel got up onto the cart again and they lumbered on up the track. No one spoke and more than once Lidie glanced over at her mother, composed now but with a set expression on her face. Once they reached the house, Sara thanked Abel and she and Lidie went inside. Martha came to greet them.

'Did you visit ...' she began but stopped when she saw their expressions.

'Is something amiss?'

'There were these strangers,' began Lidie, but Sara interrupted her.

'It was nothing. Some rude men on horseback blocking the road.'

'The Intendant's spies?'

'It was nothing,' repeated Sara. 'It is not worthy of discussion.' Then she walked towards the stairs. 'Come Lidie,' she said.

'But I ...'

'Come with me,' she repeated.

Lidie raised her eyebrows but made no more objection and followed her mother upstairs and into Sara's chamber. Sara closed the door behind them.

'Please do not speak with Abel and Martha about that incident,' she said.

'It was horrible, Mama. They were so rude. It was frightening, the way they spoke to you.'

Sara took her hand. 'I know, my love, but we must not make Abel and Martha feel afraid. If we make little of it and show that we are not affected, then it will soon be forgotten. I would not have them feel under threat. Remember, they live here all the time.'

'What did the man mean, Maman, when he said that about our land?'

Sara loosed Lidie's hand and went over and sat down on the edge of the bed.

'Idle threats. We bought this land and have the deeds to prove it and your papa has made many improvements and cared for those who live on it and who work for us. No one can take away what is legally ours.'

Though her words were defiant, Lidie heard the note of uncertainty in her mother's voice. She was about to say more but then Sara got to her feet and went over to the basin set on the table in the corner and began to wash her face. As she patted it dry with the rough cloth provided, she straightened up and faced Lidie.

'We'll have one more day here while I finish my business, then Uncle Jacob will send his carriage to pick us up and take us over to join them. It will be good to be with all your cousins out here in the country, will it not?'

Lidie smiled. 'It will,' she said, but she was still thinking of the man's words.

'How long do you think you'll be able to hang onto your land, Huguenot bitch?'

Horrible words. Horrible man. Mama should not have to endure such insults. She shivered, then excused herself and ran out of the house. She felt soiled and had a sudden pressing desire to get away from the others and be alone so she made, again, for the orchard and settled down under the shade of her favourite apple tree.

I have been cocooned in my pleasant life, surrounded by Reformist friends and relations. I have never before felt threatened.

This feeling of uncertainty had begun with the incident near the stables, when she and Cécile had been insulted by the drunken Catholic strangers, and it had come surging back after their encounter just now with the men on horseback.

She lay on her back and laced her hands behind her head, looking up through the apple leaves, to the blue sky.

Surely this land belongs to us? Surely no one can take it from us?

She dozed off briefly and in her dreams she was back again on the night of her birthday party, dancing the minuet with Samuel, but now he was dressed all in black and his face was that of the rude Catholic man shouting at her as he whirled her faster and faster around the floor, at quite the wrong pace for the dance, too fast so that she was stumbling, begging him to stop, but he would not and he was laughing and shouting insults at her.

'Mam'selle! Mam'selle Lidie!

Her heart was thudding as she swam back to consciousness. Someone was calling her. She scrambled to her feet and walked slowly back towards the house.

It was only a dream.

Martha met her. 'There you are mam'selle! I've been shouting myself hoarse. Come and eat. I have laid out some victuals for you and your mother. You must be hungry after your excursion.'

They made their way back to the house together.

'Those Catholic spies upset you, did they not?' said Martha. 'I knew at once when you came back. What did they say to you?'

Mindful of Sara's words, Lidie shrugged. 'It was nothing,' she repeated. 'Just two rude men and I have given them no more thought.'

'If you say so, mam'selle.'

'Truly, Martha. Words from rude Catholics cannot hurt us. After all, Christ Himself turned the other cheek, did He not?'

'Umm,' muttered Martha, as she followed Lidie into the house.

Uncle Jacob's carriage arrived at the farm the next morning. Cécile had come to fetch them and she jumped out of the carriage and embraced Lidie as Sara was giving last minute instructions to Abel, and Annette was bidding farewell to Martha.

Then they all clambered into Uncle Jacob's carriage. The driver flicked the reins over the backs of the two horses and they drove off down the track. Lidie and Cécile were immediately engrossed in each other's company, making plans for their time together but both Annette and Sara were quiet

As they drove further west through the fields and orchards and vines of their neighbours, all was activity. A picturesque scene of peasants labouring in the sunshine, but Sara's thoughts were with the woman whose hovel they had visited. It troubled her that she had been so blind to the fate of those who had lost their meagre livelihoods because of crippling taxes and bad harvests.

As soon as they arrived at Louise and Jacob's farmhouse, Lidie and Sara both relaxed. As usual, with the cousins, there were noisy comings and goings and Lidie was soon swept up in familiar chatter and activity. After she had greeted everyone, Cécile took Lidie up to the room they would share. She threw herself onto the bed, the ropes creaking beneath as she did so.

'How was it, at your farm?' she asked.

'It was well,' said Lidie. And she told Cécile about their visit to see the peasant woman.

'Ugh,' said Cécile, her mouth turning down. 'All that filth and smell, I wonder you could bear it.'

Lidie frowned. 'Mama and I can go back to our comfortable house,' she said. 'There is no respite for that poor woman.'

'Lidie, it is how they live. It is how they have always lived.'

'Where's your heart, Cécile? Our faith tells us to look after the poor and needy.'

'And we do,' retorted Cécile. 'Father and Mother look after those who work for them. Their lives are not so wretched.'

Lidie said nothing. She didn't want to fall out with Cécile but she felt ill at ease. She busied herself with her toilette, brushing out her tangled curls with unnecessary force.

Cécile came up behind her and put her arms round Lidie's waist.

'My heart may be harder than yours, cos, but yours is a deal too soft.'

Lidie smiled. She could never be angry with Cécile for long. She changed the subject and told her about the incident with the men on horseback.

Cécile didn't seem surprised. 'There's been talk here, too, about strangers looking over our land but no one knows their business.'

'Abel and Martha think they are Catholic spies, agents of the King.'

'What nonsense. Just peasant gossip,' said Cécile.

'The men we saw were Catholics, that's for sure,' said Lidie. 'One called Mama a Huguenot bitch.'

Cécile raised her eyebrows. 'We should not let these insults hurt us. Why, those drunks at the stable were rude to us, were they not, yet I have forgotten them already.'

Lidie didn't answer.

***

The next few days were taken up with visiting neighbours and other outings. The young people went on picnics together, walked among the trees and the vines and Lidie joined in with all the amusements in such familiar and easy company.

They saw little of Uncle Jacob who spent most of the day on farm business, checking on the crops, taking notes of what was needed and what improvements he could make for the following season, speaking to the peasants when they broke from their labours for a simple meal of black bread and cheese. By evening he was usually tired and spoke little but listened happily to the chatter which ebbed and flowed about him.

Then one evening, after they had all eaten, he broke into a lively conversation between the cousins.

'By chance I met with young Samuel Verdier today while I was near their property.'

Lidie felt herself blushing as Uncle Jacob continued. 'His father is too taken up with his patients to spare the time to come to his farm and he's sent Samuel with instructions to check on the harvest there. Samuel sought my advice when we met so I shall go round his farm with him tomorrow and I thought to bring him back here to dine with us afterwards.'

Louise clapped her hands. 'Oh yes, it will be good to have him here. He seems a splendid young man.'

'Yes, indeed,' said Sara. 'A little serious, perhaps, but that is no bad thing.'

Cécile caught Lidie's eye and winked.

63

After they had finished their meal, Lidie and Cécile wandered outside and sat on the door step watching the rays of the setting sun touch the tops of the farm buildings and listening to the sound of the cicadas coming from the poplar trees which lined the track leading up to the house.

'It is peaceful, is it not?'

Lidie nodded and picked up a smooth pebble from the ground, turning it round in her hand.

'I have always been happy here,' she said quietly.

Cécile nudged her. 'And you'll be happier still, I warrant, when Samuel comes to dine tomorrow!'

Lidie threw the pebble away. 'Cécile!'

'You liked him did you not?'

'Yes, I liked him well enough, but please make no more of it.'

'I'm sorry, cos, I'll stop my matchmaking ways!'

Lidie shifted her position a little and sighed. 'In any case, I doubt he has thought of me for one moment since my birthday celebration. He has his studies to occupy his mind and his father's farm to worry about. He'll forget about all our little lives when he returns to his studies.'

'See, you *have* been thinking of him!'

'I have *not.*'

Cécile said nothing but she smiled into the twilight and they sat there for a while longer until darkness fell and then they got up and went back inside the farmhouse. The rest of the family had gathered ready for evening prayers and as the girls joined the others, Uncle Jacob led them all in the singing of the 23rd psalm.

The Lord is my shepherd; I shall not want; He maketh me to lie down in green pastures; he leadeth me beside the still waters. He restoreth my soul: he leadeth me in the paths of righteousness for his name's sake. Yea, though I walk through the valley of the shadow of death, I will fear no evil: for thou art with me; they rod and thy staff comfort me. Thou prepares a table before me in the presence of mine enemies: thou anointest my head with oil; my cup runneth over. Surely goodness and mercy shall follow me all the days of my life, and I will dwell in the house of the Lord for ever.

Cécile and Lidie chatted as they got ready for bed in their chamber. Cécile was soon asleep but Lidie lay awake beside her for some time, the words of the psalm echoing her head. They were so familiar but she had never really considered their meaning before and now as she repeated the well worn phrases to herself she began to see how relevant they were to the people of her faith.

Here they were, indeed, in those green pastures, the still water not far away, but they were also surrounded by enemies. She had been shielded from any unpleasantness but now she was glimpsing the threat from outside that pleasant and protected life.

Her parents, her aunt and uncle, they had always been so sure in their faith, unshaken and unshakable.

Will I be able to follow their example?

She closed her eyes. 'Papa, help me to hold fast to my beliefs.'

There was a stillness in the room and it seemed, for a moment, that even Cécile's deep breathing had ceased as a calm descended on Lidie and she smiled into the darkness.

Lidie was distracted during the next day. Although she had protested to Cécile that she had no romantic feelings towards Samuel, her excitement rose as the day wore on and she tried to occupy herself by helping her mother and Aunt Louise about the house. They sent her to pick wild flowers from the hedgerows and the edges of the fields to put in a vase on the big old table in the kitchen where they all gathered to eat, for there was no fine dining room in the farmhouse.

She was grateful to be on her own for a while as she wandered round the edges of the fields, collecting wild lavender and tall grasses and late flowering honeysuckle.

Aunt Louise was there when she took the flowers into the kitchen and she gave Lidie a great earthenware pitcher and when Lidie had arranged them and set them in the middle of the table, she nodded approvingly.

'You have a flair, Lidie. One day you will make your own home beautiful.'

Lidie blushed.

Why are Aunt Louise and Cécile always talking of my future?

The evening meal at the farmhouse was a simple affair, but even so, Lidie took care with her appearance, fretting over her hair and changing into a clean dress. When she came down from their chamber she met Cécile on the stairs who said nothing but raised an eyebrow.

'What?' asked Lidie.

'I am keeping my peace, Lidie,' said Cécile, grinning as she brushed past her and went up the stairs.

Samuel had walked over from his father's farm and his arrival was unheralded until suddenly he was there amongst them having followed the sound of conversation and wandered into the kitchen where the family was gathered.

Louise, Sara and a peasant woman were all busying themselves at the stove and had their backs to the door so it was Uncle Jacob who saw him first.

'Samuel, how glad we are to have you here with us.'

Louise, too, went to greet him, wiping her hand before offering it up to him to kiss.

Then Uncle Jacob took him by the arm and guided him out of the door.

'Samuel and I have more farm matters to discuss,' he called over his shoulder, and the two of them were immediately in deep discussion, leaning in towards one another, as they walked away from the kitchen and into another room.

Cécile looked at Lidie. 'He didn't even greet us,' she whispered.

'He didn't have the chance,' said Lidie.

She continued to carry out the tasks she had been set by Aunt Louise.

He could have managed a smile at least.

Later, when they were all settled down to eat, Samuel was seated by Uncle Jacob and they continued their talk about the management of farms. From time to time, Lidie caught snatches of their conversation but to her ears it sounded dull – all on subjects of which she had little knowledge and less interest. About irrigation, ways of increasing the yield of crops, the quality of soil and suchlike.

She sighed and stopped listening, joining in again with the lively talk of the cousins.

Then Uncle Jacob rose from the table to fetch the wine and Samuel looked round at the assembled company. Lidie was chatting with one of Cécile s brothers but something made her look up and she caught Samuel's eye. He smiled at her and she blushed crimson and lowered her eyes.

As always, at the end of the day, there were prayers and Bible readings. They sang some psalms and Samuel joined in, singing quietly and reverently along with the rest of the family, then he thanked Uncle Jacob for his advice and Aunt Louise for her hospitality, and made his excuses.

'I need to return to our farm before dark,' he said.

The sun was sinking fast as they all gathered outside to see him off. The others soon went back inside but Lidie and Cécile stayed for a while, looking after his receding figure as he walked quickly away from them down the track. He stopped once and looked back, raising his hand, then as the track veered to the left, he was lost to their sight.

'Huh!' said Cécile. 'He could have been more pleasant to the rest of us. All his conversation was with Father.'

Lidie's voice was flat. 'I imagine he feels his responsibilities keenly,' she said. 'His father has charged him with attending to the farm business. And he is still only a student after all.'

'I would have thought a student would be more merry,' said Cécile. 'What age is he? He can't be much past twenty.'

'There is something to be said for a young man who is not always frivolous,' said Lidie.

Cécile hooted with laughter. 'You sound like my Mama,' she said. 'You need someone young and gay who will sweep you off your feet, Lidie, not a dull student of the law who takes everything so seriously.'

She put her arm round her cousin's shoulders. 'You are such a pretty girl, and there are plenty more young men who will come to court you, you mark my words.'

Lidie changed the subject. 'All this talk of me, Cécile, but you are nineteen, after all. You told me of this fellow you had met …'

67

Cécile needed little urging and she chatted on excitedly about some young man. Lidie had heard much talk of him but had never met him.

'Why do you not invite him to your home?'

Cécile looked down at her feet. 'I'm not sure.'

'Not sure about what?'

Cécile turned to her. 'Can you keep a secret, Lidie?'

'Of course.'

'He comes from a Protestant family but …'

'But what?'

'He is not devout in the way in which our families are devout.'

Lidie frowned. 'Do you mean that he would consider abjuring if it suited him? Is that why you said to me the other day that you could not find it in your heart to blame those who abjured if they were threatened?'

Cécile nodded and there was silence between them, only broken by the insistent noise of the cicadas.

'That would not go well with your mama and papa,' said Lidie, at last.

'He is serious in his intentions towards me, Lidie, but I fear my family would not approve if they knew that he doesn't take his faith so seriously.'

'You met him at our temple, did you not?'

'Yes, but his family are not one of our circle. They have never worshipped regularly.'

'Then how …?'

Cécile looked down at the ground. 'I confess we have met in secret. I … well, I have found a way to creep from our house without a chaperone. We see each other whenever we can. He is the one for me, I know it.' She held her hand to her heart. 'I feel it in here.'

'You've left the house by yourself? But what if you were discovered …?'

Cécile did not meet Lidie's eyes. 'I love him. I had to see him,' she said.

Lidie frowned. 'Maybe, if he meets your family and sees how they love their faith, he might change?'

'Maybe,' said Cécile, but she didn't sound hopeful.

'I will pray that God will help him come to a stronger faith.'

But as she lay in bed that night, Lidie's thoughts turned not to Cécile's young man but to Samuel.

I wish that Samuel had been friendlier to me this evening.

Chapter Six

Winter 1681

Isaac Verdier was in a coach being driven back from Bordeaux where he had personally petitioned the Intendant to allow him to continue to offer practical experience to young medical graduates of his faith. A petition which had fallen on deaf ears.

Usually the journey would have only taken a day but the roads were slow, the weather inclement and then one of the horses went lame, forcing Isaac to lodge in an inn overnight. He had hoped that the next day would bring better weather but the morning skies were leaden and the mud on the road even worse. The driving rain continued to beat against the carriage doors, the gloom outside matching his mood.

His had been an informal request but he knew he would not succeed if he were to take his case to the provincial parliament since the special chambres mi-parties, which protected Huguenot interests, had been abolished in the region by the King's order two years ago. In the past these courts had equal numbers of Huguenot and Catholic judges but now they consisted of only Catholics meaning that Huguenot cases stood little hope of a favourable outcome.

And, indeed, it had been made clear to Isaac that it would not be long before young Protestant men would be barred from entering either the medical or the legal profession unless they abjured. However, if they did abjure, then the Intendant would be delighted to welcome them as Catholic students of medicine or law, and offer them financial inducements to do so.

It was made clear, too, that if such a well loved and respected member of the community as Isaac were to abjure, then he, too, might receive considerable financial help for his infirmary.

As he was jolted from side to side in the carriage, Isaac's thoughts were gloomy.

THE KING'S COMMAND

What has happened to our people? So often I have worked in harmony alongside Catholic men of medicine in the past. We all have the interests of our patients at heart, surely?'

He sighed and shifted in his seat trying to ease some of the stiffness in his body.

Now he would only be allowed to give practical instruction to Catholic medical graduates or to Protestant graduates who had denied their faith and converted.

He smiled grimly to himself.

That may be the ruling but I am not disposed to obey it.

When at last he reached home, an anxious group of servants met him as he dismounted from the carriage, and he'd hardly had time to pay off the driver before they were questioning him.

'What news, doctor?'

'Did the Intendant accept your plea?'

'Will you be able to continue your teaching?'

Isaac handed his cloak and hat to one of the maids. 'Would you take some wine, sir?' she asked.

Isaac smiled at her. 'That would be very welcome. A glass of wine and a warm fire.'

'The fire is burning brightly already sir.'

He made to walk across the vestibule but then he stopped.

He sighed and rubbed his eyes. 'I fear, my friends,' he said, 'that it did not go my way.'

There was some murmuring among the servants.

Isaac was bone weary. He looked around at all these loyal members of his household. He was not normally given to shows of emotion but at that moment he felt himself ready to weep.

If he could no longer give practical help to newly graduated Huguenot students, they would not be admitted to the professional Guild in Bordeaux, but then, in any case, they would not be accepted unless they abjured. And if he continued to instruct those who refused to abjure, he would put them at risk as well as himself. It was a heavy burden to bear.

***

The next morning, there was a commotion at the door of Isaac's house and the pastor, Pierre Gabriac, rushed inside, not even pausing to greet anyone.

'Have you heard?' he asked, breathless after his ride from the town.

'My dear Pierre,' said Isaac, 'Whatever is the matter? Please, calm yourself. Come in and sit down.'

But the pastor paced up and down, wringing his hands.

'Dear God, Isaac,' he said, 'I cannot believe the King would sanction such evil.'

Several of the servants were present so Isaac guided Pierre firmly away into the library and closed the door.

Pierre continued to pace, shaking his head.

'Pray sit down, Pierre. I have never seen you so agitated. What's happened?'

Pierre eventually slumped into a chair and put his head in his hands. 'In Poitiers,' he muttered. 'We heard news of it just this morning, from some merchant who had met some of those fleeing …'

'You're making no sense, man. Who is fleeing?'

'It must have been de Marillac's doing.'

Isaac frowned. 'Marillac? The Intendant in the Poitou region?'

Pierre nodded. 'Yes, yes, but they say he was under instruction from Louvois.'

'The Minister for War?' But I don't understand, Pierre. Please, man, calm yourself and start from the beginning.'

Pierre took a deep breath.

'It seems that Louvois sent a calvalry regiment to Poitiers for winter quarters.'

'That is not so unusual, surely?'

Pierre shook his head impatiently. 'Of course not, but then Marillac lodged the soldiers in Protestant homes and allowed them to run riot.'

Isaac frowned as he began to comprehend what this might mean. He pulled up a chair and sat beside Pierre. 'In what way, run riot?' he asked.

Pierre stared down at the floor, fiddling with a thread which had come loose from his black jerkin.

'In every way possible,' he muttered. 'The merchant had spoken at length with some of those fleeing.'

Isaac said nothing and waited. Pierre eventually raised his head and met Isaac's eyes.

'They were dragoons,' he said. 'Rough soldiers, many of them mercenaries, not even natives of France. They were allowed to ruin their hosts, nay even encouraged to do so as a way of forcing them to abjure. Only if the head of the household signed an abjuration paper agreeing to deny his faith would the soldiers leave.'

Isaac clenched his fist. 'Go on.'

'The merchant said that the soldiers forced their hosts to feed them, they broke their furniture or sold it. They tortured the men and raped the women and even, God help us, mistreated the children. Those savages treated our people as though they were their playthings.'

'Dear Lord,' muttered Isaac. 'And this is still happening?'

Pierre nodded. 'Apparently.'

'Have any died?'

Pierre nodded. 'Some were tortured to death but many have abjured to save their families. And many have left everything behind and are fleeing.'

'Fleeing?'

'Yes, they told of unspeakable violence measured out to our people.' He turned away, shuddering. 'I cannot repeat what I have heard it disgusts me so.'

He swallowed and went on. 'The merchant said that some of those fleeing spoke of trying to find passage to England, or going to Holland or other Protestant countries even though we are forbidden to leave.'

'An impossible choice,' muttered Isaac. He rose to his feet and walked over to the window which looked out over his walled garden. It was a peaceful scene, the garden put to bed for the winter, the innocence of the naked plants and trees contrasting with the rage within him.

73

He turned. 'So it has come to this,' he said quietly. 'The King has sanctioned this cruelty.'

Pierre nodded. 'I cannot believe that His Majesty fully understands what he has unleashed,' he said.

'He may not comprehend the enormity of it,' said Isaac. 'But he must be held responsible for it with that rallying cry he causes to be recited up and down the country.'

'One country, one king, one faith,' said Pierre, spitting out the words. 'Louvois and Marillac would say they are only doing the King's bidding.'

Isaac suddenly brought his fist down on the table and Pierre started. 'It is so wrong, Pierre! We have always been loyal to the King. All we ask is to live in peace, work hard, help others and love God according to our own conscience and if we are driven out of our country because of it, it will be France's loss.'

They both stayed silent for a while, then Pierre spoke. 'How far is Poitiers from here?'

'About five days journey North,' said Isaac.

'Five days is not such a long time,' said Pierre quietly. He swallowed again and looked at his feet. 'They say that the pastors have been treated cruelly, worse than any others. The tortures …' He wet his lips. 'They have been …'

Pierre shuddered and Isaac put a comforting arm on his shoulder. 'Please, Pierre, do not distress yourself. From what you say, these were brutal acts of soldiers allowed to inflict whatever pain they chose upon innocent citizens. I cannot believe that they will go unpunished, that Marillac will not be disciplined. And we have the Edict of Nantes, after all, to protect us.'

But even as he said it, he knew his words were empty. The terms of that Edict which had kept the Protestants safe for over eighty years, were gradually being eroded. Bit by bit, King Louis and his advisers were imposing more and more restrictions.

Pierre echoed his thoughts. 'Can it really keep us safe. Isaac?'

'For now we are protected legally, though …'

Pierre looked up. 'Though?'

Isaac sighed. Pierre would find out soon enough what had happened at Bordeaux.

'I visited the Intendant in Bordeaux the day before yesterday,' he said.

'Ah, forgive me, Isaac, in all this turmoil, I had forgot. How did it go?'

Isaac shook his head. 'It is official. I am banned from teaching Reformed students from now on. Unless they abjure.'

'How can they do that!' shouted Pierre. 'How can they deny our young men the chance to learn the necessary practical skills you teach. It is wicked.'

'I suppose it is a sure way of ridding France of Protestant professionals,' Isaac said wearily. 'As you know, students of our faith are already meeting barriers to their advancement in the legal profession.

'But then there will come a time when our people will have no one to represent them, to put their case!'

'Indeed.'

'And what of your son?'

Isaac shrugged. 'Who knows what the future holds for him. He will become an avocat but I doubt he will be able to become an attorney. And there are rumours that young men of the Reformed faith will soon be banned completely from entering the profession.'

'And for you, my friend. Your wonderful infirmary, all your work with the sick. *You* never discriminate between the Protestant sick and the Catholic sick. How can they treat you so unjustly? Can they not see that all you wish to do is to pass on your skills so that the sick continue to be cared for. What will you do?' Then he frowned. 'You would never abjure would you, Isaac?'

'How can you even entertain the thought, Pierre! No, of course not. I hold strongly to our beliefs. My ancestors fought and died for them. I would never profane their memory by denying my faith.'

'But you will no longer be able to teach Protestant students?'

Isaac stretched his arms above his head, leant back in his chair and laced his hands behind his head.

'I admit I could not sleep last night for thinking about it,' he said. 'But before I make any decisions, I must go to the infirmary for I want those who work there to hear the news from my own lips.'

Pierre nodded. 'They will be appalled.'

They were both silent for a moment. Isaac glanced at Pierre who sat looking down at his lap. He was still a young man, less than 30 years old, yet he had had to bear so much. Isaac thought back to the joyous wedding of Pierre with his pretty wife, Hannah, when they were both so young and full of energy and enthusiasm and love for one another. Now that joy had turned to misery. Every year, there had been a tragedy, either a miscarriage or a child brought to term and then stillborn or only alive for a matter of days. Isaac had attended every one of these events and had seen how they had turned Pierre's wife from a trusting, lovely girl, into a trembling nervous woman who walked with her head cast down and with a constant tic to the side of her face.

'Does Hannah know of what happened in Poitiers?' he asked gently.

Pierre shook his head. 'I have said nothing of it. As soon as I heard I rode out of town to see you, but I fear she will hear soon enough and … I should be with her.'

He met Isaac's eyes. 'It will not improve her state of mind,' he said quietly.

'I fear not,' replied Isaac. Then he rose from his chair. 'I am so grateful to you for coming to tell me this dreadful news, Pierre. I would not have been left in ignorance. But I must go to the infirmary now.'

'Of course,' said Pierre. 'And I must go back into the town and consult with the Elders – and try and reassure my flock.'

The words *and my wife* were left unsaid.

Isaac saw him out and as Pierre was putting on his hat, he said. 'You must try and find a way to continue your teaching work, Isaac. Your students need you.'

Isaac clasped his hand. 'And we need you, too, Pierre. God go with you and let us pray that He has a plan for us all.'

A little later, Isaac walked round to the stables at the back of his house. He spent a moment stroking the nose of his favourite cob and whispering to him before he tacked him up, led him out to the mounting block and then heaved himself up into the saddle.

The infirmary was not far away but Isaac rode slowly, taking time to consider how to break the news and as he rode he thought back to that time, last summer, when he had saved the life of the young Catholic soldier and maybe opened his eyes a little.

As he approached the infirmary he felt a familiar sense of pride. It was small, to be sure, but well built and exactly suited its purpose. So many people had helped bring the project to fruition, not only the well off Protestants who had given money, but all the carpenters and skilled tradesmen who had worked on it.

'It must not go to waste,' he muttered.

He raised his head to the sky. 'God, healer of the sick, look down upon your unworthy servant and give me wisdom.'

There was a sudden break in the clouds and a shaft of sunlight struck the infirmary roof.

Isaac smiled to himself. If he had been a fanciful man, he might have seen this as a sign from heaven. But he was not. He was a practical man and no sunbeam was going to solve his problems. Nonetheless, his resolve hardened. He had decided on the way forward and he had no doubt at all that his decision was the right one.

At the entrance, a little knot of people was already there to greet him, having seen his approach. Adam came up and held the cob's head while Isaac dismounted.

'What news, sir?' said someone.

Isaac looked at the anxious faces and felt a wave of affection for them. His people. They trusted him, they took pride in their work and they relied on him for their livelihoods.

'Gather everyone together,' he said, 'I would speak with you all.' Then, as Adam led the cob away, he raised his voice. 'And you, too, Adam. Come back when you have seen to the horse.'

The two nurses, the cook, Marie and her brother, two other servants and Adam all gathered in the little entrance hall of the infirmary. By this time, Isaac had taken off his hat and cloak, washed his hands and face and composed himself as much as he was able.

77

He stood with his back to the wall, his eyes fixing on first one face and then another. Adam was at the back, standing awkwardly near his two children and the cook. The two nurses and the maids were near the front.

'Is everyone gathered?'

There were murmurs of assent. He cleared his throat and came straight to the point.

'I fear, my friends, that the result of my meeting in Bordeaux went against me. From now on I am forbidden to teach Protestant students.' He sighed and went on. 'As you know, already many surgeons and apothecaries of our faith have been banned from working unless they abjure, and it is becoming clear that we Protestant physicians may also soon be refused permission to practice our profession – unless we, too, convert.'

There were gasps and immediately chattering broke out. One of the nurses spoke up.

'But what will happen, sir? We need physicians.'

Isaac held up his hand for silence. 'When I became a doctor,' he said, 'I took a solemn oath to treat the sick to the best of my ability and to pass on my skills to the next generation.'

All eyes were on him as he continued: 'I cannot foreswear that sacred oath,' he said quietly. 'No squabbles between religious sects can alter what, as a young man, I solemnly swore to do for the rest of my life.'

There was complete silence in the room, then some brave soul said. 'But will you not put yourself at risk, sir, if you continue to teach?'

Isaac raised his voice. 'That may be, but that is not to say that you, my loyal friends, need to put yourselves at risk by associating with me. I will understand if you no longer wish to work for me.'

There was more hubbub among the listeners and Isaac spoke again.

'Take your time to consider your positions,' he said. 'No one, least of all me, will think less of you if you wish to disassociate yourselves from me and from our work here, and when you have given it due thought, come and tell me your decisions.'

The first to speak up was Adam. 'I am with you sir.'

Then there were others. 'Aye, me too. I'll not desert you.'

'Nor I.'

'Take your time, my friends,' Isaac urged again. 'Do not be too hasty. You must consider your decision carefully. Speak to your families. I would not have you stay through misplaced loyalty to me.'

Then he clapped his hands. 'But now we have work to do.'

The nurse spoke out again. 'We know the risks, sir, and ...' She looked round at the others.. 'We ... we heard the news from Poitiers.'

Isaac frowned. 'You have already heard?'

'It is all over the town. This morning, since the news spread from the merchant, they speak of nothing else.'

Isaac shook his head. 'It is a shocking business,' he said. 'We must pray that this was a single brutal act sanctioned by the Intendant of that region. And,' he added, 'I would urge you to remember in your prayers all of our faith who have been affected.'

'How can the King allow such brutality?'

Some heated conversation broke out then and Isaac raised his voice again. 'To work,' he said. 'There are those who need us here.'

Chapter Seven

After Isaac had finished his rounds, he walked slowly out of the back of the infirmary. The air was sharp and cold as he made his way to the stables, but the sky was a clear blue and the winter sun cast its rays across the fields in the distance, empty of labourers now, the ground waiting to be tilled and planted when Spring arrived.

In the stables Adam was forking the soiled straw into a barrow. Isaac stood and watched him for a moment, unobserved. The man worked with a furious energy, his face set.

'Adam,' said Isaac gently. 'Your son could do that. The work is too heavy for you.'

Adam leant on his pitchfork and looked down at the stable floor. 'I like being close to the horses,' he mumbled.

Isaac nodded. 'They accept us for what we are, do they not, and it is a comfort not to be judged. They do not care whether we are Catholic or Protestant.'

Adam smiled. 'I'd a deal rather spend time with the animals than with some Catholics.'

Isaac patted the nose of his favourite cob. 'These are troubled times, Adam. No one knows what the future holds, but you must not put your family at risk for my sake.'

Adam looked up. 'We would be dead if you had not come to our aid, sir. We will always serve you.'

Isaac turned quickly and started to saddle up the cob.

I am tired and distraught. I should not be so affected.

By the time he had finished, he had composed himself somewhat. He led the cob out to the mounting block.

Adam watched as Isaac dug his heels into the horse's flanks and set off at a brisk trot towards the town.

He had a need to speak with his Reformist friends, to gain strength from their company and he wanted to know details of the outrages at Poitiers from the merchant who had brought to news to the town. Rumours were rife but he needed to learn the facts and judge for himself what danger they might be in here in Castillon.

He decided to visit the merchant first.

He knew the man. Indeed he had treated his father only recently; he came from a family of weavers whose business was set up just beside the ruins of the town wall. When Isaac arrived at the place, he found a large and agitated group of people there.

'Have you heard the news, doctor? About what happened in Poitiers?'

Isaac nodded. 'I have, but I would hear it from the man who delivered it.'

Just then, a member of the weaver's family came out from the house. 'He is not here,' he said to the assembled crowd. 'He has gone to speak with others of our congregation to tell them what occurred.'

Isaac nodded and turned away. Louise and Jacob would have heard the news and he was sure that they would be able to give him a sensible account of the atrocities. He headed down into the faubourg to their house, dismounted and called for a servant to tend the horse.

He had hardly had time to scrape the mud off his boots when the door was flung open.

'Isaac,' cried Jacob. 'I saw you riding up the street. Come in, come in. This is a terrible business.'

Isaac followed him upstairs to the main reception room the scene, only last summer, of Lidie's joyous birthday celebrations. Now it was crowded with people, many of whom were known to him, and at its centre, the merchant who had brought the news. The man's hair was tangled and his clothes spattered with mud.

Jacob clapped his hands for silence.

'I have asked you all here so that our friend can tell us exactly what he has heard. We must not deal in false rumours. If we know the facts, however bad they may be, then we are prepared.'

'May the Lord have mercy on us,' muttered someone. Jacob raised his voice.

'We shall indeed call on the Lord,' he said. 'But first, let us hear what our friend has to say.'

81

'Sir,' said the merchant, looking round the room and spotting Louise, Sara and several other women. 'What I have to say …I do not think our womenfolk should hear it.'

Louise spoke up. 'We are not fainthearted,' she said firmly.

The merchant glanced anxiously at Jacob, who nodded.

The man cleared his throat and everyone fell silent. 'I was on the road,' he said. 'I had been gone a few days, trading my cloth and taking orders from my usual buyers, and I was approaching Poitiers.' He licked his lips.

'How far were you from the town?' asked someone.

'I had another day's ride,' he replied. 'But then I met the first of those fleeing.'

'Go on,' said Jacob.

'Most were on horseback or were driving carts,' he said. 'As I approached, they urged me to turn back, telling me that there was much evil being done in the town. But they said no more, just went on their way, their faces set.'

'So, did you do as they asked?' said someone. 'Did you turn back?'

'I hardly knew what to do,' said the merchant. 'I do good business in Poitiers and … and I had those in the town who were expecting me, so I rode on.'

'And what persuaded you to turn back?' asked Jacob.

'What started as a few families on the road turned into a great stream of folk,' he said. 'Not many addressed me, they were too anxious to leave the town, but those who did shouted out warnings, urging me to turn back.'

The merchant's brow was covered in beads of sweat and he paused to wipe it with a kerchief.

'At length I saw a couple from the town I recognized and begged them to tell me what had occurred.'

He shook his head. 'In truth, if I'd not traded with them often in the past, I would not have known them for my friends, their demeanour was so changed. They were dishevelled and bloodstained.' He cleared his throat. 'Their looks were wild and the wife's hands trembled. Indeed, she could hardly speak. I would not have known her as the voluble and amiable soul with whom I had done business so many times.'

He paused then and closed his eyes for a moment.

'Go on,' said Jacob gently.

'I could see that they were exhausted and I urged them to pause for a moment in their flight and tell me more, so we drew aside from the stream of people.'

He wiped his brow once more while everyone in the company stayed silent and waited for him to continue.

'I can only recount what my friends told me. I cannot say exactly what happened to other families but I suspect it was similar.' His voice started to falter.

Jacob put a hand on the merchant's arm. 'We must understand what has befallen our brethren.'

The man sat down suddenly in one of the chairs and put his head in his hands. When he raised it again, his face was tear stained.

'The dragoons came two weeks' ago,' he said quietly. 'They marched into the town and their leaders billeted them only with Protestant families. Many of the families objected to this invasion of their homes but the more they objected the worse they were treated.'

Louise spoke up. 'Did they have to feed the soldiers?'

'Not only that, they had to provide everything they wished for. The soldiers were the lowest sort. They gorged themselves on all that was in store for the winter, all the food and drink in the house and when they had finished that they demanded more. Despite being met with politeness and entreaties to forbear, they became more and more rude, swearing and treating folk with no respect. They attacked both the men and the women if they were refused anything.'

There were some shocked gasps among the company.

'And your friends?' asked Jacob.

'The husband went to the soldiers' leader in the town to beg him to control the troops, but to no avail. He was told that if he signed a document revoking his faith, the soldiers would leave his house immediately and he and all his household would no longer be troubled. If he did not, then he must take the consequences.'

'An impossible situation,' said someone.

'Indeed. My friend would never deny his faith so he returned to break the news to his wife and family. And then, having heard of his visit to their leader, the soldiers renewed their atrocities. They broke up the furniture then ripped the tapestries from the walls, they smashed and looted and destroyed everything they could find. And they made free with …'

'What exactly are you telling us?'

'The menfolk tried to protect the women,' he whispered. 'And even the wife's old father was cruelly treated. He was stripped naked and strung from the rafters, then they filled his boots with boiling oil and forced them on his bare feet.'

There were horrified looks and further murmurings which fell silent again as he continued.

'And the husband fought to protect the honour of his wife and his daughter,' he said 'but he was knocked unconscious by the soldiers and when he at last became sensible again it was to witness his son being run through with a sword while he tried to prevent one of these beasts forcing himself on his sister.'

For a while there was no sound in the room as everyone absorbed the horror of the events being recounted.

The man was still sitting in the chair and his hand trembled as he accepted a glass of wine.

Louise moistened her lips. 'Did the son survive?' she asked.

The merchant shook his head. 'No more did the wife's father,' he said flatly.

There was a shocked silence, then someone muttered 'That poor family How could those beasts be let loose on such innocents?'

The merchant nodded. 'The soldiers refer to themselves as missionary soldiers bound on converting those they refer to as heretics to the Catholic faith, but in truth they were nothing more than the lowest of men revelling in torture and destruction. Many of them were mercenaries from Germany and elsewhere. They were carrying out orders to crush those of our faith and force them to convert and they did so with a violent blood lust.'

'Did your friends know if there were many converts to the Catholic faith among our brethren?' asked Jacob.

'Many many conversions. He spoke of terrified householders lining up to sign papers to save their lives and those of their families.'

'Then it seems that this experiment carried out by Marillac and Louvois was a success. Not many would be as brave as your friend and refuse to abjure when faced with such horror.'

There were more murmurings in the room, then Jacob spoke again. 'We should pray for our brethren in Poitiers,' he said. 'We will ask the Elders to call a meeting so that we can pray to God to give strength to them in their travails and to help us here to hold fast to our beliefs.'

As everyone was nodding their agreement and urgent conversation continued, Isaac walked over to the window and stared out at the great river below. The view of the water was peaceful but nothing could calm his fear. He had reassured Pierre that Marillac was sure to be admonished for what he had allowed in his généralité, but now he was not so sure that this would happen. What if releasing these dragoons into the homes of Huguenots became an action to be repeated elsewhere as an effective way of forcing them to abjure?

When he turned away from the window, he went over to Jacob and tapped him on the shoulder.

'I'll go to Pierre now and ask him to assemble us to pray,' he said quietly.

Jacob nodded. 'I am surprised he was not among us. I sent word,' he replied.

Isaac had a good idea why Pierre was absent, but he kept his thoughts to himself.

'I'll ride over now,' he said, and made his farewells, relieved to leave the ferment of anxiety in the room and clear his head. He collected his horse from the servant at the door and rode up through the town to where Pierre and his wife lived on the other side of the market.

As he rode through the town, there were huddles of folk, some in doorways, some in the middle of the street and several people called out to him.

'Doctor, have you heard what happened in Poitiers?'

'Indeed. A sorry business,' he remarked, but he did not stop.

Pierre lived in a modest house on the other side of the market, on one of the narrow streets that ran down to the river. The buildings here overhung the street, almost meeting those on the other side, Isaac dismounted and hooked the horse's reins over the post outside Pierre's house.

He stood at the door for a few moments before knocking. He could hear voices from within, Pierre's low and steady and his wife's, shrill and edged with hysteria. Then he knocked on the door and the voices stilled.

It was a while before the door opened, and it was done very cautiously, but when Pierre saw who it was the relief on his face was almost comical and Isaac guessed that the poor man had already been besieged with visits from members of his congregation.

Isaac smiled at him. 'Not another member of your flock come to seek comfort,' he said. 'I have come to convey a message from Jacob – and also,' he added, 'to see Hannah.'

'Come in, come in,' said Pierre, and led Isaac through to the back room where his wife Hannah was sitting.

It was a sorry sight. Isaac knew that she didn't welcome company. This was no bustling, happy household but gloomy and quiet. Here was such a contrast to the house he had just left, richly furnished and full of light. Isaac approached cautiously.

'Hannah,' he said. 'How goes it with you?'

She started and her head turned slowly, eyes staring.

'Doctor,' she said, and her voice was not much above a whisper.

Isaac drew a chair up beside hers and looked at her. What a tragic change had befallen this once lovely, vivacious girl. Her face twitched and her hands were restless in her lap, folding and refolding a piece of linen.

'How goes it?' Isaac repeated.

She shook her head. 'I suffer all the time,' she said. 'I cannot sleep, I have pains, and now …' She looked up at Pierre. 'He has told me of the dreadful tidings from Poitiers. We shall be next. Pierre will be tortured or killed. They will take him away.'

The linen in her lap was kneaded faster and faster and tears were welling up in her eyes and dripping unchecked down her cheeks.

'Tell me where you feel the pain,' said Isaac, though he knew very well that the pain was in her head.

'Everywhere,' she said. 'Please give me something for it, doctor.'

Isaac took her hand and looked up at Pierre.

'I can prescribe a little more opium,' he said cautiously.

Hannah squeezed his hand. 'Oh please, doctor. It is the only thing that brings me any relief.'

Gently, Isaac removed his hand. 'I'll see to it,' he said. 'Now, I have to speak to Pierre for a moment.'

'Why,' said Hannah, her hands fluttering up to cover her mouth. 'What has happened?'

'He will need to speak with the Elders to arrange a meeting, that is all.'

'A meeting? Surely it is too dangerous …'

Isaac walked with Pierre out of the room. 'I fear she may become addicted to the drug,' he said quietly.

Pierre nodded. 'But it is the only thing that gives her peace. It seems to calm some of the turmoil in her head.' He sighed. 'If you knew how many prayers I have offered up to God for her recovery.'

'It is hard burden to bear, my friend.'

Pierre nodded, then he stood straighter and braced his shoulders. 'What is this about an assembly?' he asked.

'I have just come from a meeting at Jacob's house.'

'Ah yes, he sent word to me but ...' He gestured towards the room where Hannah was sitting.

'You were right to be with her,' said Isaac. 'The merchant who brought the news from Poitiers told us more.' He paused. 'It did not make easy listening.'

'We must pray for all our brethren so cruelly abused,' said Pierre

'It is everyone's wish,' said Isaac. 'Can you arrange it?'

'Of course,' said Pierre. 'We must all come together as soon as possible. I will spread the word once I have consulted with the Elders and found a suitable place.'

'We shall need more space than that afforded by a private house, Pierre. I am sure that every one of our faith will want to be there at this time.'

Pierre frowned. 'Are we brave enough to defy the law and meet in our temple?'

Isaac smiled. 'I hoped you would suggest it. Reformists greatly outnumber the Catholics in the town and it would show solidarity with those poor people fleeing their homes who have endured so much.' Isaac rubbed his chin. 'A symbolic gesture, to be sure, but it will be a way of showing how united we are, even in the face of such persecution. It will be a joyous celebration of our strength and of our commitment. And,' he added. 'Being in such a public place, any Catholic passers by who witnesses it will know that we stand firm.'

Pierre's brow cleared and he smiled. 'It is that faith which gives me strength, Isaac. And friends such as you who keep it so loyally. If the Elders agree I will spread the word and we shall gather there tomorrow.'

Isaac clapped Pierre on the back and smiled. 'Thank you for your courage, Pierre. We shall all draw strength from it,' he said, then he headed out of the house.

When he was beyond the town, he slowed his horse down to a walk, anxious to be alone with the thoughts which crowded into his head.

Where will it end?

Chapter Eight

Lidie had spent the morning at her Aunt Louise's house. She no longer had lessons there but after the news from Poitiers, she had felt the need for company and she joined her boy cousins and the tutor in their study of the Bible before wandering off to find Cécile who was sitting in the window seat of the main reception room, her head bent, sewing. When Lidie came in, she raised her head from her work and stretched her arms above her head.

The pale winter sun coming through the window caught at the motes of dust in the air and picked up the bright white of her coif and the gleam of the dark ringlets which fell to her shoulders.

'Lidie, are you calmed by the study of the word of God?' asked Cécile, smiling at her.

'A little,' admitted Lidie, 'Though these horrors at Poitiers …' She swallowed. 'They say that households where the soldiers found hidden bibles were treated particularly harshly. We should take more care.'

Cécile patted the space beside her and Lidie joined her on the wide window seat.

'You must not dwell on it. It is because the Catholics are ignorant. They do not study the Bible. They only hear the word of God from their priests.'

'How can I not dwell on it? Mama was so shocked when she came back to the house after hearing from that merchant. I insisted she tell me everything and now …' she shunted along to be closer to Cécile. 'Now I wish she had not.'

Cécile put down her tapestry. 'Papa says that he is sure that the King did not intend such brutality. That it was the fault of the Intendant and that he will be severely reprimanded.'

Lidie shivered. 'Let us hope it will be so,' she said. 'It sickens me to hear what those poor people suffered.'

They were silent for a moment and then Lidie took Cécile's tapestry from her lap and examined it.

'You have such a talent,' she said. 'My own stitching is so clumsy.'

'Oh well, no doubt I shall put it to good use when I have my own household.'

Lidie dropped the tapestry and looked up sharply. 'Cécile, you're not saying …'

Cécile put her finger to her lips. 'Shh! No, nothing is certain Lidie, but …'

'But what?'

'He has asked for my hand,' she said.

Lidie flung her arms round her cousin and hugged her, squashing the tapestry in the process.

'But that is wonderful, Cécile. Your parents have agreed to the match when you thought they would not. You must be so happy!'

Cécile frowned. 'Well, when I say he's asked for my hand, that's not quite true. He has asked me to be his wife but Mama and Papa have not yet met him - though he has agreed to come to the great gathering at the temple tomorrow.'

'How is it that they have not met him, Cécile? If he is of our faith and lives in the town.'

'I told you before, his family are not devout. I met him at one of our secret assemblies, but he's not attended any since, nor have his parents.'

Lidie picked at a thread which had come loose from her bodice. 'And do you think that Uncle Jacob and Aunt Louise will approve of him. Will they give their blessing to such a union?'

Cécile laughed. 'I think they'll be pleased to see me settled,' she said. Then she added, drily, 'His family are very wealthy.'

Lidie raised her eyebrows.

'Do you truly love him?'

Cécile nodded, her face serious for once. 'I mean to marry him, Lidie,.'

Lidie smiled. 'Then I long to meet him,' she said.

Cécile looked up. 'You will like him, I know,' she said. 'But in truth I am a little nervous. We have been meeting in secret without a chaperone, and I have not yet met his parents. They may condemn us for that, as may Mama and Papa.'

'Will his parents be at the gathering?'

Cécile shrugged. 'I asked him to try and persuade them to come,' she said. Then she got up suddenly. 'Let's talk no more of it now. Has there been any news of Samuel Verdier since the summer?'

Lidie coloured and shook her head. 'Samuel, no. I imagine he is away at his studies. He won't be thinking of me, I am sure of that.'

'You should forget him, Lidie. There are plenty of other young men who would seek to woo you.'

Lidie looked down at the floor. 'I know. You and Mama never cease to remind me of all the sons of families known to us. But …'

'But?'

Lidie sighed. 'It was just that he was different and … and I felt something for him.'

Cécile pulled Lidie her to her feet. 'Every Protestant family is sure to be at the gathering tomorrow,' she said. 'Your eye might alight on another young man!'

Lidie laughed. 'Tomorrow I shall be looking to meet *your* young man,' she said. 'You have never even told me his name?'

'There was a good reason for that,' muttered Cécile.

'You know that I have always kept your secrets!'

Cécile looked keenly at Lidie, 'Well, I suppose there's no harm now. You'll meet him tomorrow. His name is Charles. Charles Boucher.'

Lidie's hand flew to her mouth. 'Boucher! Is he related to the family who…'

Cécile nodded. 'Yes. His uncle is the merchant who abjured last year.'

'The family your parents were so exercised about the day after my anniversary party?'

'The very one,' said Cécile. 'But that is his uncle's family, Lidie. His own parents have not abjured.' She hesitated. 'It may be that they are not especially devout but they have not abjured – at least not yet.'

Lidie said nothing and soon after that she made her way home. At evening prayers she made an extra, silent, supplication.

'Dear Lord, help Charles Boucher hold fast to his faith'

Later that night, when the rest of the household slept and the house was silent, Susanne rose from the truckle bed on the landing and crept quietly downstairs.

The next day, from the middle of the morning, families started to stream from the town to the ruined North gate, the Porte Lavergne, being joined by others coming from the faubourg. They converged on the road to Saint-Magne where the temple stood. News of the atrocities at Poitiers had spread rapidly among the faithful and others came from surrounding villages having heard of the gathering. As the groups became larger they walked along more boldly, some even singing psalms in defiance of the law. Most were dressed soberly, the men in dark cloaks and hats and the women modestly in woollen dresses and white coifs. All were wearing warm cloaks to protect them from the chill of the morning.

Nearly all were known to one another and they greeted each other cordially, but the mood was sombre.

Lidie, Sara and Annette walked together and soon joined up with others. There was much talk of the atrocities at Poitiers but they also spoke of how their own Intendant had overseen the destruction of certain newer temples in their region.

'They say that Catholic workmen were employed to do the work and that they took the wood away for their own use,' said someone.

'Aye. Though our people petitioned the Intendant, he refused to stop the destruction.'

Here in Castillon, the temple still stood, empty now but still a fine symbol of the Protestant faith. Though the congregation had continued to worship in secret, in private homes and occasionally, in larger gatherings, in the woods near Pujols, today was different.

Today was an open act of defiance.

As they came nearer to the temple, the chattering ceased and Lidie could feel the tension in the air. She and Sara pushed through the crowd to join their family.

'Oh, there's a sharp wind today,' said Aunt Louise as she greeted them. She drew her cloak further round her. Then she, Jacob and Sara saw some friends and went over to greet them.

Cécile sidled up to Lidie and whispered. 'He has come!'

'Who?'

'Charles of course,' said Cécile. 'Over there, by the couple dressed in silks.'

'Are they his parents?'

Cécile nodded and bit her lip. 'Oh Lidie, he has seen me. They are all coming over.'

Although Charles and his parents were, indeed, headed their way, the crush of the crowd was considerable and their progress was slow so Lidie had plenty of time to observe them.

Most of the company had dressed quietly for this most solemn occasion. To be sure, Sara and Louise had lightened their plain dresses with a few ribbons, but Charles and his family stood out from the crowd, flamboyantly attired in brightly coloured silks covered by richly woven cloaks.

Charles was a well built young man. He wore no wig but sported a thick head of dark curly hair which he constantly brushed away from his face. He strode towards them ahead of his parents and when he finally reached Cécile's side, defying convention he took her hand and kissed it, smiling broadly. Then he turned to his parents who had arrived, a little breathless, to join him.

'Mother, Father, this is Cécile!'

Lidie noticed that Cécile was blushing as she bobbed a curtsy.

Charles' mother gave a brief nod and Lidie could see the disdain in her face as her eyes swept over Cécile's modest clothes. Lidie felt her own cheeks grow hot.

This is a solemn occasion. It is fitting that we dress modestly and soberly for it.

Cécile immediately introduced Lidie to Charles and his family and they smiled at her politely.

'Where are your parents, Cécile?' asked Charles' father.

Cécile pointed. 'Over there, sir, near the front.'

'Will you not take us to make their acquaintance?'

'Of course,' said Cécile, but just then the crowd hushed as Pierre Gabriac raised his voice and called for silence.'

93

'My beloved brethren,' he began, his voice sure and strong, 'We come here today to our temple where we have held so many gatherings in the past, both joyful and sad.'

Pierre cut a fine and confident figure as he stood firmly before them in his black garb and only those standing very close to him saw the beads of sweat on his brow.

'A brave man,' muttered Uncle Jacob and beside him, Louise nodded. 'He will be the one to be blamed. If it comes to the ears of the Intendant, it will be Pierre who will be accused of inciting his congregation to disobey the King's edict.

Pierre cleared his throat and continued. 'Thank you my dear friends,' he said. 'Thank you for being courageous enough to come here today to pray for our brothers and sisters in Poitiers who have been so sorely abused. I am going inside our temple to lead prayers for them and to offer psalms of praise to the Lord.' He paused. 'I hope that you will follow but if you feel you cannot flout the law in this way, I shall understand.'

Sara did not hesitate and she was one of the first to step inside the temple, Lidie at her side. Sara looked about her and then said quietly to Lidie. 'He could have done with the support of his wife today, the poor man.'

As they pushed their way inside, Lidie heard Charles' mother say to her husband, 'I hope the pastor won't speak for too long. It is not pleasant standing here among such a throng and in the cold.'

Lidie frowned.

What about all those fleeing their homes in Poitiers? They will be a sight colder.

She glanced at Cécile, but Cécile had eyes only for Charles and Lidie felt a stab of jealousy.

If she marries him, our bonds will loosen. Her affection will be elsewhere.

She sighed and looked back at Pierre who was now inside the temple. He was so steadfast in his faith, so true and without doubt.

At length, when everyone had crowded into the building, the men standing in the upper tier and the women and children on the ground floor, Pierre addressed the congregation from the pulpit. His voice rose and fell, urging the congregation to remain steadfast and saying heartfelt prayers for the afflicted. Then, as he handed over to the chanteur to lead the faithful in the familiar psalms, Lidie felt herself transported. How lucky she was to be part of this community of pilgrims with their simple faith which was so strong because it came from within each and every one of them, pared down to the core of belief and not bolstered by incense and rituals and the power of the priests. Pastors of their Reformed tradition were of the people and cared for the people, they set no store by title and fame.

Being inside this familiar building, she felt moresure than ever that how they worshipped God and how they behaved in their lives, was good and right.

The temple was so familiar but now it was as if she were seeing it anew for the first time and appreciating the fine cross beams of the ceiling and the gallery looking down on the pulpit and wooden seating below.

Sara, too, was looking about her. 'It lifts my soul to be inside this building again,' she whispered to Lidie

At length, the service was over and Lidie and Sara followed the crowd outside where they were soon caught up in conversations with their fellow worshippers.

'Didn't the pastor speak well?' said someone.

'Aye,' said another. 'He has bound us even more strongly together.'

Lidie spied Cécile who was introducing Charles and his family to Louise and Jacob.

'Who are those people with Cécile?' asked Sara. 'I don't think I've made their acquaintance.'

'That is the young man Cécile intends to marry, Charles Boucher, with his parents.'

'What! I knew nothing of this!'

'No. She has been very discreet about it.'

Sara stared at the threesome, so finely dressed compared with most of the others. She frowned. 'I have never seen them at our gatherings before.'

'No, nor I,' said Lidie.

'They seem a little overdressed for such a solemn occasion.' Then she continued. 'Boucher. Was that not the name of the merchant who abjured?'

'I believe they are related,' said Lidie. 'But I'm sure they are good people, Mama. And Cécile has told me how happy Charles makes her.'

'Well,' said Sara, 'If my niece has really set her heart on the young man, we had better get to know him.' But she didn't smile as she made her way over to them.

They had hardly been introduced when there were shouts from the edge of the crowd and people who had been chatting amiably to one another, looked up anxiously.

Jacob was the first to realize what was happening.

'Come, Louise. We should go home now.'

'What is it Papa?' asked Cécile.

'Some Catholic rabble rousers trying to cause trouble,' said Jacob shortly, and I would rather you were safely in the house.'

Monsieur Boucher followed Jacob's gaze. 'All this fuss because of religion,' he said. 'Is it really worth fighting over?'

Every member of Lidie's family heard the remark and stared at him. Then his wife took his arm. 'Come my dear,' she said. 'We don't want to become involved in any trouble.'

Charles lingered for a moment, pressed Cécile's hand to his lips and then followed his parents.

Cécile's cheeks were aflame and Lidie could not tell whether it was from embarrassment at what his Charles' father had said or the intimate way in which Charles had kissed her hand.

The noise was getting louder. There were shouts and insults coming from the group of Catholics on horseback as some of the congregation were trying to reason with them.

As Lidie and Sara and the others followed the crowd back towards the town, some of the insults reached their ears.

'Your heretic friends in Poitiers converted, did they not! You blasphemers will soon bend to the will of the King.'

When one of the congregation shouted. 'Never. We will never forsake our faith' there was some harsh laughter. 'Aye, you'll resist until it hurts your pockets, then you'll abjure soon enough.'

Then they rode their horses into the crowd, laughing and hurling insults as people jumped out of their way.

'I suspect that there may be some truth in what that Catholic said,' said Sara breathlessly as she and Lidie started to run towards the town.

And Lidie knew that she was thinking of the Boucher family.

The horsemen finally tired of harassing the congregation and rode off. Lidie and Sara slowed their pace and met up again with their family. Isaac Verdier was there, too, and Louise begged him to come back to the house for some refreshment and, after some hesitation, he consented.

'I cannot stay long,' he said to Louise. 'But a little refreshment before I continue with my work would be very welcome.'

By the time they reached Louise and Jacob's house, there was no sign of the Boucher family but Sara and Lidie went in and they all sat down, thankful to be out of the cold wind and rest for a while after the emotion of the morning.

'We must invite the Boucher family here,' said Louise as she and a servant handed round some drinks and pastries.

Isaac frowned. 'Boucher. Is that not the …'

'Yes,' interrupted Jacob. 'Boucher was one of the first Protestant merchants to abjure.'

There was silence in the room, the only sound coming from the footsteps of the servant who was offering more pastries.

Jacob cleared his throat. 'His brother's son has asked for Cécile's hand.'

Isaac turned to Cécile. 'That is joyful news indeed, my dear. May I offer my congratulations.'

Cécile smiled. 'Thank you, sir,' she said, looking anxiously at her parents.

Neither Jacob nor Louise said anything.

Sara cleared her throat. 'My dear doctor,' she said. 'We heard that your meeting with the Intendant in Bordeaux did not go your way?'

Isaac nodded. 'It is a bad business, Madame, but for now I intend to carry on as usual and I'm glad to say that all my friends at the infirmary are supporting me.'

'And there was a rumour that young Protestant men may not to allowed to study the law. Is that so?'

Isaac shrugged. 'Rumours, yes. Nothing certain.'

'What of your son?'

Lidie looked up.

Isaac sighed. 'Samuel is near to qualifying,' he said. 'I just pray that he will be able to practise, at least in some limited way, without interference.'

Then he stood up. 'Forgive me, Madame,' he said to Louise, 'but I have work to do.'

'I beg you give us a little more of your time Isaac,' said Jacob. 'Why you have hardly had the chance to get warm. Wait a while before you head back to the infirmary.'

Isaac smiled. 'You are very persuasive,' he said, 'Just a few minutes more then.' He sank back into his chair and accepted another glass of wine.

Inevitably the conversation turned to the disruption at the temple.

'Who were those men?' asked Sara. 'And how did they know about the assembly? Pierre had asked all of us to be discreet and not make it known abroad.'

'A large movement of people converging on the temple would hardly go unnoticed,' said Jacob.

Isaac cleared his throat. 'There were a lot of the Catholics and they seemed well organised. I wonder …'

'What do you wonder, sir?' asked Sara.

'Can we be sure that all our friends are loyal?' he asked.

'What are you implying?' asked Jacob.

'Only that there may possibly be informants.'

'Surely not!'

'There is a history of it, Jacob. Cast your mind back to the turbulent times of the wars of religion. Men will do much if the price is right.'

'Bribes!?'

'Aye,' said Isaac. 'Men's morals are easily turned by the offer of money.'

THE KING'S COMMAND

Chapter Nine

Summer 1683

There had been changes in the last two years. Although there had not been incidents as grave as that at Poitiers Huguenots' privileges which had previously been accorded to the Huguenots continued to be eroded and there had been a steady stream of those abjuring.

Others, however, remained steadfast to their faith, living with difficulty under the restrictions imposed upon them or escaping from the realm, at great risk to themselves, to find refuge in Protestant countries.

Cécile had married Charles Boucher and was living in a house not far from her in-laws on the other side of the faubourg from Lidie and Sara. Their wedding had been a quiet but joyful occasion, conducted by Pierre Gabriac, and Louise and Jacob had set aside their misgivings when they saw how the young couple adored one another. Then, last year, Cécile had given birth to a healthy son which had further mended any rift.

Although Lidie visited her cousin from time to time, the intimacy they had enjoyed while they were growing up had suffered since Cécile's marriage, but today Lidie was going to see her cousin, not with her mama, for a change, but accompanied only by the young maid Susanne.

After a somewhat turbulent start, the relationship between Lidie and Susanne had settled down. The girl had been with them now for three years and she had been quick to learn her duties. Though she sometimes shocked Lidie by her frankness and rough speech, she had become a valuable member of the household.

Today, however, Susanne seemed cast down.

'Are you quite well, Susanne? You are very quiet.'

Susanne shrugged.

'What is it? If something is troubling you, you can tell me.'

Susanne merely shook her head, but Lidie persisted.

'Do you miss your family in Bordeaux?'

99

The girl's head whipped up then and she gave a mirthless laugh.

'That lot! Nah! Best thing I ever did was to run off.'

'Castillon must be a quiet place compared to Bordeaux.'

Susanne grunted.

'I went there once with my father,' said Lidie.

'Aye, and I wager you saw some smart houses and pretty folk.'

'Well, yes. It is a fine city ...'

'A fine city,' repeated Susanne. 'I never saw nothing of a fine city. All I ever saw was the filthy shacks round the docks.'

'What of your parents, Susanne. You never speak of them.'

'Nothing to say.'

'And you never say how you came to Castillon, who brought you here.'

'A friend.'

Lidie sighed. She had tried, from time to time, to learn more about the girl's background but she knew, from the mulish expression on Susanne's face that she would get no further information from her. Annette, too, had always been strangely reluctant to talk about her niece in Bordeaux.

However, today the girl was not herself. For all her refusal to speak of her family, Susanne normally entertained Lidie with a constant stream of nonsense and was a great one for gossiping about others. Indeed, Lidie often had to silence her.

What ails her today? I have never known her like this.

They walked on in silence and at length stopped at a well appointed house on a wide street and were let in by a young servant. Susanne was taken into the servants' quarters while Lidie waited in the vestibule.

As she stood there, looking about her, she remarked on how much Cécile had stamped her personality upon the place. She had a sure and light touch. There were pretty tapestries on the walls and elegant furnishings.

I wonder whether I shall ever have a house to make my own?

Lidie heard voices coming from upstairs so she made her way to the nursery on the next floor. Cécile was playing with the baby when Lidie entered and she immediately handed him over to Lidie who could not help but smile as the little boy gurgled in her arms, then his nurse took him from her and left the room.

Cécile embraced Lidie, offered her refreshment and they sat down to talk. Cécile chatted on about her further plans for the decoration of the house, of the development of the baby and of diverting outings she had taken with Charles and his family.

'How is Charles?' asked Lidie and, as she felt she must, she also enquired about his parents.

Cécile looked a little discomforted. 'Oh, they are well,' she said shortly.

Lidie frowned. 'Have you had some disagreement with them?'

Cécile looked down at her hands which lay in the lap of her pretty muslin summer dress. She shrugged. 'Not really. It is their business, after all, how they worship.'

'Have they abjured?'

Cécile nodded, still looking at her hands.

'Oh Cécile!'

Cécile shrugged. 'I know how much it means to us, Lidie, to my parents and to you and your mama, but the Bouchers are not the same. They say it is too difficult to remain Reformists. They have abjured so that their business will thrive.'

'But they will have to attend mass!'

'Of course they will attend but in their hearts I have no doubt that they remain loyal to the teachings of Calvin.'

Lidie got to her feet. 'That is nonsense, Cécile! If they were loyal to our faith they would never have done that! They are simply loyal to their purses!'

'Lidie!'

'I'm sorry to say that about them, Cécile, but it is true.'

Cécile blushed. 'I cannot allow you to insult them in this way! It is insufferable.'

'And I cannot unsay what I have said. Think of all those people who have suffered by being true to their beliefs. Think of the poor people of Poitiers, of others who have been cruelly treated. Think of our own Doctor Vernier!'

'Isaac Vernier has not suffered.'

Lidie stamped her foot. 'What do you mean, of course he has suffered! Catholics are constantly harrying him, coming into his infirmary to see whether he is teaching Protestant students. The poor man has to play a game of cat and mouse to avoid them, even teaching secretly in his own home. Think of all the good he does in our town, all the lives he has saved. And your parents in law ignore the strength of someone like him, someone so admirable, just because they can make more money by pretending to adhere to the Catholic faith. It disgusts me!'

The silence between them was only broken by the distant cries of the baby in another room and the drone of the nurse's voice speaking to him.

Cécile looked up. 'How is it that you have become so serious, Lidie? Where is this passion coming from?'

'I feel strongly about my faith, Cécile,' she said quietly. 'As do your parents and my mama. You know we do.'

Cécile turned round then and faced her. 'Where is that giggling girl I knew and loved, Lidie? Where is the girl so taken up with fashions and beautiful silks?'

Lidie frowned. 'She is still here cos, but can't you see how threatened we are?'

'Of course I see,' said Cécile. 'And it is because of these threats that Charles' family have converted. To save themselves.'

'Huh! They may save their bodies, but what of their souls?'

Cécile shrugged.

'At least tell me you would never abjure, Cécile.'

Cécile didn't answer immediately and then, smoothing down her dress, she looked up. 'I truly do not know, Lidie. If Charles …'

'What!'

'How could I go against my husband? If he signed the papers then he would do so for the whole household.'

Lidie stared at her for a moment, then she said quietly. 'Do Uncle Jacob and Aunt Louise know of your in laws' decision to abjure?'

'I have said nothing to them but we live in a small town, do we not? The news will reach them soon.'

The sun was just as bright when Lidie left the house but everything seemed lifeless to her now and she hardly greeted Susanne when she joined her at the door.

Instead of seeing cheerful faces around them as they made their way home, Lidie saw only the dust swirling in the air and the weeds wilting in the heat.

She was so deep in thought as they made their way back that at first she did not register that someone had greeted her, but when her name was called again, she looked up and saw Pierre Gabriac.

'Well met, demoiselle Lidie,' he said, sweeping off his black hat in greeting, 'And young Susanne. If you are looking for fruit for the table, I have just left the market in town and there are some fine early grapes just arrived.'

Lidie smiled. 'I'll tell Mama,' she said. 'But we are not heading to the market. We have been visiting my cousin and her family.'

'Ah. Cécile. Is she well? And that bonny baby?'

'Very well thank you sir. But ...'

She glanced at Susanne, who immediately fell back a few paces.

Pierre looked down at Lidie, sensing her disquiet. 'Is something troubling you?' he asked.

'It is nothing, sir. Truly.'

'You are concerned that your cousin's faith may waver?'

Lidie was startled. 'How could you know that, sir?'

'Walk with me a little, Lidie. I am going your way.'

At first they walked on in silence and Lidie sensed that Pierre was waiting for her to speak.

'Cécile told me that Charles' parents have rejected the true path,' she said quietly.

Pierre did not seem surprised. 'I guessed as much,' he said. 'I'm afraid that the Bouchers put much store on worldly goods.'

Lidie nodded. 'If Charles does the same,' she said, 'then Cécile will have to follow. If her husband converts, she will have no choice.'

Pierre seemed to consider this, stroking his beard as he continued to observe her.

'And what of you, Lidie? Would you forsake your faith if you married a man who turned against it?'

'Never! But then I would never marry a man who did not have a strong faith, who would not fight for his beliefs.'

'You say that now, Lidie, but our faith may yet be put to further test.' He frowned, and then continued. 'Have you heard of Claude Brousson?'

'No. Forgive my ignorance, sir. Who is he?'

Pierre sighed. 'He's the famous Protestant lawyer, Lidie. He was our great hope. He has been working tirelessly for our cause and has won many cases on our behalf. He is a devout man – a zealot even – and just now he organized a conference of Protestant pastors to appeal to the King's conscience, petitioning him for their rights to practise their religion. They explained that they wanted to honour him as their sovereign, but that they could not dishonour God by going against their own consciences.'

'And was his petition successful?'

Pierre shook his head. 'Alas, it has had the opposite effect. Instead of softening the King to our plight, it has brought down further wrath. Ten of the twenty pastors who took part were captured and executed for participating in Brousson's 'treasonous project' as it was called.'

'That is shocking, sir. And what of Brousson? Was he also captured?'

'No, I am told he has gone into hiding. But it means that we have lost a powerful friend in the fight to retain our religious freedom.'

Immediately, Lidie thought of Samuel Verdier. 'You know, sir, that Doctor Verdier's son has qualified as a lawyer?'

Pierre nodded. 'I was speaking to Isaac last evening. He is very worried for the future.' He looked round to make sure he was not overheard. 'You have heard, I expect, that there are more restrictions expected?'

'I heard a rumour,' she said.

'I suspect that Isaac will continue to do his work even if there is a price to pay,' said Pierre. 'He is beloved in our town and has many friends of both faiths, but he will be in danger to be sure.' He hesitated, lowering his voice and looking about him. 'You know he continues to allow Protestant medical graduates gain practical experience in his infirmary?'

Lidie nodded.

There was a thoughtful silence between them as they continued to walk, side by side, and then Lidie looked up at him.

'And you, sir, are you in danger?' she asked.

Pierre sighed. 'I cannot deny that I am afraid. The latest ruling is that pastors should not remain in the same place for more than three years, so, in theory, I should move from Castillon but I fear it would upset Hannah so.' He hesitated. 'And now if pastors are found holding illegal public gatherings, we are to be severely punished.'

'But we come to your gatherings when you hold them in the woods. Do you mean that if you are found holding services…?' She stared at him.

'My calling is to look after my flock,' said Pierre. 'I would be failing in my duty to them and to God if I were to desert them now.'

'But to risk your life!'

Pierre looked up to the cloudless summer sky. 'The worst of it is that we cannot fight back.'

They were silent for a moment. Lidie could not know Pierre's thoughts but her own turned to the Verdier family.

'Come,' said Pierre, suddenly, 'Let us talk no more of these sad matters. He started to walk forward. 'Tell me what you do to pass the days, Lidie. I have no doubt that you are a great comfort and help to Sara in the household and that you are a fine needlewoman.'

Lidie smiled. 'I am no needlewoman, sir and, in truth, domestic life does not interest me as it should. I feel …'

'You feel?'

Lidie reddened. 'I feel I should like to do something more …'

'More? You mean more, how can I put it, more worthwhile?'

'Exactly! But it is difficult for a young girl like me. I see the Elders from our church visiting the sick and giving comfort and I almost envy them.'

Pierre raised an eyebrow. 'How do you think that the poor wretches suffering in their hovels would feel to be visited by a pretty, well born girl all dressed up in her muslins?'

Lidie laughed. 'I would not have to visit them wearing my good dresses!'

'Even so, it would discomfort them, my dear. They would not like to expose their poverty and disease to one such as you. The Elders do good work; they are not alarmed by infected wounds and stinking rags, and the poor to whom they minister gladly accept their help.'

'So you are saying, sir, that I should continue to do my clumsy needlework and instruct the servants and visit friends until some suitable young man claims me for his wife.'

'Is there no young man among our company who interests you, Lidie?'

Lidie's blush deepened. 'None who is interested in me,' she said quietly. 'The only one who interests me sees me as a skittish young girl with an empty head and an interest in the latest silks and fashions.'

'And you are not going to disclose who this is? You know that anything you tell me is in confidence.'

Lidie turned to him, almost persuaded to confide in him. She had not seen Samuel Verdier for months though she knew that he had qualified as a lawyer and was working some way away, under the tutelage of another, but knew no more

She had tried very hard to forget him.

'No, sir, I am not going to tell you.'

'Then I shall respect your decision, Lidie. But to go back to your desire to do something worthwhile in the community, let me give the matter further attention. You are a clever and thoughtful young woman and it should be possible to find a way of using your talents.'

'You really think so, sir?'

Pierre smiled down at her. 'I am sure of it, Lidie. But now our ways part. I have to see a troubled family who live in this street. Give my regards to your mama.'

Lidie watched him turn into a side street and stride away down towards its end

When she and Susanne reached home, they found Sara with Annette in the kitchen, sitting at the large kitchen table shelling

106

some newly harvested peas. They greeted Lidie and Susanne and then they, too, helped with the shelling, Lidie finding comfort in the mundane job.

Later, Sara and Lidie went to sit together in the panelled room.

'How did you find Cécile and the baby?' asked Sara.

'Oh, they are well enough.'

'And Charles?'

Lidie glanced at the portrait of her papa. 'I did not see Charles,' she said. 'But I believe he is well.'

'And his parents?'

'I assume they are well.' She paused. 'Cécile tells me that they have abjured.'

Sara's head shot up. 'Oh no!'

Lidie nodded. 'There was some matter of business,' she said, flatly.

'How did Cécile feel about that?'

'In truth, Mama, she did not seem particularly exercised.'

Lidie could see the shock in her mother's eyes.

'But how could she not be exercised? She is my niece, our family has fought for years for the freedom to worship as our consciences tell us.'

'I know, Mama. But she has married into a family who do not take their faith so seriously.'

'Do you think that Charles would abjure if it suited him?'

Lidie nodded. 'I think it very likely and if he did then Cécile would follow him.'

Sara stretched across the table and grasped Lidie's hand.

'Promise me that you would never do that.'

'With all my heart, Mama.'

Sara's brow cleared. 'I see a change in you, Lidie, these past two years. You are more thoughtful, more sure in your faith.'

'We have all had to think more deeply about our beliefs, have we not?'

'Indeed,' said Sara. Then she smiled. 'I was visited earlier by the Master Silk Weaver and he has left his book of patterns for us to peruse. I hope this new affirmation of your faith does not mean that you have lost your eye for fashion!'

Lidie laughed out loud. 'Never!'

'Then let us inspect the book and forget all this unpleasantness.'

So, for a happy hour, mother and daughter looked through all the patterns and discussed the colours and how the silks might be made up.

Having made their decisions they chatted together amiably while waiting for the return of the silk weaver and, having placed their orders with him they continued to speculate how the silks would look when they were woven.

'You will look well in the silks you have chosen, Mama,' said Lidie. 'You are still lovely. Maybe, one day …'

Sara smiled. 'I know what you are thinking, Lidie, but I could never love any man in the way I loved your papa.' She paused and then said quietly, 'I pray that you, too, will find such love.'

***

A few days later, Pierre Gabriac called on Sara. His dark pastor's garb was unsuited to the heat of the day and he mopped his brow when he took off his hat.

'Pierre, come in,' said Sara, immediately instructing Annette to bring him some refreshment.

'I cannot stay long,' he said, but I have come with a message.' He sat down at the table and the morning sun streamed in from the windows, striking his face and emphasizing its pallor.'

As Annette brought in some drink, he asked after her health and that of Susanne and then, when she had left, he said. 'Is Lidie not here?'

Sara shook her head. 'She is visiting friends,' she said.

'Ah. Good. I would speak with you first, Madame.' Pierre fussed with the white collar at his throat. 'She asked me if I could put some work her way.'

'Work? What can you mean?'

Pierre frowned. 'It seems,' he said carefully, 'that she feels she could do more to help those less fortunate than herself.' He looked up at Sara.

'But we do what we can, Pierre, as you know. We send food to those in need in the town and we help the peasants on our farm.'

'I know, Madame. You are generous to a fault. But I think Lidie would like to … how can I put it? I sense she would like to be at the side of those in trouble.'

'How would that be possible, Pierre. The Elders of the church visit the poor but we women are not encouraged to do so.'

'No. Lidie did suggest she could help in this way, but I told her it would likely make them uncomfortable to have a young girl ministering to them. However,' he continued. 'Since then I have been speaking with Dr Verdier.'

'Ah, poor Isaac. He is under great strain, caring for the sick while avoiding the attentions of those Catholic magistrates trying to catch him out. It is so unjust.'

'Indeed.' Pierre cleared his throat. 'I spoke to him about Lidie's wish to help and he has agreed, if you permit it, to let her help the two nurses at the infirmary.'

Sara frowned. 'But, Pierre, I was of the belief that Isaac has always discouraged those of our class to get involved with his work.'

'He has not had happy experiences in the past, it is true,' said Pierre carefully. 'So often, gentlewomen are unsuited to the work and they faint with horror when confronted with blood and gore.'

'Then why should he think that Lidie would react any differently?'

Pierre shrugged. 'I was surprised myself. I only asked him in passing if he could think of a way in which Lidie could be useful in the community and he himself suggested that she help his nurses.' He paused. 'Maybe he sees some steel in her character.'

'But to be confronted with such sights …'

'Would you agree to speak to her about it?'

'If you wish. But I am convinced it would not suit.'

They were silent for a moment and then Pierre said. 'You should be proud of her Madame. She's a gay young woman but there's a thoughtful head on her shoulders.''

Sara smiled. 'Oh, and there's a deal of frivolity in that head, too!'

As Pierre finished his drink and rose to take his leave, Sara said quietly, 'How goes it with Hannah.'

Sara was horrified to see Pierre's expression change and as he tried to compose himself, he stuttered. 'Forgive me Madame.'

'Forgive *me*, Pierre. I should not have been so insensitive.'

'She is no better,' he said. 'She is frightened of everything, her head is full of who knows what monsters and I am unable to comfort her.' He paused. 'She flinches whenever I try to hold her close.'

'I am so sorry. I will pray for her.'

'I pray for her every day but I think that God has burdened me with this unhappiness for the good of my soul for my prayers are never answered.'

Before leaving, he said. 'Next time you visit your farm, Madame, shall we meet again for worship in the woods? It is not ideal but, by God's grace we shall not be disturbed.'

'Of course. We shall look forward to that. And when winter comes, you know you are welcome here to gather.'

'You will put yourself in danger, Madame. The Catholics are becoming more vigilant at reporting private gatherings. And I fear there may be spies …' He did not finish the sentence.

Sara nodded. 'I know,' she said quietly. 'I understand the risks.'

After Pierre had left, Sara drew close to her husband's portrait. The artist had captured both the restless energy of the man and his humour.

She put her finger to his lips where the smile she had loved so much still hovered.

'How could I ever love another?'

Then her thoughts turned again to Pierre. So young, and now not even able to reach his wife through physical union. Life was indeed cruel.

While she was still standing in front of the portrait, the front door opened. She called out and Lidie came in.

'It is fiercely hot out there,' said Lidie, flopping down onto one of the chairs.

Sara looked from the portrait to Lidie and back again.

'Now you are older, I see more of him in you,' she said. Then she went over to Lidie and sat down beside her.

'The pastor has just left,' she said. 'He told me of your desire to do something of worth.'

Lidie coloured. 'I meant to tell you, Mama. I did not wish you to be offended, but I am restless.'

Sara smiled. 'And your needlework does not absorb you?'

Lidie grimaced. 'You know it does not!'

'And is there no young man in our community who …'

'No,' said Lidie shortly, then she added quietly, glancing up at the portrait of her father. 'At least none to whom I could give my heart.'

Sara sighed. 'Well, Isaac has said you can help his nurses,' she said, observing Lidie closely. 'Though I doubt …'

But she couldn't finish her sentence because Lidie had leapt up and embraced her.

'Oh Mama, that is *exactly* the sort of work I need,' she said. 'Did he say when I can begin?'

'Not so fast, Lidie,' said Sara, disentangling herself. 'I think we need to find out more of what he expects from you.' She paused. 'You have never been exposed to those with severe sickness, with sores and blood and suchlike. You may find it impossible to stomach such sights.'

'But Mama,' said Lidie. 'Surely, wanting to do good for others is at the core of Calvin's teaching, is it not? And I want to feel useful, can you not see that?'

'You may be of no use to Isaac's nurses. You may be an encumbrance and let him down. You would not wish that, surely?'

'Let me try.'

'Is this truly what you want?'

'Truly.'

Sara sighed. 'Very well. We shall go and see Isaac this very afternoon, but I am sure that this kind of work will not suit you.'

***

In the kitchen, away from other members of the household, Annette and Susanne were engaged in a furious, whispered argument, Annette standing over Susanne, her arms folded and her face flushed.

'I thought you'd learnt better ways since you've been here. I should have known you would disgrace me! I should have sent you packing when you first came, wheedling and whining and begging me to help you. What shame you will bring down on me...'

Susanne was biting her lip, trying to keep the tears at bay. 'Aunt. Let me explain ...'

'What is there to explain?' Annette's cast her eyes on Susanne 's belly. 'You're but a common slut, no better than any of the rest of your cursed family. I've seen the way you flash your eyes at that young stable boy: I suppose the child is his?'

Susanne clutched Annette's arm but Annette drew away with such violence that the girl tumbled onto the floor.

'Aunt ...'

'Don't you call me Aunt. I wash my hands of you. You repay my kindness in this way. I begged the mistress to take you in ...'

'The child is not his.'

'Huh! So you have been putting yourself about the town, is that it?'

Susanne scrambled to her feet. 'No. I swear it! Aunt, I still had my maidenhead and this man forced himself on me ...'

'What man?'

Susanne wiped her eyes with the back of her hand. 'I cannot say ...'

'What do you mean, you cannot say? If you know what's good for you, girl, you had better start talking.'

Susanne said nothing.

Annette grabbed the girl's ear and twisted it. 'Well?'

'Ow! Let go!'

'What's his name?'

'I'll tell you, Aunt, I swear. Please .. let me go!'

Annette loosed her grasp and Susanne moved away, cowering in the corner of the room.

'Well?'

'The man from Bordeaux,' whispered Susanne.

'What are you talking about girl? What man from Bordeaux?'

Susanne sniffed. 'The man who first brought me here.'

Annette narrowed her eyes. 'Huh! So that was how you made your way here.'

'I was desperate, Aunt. I had to get away ... you know what goes on in my mother's house.'

'I can guess.'

'I was only a child when I came here but I knew what I would become. I had seen my sisters debauched on the street and the violence all around me and then ...'

'And then some *kind* man offered you free passage in his cart to Castillon when

you told him that your great aunt lived in a respectable Protestant household and would take you in.'

Susanne said nothing.

'And would this man be a Catholic?' Annette was breathing heavily.

'I ... I think so. He comes often to Castillon. He does some trade here.'

'And you had no way of repaying him for his kindness, did you?'

Susanne shook her head. 'I did not understand ...'

Annette closed her eyes for a moment. 'You *stupid* girl,' she hissed.

Susanne swallowed. 'At first he was kind when he sought me out,' she said. 'He asked after you and the household ...'

'Oh, no doubt!'

'I did not realise ...'

'You did not realise that he was a Catholic spy?!'

Susanne shook her head. 'NO! of *course* I did not. Not ... not until ...'

'Go on.'

'He started to ask about secret gatherings. The meetings you hold in the woods and in houses. He said he wished to come along, that he had a mind to convert.'

Annette raised her eyes to the ceiling. 'God in heaven! What Catholic would convert to our faith in these times?'

Susanne nodded. 'I was a fool to believe him.'

She moved closer to Annette. 'I have been happy here. It is the only place where I have known tranquillity. And … and I am fond of Mam'selle Lidie. I did not mean to betray you.'

'But you have, have you not?'

Susanne hung her head. 'Only when I did not realise it. Then, when I heard of meetings being disrupted, of mobs going into the woods … it was then I refused to give him more information …'

'And then he showed his true character, eh?'

Susanne nodded. 'If I had nothing to tell him, he beat me, so I started to tell him falsehoods to keep him from harming me.'

'And when did he ….?'

'A few months ago he realised I was deceiving him and then...' She started to cry and Annette's fury began to subside.

She's still hardly more than a child herself. What things she has endured.

At length, Susanne continued. 'I fought to keep my maidenhead, Aunt, but he was so strong. I could not prevent him. And he said … he said that if I did not let him have his way with me he would make sure you knew I had betrayed the household and …'

Her voice rose and she stuttered between the sobs. 'He said I would be worse off because the mistress would throw me out on the street where any man could have me.'

'The brute,' muttered Annette.

'What am I to do?' whispered Susanne.

'Does this man know you are with child?'

'No. He has not been in the town for some time.'

Annette sighed deeply and then put her arms round Susanne.

'We have to tell the mistress,' she said. 'We cannot keep this from her.'

Susanne raised her head from Annette's bosom. 'She will dismiss me.'

'Soon you will not be able to hide your condition. She will have to know the truth.' She pushed Susanne away from her. 'Now I have work to do, child, and so have you. Let me take time to think on this and meanwhile, do not leave the house unless in company, do you understand?'

114

Annette bent over to take some bread out of the oven. Then she turned back and said, more gently.

'I will speak to the mistress, but I cannot tell what she will do.'

Chapter Ten

Lidie changed into a plain dress and one of her most severe coifs, then ran down the stairs to await the carriage.

Sara was already at the door and she turned to greet her.

'You are the picture of modesty!'

'I want to give the right impression.'

Sara raised an eyebrow. 'Which is what?'

'That I am ready to work.'

Sara didn't answer because at that moment the carriage had drawn up outside.

They rattled along, through the faubourg, out along the road towards Saint-Magne and past the temple, standing deserted and forlorn. The last gathering there had been two years ago when they had all come together to pray for their brethren in Poitiers.

'It still stands, at least,' said Sara.

Lidie nodded. 'It was brave of Pierre to defy the law.'

A 'but' hung in the air. Since that act of defiance, Castillion had attracted unwelcome scrutiny.

The sun's heat was beginning to gather intensity as the carriage drew up outside the infirmary and Sara asked the driver to wait for them, but she hesitated before descending.

'I have never visited it before. It is hardly extensive but it is a sturdy building. And built by those of our faith. Your Aunt Louise and Uncle Jacob helped to fund its construction.'

As they alighted, a peasant woman, her simple clothing covered by a white apron and her hair neatly hidden under a coif, hurried out to greet them. She bobbed a quick curtsy and asked them their business.

'We have come to see Dr Verdier,' said Sara, making to go in through the door, but the woman barred her way.

'Dr Verdier does not see visitors,' said the woman.

Sara frowned. 'Madame, we are friends of the doctor's and my daughter here has offered to help tend the sick. An offer which I believe he has accepted.'

The woman glanced at Lidie but she didn't smile. Lidie blushed and looked down at her feet, feeling overdressed. She could sense that she was being assessed and was found wanting.

There was an awkward silence, then the woman said. 'Wait here if you please.'

Sara and Lidie looked at one another. 'Not much of a greeting,' said Sara.

They stood outside the building for some time and eventually moved to where their carriage was parked, under the shade of a large tree.

At length, the same woman reappeared and came over to them. 'Follow me,' she said.

She led them round the side of the building to the back and there, beside the herb garden, stood Isaac. He was speaking to an old bent peasant who was leaning on his hoe and nodding.

Isaac looked up as they approached and Sara was immediately struck by how much he had changed since they had last met. He was much thinner, the strain of living under constant threat showing in his face and in his bearing and although he greeted them with courtesy, his eyes were watchful.

He bowed briefly. 'Forgive the less than fulsome welcome,' he said, with a wry smile, 'but in these difficult times, I have to be careful. We have visits from magistrates and, though they say they come to give comfort to the sick, in truth they are no more than spies of the Intendant.'

'I am so sorry, sir,' said Sara. 'And I am told that restrictions have been further tightened.'

Isaac nodded. He was about to speak but there was a sudden noise from the front of the building and he frowned. 'Madame, forgive me if I keep our conversation brief.' He turned to Lidie.

'Is it true that you would help?'

'Yes sir, if you think I am able.'

Isaac smiled and for a moment his shoulders relaxed. 'I am sure you are able, my dear,' he said, 'But the work is arduous and there are many sights and sounds and smells which are unpleasant. You will see such things as are not usually observed by young women of your class.' He put his hand under her chin and looked her in the eyes. 'Are you sure about this? Would you not rather be continuing with all your pleasant pastimes?'

'In truth, sir, I tire of my pleasant pastimes. Our Lord instructed his followers to care for the sick and the poor and I would like to try and carry out His will.'

Sara looked up in surprise but Isaac continued. 'Very laudable sentiments and I applaud them, but you may find the reality disagreeable and, if you do, then no one here would blame you if you cannot stand it.'

'I promise to do my best,' said Lidie.

'You will have to learn humility, my dear. My two nurses may come from a different social class than yours, but they have a lot of knowledge and,' he hesitated. 'And they may look on you with suspicion.'

Lidie swallowed. 'I understand, sir.'

Then Isaac smiled. 'It is good you do, Lidie. If you can overcome any hostility by being humble and ready to learn, then I feel sure that you will be an asset.'

He bowed briefly. 'Now, I must leave you. I am so often disturbed by unwelcome visitors that I have to use my time here wisely and patients are waiting. I will call someone to show you what to do.'

'You mean she should start at once?' said Sara.

'No time like the present,' said Isaac. 'My nurse will be here in a moment.'

As Isaac walked back into the infirmary building, Sara noticed the weariness in his gait.

'The poor man is exhausted,' she said. She came closer to Lidie and spoke in a low voice. 'Are you sure this is what you want, Lidie? I fear that you are not well equipped for the task. And Isaac … well, he was a little abrupt, was he not?'

'Quite sure, Mama, and it is well to start at once, is it not – and to be told how things stand.'

They stood watching the old peasant hoeing the herb garden. He was slow in his movements but he worked steadily and while they waited, a young woman emerged from the kitchen bringing him

THE KING'S COMMAND

some refreshment. She bobbed a quick curtsy to Sara and then disappeared back inside.

At last the nurse appeared. She was holding a clean white apron which she gave to Lidie.

'Put this on mam'selle,' she said. 'And roll up your sleeves.'

Lidie did as she was told and Sara watched.

'You may go now, Madame,' said the nurse.

Sara nodded. 'At what time should I send the carriage?' she asked.

Lidie frowned.

The nurse will never have the luxury of travelling by carriage to her work.

There was a brief silence, then the nurse shrugged. 'Whenever it suits you, Madame.'

'I will work the hours that you work,' Lidie said.

The woman looked at her for a long moment. 'I shall be here until six in the evening,' she said. 'Or thereabouts.' She hesitated. 'Caring for the sick is not something that can be precisely timed.'

Lidie blushed. 'Send the carriage at six, Mama. And if the driver has to wait, then so be it.'

When Sara had left, the nurse stood over Lidie as she washed her hands thoroughly and then set her to changing bed linen and swabbing down the floors.

Lidie had never done such work but she set to it without complaint, aware that she was being keenly observed.

They think I'll not last the day.

While she was going about her duties, she witnessed dressings being changed and she had to stop herself from gagging at the smells of body excrements and infected wounds. Some of the patients had visitors at their bedsides and she recognized two of the Elders from their congregation who were praying with them. They looked up in surprise when they saw her, but Lidie simply nodded at them and continued with her work.

During the afternoon there was a visit from a group of magistrates who elbowed the nurse aside and talked earnestly to those trapped in their sick beds.

Lidie kept well away from them but she couldn't help hearing snatches of their conversations.

'Come to the true faith …. Be well rewarded …. It is your King's wish.'

She worked on grimly, not daring to let up in case she was seen as weak. When the nurse came to tell her that there was some refreshment laid out in the kitchen, Lidie could have wept with relief. She was exhausted; her back ached fearfully and her hands were raw with all the washing, wringing out and scrubbing she had done. Gratefully, she took her bucket of dirty water out to the garden to pour onto the parched earth and went into the kitchen.

The nurse pointed at a chair set at a large wooden table and Lidie sat down. She had never been more thankful to take the weight off her feet. The nurse sat down beside her and, for the first time, she smiled.

'You worked well, mam'selle.'

Lidie had never valued a compliment more.

The young peasant girl she'd seen earlier set a plate of bread and preserves in front of Lidie and poured a drink from a pitcher. Lidie looked up.

'Thank you,' she said. Then, 'What is your name.'

'Marie, mam'selle,' she said.

'Please, call me Lidie.'

Marie looked awkward and glanced at the nurse, who nodded briefly.

'We do not stand on ceremony here.'

Just then, two young men came into the kitchen. They started when they saw Lidie and made to go out again, but the nurse stopped them.

'She is from our faith,' she said quietly.

The relief on their faces was almost comical. Lidie turned to them. 'Are you graduates from the school of medicine?' she asked.

One of them smiled at her and put his finger to his lips. 'Aye, mam'selle, but I beg you pretend you have not seen us.'

'How is it that you can …?' began Lidie.

'By keeping out of sight and avoiding those tiresome magistrates who appear from nowhere and try and force the sick to abjure with bribes and fearful threats of eternal damnation.'

'It cannot be easy for you, or for the doctor.'

'He is risking a deal more than we are,' he said. 'But he wants to pass on his skills and we are blest to be taught by him.

'Aye,' said the other one. 'Whatever befalls us we shall have benefitted from his knowledge. Meanwhile,' he continued, breaking into a broad smile, 'we have become experts in the art of vanishing.' He clapped his companion on the shoulder. 'We are some of the lucky ones,' he went on. 'There are many in the profession who will not risk the consequences of continuing to teach Huguenot graduates. Dr Verdier is a brave man.'

The nurse nodded gravely and turned to Lidie. 'Now mam'selle.'

'Lidie, please call me Lidie.'

She smiled. 'Now Lidie, we should get on with our work. These young men have come to the kitchen for some repast and we must let them eat.'

Trying not to show how weary she felt, Lidie scraped back her chair and stood up.

For the rest of the afternoon, the work was unrelenting. As well as continuing to scrub and change linen, Lidie was set to washing one of the women patients and also watched as the nurse cleaned a festering wound and put on clean bandages. From time to time, as the nurse was working, she glanced up at Lidie to explain what she was doing but also, Lidie guessed, to make sure she wasn't flinching from the sight.

By the end of the day, Lidie's hair was damp beneath her coif and it seemed that every bone in her body ached, but she felt triumphant.

They have not rejected me.

While she stood under the tree outside the entrance to the infirmary, awaiting the carriage, Isaac came out of the door and walked over to her.

He smiled. 'Well done, Lidie. My nurse tells me you were of real help to her and that you did not faint away with the horror of it all!'

'I have much to learn, sir.'

He nodded. 'The greatest lesson is that of humility,' he said. 'And from what I hear, you have learnt it already.'

He looked up into the branches of the tree and stretched. 'It is pleasant here, is it not. I will wait with you until your carriage arrives.' They were quiet for a moment and then he said. 'You met my graduates?'

'Yes. They seemed cheerful young men.'

Isaac sighed. 'Unless they abjure, they will never be accepted into the Bordeaux Guild, though they may be able to work in some smaller places, but they are eager students, and discreet, too.' Then he turned to face her and his expression was solemn. 'Lidie, you understand that you must not talk about their presence here? To do so would endanger them.'

'Of course, I will say nothing to anyone.'

'Good. One never knows when spies are listening.'

Lidie frowned but then, when she saw her carriage coming down the hill towards them, all thoughts of spies were banished from her mind as she anticipated her arrival back into the comfort of her own home where she could change and wash and rest her weary limbs.

As they watched the coach's progress, Isaac said suddenly. 'There is some good news to impart, at least.'

'What is that?'

'My son Samuel is coming home and intends to set up a practice here.'

Lidie could not conceal the blush that rose to her cheeks. 'That is good news, indeed, sir,' she stuttered. 'You will be glad of his company. But will he be allowed? I heard that lawyers of our faith are under some threat.'

Isaac continued to stare at the approaching coach. 'You are right, there are rumours. Already Huguenot junior offices of justice and notaires are banned from employment but Samuel is a fully trained barrister. For now he is free to practise, though I fear that nothing

122

is certain in these times. The sands shift every day and we hardly know where we stand.'

But he is coming back to live among us! He will be here in the town!

Isaac was still lost in thought as he closed the carriage door for her, his fingers idly tracing the pattern of its decoration. Then he turned and walked slowly back to the infirmary as the driver made a great circle and headed back down the track.

Lidie stared out of the carriage window and of a sudden, it seemed to her that the heat was less oppressive, the countryside more lovely and the evening sky more colourful.

When Sara greeted her, she was surprised to see Lidie so full of life.

'I quite expected to see you bowed down with weariness,' she said, 'But you look quite fresh and lively.'

Lidie hugged her. 'It is hard work, Mama,' she said. 'But I think I showed that I would not shirk it.'

'Will you go back?'

'Of course. I plan to be there every day.'

'Every day? Surely not, Lidie. We are soon to visit the farm. You shall want to do that, at least, and see Martha and Abel and visit your cousins?'

'Possibly,' said Lidie.

But a visit to the farm seemed to hold less appeal than usual.

Chapter Eleven

Some days had passed since Lidie had started to work at the infirmary but on this particular morning, Sara urged Lidie to stay at home as the carriage was not available.

'It is still early, Mama,' she said. 'It will not be so hot. The walk will do me good.'

Sara frowned. 'It is not the exercise that worries me, Lidie, but the empty road beyond the town. If you must walk, then make sure a servant goes with you.'

Lidie laughed. 'Both the nurses and Marie and her brother travel to the infirmary on foot from the town. I will have company along the way and I am well equipped for walking.'

Sara looked with distaste at Lidie's tightly laced leather shoes.

'Those are peasant shoes!'

'I cannot minister to the sick wearing fashionable shoes!'

Sara took one of Lidie's hands in hers and turned it over. 'You must take more care of your hands, my love, they are becoming rough and raw. You shall soak them in almond oil tonight.'

'Working hands, Mama.'

As Lidie walked out of the faubourg and onto the Saint-Magne road she met a man she knew who was one of their secret congregation.

'Take care on the road, mam'selle,' he said, frowning. 'Why is it that you have no company?'

'I shall have, sir. I am on my way to the infirmary and others will join me soon.'

The man didn't look convinced and Lidie felt a frisson of unease.

'I would accompany you,' he said, 'but I have pressing business in the town.'

He held his hand up in a gesture of farewell as she walked down the road away from him and when she looked back a few minutes later, he was still standing there, shading his eyes, watching her progress.

Although Lidie had assured her mama that she would soon be joined by others, she realised that she had misjudged the time. It had taken her much longer to walk the distance than she'd anticipated, and there was no sign of the nurses nor of Marie or her brother.

They must be ahead of me.

Earlier, a few farm carts had passed her but now the track was empty. The sun was climbing in the sky and the day was beginning to warm up. Lidie kept her eyes on the ground on front of her, anxious not to let the sun burn her skin. She did not see the three men emerge from a ditch at the edge of the track until she was almost upon them.

As soon as she did, she made to skirt round them, but they moved as one and blocked her way.

Lidie's heart started to beat fast but she looked up and met the eye of one of them. He was grinning and moving his tongue around his lips.

'Let me pass please sir,' she said, trying to keep her voice level.

The man did not move but put his hand under her chin and when she twisted to free herself he held it tighter.

Without turning his head, he said to his companions. 'Here's a pretty little wench out all alone.'

The other two men laughed. 'No one to help you here, girl,' said one, coming closer and lifting up Lidie's skirt. 'Let's see what's under here!'

Lidie kicked out at him. 'Leave me alone!'

'Ha, she's full of passion!' He reached out and pulled at her bodice. 'Lovely little bubbies,' he said, putting his hand over her breasts.

The other two men were beside her now, pawing at her, doing their best to rip her clothes off. One forced her coif from her head and her hair fell loose over her face.

Lidie screamed as loudly as she could and her eyes searched desperately for help, but there was no one about and the three men were starting to drag her down into the ditch. She was sobbing, helpless against their strength.

'Bloody little Huguenot,' said one, as he started to unbutton his breeches. 'Needs a good fuck, I'll warrant.'

Lidie was on the ground now, but she was still fighting. She thought she heard a distant sound of hooves on the track and she tried to raise her head. She screamed again, with the strength of pure terror, hitting out and scratching the men who only laughed as they pinned her to the ground.

It was no good. Her resistance just seemed to fire them up and when she tried to scream again, one of them put a rough hand across her mouth and she bit down on it as hard as she could. He reared back swearing and sucking blood from the wound.

'Vicious little she cat,' he said, straddling her and tearing at her clothes. I'll fuck you all the harder for that.'

'You give it 'er,' said one of the other men. 'Give the tight little cunt a ride, then I'll have my turn.'

Lidie tried in vain to twist her body this way and that, away from the man on top of her and away from his hand which he was trying to clamp over her mouth.

There was so much swearing and noise that no one heard the sound of a horse's hooves, coming very fast, at a gallop now, down the track.

And then there was a slithering of hooves above the ditch and another voice shouting at the men as a horse was driven forward down into the ditch and someone was laying about the men with a riding whip and yelling about the full force of the law.

Suddenly, Lidie was freed. The man on top of here had heaved himself off her and was stumbling to his feet and he and his two companions were scrabbling up the ditch and running away over the fields.

She was sobbing as she got to her knees and looked up. The rider had dismounted from his horse and he bent down and offered her his hand but she shrank away from his touch.

'Mam'selle,' he said gently. 'I am so sorry. What have those brutes done to you?'

Lidie was still shaking and she couldn't answer.

'Do you know them?'

She swallowed and shook her head.

'I'd recognize them again,' said the man. 'They won't get away with this.' Then he put his hand out once more. 'Come, let me help you up.'

She took his hand this time and got to her feet, trying to protect her modesty by holding her ripped bodice tightly together.

Then, when she raised her head, the man saw her properly.

'Lidie!Lidie. It's Samuel. Samuel Verdier.'

She dropped her eyes to the ground.

'I'm so sorry …' she gulped.

Samuel took off his cloak and put it round her shoulders. '*You* have nothing to be sorry for,' he said.

'I should have heeded my mother's words and … and if you'd not come.' She was shaking so hard that she could hardly speak.

'I am heartily glad I did come. And not a moment too soon, I warrant.'

Then he continued. 'What were you doing, walking on this lonely track on your own? These are dangerous times.'

'I was on my way to the infirmary,' she whispered.

'The infirmary? Is someone in your household sick?'

She shook her head. 'I am helping the nurses,' she said.

'I did not know. I only returned last evening. That is indeed good of you, but surely your mother could have sent you in the carriage?'

Lidie was too cast down to explain. She simply shook her head. Her legs were so weak that she thought she would fall.

'Come,' said Samuel. 'I will lift you onto the back of my horse and take you back to your house.'

'No! Please.' Lidie gulped and she spoke more loudly. 'Please don't take me home. If Mama hears what has happened, she will forbid me to continue working for your father.'

'But we need to pursue the men that attacked you and bring them to justice.'

Lidie looked up at him, at his face so full of anger.

'But think what that will do to my reputation, Samuel. I shall be condemned for putting myself at risk, for disobeying my mother. There would be rumours that … that I was defiled.'

He frowned, looking out across the fields. 'Those men …'

127

She swallowed. 'I will not walk alone here again,' she said quietly. 'They were ignorant Catholic brutes and there may be others like them abroad, feeling that they are free to insult all Huguenot women. I have learned my lesson.'

Samuel said nothing for a moment but just looked at her and Lidie blushed under his gaze.

'You are very brave, Lidie,' he said at last. He clenched his fists. If I ever see those men again …' He cleared his throat. 'Shall I take you back to my father's house?'

She shook her head. 'If you would take me to the infirmary,' she said. 'I'm sure the nurses can find me fresh clothes there. I will say … I will say I stumbled and fell.'

He nodded, then as he held her close to lift her onto the horse's back, Lidie allowed herself to relax a little and lean into the safety of his arms.

When she was settled, he led her at a sedate pace down the track. For a long while neither said anything and it was Lidie who finally broke the silence.

'I have not ridden astride a horse since I was a child at the farm and my papa led me round.'

Samuel turned to look up at her. 'He was a fine man, your papa.'

'I did not think you knew him.'

'No, I never met him, alas, but I remember my father speaking of him when he was so sadly taken from you. I think they had some dealings with one another.'

The infirmary finally came into sight and Samuel halted.

'Are you sure you want to …?'

Lidie nodded. 'I need to put this behind me and set to work. I refuse to dwell on it.'

When they reached the infirmary, Samuel lifted Lidie down and continued to hold her round her waist. 'Shall I come in with you?' he asked.

She shook her head. 'You have been kindness itself,' she said. 'And if …' She didn't finish the sentence.

'Thank God I was there, Lidie,' he said quietly, and there was a slight break in his voice. 'How will you return home?'

'The carriage will come for me,' she said. 'It was only this morning ….'

He loosed his hold on her then. 'I shall be in the town all day. I'd … I'd like to call on you and your mama this evening.'

She looked up, alarmed. 'You won't say anything …?'

He shook his head. 'If you wish me to say nothing about your attackers, then I promise you I will not, but I want to reassure myself that you are … that you are recovered. I will simply say that you tripped and I found you and helped you here.'

'Promise?'

'I promise.'

She took off his cloak and handed it back to him. 'I hope I have not delayed you too much.'

He smiled at her then. 'My business can wait. Your safety is of more importance.'

He watched until she was inside the building and then he headed away, back up the track.

Lidie knew that there would be people watching out for unwelcome strangers, so she braced herself as she entered the main door of the infirmary.

'Lidie,' said one of the nurses, looking at her in alarm. 'Whatever has happened to you? And who was that man on horseback?'

'I was walking from the town,' she said. 'And I tripped and fell on the road. Dr Verdier's son came to my aid.'

Lidie had managed to straighten out her clothes but there was no disguising that her bodice had been badly ripped. The nurse said nothing but she stared at it.

'I fell into a savage thorn bush,' said Lidie. 'I fear I tore my bodice as I sought to free it.'

The nurse frowned and seemed about to say more, but Lidie interrupted her.

'Are there some clothes ,,,'

'Of course. Go and see what you can find in the charity box.'

Lidie nodded. She knew that wealthy folk left discarded clothes for the infirmary. Often the linen shifts were torn up for bandages, but there were spare plain clothes there, too, for the nurses when their clothes became soiled. She rummaged in the box and found a plain skirt and bodice about her size and changed into it with all speed, putting a white apron over it. And as she changed, she noticed the bruises coming up on her breasts and caught her breath at the sudden memory of those revolting hands kneading them as if they were so much pastry.

She shuddered, then she bundled up her own clothes and set them aside to take home later.

For the rest of the day, she forced herself to do whatever work she was set with the utmost diligence but by the time the carriage arrived to take her home, she was trembling with fatigue.

She was relieved that Sara was not at home when she arrived back, and she took her damaged clothes straight to Annette.

'I fell on the road,' she said. 'Could you ask one of the servants to mend my bodice, Annette. I … I landed in a thorn bush and I fear it is badly torn.'

Annette took the bodice from her and when she saw how it was ripped, she said. 'This is not damage from any thorn bush.'

'It *is!*'

'If you say so, mam'selle,' said Annette as she took the bodice. She frowned. 'I will see to it myself.'

Then she put her hand on Lidie's arm. 'You look pale, mam'selle, are you sure you …'

'I am quite well, Annette,' said Lidie. 'A little fatigued, that is all. When is my mother expected?'

'Very shortly,' said Annette, then, with another searching look at Lidie, she took her leave.

Lidie ran up the stairs to her chamber, refusing the assistance of Susanne who went to follow her. She sat on the edge of her bed for a few moments, composing herself before changing into one of her prettiest muslins. The bodice was high cut and the bruises which were coming out on her breasts were hidden, but Lidie could not help shuddering as she observed them.

I will not think of it.

She began to brush her hair vigorously and then put a soft coif over it.

Sara was just coming in through the front door when Lidie came down the stairs and she enquired after Lidie's day, but she seemed distracted.

'It was well, Mama, thank you.'

'Good. Good.' But Lidie could tell that there was something on her mind.

'Is something the matter?'

Sara frowned. 'I do not know how I can contest this,' she muttered.

'Contest what?'

Sara hesitated, then she said quietly. 'Come, we should perhaps talk of this privately. I would not want the servants to be alarmed.'

When they were out of earshot of the servants, Sara turned to Lidie.

'The curé called on me while you were at the infirmary,' she said.

'The curé!' Lidie frowned.

'Huh!' said Sara. 'He delighted in the news he had to impart. I have no doubt he gloried in my discomfort.'

'What news?'

Sara started to pace up and down the room. 'It appears that the Intendant himself has sent word that if I do not abdure, our farm will be seized.' And then, when Lidie continued to frown, uncomprehending, she repeated. 'They will take our land, Lidie. The King will take ownership of it. That toad of a man said to me that we Huguenots will soon be dispossessed of our land unless we abjure. And he could hardly keep the smirk from his face.'

'But that is ridiculous, Mama. Our farm was purchased by Papa and you are his widow. He paid for it. It is ours.'

Sara stopped pacing and stared out of the window.

'When the food came over the river from the farm this afternoon, Abel sent a message with it. It seems they have had more visits from representatives of the Intendant questioning its ownership.'

She continued her pacing, her hands clamped either side of her head. 'I should have anticipated this,' she sighed. 'I should have realized that it was only a matter of time. 'You remember, Lidie, when those men approached us at the farm? Those spies who forced us off the track?'

Lidie nodded. 'But that was a long time ago.'

'Maybe, but I suspect they reported back to the Intendant who has been biding his time until the King has given approval to seize land from us unless we abjure.'

'And has he that approval?'

Sara shrugged. 'Perhaps he has, the curé was muttering something of another Edict but in tuth, Lidie, there have been so many of these Edicts that I couldn't tell whether he was speaking the truth or not.'

She sat down heavily on one of the tapestry covered chairs.

'I have just come from conferring with Louise and Jacob,' she said. 'They are as horrified as I about what has happened. And if it is true that we can no longer own land unless we deny our faith, then they have a deal more to lose than I.'

Sara adjusted her coif which had loosened with all the agitation. 'Jacob is going to look into the matter,' she said. 'But he said we shall need a lawyer to prepare a case for us.'

Lidie smiled. 'I know someone who could help you, Mama!'

'A Catholic lawyer would be no good to me and I doubt we'd find a lawyer of our faith now.'

Lidie hesitated. 'Did you know that Samuel Verdier is home?'

'No! How did you come by this knowledge, Lidie?'

Lidie felt herself blushing but Sara, for once, was too concerned with her own troubles to notice.

'I met him by chance this morning when I was on the way to the infirmary. I ... I tripped on the road and fell and he was passing and insisted on putting me on his horse and taking me to the infirmary.'

'You're not telling me you rode astride?'

Lidie nodded. 'It took me back to when Papa would lead me round the farm on one of the carthorses.'

'I knew you should not have walked all that way. Are you hurt?'

'No. I ... I was not looking where I was going. It was not grave, but Samuel was kind and he insists he will call in later to make sure I am recovered.'

132

Sara looked at her and smiled. 'Indeed,' she said. 'Very kind. And is this why you have changed into your prettiest muslin?'

Lidie blushed. 'Mama!'

'I am teasing, Lidie. In truth it will be good to see him and he can perhaps advise me on this matter of the farm.'

Chapter Twelve

It was evening when Samuel Verdier called. Lidie greeted him at the door and said in an undertone: 'Please say nothing about what happened earlier.'

He shook his head. 'Of course not, Lidie, but how do you fare? I was so worried about you when we parted. It was a horrible …' He swallowed. 'Those brutes. They should be punished.'

Lidie put her hand on his arm. 'I beg you, Samuel, say nothing of it.'

Just then Sara appeared and they all went into the panelled room.

'This is a fine room,' said Samuel. He pointed to one of the portraits. 'And an excellent likeness of you, Madame, in that painting.'

Sara smiled. 'Yes, they are well crafted, are they not. Lidie is to sit for the portraitist soon.'

Samuel looked across at Lidie. 'She will make an excellent subject.'

Sara did not reply but a slight smile played around her lips. Lidie looked down at her feet.

Then Samuel told them of what he had been doing during the day and how he had found a room in town that he could rent and this led naturally on to Sara confiding in him about the ownership of the farm.

Immediately he was all attention. 'This is just the sort of case we need to fight,' he said.

'Jacob and Louise have a deal more land than I and if they refuse to abjure then no doubt that, too, will be forfeit. They were very worried to hear of the curé's visit to me. No doubt he will be at their door, too, before long.'

Samuel nodded. 'They have good reason to be worried. As will my father be. The situation regarding land owned by those of our faith interests me greatly, Madame. With your permission I should like to look into your case further.'

Sara didn't reply. The serious young man before her looked so young.

Sensing her uncertainty, Samuel went on. 'I worked on some cases of this nature when I was under tutelage,' he said. 'I have recent experience.'

'I'm sure you would be in good hands, Mama,' said Lidie quickly. 'And … and Samuel is staunch in his beliefs.'

'Madamoiselle Lidie is right, Madame. One of the reasons I became a lawyer was to represent the people of our faith and to try and ensure they receive justice, but now that the parlement mis parties has been dissolved and all the judges are Catholic the situation is precarious, to say the least.'

Sara looked from one to the other. 'Then I accept, Samuel. It will be good to have such expert help.'

The sun had almost set by the time Samuel left them. He rose to his feet and took his leave.

'It has been such a pleasant evening,' he said, 'but I must leave now for my father's house.'

Lidie came to the door with him and suddenly he took her hand and kissed it and she was momentarily startled at this intimacy.

'I have been worrying about you all the day, Lidie. Would you not confide in your mother about what happened?'

She shook her head. 'She has enough to think about. I would not burden her further. I … I will put it out of my mind.'

'Is that so easy? Would you not trust me to pursue …'

She met his eyes. 'No. please, Samuel, I will forget the horror of it more easily if we can keep it between us.'

He put his hand over hers. 'Not all men are such beasts,' he said softly. Then. 'You are shaking, Lidie!'

'In truth, it is difficult to forget,' she whispered. 'And I am for ever in your debt.'

He smiled. 'Then I shall reclaim that debt by visiting you as often as you allow it.'

And with that he clattered down the front steps and out into the street where his patient horse was tied to the post outside. Lidie followed him out and stood on the bottom step as he untied the reins and leapt into the saddle. Then he leant down, caught her hand and kissed it again.

'Good night Lidie,' he said.

She was still smiling when she went inside to re-join her mother.

That night, Lidie dismissed Susanne after evening prayers, afraid that the girl's keen eyes would see the bruises if she helped her undress. She had found it impossible during prayers to thank God sincerely for the blessings of the day, but when she was in her bed she addressed her papa and although the night was warm she was shivering as she confided to him what had happened on the road that morning.

'I know all men are not like that when they are aroused, Papa,' she said. 'But it sickened me. I cannot put it from my mind.'

She lay there for a long time trying to find some peace but the terrifying image of the man on top of her ripping her bodice and pawing at her breasts, kept coming to the front of her mind.

She tossed and turned, wishing with all her heart that Samuel had not seen what had happened to her but then, when she calmed a little, she thought back to how he had smiled at her and kissed her hand.

'Not all men are such beasts,' he had said, and she knew this to be true. She had seen the love and affection which was so evident between her parents, how gentle her papa had been with her mama and even as she felt the tenderness of her bruises, she knew, with certainty, that Samuel was a gentle man.

She slept fitfully, more than once waking from nightmares, and as dawn was breaking, she rose and dressed, determined to put yesterday's horrors behind her. There was no one about when she crept down the stairs but then she heard some movement in the kitchen and found Annette there taking the first batch of bread from the oven.

'You are up very early, ma petite,' she said. 'Did you not sleep well?'

Lidie shrugged. 'Just a few bad dreams. Nothing of note.'

Annette placed a hunk of warm bread in front of her together with a choice of preserves. 'Eat up, mam'selle. You need your strength for the work you do at that infirmary, I warrant.'

Lidie nodded and forced herself to eat, though she had little appetite.

'I have mended your bodice,' said Annette. 'I took it upon myself to do the work,' she added, looking hard at Lidie.

'Thank you.'

'A mighty job it was, too.'

'I am in your debt, Annette. I wish my stitching was more accomplished, then perhaps I could have done it myself.'

Annette did not smile and there was an awkward silence between them. Then suddenly Annette turned to face her.

'You were attacked, were you not?' she said.

Lidie blushed. 'What! Have you taken leave of your senses, Annette?'

Annette folded her arms across her chest and met Lidie's eyes.

'That bodice was ripped by a man's hand.' She put up her hand to stop Lidie who had begun to protest again. 'No, mam'selle, I am not a fool. Do not try to deceive me.'

'I …' Lidie tried to speak but could not. She lowered her eyes and Annette continued, her fists clenched. 'Has some man violated you?'

Still Lidie said nothing and Annette knelt beside her.

'Tell me what truly happened,' she said.

'You will not tell Mama?'

'Not if you do not wish it.'

Lidie sighed. 'I was attacked on the road yesterday morning when I was walking to the infirmary,' she said. 'There was no one else there and they …' she swallowed. 'They came up from out of a ditch and …'

Annette put her hands up to her face. 'Oh no, my poor child,' she said. 'Tell me they did not take your maidenhead?'

Lidie shook her head. Then she gulped. 'They were about to, Annette. They had me pinned to the ground.' She started to cry soundlessly.

'And someone came to your aid before …'

Lidie nodded through her tears. 'Samuel Verdier rode up and drove them away.'

Annette put her arms round Lidie and held her close, rocking her gently.

137

Lidie sniffed and started to draw away. 'I was foolish. I should not have walked on my own. I thought … I thought there would be others on the road.'

Annette did not let go of her but instead lowered her voice. 'Then perhaps, mam'selle, you will look kindly on one who was not so lucky. One who had no one to rescue her.'

Lidie looked up. 'What can you mean?'

Annette glanced quickly around the kitchen and whispered. 'Have you not noticed the change in Susanne?'

Lidie frowned. 'She has been subdued of late but … what! You cannot mean that she …'

Annette nodded. 'She, too, was taken by force, but she had no one to save her.'

'She is with child?'

Annette let go of Lidie and glanced again towards the door. 'Aye,' she said quietly. 'And she is out of her wits with worry. She is certain that your mama will dismiss her.'

'What of the man who used her so cruelly?'

'She will have nothing to do with him. He is a Catholic spy, mam'selle. He was using her to gather information.'

'No!'

Annette moved closer and took Lidie's face in her hands. 'Please mam'selle, please speak to your mama on the girl's behalf. She was duped. She thought the brute was taking a kindly interest in her when all the time he was finding out about the household.'

'But why?'

Annette raised her eyes to the ceiling. 'Are you as blind as Susanne? To get news of secret gatherings, to hear if we keep a Bible in the house. To gather evidence to pass on to the King's agents.'

Lidie's face was pale. 'We have been discreet but she could have overheard I suppose…'

'She did nothing out of malice, mam'selle. I know her; she is my great niece after all. And she is happy here. She has had such a turbulent life. She would never knowlingly betray you.'

Lidie was still looking shocked and Annette continued. 'Once she understood what he was doing she started to give the man false information and when he found out.' Annette swallowed. 'Then he took advantage of her, saying that if she did not let him have his way with her he would make it known to you and your mama that she had been betraying you.'

Still Lidie said nothing.

'It could have happened to you, mam'selle.'

'What do you mean?'

'If Monsieur Verdier had not rescued you …'

For a few moments, Lidie looked furious and then the tension drained from her.

'Aye. I'd not considered that. If I had been violated I, too, could have been in Susanne's condition.'

'And equally disgraced and shunned by society.'

Lidie nodded.

'Then will you speak to your mama about Susanne ?'

'I'll put her case as well as I can but I cannot judge how Mama will react.'

'And for my part I will say nothing of what happened to you on that lonely track.'

There was a long silence finally broken by Annette.

'Well,' she said. 'There is at least some good that has come out of the sorry business.'

Lidie frowned. 'What do you mean?'

'You have become reacquainted with the young lawyer.'

'Yes, there is that.'

'Do not look so coy, mam'selle. I know you have feelings for him. You have always had feelings for him, ever since you met on the night of your sixteenth anniversary.'

Lidie blushed deeply. 'How can you say that, Annette? How could you possibly …?'

Annette laughed out loud then. 'I watched you dance together when I was helping clear the tables at your birthday celebration. And I said to myself then that one day that would be an excellent match.'

'Annette!'

As she stepped into the carriage later that morning, Lidie was still turning over in her mind how to tell her mama about

Susanne's condition and to predict how she might react but she was not so deep in thought that she did not shudder when the carriage passed by the place where the attack had taken place.

While Lidie was at the infirmary, she was almost able to put aside all other thoughts as she went hither and thither, helping the nurses, emptying slops and giving comforting words to the sick. She had learnt how to clean wounds and had trained herself not to flinch at the sights and smells as she went about her work and put on clean bandages.

As ever, the two young Huguenot medical graduates went about their business, usually with Dr Verdier on hand to test their knowledge or oversee their actions but they, and the doctor, were always watchful and relied on someone to warn them if the magistrates were visiting, in which case, the two young men melted away out of sight.

Two Elders from their own congregation visited during the morning, too, and Lidie smiled at them and exchanged pleasantries with them.

Everything was as normal, and she was glad of it.

In the kitchen, Marie gave her the mid-morning refreshment and they talked easily together, then Lidie went out of the back to take the air for a few moments before going back to her labours. As she was stretching and taking some deep breaths, Dr Verdier came to join her.

'Ah Lidie,' he said. 'Samuel tells me that he spent a happy evening with you and your mama.'

Lidie blushed.

'He told me you had a fall on the road. Are you quite recovered?'

'Quite, thank you. I was not paying heed to where I was going. It was my own fault and Samuel was kindness itself.'

They stood in silence for a few moments, looking across the peaceful countryside and hearing only the buzz of bees in the herb garden and the distant sound of activity and conversation coming from inside the infirmary. Then Isaac said.

'My nurses tell me that you are quick to learn, Lidie, and not afraid of hard work. I am grateful to you.'

Lidie smiled. 'I am glad to be of use, sir. I was afraid I would be considered a hinderance.'

'I confess that at first I was reluctant to have you here. However, I am glad that our pastor persuaded me to give you a trial. You are stronger than you appear, Lidie, both in mind and body.'

He paused then, frowning. 'I wonder,' he began and, when Lidie looked at him, questioningly, he went on. 'None of my nurses have your education Lidie,' he said, 'And I find myself increasingly bowed down with wearisome matters ...'

'What sort of matters?'

Isaac sighed. 'Not only the ordering of supplies from the apothecary and such, but correspondence with colleagues and with officials. We Protestants are meeting obstacles at every turn, having to comply with petty rules.'

Isaac rubbed his eyes, yawned and then continued, 'Samuel told me of your mama's predicament and I fear it will only be a matter of time before I too shall be receiving a similar demand from the Intendant.'

'She is much exercised about it sir, but Samuel has promised to look into it on her behalf.'

'Yes, he told me as much.'

Isaac stifled another yawn. 'Forgive me, Lidie, I was up late into the night dealing with some tedious correspondence.'

'And is it this tedious correspondence you would like help with, sir?' If you show me what to do then I should be happy to help.''

Isaac rubbed his hands together. 'Excellent! That is a burden off my shoulders, Lidie. I shall inform my nurses that they are to make sure you have enough time to help me in this way.'

When Lidie reached home at the end of the day, she told Sara of this new arrangement.

'I think you will be well suited to it,' she said. 'And perhaps your hands will be less raw.'

'I shall not cease my other work, Mama.' She grinned. 'My raw hands will merely be stained with ink!'

Sara sighed. 'Do not take on too much, Lidie.' Then she went on. 'Samuel is to call in a little later and discuss matters about the farm with me. I have invited him to dine with us.'

Lidie felt a blush coming to her cheeks and she turned away from her mother and removed her coif, shaking out her dark hair.

'It is good that he is pursuing this matter for you.'

'Yes indeed,' said Sara, and Lidie did not see the smile on her lips as she added. 'I confess that I was a little surprised at how swiftly he seems to be acting.'

Lidie abruptly changed the subject. 'Have you heard yet from the dressmaker, Mama? Are our new silks near completion?'

For the next little while they discussed the new silks they had ordered and then Lidie escaped up to her chamber, still not calling for Susanne. As she undressed to change out of her plain garb, she saw how the bruises on her breasts had developed, leaving blue black marks which were stark against her pale skin. She washed herself carefully and brushed out her hair, then changed into a high cut bodice she'd not worn for a long time and laced it tightly.

Samuel was with her mama when she came downstairs and she heard them talking together, so she did not disturb them and later, her Uncle Jacob called in.

He embraced Lidie. 'I am glad that your mama has asked young Samuel to assist with this tedious business about the farm,' he said. 'I said I would call in to hear his advice.'

Lidie showed him into the panelled room where Samuel and her mama were scrutinizing maps and documents. Samuel rose to his feet, smiling at her as Jacob went to join them. Just then, Annette appeared with a tray of wine and set it down on the table. As she left the room with Lidie she whispered. 'I wonder why the young lawyer is so eager to help your mama!'

'Annette!'

They had a simple and relaxed evening meal, gathered around the large table in the kitchen. Jacob stayed to eat with them and there was much general discussion about land ownership, further restrictions being imposed on their people and how Samuel and other Protestant lawyers would fare in the future, but every now and again, Samuel would look across at Lidie and meet her eyes, and they smiled at one another, which did not go unnoticed by Sara or Jacob.

At length, Samuel took his leave and Lidie left her uncle and mama talking and, as on the evening before, she saw Samuel out.

He took both her hands in his. 'You still look pale,' he whispered.

She did not remove her hands. 'I confess I had a disturbed night,' she said.

His eyes left her face and he looked at her chest. 'And the …' He paused, glancing briefly at her bosom and then looked away. He swallowed. 'And the bruises?'

'Horrible. But they are well hidden, are they not?'

'Oh Lidie,' he said suddenly, with a break in his voice, how I wish …'

'Do not concern yourself Samuel. You were there. You saved me and I am recovered.'

He smiled then. 'I shall be back often to visit your mama,' he said. 'I am eager to pursue this matter for her.'

Lidie said nothing but she couldn't help returning his smile.

'It is a happy chance,' continued Samuel, his voice quiet, 'that I have such an excuse.'

Lidie looked up at him.

He laughed then and it was a joyous sound. 'I … I suspect that you know what I mean, Lidie.'

When Samuel and Jacob had left, Lidie found a moment to speak to Sara privately.

'Mama, there's a matter I need to …'

Sara turned to her, smiling. 'That was a happy evening, was it not? I am much relieved that young Samuel is helping. Why, with his legal knowledge, surely he will …'

Lidie interrupted her. 'Mama, there is something I must tell you.'

Sara was still smiling. 'Is it that you have feelings for Samuel,' she said. 'I had suspected …'

'No. No, it is not about Samuel. It is about Susanne.'

'Susanne!' Sara frowned.

'Listen, Mama, this is a grave matter. You must hear me out. Sit down for a moment.'

But Sara was making her way towards the stairs. 'I am tired Lidie, surely it can wait until morning.'

143

Lidie grabbed her arm. 'Susanne is with child.'

'Sara stopped then and turned to face Lidie, her expression hard.

'What! Wretched girl. I should never have let Annette persuade me to take her on. She clearly has no morals. She will have to go.'

'No!' Lidie clung onto Sara's arm. 'No Mama, do not be so quick to judge her. Hear me out. You need to listen to what befell her.'

And so, at the foot of the stairs, Lidie recounted the sorry tale to Sara.

'So she's a spy as well as a slut,' said Sara. 'All the more reason for her to leave our household.'

'Mama!'

'You are too naïve, Lidie. No doubt she fabricated this fanciful story so that you felt sorry for her.'

'I am sure she speaks true, Mama, and I wish her to stay,' said Lidie.

'And I wish her to leave,' said Sara.

Lidie thought back to those brutes who had so nearly defiled her and her resolve hardened.

It could have happened to me.

'Where is your compassion, Mama? The girl has nowhere to go. And did not our Lord help the poor and forgive the woman taken in adultery? Would you not follow His example and show mercy.'

Sara stood still for a moment. 'But she has *spied* on us!'

'Not knowingly. It was she who was naïve, Mama, taken in by that vile man. It is she who has been abused trying to protect us when she realised what he was doing.'

Sara kept silent.

'Please, Mama. I am fond of her and she is good at her tasks.'

Still Sara said nothing.

'She may have rendered us a favour, Mama.'

'What!'

'We know, now, that there are those spying on our household. We can be more vigilant.'

Suddenly, Sara sat down on the first step of the stairs and put her head in her hands. After a moment, Lidie sat beside her.

'Perhaps we can come to a compromise, Mama. Thinking on it, the man could pursue her if she stayed in Castillon but I doubt he'd bother to go further afield. Could she perhaps go and live on the farm with Abel and Martha, at least until the child is delivered?'

***

At length, Sara was persuaded to send Susanne to the farm to see out her confinement.

In the weeks following, Lidie often pondered whether she would have shown such sympathy for Susanne's plight if that vicious attack on her own body had not happened. Or whether she and Samuel would have become intimate so quickly.

At harvest time, Sara, Lidie and Annette visited the farm. They were greeted by Abel and Martha and standing a little way behind them, Susanne, now great with child.

Susanne kept her head lowered and said nothing but Lidie addressed her.

'Susanne, is all well with you? Your time has almost come, has it not?'

Susanne nodded but said nothing.

When she had been sent off to do some errand, Lidie asked Martha about Susanne.

'I hope she is of some help to you?'

Martha smiled. 'I confess at first there was an awkwardness between us. She is not familiar with our country ways but she is grateful to have a home, mam'selle, and she tries to please, though it must be dull for her here.'

'And the babe, when it arrives? How will you manage?'

Martha sighed. 'We shall welcome it and see that it is cared for, mam'selle.'

'We are asking a lot of you.'

Martha was quiet for a moment, staring out of the window. 'Abel and I were not lucky enough to bring a child to term,' she said. 'I have compassion for young Susanne. Why she is hardly more than a child herself and she has been ill used. If the babe survives, it will be a blessing.'

'And a disruption to your lives.'

Martha smiled. 'Aye, it will be that and no doubt Susanne will need a deal of help.'

She paused. 'Who knows what the future holds for her, or for her babe.'

'Or for any of us,' muttered Lidie.

Later, when Lidie was alone with Susanne, the girl was more forthcoming.

'I thank God every day that you helped me, mam'selle. I am truly grateful.'

Lidie smiled. 'I know it is dull for you here in the countryside, Susanne, but at least you can have your babe in safety and be well cared for.'

The girl looked down at her stomach. 'I am afraid, mam'selle.'

'That is natural, Susanne. Childbirth is …'

'No, it is not the birth I fear. I fear that I will not love the child whose father I loathe.'

'The babe cannot help its parentage and the child will have your blood, too. I warrant you will love it.'

Susanne looked doubtful.

***

It was not long before Samuel also came to check on the harvest at his father's farm and soon after arriving he came over to visit them.

When he arrived, Sara was out but he found Lidie in the orchard and they spent a happy time walking and talking together, talk which in due course turned to Samuel's plans for the future and of the daily threats to those of their faith.

'They are coming to me every day now,' said Samuel. 'So many wanting me to plead their case for them. It is overwhelming.'

'And will any of their cases succeed?'

Samuel stopped and leaned against an apple tree, looking up through the leaves to the sky. 'I fear most will fail, but I do have some good news at least. It seems that the curé was not well informed when he visited your mama and in his eagerness to convert her, he interpreted what was a mere rumour as fact. As yet there is no law passed to ban Huguenots from owning land.'

Lidie clapped her hands. 'That is good news indeed!' She looked round at the familiar landscape. 'Oh how happy I am that we shall not lose all this,' she said. 'My father loved this place and every time we visit I can feel his presence.'

Samuel frowned. 'I fear it is but a stay of execution. No doubt there will soon be another edict posted to say that no one of our faith may own land.'

'But for now, at least …and do you fear for your own profession?'

Samuel nodded. 'It is possible that I shall have to find another way to make a living.'

'No! Surely not, after all your training!'

'I hope with all my heart that it will not come to that but I must think ahead. If the worst happens and I can no longer practise, then …'

She said nothing but moved a little closer to him.

'My sister is married to a textile merchant in Montauban,' he continued. 'I plan to visit them soon and see if there is a way in which I can involve myself in that trade.' He sighed. 'Oh, it is all so frustrating. I have been trained in the law, it is what I know and now …'

Lidie snatched at a blade of grass and chewed on it. 'The pastor was telling me about the work of the lawyer Claude Brousson,' she said. 'It is sad that he has had to go into hiding.'

Samuel's eyes lit up. 'He is my hero, Lidie! Brousson has done more than any to fight the injustice meted out to our people. I have never met him but I would dearly like to, though I fear now that he will flee the country and I never will. He is a brilliant lawyer and not only that, he studied at the School of Theology at Nimes before he turned to study law so he is a committed Protestant with a true understanding of Calvin's principles.'

Lidie had never seen him so animated. 'You feel his plight sorely, do you not?' she said.

He nodded. 'I was enraged when I heard what happened to those poor pastors who supported his petition. Indeed, all our pastors are in danger. They try to lead their flocks and keep their faith but they are harassed at every turn. In truth, I do not know where this will all end.'

'Is our future really so bleak?'

Samuel looked up, then took her shoulders and turned her towards him. 'Our future?'

Lidie blushed and looked away. 'I mean, the future of those of our faith,' she said, stuttering slightly.

Samuel continued to hold her. 'I know that my future will not be bleak if you are with me,' he said softly and at last she looked up and met his eyes.

He cleared his throat. 'I have never met any girl like you, Lidie. You have a real understanding of what is befalling our people, a real concern.' He hesitated. 'Perhaps I should not speak so soon?'

There was a long silence as they looked at each other while the sounds of the birds and the workers in the fields filled the air.

'I love you Lidie.,' he whispered. 'I want you with all my being. Please say you will be my wife?'

'Of course I will, your foolish man!'

'Then you do return my feelings?'

Lidie put her hand to his face. 'I have loved you from the moment we danced together at my sixteenth birthday but I thought you considered me silly and frivolous.'

He grasped her hand and held it fast 'You were so young,' he said, 'And so lovely. I thought myself too dull for you and I was sure you would find some other suitor while I was away at my studies.'

He drew her to him then and kissed her and she relaxed into his embrace, her heart bursting with happiness and when at last, they disentangled themselves, he took her face between his hands.

'I will always protect you, Lidie,' he said. 'I promise that I will never let anyone harm you.'

I will always protect you.

Brave words that Lidie had cause to reflect upon many times in the years to come.

Sara gave her own consent and wrote immediately to her husband's cousin, who stood as Lidie's guardian after her father's death. He, too, consented to the match and Isaac, too, was

148

delighted. In a quiet moment, when he had his son to himself, he said.

'She is a lovely young woman, Samuel, and she has a steadfast heart, of that I am certain.'

Samuel smiled. 'I know that, Father,' he said. 'I am a lucky man.'

'Indeed you are,' said Isaac.

When they returned to town, there was much discussion about future arrangements and it was decided that Samuel and Lidie should live with Sara. It was a large enough house and it was close to Samuel's rooms. Sara had offered it to them with some misgivings, thinking that perhaps the young couple would rather somewhere smaller but more private, but they had accepted the arrangement with alacrity and the household was re-ordered to give them their own quarters.

Pierre officiated at the wedding. It had to be a quiet and private affair, in the late evening, as so many Huguenot gatherings were being broken up by Catholic spies, but it was joyful, nonetheless, as the happiness of the young couple and the affection between them was evident for all to see and for a few hours at least all fears and threats to their future were put to one side.

As Cécile and Charles were taking their leave, Cécile hugged Lidie.

'I am so happy for you, Lidie. I had thought him too serious, but now I see you together, I know he is right for you.'

Chapter Thirteen

<u>Spring 1685</u>

'Push, my darling, push!'

Sara was gripping Lidie's hand as she writhed on the bed.

'You are nearly there, ma petite,' said Annette. 'I can already see the head. Now you need to push again.'

'Be brave,' said Sara, wiping the sweat from Lidie's brow. 'Not long now I promise you.' She looked anxiously at Annette.

Lidie closed her eyes, clamped her jaw tight and pushed with all her might.

When will this agony end?

'The head is out!' said Annette. 'Just one more push!'

And at last Lidie felt the slithering emptying of her womb and the pain had suddenly and magically ceased but at first there was no sound of a cry.

'Is the child alive?' whispered Sara.

Then the most welcome sound in all the world. A fierce little cry and then another, loud and protesting.

Annette wrapped the baby in a towel, wiping tears from her cheeks.

'You have a beautiful boy!' She showed him to Lidie who stretched out her arms for him and cradled him in the crook of one elbow kissing the top of his head.

'Where's Samuel?'

Sara sniffed. 'I will go and fetch him directly,' she said. 'And Isaac too. They are both downstairs.'

But no fetching was necessary. Samuel had heard the baby's cry and was already bounding up the stairs and in moments he was through the door and had rushed to Lidie's side kissing her cheek and smoothing the damp hair back from her head and all the while staring in wonder at the little creature in her arms.

Lidie looked up at him. 'I fancy he favours you,' she said, smiling.

'Poor boy!' said Samuel, laughing and crying at the same time. He took Lidie's hand in his. 'How are you?'

'Weary,' said Lidie. But happy to have given you a son.'

'Little Elias,' said Samuel, stroking the baby's soft downy cheek. 'Welcome to the world.'

Then Isaac was there beside them.

'May I see my grandson?' he asked, and Lidie handed him the baby. He unwrapped the towel and quickly inspected the baby then handed him back. 'All is well, Lidie. He looks to be a sturdy little fellow.'

Then he turned to his son. 'Now, off with you, Samuel. I need to examine Lidie and Annette will want to put everything to rights here. You can go downstairs and tell the household.'

Moments later they heard Samuel clattering down the stairs, shouting out the good news to the servants.

'A son! We have a son!'

In the chamber they could hear joyful cries coming from below as the news spread. Lidie handed the baby to Sara whose cheeks were still wet.

'I was so afraid for you my darling,' she said. 'I fear that I was remembering my own unhappy experiences, but you have produced a strong little boy.'

As if on cue, Elias let out a squawk and Sara smiled through her tears. As she put the baby to Lidie's breast and watched him seek for the nipple with his mouth and then latch on as Lidie winced briefly, she stroked the damp curls on Lidie's brow.

'Will you promise me that you will bring him up in our faith?' she said.

Lidie didn't take her eyes off the baby. 'How could you even ask that, Mama?'

Annette was busying herself cleaning up the bed and she gently moved Lidie so that she could reach the soiled linen.

Lidie put a hand on Annette's arm, 'I warrant you were more skilled than any Catholic midwife,' she said.

Annette paused in her work for a moment. 'I thank God we had no need of one,' she said. 'A Catholic midwife would have had that babe baptized into their faith before he'd had a chance to suckle.'

Lidie nodded. 'But now we shall have him baptized as a true Reformist,' she said, holding Elias close and watching as his little lips sought out her nipple once more.

Sara left the chamber and went downstairs where she waited for Isaac to descend. When he came to see her some time later he took both her hands in his.

'A joyful outcome indeed,' he said.

Sara looked at him fondly. 'Why Isaac,' she said. 'If I did not know you better I would swear that there was a tear in your eye!'

He did not deny it and continued to hold her hands in his.

'Am I not allowed to weep for joy at the safe birth of our grandson?' he asked.

Gently she prised her hands from his grasp. 'Let us pray that the babe will thrive.'

Isaac nodded. 'He will not be lacking love,' he said quietly. 'And between us all we shall afford him all possible care.'

For the next few weeks, Lidie was so enraptured by her little son that she thought of nothing else. She had Sara and Annette to support her and give her time to rest and recuperate. Sara, ever watchful and only too aware of the fragility of a baby's life, began to relax as she saw how Elias grew stronger by the day.

Samuel, too, was in a daze of happiness at the survival of both his son and his wife and, for a little while, lived in a sheltered world filled with wonder and love, only half engaging with the desperate discussions which were taking place amongst his fellow Huguenots.

Rumours were rife that the King planned to revoke the Edict of Nantes which had protected those of their faith for nearly ninety years, during which time they had thrived. The future was so uncertain that although Samuel continued to practise as a lawyer, he had also joined his brother-in-law's textile business in Montauban and was learning the trade.

In the Spring of the year, the custom of billeting dragoons in Protestant homes had resumed. The rough soldiers were no longer restrained and indeed their bullying tactics with householders were encouraged. They committed untold atrocities and ransacked homes unless the head of the household abjured. Because of this there had been thousands of 'conversions' to the Catholic faith in Bearne and Grenoble.

More temples had been destroyed, too, and there had been many false charges laid against Protestant pastors.

A few weeks after Lidie had given birth, Isaac was visiting and the family was dining together.

'You look fatigued, Isaac,' said Sara. 'You work too hard.'

'It is not so much the work,' replied Isaac. 'It is being constantly on my guard. I worry for those who work for me. It is a great burden for them to know that I teach illegally. If I am discovered, they will all suffer, I fear.'

'Huh! What is illegal is the way these laws are passed,' said Samuel.

'Aye,' said Isaac, taking a long draught of wine. I fear that the time is fast approaching when our professions will be barred to us, Samuel, and you are wise to become familiar with commerce.'

Samuel gave a mirthless laugh. 'All that training,' he said bitterly. 'And soon I may be but a merchant and a farmer.' He tipped back his chair and stretched his arms above his head. 'And I warrant we'll not be farmers for long either.'

Sara looked up. 'Has it come to this? Shall we lose our land if we do not abjure?'

'If the King revokes the Edict of Nantes, we shall lose every privilege we ever gained,' said Samuel.

Isaac interrupted. 'Let us not dwell on what has not yet happened,' he said firmly, seeing the look of anxiety on Lidie's face. 'We must rather be inventive and think of ways we can continue to thrive and yet to be true to God.'

'Aye,' said Sara. 'With God's help we shall surely find a way.'

Isaac looked across at her and smiled and for a long moment they locked eyes. Then Sara looked away 'And, after all,' she continued. 'We have much to celebrate, do we not? The birth of a new baby to uphold our faith.'

They all turned to look at Lidie. 'Motherhood suits you my dear,' said Isaac. 'You grow more beautiful by the day.'

'I will drink to that,' said Samuel and he raised his glass. 'To my beautiful wife and our lusty young son.'

They all repeated the toast and Lidie smiled back at them.

There was an amicable silence for a few moments and then Samuel turned to Lidie. 'I have neglected my business in Montauban,' he said. 'I should go and visit my sister and her husband and collect a new supply of textiles to sell, but if you still need me here, then I will delay my departure.'

For a moment, Lidie looked alarmed, then she recovered. 'Of course you must go,' she said. 'I am surrounded by those caring for me. Do not give it another thought.'

Isaac frowned. 'I worry about Montauban,' he said, 'And for my daughter and her family. There is such a great population of our faith in the city.'

'But the textile trade thrives there,' said Samuel. 'And it offers me a living if I can no longer practise the law.'

'We have always been a resourceful and hard-working people,' said Isaac thoughtfully, 'And now we shall need every scrap of that resourcefulness.'

Then Isaac and Samuel spoke of their plans for their land. Over the last two seasons, they had studied water usage and planted maize, the crop come over from the New World. Last year's yields had been good and this year's promised to be even better. Samuel's legal mind was well suited to analysis and the interpretation of figures.

Lidie was able to contribute a little to this conversation as she had written letters to grain merchants and other dealers on Isaac's behalf, but Sara looked solemn.

'Jacob and Louise are very worried. His business is suffering because of his faith. He has much to lose. And Cécile's conversion hit them hard.'

'Charles is very successful, I'm told,' said Isaac.

There was an awkward silence, then Sara spoke up. 'Yes,' she said slowly, 'It seems that since he and his parents abandoned their faith, many fruitful contracts have come their way.'

'Is Cécile's conscience troubled I wonder' said Isaac.

Louise tells me that Cécile remains steadfast in her heart,' said Sara quietly. 'But I do not think that Charles had much difficulty in persuading her to agree to his decision.'

Lidie changed the subject. 'When do you plan to leave for Montauban?' she asked Samuel.

'Probably next week, if you are sure you are well enough here?'

'Of course,' said Lidie.

Isaac looked across at his son. 'Do you really need to go?'

Samuel smiled. 'I must make myself more familiar with the textile trade if it is to be my work in the future, Father.' He got up from the table and went over to stand behind Lidie, his hands on her shoulders. 'If the law is closed to me, then I must make a living somehow if I am to feed my wife and family.'

Isaac sighed. 'Well, if you are determined. It will be well to hear news of Montauban and that my daughter and her family are safe.'

'Why should they not be safe?' asked Lidie.

'No reason my dear,' said Isaac hastily. 'It is just that Montauban has been under attack in the past and ... and I fear that it is vulnerable in such uncertain times.'

A week later, Samuel set off. Montauban was more than two days' journey from Castillon and he had hired a large coach with a driver so that there would be plenty of room for the textiles he planned to bring back with him and sell in the region.

It was only a few days later that the rumours began to circulate, spreading quickly among the Protestant households of Castillon.

Merchants coming back from Montauban said they'd heard that dragoons were approaching the city. They reported that already the place was in a ferment as Protestants prepared themselves for an invasion.

Isaac had used his contacts to make sure he was kept informed and the tight knit group of the faithful in Castillon prayed fervently for the safety of their brethren. Sara opened her doors to Pierre and they were joined by Jacob and Louise and many other members of their faith. They prayed quietly and said psalms, not daring to sing them in case spies reported them.

As the days went on, the reports brought back became more lurid. Stories of brutality against Huguenots, of soldiers billeted in their homes, abusing their hospitality, terrifying their women and servants. And of many many abjurations.

'How can they?' said Sara. 'How can they desert their faith like that?'

Lidie frowned. 'We cannot know how we would feel if we were treated so harshly, Mama.'

'There are no circumstances in which I would betray my faith,' said Sara firmly. 'Nor you, Lidie.'

Lidie shook her head. 'I hope I would be able to remain strong,' she said, looking down at baby Elias in her arms.

When he next visited, Isaac looked haggard. 'I would have expected Samuel back by now,' he said quietly, when Sara let him in.

She nodded. 'Lidie pretends unconcern,' she confided. 'But I know she is hiding her true feelings.'

Another week went by and still there was no news of Samuel. In the household, everyone went about their business and meals were prepared and routine tasks undertaken, but they were all waiting for the rattling of the coach on the cobbles outside and the sound of Samuel's voice.

Isaac seemed to have aged years in those days. He came every day to the house to see them, even though there was no news to impart.

'Nothing,' he would whisper to Sara as she let him in. Then as Lidie came running, he would smile broadly. 'Nothing to report, Lidie, but I am sure that Samuel is merely delayed leaving the city. There will be guards at the main gates and so on. No doubt there will be much confusion, but he will return, I am sure of it. Now, let me see this grandson of mine.'

And then, one evening, nearly three weeks after Samuel's departure, while they were sitting in the kitchen saying grace before they ate their evening meal, there was the sound of a coach outside and they heard the coachman's voice.

'Woah. Woah there!'

Isaac, Sara and Lidie, closely followed by Annette, all rushed to the door.

156

THE KING'S COMMAND

The coachman looked at them. 'You'd best help him out,' he said gruffly.

Lidie was the first to the door of the coach. She wrestled with the handle, her hands shaking, and finally managed to open it.

'Samuel?'

In the gloom of the coach's interior, she saw that Samuel was heaving himself out of the seat with great difficulty.

'Help me out, Lidie,' he gasped.

She climbed into the coach and took his hand firmly in hers.

'What ails you?'

'Just help me,' he said.

By now, Isaac was by her side and together they managed to lower Samuel from the coach, but when his feet touched the ground, he staggered. Isaac took one arm and Lidie the other and slowly they managed to get him up the steps to the front door while Annette called for servants to come and empty the coach of luggage. The coachman looked on and when he saw all was unloaded, he made to set off again. But Samuel, with a huge effort, turned his head.

'I owe you my life,' he said. 'You will be rewarded, I promise.'

'He risked everything to get me safely away from the city,' he whispered to Lidie. 'I wondered … I truly wondered whether I would ever see you again.'

Lidie's heart twisted when she heard his voice, so weak and defeated.

They helped him into the vestibule and sat him down. His clothes were stained and he winced in pain when Lidie tried to take off his outer garments.

'What is it my love? Where are you hurt?'

Isaac was beside him. 'Tell me your sister is safe,' he said.

Samuel nodded. 'They are safe,' he said shortly, and there was something in the tone of his voice that brought Isaac up short.

'But is there something else?'

Samuel sighed. 'I have been sorely used and am bruised and battered, Father. Just let me rest and give me some victuals. We were on the road and only stopped to rest the horses. I have hardly eaten for two days.'

157

The household fussed around him. Lidie helped him upstairs to change his clothes which were torn and bloodstained and when she took off his shirt she gasped for his chest was covered in bruises and scratches.

'What happened to you? Who did this to you?'

'I'll tell you everything directly, Lidie, but for now, just attend to these for me I beg you.'

Gently she bathed his wounds and helped him into fresh clothes and combed out his hair and his beard.

He took her hands in his then. 'Thank God I was able to come home to you.'

She said nothing but kissed his cheek.

At length, he and Lidie came slowly down the stairs and entered the kitchen where Annette had set out some food.

Samuel sat down very carefully and they could all see what pain it caused him but he smiled at Annette and thanked her warmly.

As Samuel ate, Isaac took Lidie aside. 'How badly is he hurt? Should I look him over?'

She shook her head. 'There's no doubt that he has been beaten,' she said. 'But no bones are broken.'

Isaac clenched his fist. 'I must find out what happened,' he said.

Lidie put a hand on his arm. 'Let him eat,' she said quietly.

'You are right, Lidie. But I need to know about my daughter and her family. He has said they are safe but how can they be?'

THE KING'S COMMAND

Chapter Fourteen

Samuel slept for a long time and everyone in the household made sure not to disturb him, but there was much speculation.

'Did he say what had happened?' Annette asked Lidie.

She shook her head. 'Only that the dragoons were all over the city.'

'Those rough soldiers will be here next, mam'selle. We'll all be murdered in our beds.'

'Hush Annette, do not speak like that. Castillon is but a small town, not a city like Montauban. I doubt the King would bother billeting soldiers here.'

Annette did not look convinced. 'Who is to tell,' she muttered. 'Everything is turned upside down. Why, the man coming up from your farm yesterday was telling us of how Abel and Martha are being pestered.'

Lidie frowned. 'How pestered?'

Annette shrugged. 'Nowhere is safe,' she said. 'You would think in the countryside our people would be left in peace but the man said there is danger even there.'

Lidie decided to say nothing to Sara about Annette's chatter.

It was not until the evening when they were all gathered together, that finally Samuel spoke. He sat at the table crumbling his bread and staring ahead.

'We had been warned they were coming,' he said. 'Impossible to keep quiet about an invasion of that sort. We knew they were on their way.' He paused. 'People were so fearful that many signed abjuration papers in anticipation of their arrival.'

The rest of them exchanged glances.

'I was in my sister's house,' he said. 'She and her husband had hidden some of their precious goods. Everyone was waiting. No one knew what would happen but the air was heavy with fear.'

He took a gulp of wine. 'It was the boots we heard first. The hobnailed boots of the soldiers on the cobbles, coming closer and closer, and their ribald songs and shouts. And then the banging of the door knockers on doors all along the street.'

159

Sara gripped the arms of her chair.

'We knew they would come to us,' said Samuel. 'They had knowledge of all the wealthy Huguenot families in the town.'

Lidie could see that Samuel's hand trembled.

'My sister and the children went upstairs as soon as the soldiers came,' he said. 'And my brother in law and I opened the door to them. We had no choice.' He swallowed. 'We were polite and asked their business, though of course we knew what it was. My brother in law protested but it made no difference.'

'It used to be that soldiers were only lodged with the lower classes,' said Isaac, 'And then only in times of conflict.'

'We all protested but the Lieutenant had a billeting paper and there was nothing we could do.' Samuel looked at his father. 'The dragoons have but one purpose,' he said. 'To lodge with Huguenots, demand food and wine and disrupt the household in whatever way they choose - and stay until the head of the house signs an abjuration certificate.'

'How many soldiers were there that came to the house?' asked Isaac.

'Eight great brutes of men,' he said. 'They pushed their way past us, said they'd find their accommodation themselves and went up the stairs before we could stop them.'

'What of your sister and her children?'

'They pushed them aside like so many cattle and made themselves at home in their chambers.' Samuel shuddered. 'Their language was foul and their habits … I can hardly describe how they behaved. They demanded food and wine, and more and more of it. They belched and threw objects around and when they were too drunk to stagger out to the privy, they relieved themselves in the corner of the room.'

Sara gasped.

Samuel turned to her. 'I know and I am sorry to have to tell you all this, but I'm afraid worse was to come and I need to explain …'

Isaac was looking grim. 'I pray that you are not going to tell me that your sister and her family abjured?'

'Father, you were not there. The soldiers broke their furniture and made more and more demands. And one of their maids …'

'What! Did they force themselves on the womenfolk?' Isaac scraped back his chair and stood up. He put his hands on the table and stared across at Samuel.

'You are telling me that they abjured? My daughter and her husband. I cannot believe they would have done such a thing!'

'Hear me out, Father.'

Isaac sat down, defeat and shock showing in his face.

'It went on for three days,' said Samuel. 'The soldiers demanded more and more, to eat and to drink. When they were told there were no more supplies, they started to ransack the house, putting furniture on the street for anyone to buy for a pittance and pocketing the money. And ripping the tapestries from the wall, bundling them out of the door for scavengers to pick up.'

'Not your mother's tapestries?'

Samuel nodded. 'The very same. We were powerless to stop them. The family urged me to complete my business and leave so I went to the warehouse on my own. We did not dare leave the womenfolk and children unprotected. I chose the cloth and arranged for a coach but when I returned to the house I …'

He faltered then and took a gulp of wine.

'All the servants had fled,' he said quietly. And my brother in law was being restrained as one of those brutish soldiers was attacking my sister.'

Isaac lowered his head and closed his eyes.

Samuel licked his lips. 'In front of the children,' he whispered. 'They were terrified and the soldiers merely laughed at their terror. They called them spawn of Satan, Huguenot whelps.'

For a moment, Samuel could not continue. The others waited in silence.

'I was no match for them. I tried to protect them, Father, but then the soldiers decided to have some sport with me and when they'd finished …'

Lidie looked up. 'He is covered in bruises and scratches. They used him ill.'

'They knocked me unconscious,' said Samuel.

'But, the family has survived?' Isaac raised his head and his hands gripped the edge of the table. 'You would have told me last night if any …'

'They survive, Father, but I fear nothing will ever be the same for them.'

'And when you regained consciousness, Samuel,' said Sara. 'What happened then?'

'My sister was kneeling by my side. She was weeping and bathing my head with a cloth. And there was calm in the room and a new voice speaking.'

Samuel put his hand to his head.

'Do not continue if it is too distressing,' said Lidie. 'We know they live. That is enough for now.'

'No. I should explain.' He took a deep breath. 'I was able to sit up, with my sister's help, and I saw that there was a mild-mannered man at the door, speaking with my brother in law. It seemed he had some authority over the soldiers as they had ceased their attacks. I learned later that he was a so-called missionary officer sent out to Huguenot homes from the Intendant.'

Sara frowned. 'Missionary officers. What can that mean?' she asked, turning to Isaac, who shook his head.

'Sent to reason with the heretics,' said Samuel bitterly.

'What did this man say.'

Samuel sighed. 'He looked like a scholar,' he said. 'He was older, with a grey beard. He wore sober clothes and he was holding this certificate.

'A certificate of abjuration,' said Isaac, grimly.

Samuel continued. 'He said that all he needed was the householder's signature and the soldiers would leave immediately and order would be restored.'

'I can see the temptation,' said Sara quietly.

'When I heard his speech, I tried to struggle to my feet to beg my brother in law not to give in to the bribes, but I was too weak. I was so dizzy that I fell back again, and I heard the man drone on about how His Most Christian Majesty the King only wished to unite his kingdom.'

'And was that when …?' asked Lidie.

THE KING'S COMMAND

Samuel shook his head. 'I think it was what the man said next that persuaded my brother in law. He said, as if he was regretful, that further privations should be visited upon the household, that if they did not sign the certificate, then the soldiers would remain and if they could not be properly fed then he understood that there was this farm the family owned in the plains …'

'What did he mean by that?' asked Sara.

'He did not spell it out, but it was clear that cattle would be taken by force from the farm and used to feed not only those billeted with the household but others in the city.'

'So that was when he signed it?' said Isaac, his voice flat.

Samuel nodded. 'He was not only thinking of the fate of his own household but also of those who worked his land.'

There was complete silence in the room apart from the buzzing of a fly at the window.

'I was too weak to travel earlier,' said Samuel. 'The soldiers left immediately, laughing and swearing and shouting insults, and then I was put to bed while they tried to put the place to rights and reassure the children. We were all very cast down, as you can imagine, and my sister and her husband ashamed that they had not been strong enough to resist the temptation to deny their faith.'

'How many did the same?' asked Isaac.

'Many many thousands, I'm told,' said Samuel. 'You cannot blame them father.'

Isaac said nothing so Samuel continued. 'The paper is meaningless. They are no more Catholics than you or I.'

Isaac's eyes narrowed. 'In all the years of the wars of Religion, Samuel, no Verdier has ever recanted. Verdiers have died for their faith. They have never *ever* denied it.' He stood up then and addressed them all. 'My daughter and her husband will have to attend mass and their children will have to be brought up as Catholics. I have never felt such shame.'

He paced up and down the room and the others could see that he was trying to control his emotions. At last he turned back to them.

'Samuel, I hope that I can rely on you and Lidie never to renounce your faith?'

163

Lidie answered immediately. 'Of course I would not, and I pray that little Elias will grow up to be strong in our faith, too.'

'Do you need to ask, Father?' said Samuel.

Lidie was watching him as he spoke but his expression was unreadable.

Is he wondering how brave we would be if we, too, were so sorely tested?

Then he spoke again. 'In Montauban, there was some talk of a new edict.

Isaac sighed. 'That is hardly news,' he said. 'It seems there are new edicts every time the clock strikes.'

'There was such confusion in the city, so much loose talk, but this new edict, the Edict of Fontainebleau, they say it will be official any day now.'

'Yet another edict to put yet more constraints on our freedom, no doubt,' said Sara.

Samuel turned to her. 'If the rumours are true,' he said slowly. 'Then it would be worse than that.'

He had their full attention then.

He went on. 'They are saying that this new edict will replace the Edict of Nantes and that the Edict of Nantes will finally be revoked.'

Isaac stopped pacing and sat down suddenly, putting his head in his hands. 'Dear God,' he said. 'Has it really come to this? That Nantes Edict is the only way our people have been kept safe for over eighty years. It was signed to put a stop to the wars of religion, to give us the freedom to worship as our consciences dictated, to trade freely, to live alongside Catholic citizens with equal privileges!'

'We know all that, father, said Samuel, 'And it has indeed allowed us to flourish until now.'

'Aye,' said Isaac, his voice full of bitterness. 'Until this King became obsessed with uniting the realm under one single religion.' He leapt to his feet again and continued his pacing. 'If he finally revokes the Edict of Nantes, what will be left for us?'

'Did you learn anything of the contents of this new edict?' asked Sara.

'I had hoped to consult with some of my legal colleagues in Montauban,' said Samuel, 'but once the dragoons swarmed through the city, all was chaos. However, if the rumours are true, then I doubt the new edict will be anything but harmful to us.'

'At least, during the wars of religion, we were able to meet force with force,' muttered Isaac.

'Would we really want to go back to those times.' said Sara quietly. 'Our generation has at least been spared the horrors of civil war.'

Isaac sighed. 'I too abhor war,' he said. 'But I find my loyalty to King Louis sorely tested. Until now he has had my faithful allegiance, but how can we condone this brutal policy of trying to stamp out the word of God by sending in brutish soldiers to disrupt peaceful households. When will this harassment cease?'

'Not until it has achieved its ends, I warrant,' said Samuel, softly. 'And it is evidently very successful, as I saw with my own eyes.'

They were all silent then and there was an atmosphere of despondency in the room until it was broken by Elias's cries. Lidie went to tend to him and then brought him back to the company which at least raised their spirits as he was handed from one to the other.

'Pray God that you will be able to live in peace, little one,' said Sara, holding the baby close to her.

Chapter Fifteen

October 1685

They did not have long to wait to hear the terms of the formal revocation of the Edict of Nantes. The edict which replaced it, The Edict of Fontainebleau, confirmed many of the restrictions already visited upon Protestants but now that the Nantes Edict was revoked, the last of their protection was taken from them.

And for the Castillon family, the news they had all dreaded, the confirmation that from henceforth, neither Huguenot doctors nor lawyers would be allowed to practise unless they abjured.

Isaac had travelled with Jacob and Samuel to Bordeaux to hear the formal declaration and they returned home in low spirits

Samuel came immediately to tell Sara and Lidie what he had learnt, and though he spoke in the clear and dispassionate voice of a lawyer, consulting the notes he had made, Lidie could sense his fury.

'Let me first read the King's declaration,' he said.

"I cannot doubt but that it is the Divine will that I should be His instrument in bringing back to His ways all those who are subject to me. The best and greatest part of our subjects have embraced the Catholic faith and as by reason of this the execution of the Edict of Nantes is useless, we have judged that we cannot do better, to efface entirely the memory of the troubles, the confusion and the evils that the progress of the false religion have caused in our realm … than to revoke entirely the above edict."

Lidie glanced over at Sara, so upright in her chair, her hands clutching its arms.

Samuel continued, scanning through his notes. 'Let me just read out the main points,' he said. 'Here …

"On condition that they do not practise their religion, Huguenots may remain in the realm without abjuring until it please God to enlighten them."

'What arrogance!' spluttered Sara. Then she added. 'Is the King to be believed? Will he really allow us to remain in the realm without abjuring?'

Samuel shook his head. 'Who can tell,' he said. 'But I confess to feeling some scepticism on that point.' Then he continued.

"All Huguenot children to be baptized, brought up and educated in the Holy Roman Apostolic Catholic Church."

'We already knew that,' said Lidie.

Samuel nodded. 'It is but confirmed.' He looked across at Lidie.

'Never,' she said. 'We shall never allow Elias to be brought up a Catholic.'

'It goes on,' said Samuel. 'There are financial bribes for new converts or for those reporting illegal gatherings among those of our faith and the ban on Protestants leaving the country is repeated.'

Sara frowned. 'So, the King is putting all these restrictions on us yet still not allowing us to leave the realm and seek to live in a Protestant country where we might be made welcome.'

Samuel nodded. 'It seems that the King is anxious to convert us yet he does not wish to lose our skills – or at least those of the artisans and professionals.' He went on looking down the papers in his hand. 'From now on, there will be fearsome penalties if those of our faith are caught trying to leave the realm. For the men, the galleys or execution, for the women, imprisonment and their children declared orphans and sent to Catholic schools or to nunneries.'

Sara and Lidie looked at one another in horror. .

'And as for our pastors,' he said quietly. 'They are ordered to convert within two weeks or leave the country.'

'What! So they are to be expelled but their congregations are to stay!'

'No doubt the King thinks that if he exiles the pastors, then our faith will die without them.'

Sara sniffed. 'It will but make us more resolute,' she said.

'And if the pastors do not abjure or leave the country?' asked Lidie.

'Then they will face death,' said Samuel.

'What will Pierre do? How can he subject Hannah to a journey of that sort. Yet how can he stay?'

'We must go to him at once,' said Sara. 'We must offer him whatever assistance we can.'

Lidie nodded. 'How has it come to this? We all lived together more or less peacefully, did we not, and we supported the King before he began to choke the life out of our beliefs.'

Sara nodded. 'The ruling that we may not employ Catholic servants saddens me. Some of them have worked for my family for years and now we are forced to let them go.'

Samuel sighed. 'It is another way of dividing us,' he said.

'Dear God,' said Sara. 'It is too much. How shall we bear it.'

'He will show us a way,' said Lidie. 'You have taught me always to put my trust in His divine will, Mama. He will lead us.'

Sara nodded and bowed her head. 'Let us ask for His guidance,' she said.

My soul waits for God alone. He alone is my rock and my salvation. Trust in him at all times.

Samuel and Lidie repeated the words after her.

Later that day, Sara and Lidie went to visit Pierre and found the household in disarray with Pierre at its centre trying to spread some calm.

'I am so grateful for your presence,' he whispered to them. 'I am wracked with indecision. If I leave and seek refuge abroad, I am not sure that Hannah would survive the journey, yet if I stay I would either have to go into hiding or face death.'

'I am sure you have asked God for guidance,' said Sara.

'I am in such turmoil that I can find no quiet space in which to pray.'

They could hear Hannah's cries coming from another room. Sara looked up in alarm. 'Should I go to her, Pierre?'

He nodded. 'It may calm her,' he said. He paced up and down, glancing in the direction of the cries from time to time until, at length, they ceased and there was only the quiet murmur of voices.

Pierre sat down and put his head in his hands.

Lidie sat opposite him. 'If you leave, where would you go?' she asked gently. 'Have you given any thought to where you might seek refuge.'

He looked up at her then, his face ravaged.

He is still a young man yet he looks so weighed down and old.

'I have contacts in London,' he said.

Lidie frowned. 'But they have a Catholic king, do they not?'

Pierre nodded. 'Yes, King James is our own king's cousin, but I am told he is not popular with the people and that those of the Protestant faith are not persecuted in the way they are here.'

'But still, Pierre, would it not be easier for you to go to Switzerland or Germany, perhaps? Samuel tells me that the exiled lawyer, Claude Brousson is helping to establish Protestant churches there.'

'Truly, Lidie, I do not know. The journey would not be so arduous for Hannah, perhaps, and I have heard that Brousson is doing good work in those countries, but I have friends in London and I know we would be made welcome there.'

'And if you stay?'

'My conscience tells me that I should stay and comfort my flock in these dreadful times. My life is of no consequence, but then Hannah …'

Lidie leaned forward. 'Your life, Pierre, is of great consequence, and you cannot minister to your people here without putting yourself and them in the utmost danger.'

Pierre met her eyes. 'But to desert in this way …'

'If you leave and reach somewhere of refuge, then you will be able to continue to do God's work and follow your conscience even if you are in another country.'

He continued to stare at her. Lidie bit her lip and continued, amazed that she should be giving advice to this man who had been a mentor to all those of their faith. She chose her words carefully.

'Would it not be better to continue to do God's work? To spread His word and the teachings of Calvin, even if you are not in your own realm?'

He did not drop his eyes from her face. Gradually, his shoulders relaxed and his foot stopped tapping.

'I do believe that He has shown me the way and that you are his vessel, Lidie.'

He got shakily to his feet, giving her a weak smile.

'Thank you my dear,' he said quietly.

'You know that we will help you in any way we can,' she said. 'My uncle can perhaps find a vessel from Bordeaux and could lend you the coach and driver to make your journey more comfortable.'

Pierre took her hand then and kissed it. 'What would I do without friends such as you and your family, Lidie. I thank you from the bottom of my heart.

It was just as Sara and Lidie were leaving his house that Pierre asked them to wait.

'I have something for you,' he whispered.

A few moments later, he reappeared and handed Sara something wrapped in cloth. She took it, frowning.

'Unwrap it.'

Sara unwrapped the cloth and she and Lidie both stared at a few small coins.

'Mereau coins,' she said. 'But surely the Elders give these out to those deemed worthy of taking Holy Communion. I do not understand. Why…?

Pierre came closer. 'I am a pastor being forced from my home; I shall have no more need of them but in case … in case you or members of your family decided to leave the country, they could be of use to you.'

Pierre was still speaking quietly and the two women had to lean in close to hear him.

'Further supplies have been made in secret by our brethren for just this eventuality,' he said. 'To show a mereau coin to fellow Protestants is to prove that you are, indeed, of our faith and not a Catholic spy.'

'Sara smiled. 'But my dear Pierre, we have no intention of fleeing abroad. Our home is here in Castillon.' She made to give them back to him but Lidie stopped her.

'Mama, the revocation has changed everything. Who knows what the future holds for us.' She turned to Pierre.

'Thank you, sir,' she said simply. 'We shall take them and pray fervently that we shall never need to use them.'

A week later, Pierre and Hannah set off for Bordeaux. Jacob had decided to accompany them to ensure that his contact there honoured his promise of a berth on board an English vessel and to leave Pierre free to attend to Hannah, who was dreadfully fearful of the journey and was so confused in her mind that she could not understand why her husband was forcing her to leave her home.

As a small group of friends gathered to see them off from their home in Castillon, Sara turned to Louise.

'Jacob is leaving you unprotected. You will take every precaution, Louise, will you not.'

Louise shrugged. 'In truth, I am more worried about the journey that those others are taking,' she said, pointing at the coach as it moved away. 'I pray that they will be able to get safely on board. And I have my sons to protect me and sturdy locks on the doors.'

Lidie smiled and as the coach turned the corner out of their sight, she said. 'Indeed, the boys are no longer boys, Aunt Louise. They are almost grown men.'

Sara and Louise were in and out of each other's houses during the next few days, seeking comfort from one another and making arrangements for the Catholic servants in their employ.

Annette was very agitated.

'Lord Madame, how shall we manage? Besides me and Susanne, there is but one maid and one manservant left to run the house.'

Although Susanne had been given every care at the farm, her child, a little girl, had been sickly and had not survived. Susanne had begged to come back and serve the Castillon household and Sara, remembering her own babes who had not thrived, could not find it in her heart to refuse her.

'We shall manage, Annette,' said Sara. 'The Lord will provide.'

'The Lord won't get the laundry done or prepare the vegetables,' muttered Annette

Sara smiled. 'Lidie and I will help you, and no doubt there will be Protestant servants looking for new employment, too. We shall have to adapt.'

Samuel was hardly at home. He was much taken up with explaining the terms of the new edict to those who came to his rooms in town.

'Crowds of them come. They seek advice all the time,' he told Lidie and Sara. 'I do my best for them but this edict means so many changes for us all, it is hard to know where to turn.'

'And with no pastors to guide us,' said Sara.

'There will soon be no temples left. They are all being destroyed now,' said Samuel. 'In some places, I've heard that those of our faith are being forced to destroy the very temples they built.'

'We shall continue to pray,' said Lidie. 'Even though we are forbidden, there is none to stop us praying in the privacy of our home.'

'Louise told me that there is talk of another gathering in the woods around Pujols,' said Sara.

Samuel looked up. 'It will be very dangerous to attend such a gathering, Mama.'

'We shall take all care, I assure you.'

'Even so, with these financial inducements, there are those who may claim to be true Reformists but are spies sent to report such illegal practices.'

Sara frowned. 'Surely we would know if there were spies among us?'

Samuel shook his head. 'I am only saying that, now that this new edict is in force, to gather together in this way would be to take a great risk.'

Lidie walked over to him and put her hand on his shoulder. 'Should we not stand up to those who persecute us, my love?'

Samuel looked up at her and smiled. 'You speak like the lawyer Brousson,' he said.

'Then that is a compliment, is it not?'

'Aye. He is a very brave man and as you know, I admire him above all others. But his bravery cost him dear and he had to flee to avoid death.'

'But we will not be forced to flee, will we? We will stay in our homes and continue to live our lives in the way we have always lived.'

'As much as we are able, Lidie,' said Samuel.

'What of Elias?' said Sara.

Samuel frowned. 'Elias is but a babe but indeed, in the future it will be hard to bring him up in our faith.'

'What! Are you saying …'

'No. Of course we shall never waver but I am just warning of the difficulties ahead. Every obstacle will be put in our way.'

The following day, Jacob arrived back from Bordeaux and as soon as they heard the sound of the coach, Sara, Samuel and Lidie made their way with all haste across the street to hear how Pierre and Hannah had fared. Isaac had just arrived, too.

Jacob had hardly descended from the coach, his wig awry and with streaks of mud on his cloak, when he was bombarded with questions.

'Did they board safely?'

Jacob nodded. 'They did.,' he said. 'We came back with all haste from Bordeaux as I knew you would be anxious.' He turned to Lousie. 'I am parched, my love. Will you not fetch me something to drink.'

Once he had taken off his cloak and hat and was sitting down in the house quaffing a draught of wine, they all gathered round him.

Jacob rubbed his forehead. 'There was such a crowd at the harbour,' he said. 'It took me a long while to find my contact.'

'The English sea captain?'

'Aye. But then at last I located him. He was as good as his word and promised Pierre and Hannah a berth.' Jacob took another long drink. 'It was as well I was there,' he went on. 'Hannah was hysterical and I thought that the captain might refuse to take her.' He looked across at Isaac. 'I finally helped Pierre to administer that further draught of the opium you gave me and it calmed her somewhat.'

'Did you see them on board?' asked Samuel.

Jacob nodded. 'I found a sailor to row us out to the vessel but there was a crowd of small boats full of folk all trying to persuade the captain to take them and the poor man only just succeeded in hauling Pierre and Hannah on board.'

'Were they all pastors?' asked Isaac.

173

'Most of them, but some I warrant were merely dressed as pastors so that they could flee without the guards arresting them.'

'There were guards!'

'Aye, the King's guards were there in force and they were keenly alert to any Protestants trying to leave who were not pastors.' Jacob stroked his beard. 'I saw them arrest many other parties and, believe me, they treated them harshly. I would even go as far as to say that they enjoyed mistreating them.' He paused for a moment and then went on more quietly. 'I warrant that any of our faith who try to leave the country now will not find it easy.'

Isaac cleared his throat. 'Poor Pierre will have much difficulty calming Hannah when they set sail.'

Jacob nodded. 'I don't doubt it, but at least I know that they are on their way. I waited until the ship sailed out of the harbour on the next tide.'

'We must pray that they reach England and safety,' said Louise, 'But how we shall miss them.'

'Perhaps Hannah will fare better in London?' suggested Lidie.

'Perhaps,' said Isaac. But he did not sound hopeful.

Chapter Sixteen

1686-1689

After the Edict of Nantes had been revoked, King Louis announced that the Protestant religion had been purged from the realm and boasted that he had done in one year what others had been unable to do in a century.

And at first, it looked as though he was right. In the Bordeaux généralité
priests were bombarded by Huguenot converts seeking to be admitted to the Catholic faith.

However, all was not as it seemed. Although the King had made these pronouncements, there were many thousands of Huguenots who had, in theory, recanted, but still held firmly to their beliefs and only signed the abjuration papers to spare themselves and their families from ruin. They may have paid lip service to Catholicism and attended mass, but they still held true to Calvin's teachings.

Even Jacob, who the family had considered the most steadfast of Huguenots, had bent under the pressure and signed the abjuration papers. It was the cause of deep division in the family.

When Louise told Sara, there was a stunned silence in the room and both Sara and Lidie stared at her, uncomprehending.

'Uncle Jacob,' stuttered Lidie, 'I cannot believe it!'

Sara rose from her seat and went over to her sister. 'Tell me this is not true, Louise. How could he …?'

Louise was weeping. 'We have had so many harsh words and sleepless nights. I have tried to dissuade him, to remind him of all that our faith means to us, of how our forebears fought for the right to worship as their consciences bid them.'

'Then why?'

'Believe me, he has wrestled with his demons day and night and, in truth, I do understand his reasoning even though I abhor what he has done.'

Louise sniffed and wiped her eyes. 'He has not done this lightly,' she said. 'He has visited the Intendant to plead his case. He has known him for years but the man was adamant. He must convert or no longer run his business.'

Lidie and Sara continued to stare at her.

'Do you not understand what this means?' Louise's voice rose.

'Sister, I cannot …'

Louise stamped her foot. 'We would face penury, Sara! He would no longer be allowed to trade, our land would be forfeit and even our house, no doubt.'

'But how will he face his God? How will he be able to pray?'

Louise started to weep in earnest then. She collapsed onto the window seat and put her head in her hands.

Lidie turned to Sara. 'What sort of example is this?' she asked quietly. 'Uncle Jacob is of such influence in this region.'

Louise looked up, wiping her tears away with her fist. 'He is not a Catholic, Lidie. He will never be a Catholic. He has signed the papers to save his employees, to save his family – and yours!'

'No!' said Lidie, jumping to her feet. 'Do not say that, Aunt. Mama and I will never convert.' She turned to face Sara. 'Even if we are forced to flee the country.'

'Oh, it is easy for you to say that, Lidie, but have you been subjected to any pressure?'

Sara interjected. 'The curé visits and threatens us,' she said. 'And we have had to dismiss our Catholic servants.'

'Huh!' exclaimed Louise. 'Small privations by comparison.' Then she continued, her voice softer. 'You perhaps do not realise the size of Jacob's business. It is extensive and many of those he employs are Catholics. If he had not signed those papers he'd be banned from trading, not just here but overseas.'

She sighed. 'I am guilty, too, for not taking enough interest in his work. Since the revocation he has been trying to play this game of cat and mouse with the authorities and his goods have somehow found their way onto the ships at Bordeaux through the good offices of new converts who were sympathetic. But now everything has tightened up and even though he brings such profit to the town's coffers, he can no longer run his business without converting.'

Neither Lidie nor Sara spoke.

Louise looked at them. 'Like you, I am appalled,' she said. 'But I know what a struggle the poor man has had with his conscience. He has been walking a tightrope these past months and has been subject to countless threats and insinuations.' She sniffed. 'My poor husband has been harassed every day, every hour.'

When Louise had left, Lidie and Sara sat for a moment in shocked silence.

'Jacob of all people,' said Sara. 'I would never have believed …'

'Do not judge him too harshly.'

Sara shook her head. 'I cannot do otherwise.'

'He is still a Reformist at heart.'

Sara did not answer and Lidie came and knelt beside her. 'Think of all the kindness he has shown us. Think of how he has helped us since Papa died, of all his generosity, all his love towards us. Do not forget that. Do not cast him out of your heart.'

'How can I not?'

'We heard from Aunt Louise how he has wrestled with his conscience. He has done what he has done to save others.'

Sara turned in her seat and looked up at the portrait of her husband. 'What would your papa say, Lidie? How would he have acted? Can you contemplate that he would have rejected his faith in this way?'

Lidie turned to follow Sara's gaze.

'But he was not tested, Mama.'

Later that day, when Samuel came back to the house, Lidie greeted him at the door and told him the news of Jacob's abjuration but, to her surprise, he did not react with the shock that she had expected.

'I cannot find it in my heart to blame him, Lidie,' he said, wearily. He took off his hat and wig and put his hand through his hair. 'He feels his responsibilities keenly and he will not have done this lightly.'

'No, but even so …'

Samual stroked her cheek. 'I hope you will still make him welcome here Lidie,' he said.

177

She hesitated. 'I … I do not know if Mama will make him welcome. She is very shocked.'

***

Although King Louis had pronounced that he had purged his country of the 'false' religion, there was still resistance.

There were uprisings against the King's troops and in some places where there were large Huguenot populations, they were repelled.

There were brave pastors, too, who had remained in the country, at risk to their lives, and held meetings and prayers in secret, sometimes in private homes but more often deep in the woods, surrounded by nature, where they still prayed and sang psalms and worshipped simply and devoutly.

But to hold such meetings was to court disaster and news came of Huguenots betrayed by spies, surrounded by soldiers and killed as they knelt at prayer. There were horror stories of men hanged from trees in the forests and pastors being dragged away from their flock and executed. And of womenfolk flung into prison, their sons sent to Catholic schools and their daughters to nunneries.

Gradually, Sara accepted Jacob's overtures and, although it was not as before between them, both Lidie and Samuel had welcomed him into the house and the atmosphere between the families had thawed slightly.

One evening, when they were all gathered together, Jacob told the family of some of the horrors he had witnessed at the harbour in Bordeaux.

'So many of our brethren are ruined,' he said, 'And they see no way forward but to leave and seek their fortunes elsewhere but in Bordeaux the guards are very vigilant. In whatever way our brethren are disguised, the guards spot them and drag them off the ships. The sea captains hide them in the holds of their ships but now the guards have taken to going on board and letting forth some poisonous gas into the hold so that the poor wretches have no choice but to come out of hiding or die in the hold. Either way, their fate is sealed.'

'How can they be so cruel?' asked Louise.

Jacob turned to her. 'That is not the worst of it, my dear,' he said. 'Some of the sea captains are rogues of the worst kind.' He sighed and mopped his brow with his kerchief. 'Why I have been told that in some cases, once the ship has sailed, the captain will order his sailors to attack the poor families who have paid handsomely to be smuggled on board, take any valuables from their persons and then toss them overboard to drown, and divide their goods between the crew.'

Lidie gasped. Jacob continued. 'Should any of our faith contemplate leaving,' he said slowly, 'It is a path fraught with difficulties.'

Then he told them how he had witnessed gangs of captured Huguenot men, chained to one another by the neck, being forced to wear red caps, shuffling through the town being spat at and pelted with rotten vegetables and other disgusting missiles, as they were en route to row as galley slaves in the Mediterranean fleet.

'That is a life sentence, is it not?' asked Sara.

Jacob nodded. 'Aye, they are so harshly treated by the slave master that most do not survive for long and are tossed overboard to join the fishes.'

Lidie shivered and sent up a silent prayer for the souls of the poor wretches and asked God to protect her own family.

For her family was growing fast. Another little boy, Jean, and baby Esther,

had all followed the birth of Elias. Lidie worried constantly for their future. When Elias reached the age of five they would be expected to hand him over to be taught by the Catholics and although she and Samuel had sworn that he should be brought up in the Protestant faith, it would be hard to know how they would avoid the attention of the priests. It had been decreed that all children of unconverted Huguenot families who were between the ages of five and sixteen, should be placed in the custody of a Catholic family or of a Catholic person appointed by a judge.

As Lidie thought on this and prayed for guidance, she recalled that at least some of her prayers had been answered. It was not long since they had heard from Pierre Gabriac in London. It was increasingly difficult to gather any news from abroad and they had heard little since he had let them know that he had arrived and was safe, but lately Jacob had received a letter from him through one of his contacts.

Pierre's words were guarded but it did give them an impression of his new life. He told of the growing population of French Protestants in London and of the welcome that he and Hannah had received. He told them how he had been invited to preach and also that he was involved in the building of more French churches both within London and on its outskirts, to meet the needs of those who had fled from Louis's France.

He also spoke of the committee which had been set up in London to distribute alms and comfort to the French refugees and hinted at the increasing unpopularity of the Catholic king, James II, among the people.

As Jacob was reading the letter to the rest of the family, he paused, stroking his beard, and looked up.

'I had heard as much,' he said thoughtfully. 'Pierre would not say anything indiscreet in a letter which could be intercepted, but it could be that our king's cousin may not be on the English throne for long.'

'What would that mean?' asked Samuel. 'Would their parliament go against the King James?'

Jacob shrugged. 'Who can tell? But if there were to be a Protestant king to replace James …'

Samuel finished the sentence for him. 'Then England would be even more safe for those of our faith, would it not?'

Isaac looked up. 'It is all speculation,' he said drily. 'Politics is a slippery business. How could we have known that the King here would treat us so ill? If we could not foresee the extent of his repression of us in our own realm, how can we guess what will happen in another country.'

Lidie changed the subject. 'Pierre says nothing of Hannah's health?'

Jacob shook his head. 'No, there's no mention of that and I fear we can assume that she is no better for if she had recovered then he would have told us that we could rejoice with him.'

'Poor Hannah,' said Sara. 'But she is safe, at least, and Pierre sounds to be in good spirits and well employed.'

Pierre's letter had unsettled Lidie. It had made her wonder even more about their uncertain future and that of their three children.

Then, one evening, she broached the subject that had been on her mind for days. She chose her moment carefully. It had been a particularly happy day, Samuel was more relaxed than usual and his worries had not seemed to hang so heavily upon him. He had spent time laughing and playing with the little ones, and they had been long and passionate in their lovemaking when they retired to their chamber.

As Lidie lay in Samuel's arms she whispered. 'Would you ever think of leaving here, my love?'

She had half expected a violent dismissal of any such thought but instead, his reaction took her by surprise. He leant over her, looking earnestly into her face in the soft light of the candle which flickered on the chest by their bed.

'In truth, I have been considering it,' he said.

Lidie sat up in bed, hugging her knees. 'I am thinking of our little ones,' she said. 'And hearing that Pierre lives in safety …'

'Aye,' said Samuel. 'But Pierre was forced to leave, encouraged to leave. If we ever thought on it, the dangers would be terrible, Lidie. And the consequences dire should we be caught.'

'I know, you are right. It is too much of a risk. I understand that - and your father …'

'I doubt that my father would ever leave here,' said Samuel. 'If we did succeed in leaving, then we should be unlikely ever to see him again. Or your Mama.'

'I think Mama might follow wherever we went.'

'Even if she wished to, surely you wouldn't want to put her through such a trial?'

Lidie turned to him, smoothing back a lock of his hair which hung over his face.

'It would be Mama's dearest wish to be able to practise her faith openly once more among fellow Protestants, not creep about secretly as we do here, but you are right. She is getting older …If

181

we were to reach England, would you be able to practise as a lawyer there?'

'I do not know the language and the laws are different. It would mean retraining, I warrant.' He smiled into the darkness. 'But I know plenty about textiles now.'

'Aye. A true Huguenot merchant!'

'Reformist merchant!' he corrected her, kissing her fondly on the neck, at first gently and then with rising passion as his lips moved onto hers.

'Lidie!' he breathed, pushing up her shift and moving his hand again slowly up her thigh to the cleft between her legs. And then, all thought of flight was forgotten as they fell upon each other once more and as Lidie reached another shuddering climax, she cried out. 'Never leave me!'

The next morning, before they went downstairs, Samuel held her to him.

'We will not speak of flight to the others,' he said.

She shook her head. 'It was only a wild fancy,' she whispered.

'Aye. There is so much here that we hold dear, but it might be wise to think how we might prepare, should we need to leave.'

As the months went on, Lidie often thought back to their conversation that night and she took to wandering around the house, mentally selecting what she might be able to take with her.

The portraits, to be sure. Of herself and Samuel and of her parents. She could take them out of their frames and roll them up and put them inside a leather tube. And jewels she could sell, and silver coin. She said nothing to Sara but she listened carefully to stories about how others had fled. But her mind balked when she considered the enormous difficulties which would face them and the very real risk of capture.

So, for now, they continued to live quietly and modestly. They sometimes dressed up in their silks for a family meal, to raise their spirits, but they went about the town in sober clothes, anxious not to attract attention to themselves.

Samuel had persuaded Sara to make over her land to Jacob to avoid the risk of having it confiscated and eventually she gave in and agreed and Jacob was then able to continue to provide an income for her and her household.

Others were not so lucky. They heard of many landowners who had fallen foul of the inducements offered to those who betrayed them. In trying to sell their land, they immediately laid themselves open to suspicion. Why were they disposing of it? Were they planning to flee? If any had betrayed their plans, then their land was confiscated and half of its value given to the betrayer. A rich temptation indeed and it had become more and more difficult to know who to trust.

Sara was still very conflicted about this arrangement with Jacob. 'I suppose I am lucky to have been able to do this quietly and that dear Samuel has helped smooth the way to bring it about,' she said to Lidie, 'But I feel I am colluding in Jacob's betrayal.'

'Mama! I know it grates with you, but those who have abjured hardly have it easy. Why, Samuel tells me that even when law students or medical students 'convert' they are still obliged to present a certificate signed by a priest certifying good Catholic behaviour. Without this they cannot graduate.'

Sara said nothing and Lidie continued. 'These new converts are watched and hounded all the time. And it is not as if they can leave the country either.'

Sara raised her eyes to Lidie's. 'What will become of us, Lidie? It will not be long before the priests will be demanding that Elias is educated at that new Catholic school in the parish. How will you avoid him being forced to attend?'

Lidie had no answer.

She had employed a nurse to attend to the children and had also given employment to two new Huguenot maids who had been dismissed from Catholic households. Susanne, too, had proved a steady and reliable member of the household so Annette's duties were less arduous now and she would sometimes help mind the babes, so Lidie had a little more time to do some work for Isaac.

He had aged considerably in the years since the revocation. He was no longer permitted to practise as a physician, so, after a considerable wrestle with his conscience, he had handed the running of the infirmary over to a Huguenot physician who was one of the newly converted.

'The man's a pragmatist,' he sighed. 'A colleague I have known these many years; he may have signed the abjuration papers but he is as closely watched by the priests and Jesuits as if he had not. And I dare not show my face there now. It would simply put him in danger.'

'You must feel it keenly,' said Lidie.

'I had such loyal helpers and now I have had to abandon them all.' He cleared his throat. 'Samuel tells me that I may be due compensation for losing my médecin du roi status, but that will be but an empty victory if I do pursue it and it will no doubt involve a long legal wrangle for which I have no appetite.'

He was pacing the room as he spoke, his hands clasped behind his back and Lidie observed how his shoulders were bowed.

'But you have followed your conscience, Isaac,' said Lidie. She looked about the room as if there were a Catholic spy in their presence and lowered her voice, 'And it is not true that you have abandoned all your helpers. You continue to employ Adam and his family at your house, do you not? And I know you still continue to help the sick.'

It was true. He had secretly moved some of his equipment to his own house and he never refused help to those who came to his door. He kept in touch, too with some of the young Huguenot graduates he had instructed and heard that some had abjured while others had managed to flee the country. And, although he had told no one, to his astonishment there were still young Huguenot graduates who sought to be instructed by him, coming secretly to his home, although this put both him and them in danger.

Neither had Isaac ceased to correspond with colleagues. He was frequently in the company of Lidie and Sara of an evening, bringing letters for Lidie to copy in her fine hand. Letters to men of medicine all over the realm, and some abroad, too, comparing treatments and new ideas.

Lidie took a keen interest in these letters and often asked Isaac to explain things to her, so their collaboration was fruitful to them both. She would become intrigued as he taught her something of his profession and he, in turn, wondered at the way she turned his scrawl into clear and readable script.

'You have such a beautiful hand, Lidie,' he said. 'The script of us men of medicine

is almost illegible. We are notorious for it, always dashing off our thoughts with scant regard for the poor reader.'

'I enjoy it,' said Lidie. 'It gives me pleasure that I can still do a little to further your research.'

So they all gradually adjusted to a different way of life, more enclosed, less sociable, more wary, and Lidie was constantly grateful for the distraction of her babes, tumbling noisily about, unaware of the great cloud which hung over them all.

Chapter Seventeen

1690

The pressure on Isaac to abjure was unrelenting and he suffered constant visits from the local curé and from other prominent Catholic members of the community. And a more subtle pressure came from the newly converted physician who was now running the infirmary.

He called frequently and Isaac, though ever courteous to the man, began to dread his visits.

'Isaac, old friend, your knowledge would be of such benefit to the community. Were you to abjure, you could continue to apply all that learning to our patients. And a new crop of young Catholic graduates will arrive soon. Why would you not abjure so you could return and teach them?'

'You know very well why.'

The man had raised his eyebrows and leaned forward. 'It is only a piece of paper that stands between you and your ability to continue your profession, Isaac. A meaningless piece of paper.'

'The abjuration paper is far from meaningless and you know very well that to sign it or to attend a Catholic mass would go against my conscience.'

'Then I would say that your conscience is a vain thing, Isaac, if it is all that prevents you from benefiting so many.'

Isaac said nothing.

'Truly, it would be good to have you back amongst us, in that infirmary you founded and love so much. Your instruction to these young men would be so beneficial.'

Then the man had wagged his finger in Isaac's face. 'Though I should have to watch you, of course! I could not have you passing on any of your more radical ideas.'

Isaac had sighed and made some comment about new ideas needing to be embraced by a new generation and this had angered the man.

'New ideas of which the church expressly disapproves,' he said. Then his eyes swept the room and lighted on some medical books on a desk in the corner.

Isaac had followed his gaze. 'They are for my own research and instruction only.'

'I sincerely hope you speak the truth, Isaac.'

It was said very quietly but the comment hung in the air before the man continued speaking.

'You know,' he said, leaning back in his chair and lacing his hands behind his back. 'Even the magistrates acknowledge what good you did at the infirmary and noted the success of your treatments. Your reputation as a physician is high.'

'It is of no use to flatter me,' said Isaac, on the occasion of the man's most recent visit. 'My position will not change.'

There had been a long silence.

Finally, the man spoke. 'You know that I have been charged with attempting to change your mind. That they come to the infirmary almost daily and ask if I have succeeded?'

Isaac nodded. 'I know. You have been put in a difficult position my friend.'

'If I do not succeed, then things will not go well for you, Isaac, and I am fond of you. I would not wish …' The man looked away and Isaac noticed, for the first time, the fear in his eyes.

'I cannot go against my conscience,' repeated Isaac. 'However much you come here with enticements and flattery, that will not change.' There was another long silence and Isaac went on. 'I enjoy nothing more than passing my skills on to others, but if the only way I can do that is to abjure, then the matter is closed. I will never abjure.'

The man left soon after and at the door he embraced Isaac. 'I admire your resolve, Isaac, but it will be the ruin of you.'

Isaac did not answer but after he had watched the man ride away, back to the infirmary, h raised his eyes to the sky.

'Make me strong in my resolve, Lord,' he prayed. 'My life is of no importance but grant me the strength to face whatever lies ahead with dignity.'

187

He knew that he had finally convinced his colleague that his resolve would not be broken and he knew, too, that this would mean more threats, more hounding by Catholic agents and more privations visited upon him and his family and household. From now on he would be under constant scrutiny – or worse. Already he was playing a game of cat and mouse to make sure that no Catholics who visited his home came across the young Reformist graduates there. He had become very fond of these young men who still refused to abjure and they were keen to absorb knowledge even though, unless they recanted, they would never be able to practise their profession openly. He often questioned why they had not denied their faith and was humbled by their passionate resolve.

The Huguenot staff at the infirmary had abjured and both the nurses had visited him to ask for his understanding and to beg him to do the same so that he could come back to them. He had not condemned them but he had made it very clear that there were no circumstances under which he would deny his faith.

Both the nurses knew that he had secretly been instructing Huguenot graduates at his home and had not betrayed him – and nor had the servants at his house. However, from now on he would have to be extra vigilant, for not only was he teaching illegally but he frequently treated those who came to his door seeking his help.

So, later that day he gathered his household together and repeated to them the need for secrecy.

'As you know,' he began, 'I have been instructing some young Huguenot men of medicine here in the house.'

There were nods and whispers of 'Aye sir.'

'And you, my friends,' continued Isaac, 'have made that possible by your loyalty and your discretion.'

No one spoke at first and then one of his servants spoke up.

'It is wicked not to let Protestants learn to be doctors.'

Isaac nodded. 'It saddens me that they will never be able to practise in our realm,' he said. 'If they wish to qualify and remain true to their faith, then they will have to go abroad to do so.'

'Unless the King changes his mind.'

'A vain wish!'

'He'll never do that!'

Isaac looked round at the little group gathered before him. Despite the harassment, not one of his servants had deserted him. And as he was forbidden to employ Catholics, not one had abjured. He felt a fierce loyalty to them as they did to him and he hated to put them under further strain.

'As you know, I have been living a quiet life here since I was ousted from the infirmary, keeping us all out of sight, as far as is possible, from the Catholic agents of the Intendant, hoping that they will forget about me.'

'We are grateful for your protection, sir,' said someone.

Isaac smiled. 'My protection no longer counts for much, I fear, as an unrepentant follower of our faith, and now that my colleague at the infirmary has finally understood that I will never abjure, I shall become even more the focus of attention from the authorities.' He hesitated. 'I feel I should warn you that …'

'Will the Intendant send his agents here, sir?' asked one of the older members of his household., 'Or his soldiers?'

'I sincerely hope not,' said Isaac, but we must be prepared to face that possibility.'

They were all looking at him. He shut his eyes for a moment and then stood a little taller and spoke out in a clear and confident voice.

'No doctor should refuse to treat a sufferer,' he said firmly. 'In all my years practising medicine, I have never refused treatment to any human being. Their views, their religion, are not relevant. A doctor should see a patient as a man or woman who is suffering. That should be how these students see any patients they encounter and it is my fervent hope that I can instil these principles in them.'

They still continued to look at him.

'I know I put you all in danger by continuing to do what I am doing,' he said. 'But in all conscience, I cannot do otherwise.'

No one spoke and Isaac went on 'You may be in danger by continuing to work for me and though I would not wish to lose any one of you, I would understand if you choose to abjure and seek employment elsewhere.'

There was a muttering then and Adam, who was standing at the back, leaning on a stick, said. 'I will never leave you, sir.'

'Nor I,' came other voices. 'We are with you, sir.'

Moved beyond measure, Isaac could only nod. Then he passed among them, shaking hands, gripping shoulders, pressing the hands of the maids, and to each one murmuring his thanks.

They had no warning when the soldiers came. It was early in the morning and the household was not long risen when there was a sudden disturbance at the entrance of the house.

'Let us in in the name of the King!'

'What do they want with us?'

'This will not end well I warrant.'

But after the initial shock, they all continued with what they had been doing. One of the older servants saw that a young maid was wide eyed with fear and standing still as a statue, clutching a broom to her chest.

'Get on with you work!'

The girl began to sweep the floor but her hands were shaking.

Isaac had two young graduates with him. You know what to do,' he said quietly. They nodded and crept away to their usual hiding place.

The banging on the door and the shouting became ever more insistent until a maidservant opened up.

There were a group of about ten soldiers and one of them waved a piece of paper under her nose.

'We have orders to search the place,' he said, pushing past her.

'You know the drill,' he said to his soldiers. 'Search every nook and cranny of the building. Open up every cupboard, every room and go into the outhouses and stable. They are canny these lousy Huguenots, creeping into corners to get away from us.'

The soldiers all laughed and at that moment, Isaac arrived.

'Can I ask your business here, Sir?' he said. His voice was calm but there was a twitch in his eye that betrayed his fury.

The soldier in charge looked him up and down.

'Who are you?'

'I am Doctor Verdier,' said Isaac, stretching out his hand.

190

THE KING'S COMMAND

The soldier ignored Isaac's hand. 'So you're the one disobeying the law?'

Isaac didn't flinch. 'And what law would that be, sir?'

'Huh! Don't play the innocent with me.' He spat on the floor and Isaac had to stop himself reacting with disgust. 'We know what you're doing *doctor.*'

Isaac frowned. 'I am living quietly in my own home, my friend,' he replied evenly. His calm voice seemed to madden the soldier, particularly as some of his men had started to snigger.

'Go!' he yelled at them. 'What are you waiting for? You have your orders. And don't come back until you have found them.'

His men dispersed and he turned his attention back to Isaac. 'We hear you've been teaching Huguenot students,' he said. 'And that is against the King's express command.'

The soldier folded his arms, a slow smirk on his face, but Isaac did not flinch.

'You will find no students here my friend but you are welcome to seek for them if you have orders to do so from the King.'

'Huh!' The soldier spat again, with deliberation, this time while he was looking at Isaac, and some of his slimy phlegm landed on Isaac's arm. 'Don't come at me with your airs and graces, *doctor,* you're just another lying Huguenot heretic.'

'Would you like me to accompany you round my house?' asked Isaac.

The soldier made a rude gesture and turned on his heel. He looked over his shoulder as he walked off. 'My job is to find these traitors,' he said, 'And make no mistake, we shall find them soon enough. We've had practice in smelling out any filthy Huguenot scum. We'll soon winkle them out of their hiding place. And then, *doctor,* you'll be in serious trouble.'

'Search all you like,' said Isaac, to the soldier's retreating back. 'You'll find no Huguenot students here.'

As the soldier strode away to join his troops, Isaac let out a great shuddering breath and prayed that his students would not be discovered. His hands were shaking and for the first time he felt real terror at what might happen if they were. He walked out into the garden to calm himself. A wise word from Adam might soothe him, but when he stepped outside into the back garden, he found the old man sprawled on the ground, his hoe beside him, with a soldier standing over him shouting obscenities at him. Adam had covered his ears with his hands and he was trembling. All Isaac's pent up fury erupted.

He lunged at the soldier, pushing him away.

'Have you no shame!' he shouted. 'How dare you treat a frail old man with such violence.'

The young soldier was caught unawares and had stumbled, but he rose quickly, full of bravado. Isaac looked at him. He was hardly more than a boy.

'What would your mother think of you, treating a defenceless old man so roughly?'

A blush rose to the boy's cheeks and Isaac pressed his advantage.

'I understand you have your orders,' he said more gently. 'But bullying the old and weak is not manly and will serve you no advantage.'

The young soldier hesitated then dropped his eyes from Isaac's steady gaze and shuffled off towards the stables without a word.

Isaac gently helped Adam to his feet. 'Are you hurt, Adam?'

Adam leant on Isaac's arm. 'Not badly. A little winded.'

They both looked towards the stables. 'Do you think they will find them,' whispered Adam.

The students' preferred hiding place was in the loft above the stalls in the stables. There was a narrow gap under the eaves of the roof where the wooden beams met the floor of the loft. They could squeeze into this and stay undetected, especially at this time of year when the loft was full of newly harvested hay, neatly stacked and ready for the winter.

'Pray God that they will not,' said Isaac.

But as they stood there, they heard a shout coming from the stables.

'Search the loft. They could be lurking up there.'

Isaac and Adam looked at each other.

'They should not see them,' whispered Isaac. 'It is a good hiding place, even though it is cramped.'

'As long as they make no sound,' said Adam.

Suddenly there was the sound of neighing and clattering of hooves coming from the stable.'

'They are disturbing the horses,' said Adam. 'I'll go and calm them.'

'We'll both go,' said Isaac. 'I'm not leaving you at the mercy of those thugs.'

There were four horses in the stalls and all of them were nervous, their eyes wild, alarmed at the noise of the soldiers stamping about and shouting. Isaac and Adam went to the animals and stroked them, talking to them calmly. They heard the sound of hobnailed boots banging and crashing in the loft above the stalls and one of the horses reared up and struck out.

'Hush there,' said Isaac, holding its head steady and stroking its neck.

Above them they heard grunting and cursing.

'They are moving the hay away from the sides,' said Adam. There was terror in his eyes as he looked at Isaac.

'Keep steady, Adam,' said Isaac quietly. 'Tend to the horses.'

More noise and cursing came from overhead. It seemed as though the soldiers had been up there for hours, shifting the hay, grunting, shouting to one another and Isaac was certain that at any moment there would be a shout of discovery. The two students only had to shift slightly, to sneeze or cough, and their hiding place would be uncovered, they would be arrested, accused, punished and he, too, would be confronted with the full force of the law.

At last, the soldiers started to come down the ladder, one at a time. They were sweating and covered in wisps of hay and they stood on the cobbles and brushed themselves down.

'Have you finished your fruitless search?' asked Isaac. 'You have found nothing and only succeeded in unsettling the horses.'

'They'll be somewhere,' said one of the soldiers. 'We'll flush them out, you mark my words.'

They all went then except one soldier and as the others left he stood at the bottom of the ladder, listening.

'Come, Adam,' said Isaac loudly. 'The horses are calm now. We should both get back to our work.'

The soldier turned to look at Isaac and at the moment when they locked eyes there was a faint sneeze from the loft above.

Isaac tried to keep steady but beside him, Adam let out a whimper.

But the soldier seemed not to have heard anything and continued to stare at Isaac and a faint stir of recognition registered in Isaac's mind.

'Did I treat you once?' he asked.

'Aye,' said the soldier.

'A few summers back,' said Isaac. 'You had been in a fight... we spoke ...'

The soldier nodded. 'You saved my life,' he said.

Then there was another sneeze, louder this time, and Isaac closed his eyes, resigned to his fate.

It was obvious that the soldier had heard it and he even looked towards the sound. For a long moment no one spoke, then the soldier smiled. 'I wish you good day, sir,' he said. 'You may leave the horses now, we will not disturb them again.' He looked up once more towards the loft. 'There are no Huguenot students here. We have searched the place thoroughly and are quite satisfied.'

But just before he walked away to join his colleagues, he stopped and turned back to Isaac.

'You know, doctor, that you will be visited again.'

Isaac said nothing and the man raised his hand in farewell and walked briskly away. Isaac put his arm round Adam's shoulders to still his trembling.

Chapter Eighteen

They were all unnerved when Isaac told the family what had happened.

'You cannot risk teaching more students, Father,' said Samuel. 'The soldiers will be back. They will not leave you alone.' He began to pace up and down the room. 'It is so wrong,' he muttered. 'We are losing so many talented folk.'

'And you, my son?' asked Isaac. 'Would you consider leaving? I know that you still advise those who come to you but do you not wish you could fully practise your profession instead of working as a cloth merchant?'

This was the first time that Isaac had spoken of flight and Samuel looked across at Lidie. 'I ... we have sometimes thought on it,' he said quietly.

Sara gasped. 'Lidie? Surely you would not put yourselves and the children at risk?'

'I ... in truth, I do not know what we should do, Mama.'

'But the dangers if you try and flee!' said Sara. 'If you were caught! I cannot bear to think on it.'

'It is the price we pay for refusing to abjure,' said Isaac slowly. 'How much easier it would be for us if we did so.'

Sara nodded. 'So many have abjured. Cécile's household, Jacob's ...'

Isaac sighed. 'And my daughter in Montauban,' he said. He looked across at Samuel. 'I know you witnessed the ruin in their house four years ago, and she assures me that she is still a Protestant at heart, but still, my own flesh and blood to deny our faith.'

'We will never abjure,' said Samuel, going to Lidie and taking her hand.

She shook her head. 'Never,' she said. 'Our children will be brought up in our faith.' She looked across at Sara. 'I intend to keep the vow I made when Elias was born.'

Sara sighed. 'But at what cost?' she said quietly. 'And how?'

Isaac walked over to the window. The sun was setting over the river, turning the water to liquid gold.

'Then, if you are both determined to be true to your faith, you might be wise to consider flight.'

Sara leapt to her feet, spilling the embroidery in her lap on to the floor. 'No Isaac, you surely would not advise ...'

Isaac interrupted her. 'I would never leave,' he said. 'But I do not have young children to think on. I have only to worry about myself and my servants and I like to think that my skills are still of value. And for the moment I have my farm - though God alone knows for how long that will be.'

'Father,' began Samuel, but Isaac held up his hand.

'I am thinking what would be best for you, Samuel. You and Lidie and the children have your lives in front of you. If you could get to another country where you could practise your faith openly and perhaps as a lawyer, too, then maybe ...'

'Then,' said Samuel slowly. 'If we fled, we would have your blessing?'

Isaac nodded. 'It would sadden me more than I can say but, yes, if it came to it, then you would have my blessing.'

'And you, Mama?' asked Lidie.

'I could not bear to lose you,' said Sara. 'If you decide to leave, then I will come with you and help you. I am still in good health. I could be of use ...'

'But the dangers, Sara!' said Isaac.

'I would rather die protecting my family than never see them again.'

'Things might change,' said Isaac. 'No King lives for ever. It may be one day that we are able to travel freely again, go abroad again.'

Sara looked at him fondly. 'You say that to comfort me, Isaac, but we both know that change will not happen in our lifetimes.'

Isaac didn't answer and they all fell silent. Then at last he said. 'I must make my way home.' Then, as he turned to go, 'You must not speak of this to a living soul, no one must know that you think on fleeing.'

THE KING'S COMMAND

The rest of them looked at one another. Sara cleared her throat. 'If we did make plans to leave,' she said slowly, 'then I would need to tell Jacob and Louise.'

Isaac stopped in the midst of shrugging on his cloak. 'Is that wise, Sara?'

'Jacob has taken over my land to save me losing it,' she said. 'I would not like this house to fall into other hands.'

Lidie looked puzzled. 'Could we not sell …?' But Sara interrupted her. 'If we tried to sell, that would only attract suspicion.'

Isaac walked towards the door. 'There is much to think on,' he said. 'But do nothing in haste I pray you.'

After he'd left, the three of them sat up late into the night. Lidie was relieved that they had let Sara into their confidence but it pained her to see her mama so sad as she looked round the room at all the familiar furnishings, the place she had made a home for her husband and daughter.

They discussed all possibilities late into the night. Of staying under so much threat, of leaving and facing so much danger.

At last Samuel rose and stretched. 'Whichever decision we make,' he said, 'Our path ahead will be fraught with difficulties.'

And then Sara reminded them of one of the firm tenets of their faith.

'Remember, my children,' she said quietly. 'We followers of Calvin's teachings believe in pre-destination. God has set out a path for every one of us. We must trust in Him and follow His way.'

She then started to sing one of their favourite psalms, very quietly, and Lidie and Samuel joined in. When they had finished, she smiled at them.

'Even if we face death,' she said. 'We shall know that we have been true to our faith and we must pray that God, in His mercy, will find us a place in His eternal kingdom.'

Her words comforted Lidie a little. How much those of their faith had suffered these past years, yet so many had borne it gladly because they knew, with certainty, that they had followed God's word faithfully and lived in the hope that they would be received into a better life. There had been so many stories of their people suffering ill treatment with courage and steadfastness and even going to their deaths singing joyful psalms.

As she lay in bed that night, Lidie asked God to give her courage and to show them the right path to take.

Some days later, Sara asked Jacob and Louise to visit. Samuel was out and Lidie and the children were upstairs with the nurse. When Annette had brought them a little refreshment, Sara closed the door.

Quietly, she spoke to them about the possibility of fleeing the country. Louise was horrified. She flung her arms round her sister.

'We could not bear it, Sara. We should worry so much about you all. And we might never see you again. Please say you will not consider it?'

But Jacob's reaction was different. 'I know that both you and Lidie are steadfast in your faith,' he said. 'And I can see that there will be conflict ahead if Lidie's children are not brought up in the Catholic faith.'

'And there is Samuel,' said Sara. 'He cannot practise the profession for which he is trained. His only income comes from the textile trading he does for his brother in law. He does not complain, but I know he finds it frustrating.'

Jacob stroked his beard. 'Aye, he is young and talented and no doubt restless, but the dangers, Sara. It is much harder, now, to find passage to another country. The ports and borders are watched constantly and the Navy and the Army arrest fleeing Protestants every day.

'It is impossible to know what to do for the best,' said Sara. She looked around the room. 'It breaks my heart to think we might have to leave this house.'

'If it does come to that,' said Jacob, looking across at Louise, 'Then we would take over the house for you so that it would remain in the family and be here for you should you return.'

Louise stared at him. 'How can you encourage this foolishness, Jacob?'

Jacob shrugged. 'I am being practical, my love. If the house remains empty, it would soon be requisitioned by the authorities.'

He went to stand by the fire burning in the great fireplace at the end of the room. He put an arm on the marble mantelpiece above it and turned to face the two women.

'Perhaps we could set up our boys here in this house and that way we could keep your servants in employ, Sara.'

'Boys!' murmured Lousie. 'They are hardly that now. Great lumbering men they are!'

'Exactly,' said Jacob. 'Would you not be glad to have them set up here?'

Louise frowned. 'I cannot think on it,' she said. 'Let us pray God that it will not come to that.'

'But if it did,' persisted Sara. 'Could you make some enquiries on our behalf, Jacob? You are always visiting Bordeaux. You know what goes on at the port. You are in communion with sailors and ships' captains.'

'I have to be careful, Sara. I cannot be seen to make enquiries of this kind, but I can keep my eyes and ears open for you, to be sure and you are right, I do have trustworthy friends among some of the sea captains and fishermen.'

'I would not ask you to put yourself in danger.'

Jacob smiled. 'We are in danger every day my dear,' he said. 'We may have signed the abjuration papers but you know where my heart lies, as do the agents of the King, and they continue to watch me.'

'You will say nothing of this to anyone?' said Sara.

'Of course not. If nothing else, these last years have taught us the value of keeping secrets,' said Jacob.

'And you will think on what we have discussed?'

Jacob nodded. But Louise turned away. 'I cannot bear the thought,' she said. 'My only sister. Would you not go against your conscience …?'

Sara came over to her and held her. 'You know that I would not.' She looked over Louise's shoulder at Jacob who met her gaze for a moment and then hung his head.

There was a beat of silence, then Lidie cleared her throat.

'Would the boys want to live here?

Jacob turned and smiled at her. 'They will be heartbroken if you leave,' he said, 'but they will understand and I am sure that they will care for your home.'

He looked up at the portrait of Lidie's father on the wall. 'I wonder what he would have done in these troubled times.'

'He would never have abjured,' said Sara, a flush covering her cheeks. 'How can you think it?'

'We cannot know that, Sara,' said Louise.

'I know it! I know it in my heart.'

But Lidie was not so sure.

Would he have remained steadfast? Perhaps he would have made us flee earlier? He had so many contacts abroad.

Jacob was continuing to talk about the plans he had for his sons. 'They have joined my business now and I will teach them all I know in the hope that in time I shall be able to fade into the background and live a peaceful life.' He sighed. 'I confess I have less appetite for the work these days.'

During the next few weeks, Sara and Lidie began to make discreet preparations.

'It may never happen,' said Lidie, coming across Sara holding a beautiful piece of Venetian glass, a present from Lidie's papa, knowing that she would have to leave it behind.

'We may yet find a way round our dilemma, Mama.'

Sara shook her head. 'Do not try and humour me,' she said sharply.

Gradually, they sold a few trinkets to trusted merchants and bought sturdy footwear and sorted out warm plain clothes for themselves and the children. They hid these in the back of armoires in the house where they knew the servants would not look.

Every day Sara would look lovingly at the portrait of her husband.

'It is all I have of him. Could we find a way of taking it? And those lovely ones of you and Samuel?'

Lidie's little girl, Esther, was sitting on her knee, fiddling with Lidie's hair. Absently, Lidie unlatched child's little fingers and kissed them. 'We can take them from their frames, Mama. No doubt we could roll them up into leather tubes for safety, but then Annette would notice…'

'I think we should take Annette into our confidence,' said Sara. 'She has been with this household a good part of her life. Does she not deserve to know of our plans?'

'Mama! I love Annette with all my heart but she is not discreet, you know how her tongue wags!'

Sara fell silent and Lidie looked up at her father's likeness and an idea came to her. 'We could tell Annette that we are hiding some of our valuables in case the King's dragoons come to the region again, in case the house is invaded.'

Sara clapped her hands. 'Oh that is a capital idea, Lidie. We must speak to her directly.'

The next day when they called Annette into the reception room and told her, in strict confidence, what they intended doing, she was horrified.

'Oh Madame, surely the soldiers won't come to the house? How could we bear such an invasion?'

Sara hated lying to her but she made a convincing case. 'We hope very much that it will not happen, Annette, but these are such uncertain times and we want to safeguard the possessions we care about most.'

Annette looked thoughtful. 'Indeed, it would be a tragedy if the Master's portrait was to be ruined,' she said, looking up at it. 'Every time I am in this room I am reminded of him and smile at his likeness.' Then she went on. 'In truth, Madame, I had wondered why you had removed some of your trinkets from the house already.'

Lidie and Sara exchanged a brief glance. It had been the right thing to give Annette a reason for their actions.

'We would not want to spread alarm so we have told no one else in the household, Annette,' said Sara. 'I'm sure we can rely on you to say nothing of this to anyone else.'

'So the nurse knows nothing of this?'

Sara shook her head and Lidie turned away to hide her smile. There was little love lost between Annette and the nurse.

Chapter Nineteen

The season of Autumn progressed and one crisp morning, the curé pounded at the door, demanding to see Samuel.

Samuel was not at home so Lidie ushered the man into the house and Sara joined them.

Outwardly, both women remained calm, offering the man refreshment and making sure he was seated comfortably, though, to be sure, this welcome was somewhat spoiled by Annette's entrance with a glass of wine which she slammed down so hard on the table beside him that some of the liquid spilled. She did not apologise and left the room muttering something under her breath.

The curé raised an eyebrow and the corners of his mouth turned up in a mirthless smile, then he addressed Lidie, coming directly to the point of his visit. 'Your eldest son, Madame,' he said, taking a sip of the wine. 'Young Elias, is it?'

Lidie did not answer.

The curé took another sip. 'Five years old, I believe?'

Still Lidie said nothing.

'And his schooling has begun?'

'What schooling he has is here at the house,' said Lidie.

'Ah, but not with a Catholic tutor, unless I am misinformed. And I hear that there is no record of his attendance at the Catholic primary school set up in the town for new converts.'

Lidie's heart began to race but she answered evenly. 'He has no tutor, sir. His learning is from his parents and his grandmother.'

The curé began to drum his fingers on the table. 'But no instruction in the Catholic faith?'

Lidie did not answer.

'You know, Madame, that you are breaking the law,' he said quietly.

Still she did not reply.

He took another sip of the wine. 'Excellent wine,' he remarked. 'I'd wager that this is from the vines on your land is it not?'

Sara found her voice. 'I am glad you are enjoying it, sir. Yes, indeed it is from our farm.'

'*Your* farm?'

'No, it is no longer our farm,' she said quietly. My brother in law owns the land now.'

'Ah yes, your rich and successful brother in law who has so sensibly abjured and rejected the path of blasphemy.'

Lidie looked across at Sara whose face had turned red.

Do not react Mama.

Suddenly the man rose from his chair. 'You would do well to follow his example Madame,' he said, addressing Lidie again. 'For if you do not, your son will be taken from you and placed with the Jesuits.'

Sara gasped. Lidie's nails were digging into the palm of her hand but she forced herself to stay quiet.

'If you do not renounce your heresy, you, too, will suffer. Both of you and your foolish husband. Your uncle cannot protect you.'

Neither Lidie nor Sara moved as the man made for the door.

'When your husband returns,' he said. 'You may recount to him all I have said.' He picked up his hat. 'And tell him that if he does not sign the abjuration papers, he will lose his son.'

As they heard the front door slam, Lidie put her head in her hands. Sara moved to be beside her and put her arms round her. 'We shall have to flee, Lidie,' she said.

Lidie held onto her mother's hand. 'I know,' she said quietly. 'We no longer have any choice. I will speak to Samuel as soon as he returns.'

When Samuel heard about the curé's visit he, too, agreed that they must make arrangements to flee and Jacob was asked to make discreet enquiries for them from among his seafaring contacts.

'Are you sure you are determined on England as a destination?' Jacob asked, one evening. 'The journey across the water will be hazardous. You would not perhaps consider Switzerland or Holland or even Germany?'

Sara and Lidie were adamant, and Samuel agreed. 'We have contacts there,' said Sara, 'And Pierre Gabriac will look after us and see us settled, we can be sure of that.'

But it all seemed unreal. Here they were, continuing their daily lives much as usual, bearing the burden of the restrictions imposed upon them, buying necessities from the market and with supplements of fruit and vegetables coming up from the farm, the children growing apace and affording them all such pleasure. Lidie found it impossible to imagine that they might suddenly leave all this behind them and thrust the children into suffering the horrors of such a journey.

But then all thought of flight was put to one side when Samuel came home one evening in a state of great excitement. He had been away on business for his brother in law for a few days and he burst into the house, embraced Lidie and then dragged her into the reception room and closed the door.

'Lidie, such news!' he breathed. Lidie had seldom seen him so animated.

She freed herself from him, laughing. 'What is it, my love? And why the secrecy?'

'It is Brousson,' he said.

'The lawyer who fled to Switzerland? What of him?'

'He has returned, Lidie!' Samuel shook his head. 'Truly I can scarce believe the courage of the man. He has been toiling ceaselessly since he was driven out of our realm. He has helped refugees gain permission to settle and establish churches in Germany as well as in Sweden and Denmark and he has even visited those of our faith who have fled to Holland and Ireland and England and he has been in constant correspondence with pastors who fled abroad.'

'I know his writings have been widely circulated among our people,' said Lidie. 'But to risk returning! Surely that is to court disaster? Once it is discovered ...'

Samuel nodded. 'Indeed. He is considered a threat to the Catholic church and once they hear news of his return they will do everything to run him to earth and punish him. He risks his life every day he stays in the realm.' Samuel shrugged his cloak off his shoulders. 'That is why his return has been such a closely guarded secret.'

'I wonder why he should put himself in such danger,' said Lidie, frowning.

'He is a man of such pure conscience, Lidie. He knows how we suffer with no pastors to guide us, how we live in a spiritual drought, and he feels that God has called him to nourish the souls of the faithful.'

'We could all do with such nourishment, that is certain.'

Samuel put his arms round Lidie. 'Hearing about his courage and determination has already renewed my own resolve. With his wisdom and enthusiasm, we may yet rekindle the flames of those who have forsaken their faith.'

Lidie looked up at him and felt a surge of love for this husband of hers who had never once wavered in his faith despite being banned from his profession. She put her hand up to stroke his cheek.

'But how will he reach our people to inspire them?' she asked, gently.

Samuel looked towards the door, and Lidie laughed. 'No one here is likely to break any confidence my love!'

He smiled. 'I know. It is a habit I have caught during my travels. I always suspect there may be listening ears.' Then he continued.

'You have heard of the church in the desert?'

She frowned. 'You told me of the rumours of gatherings in some mountainous regions. Is this of what you speak?'

'Yes, indeed,' said Samuel, the excitement obvious in his voice. 'I have learnt so much more just now on my travels. I found out that Brousson and his companions left Lausanne at the end of July to travel south to the mountain district of the Cevennes and since they arrived there it is said that they have already preached to more than two thousand of our faith.'

'But I thought that Brousson was a lawyer, not a pastor?'

'You are right, my love, but he is accompanied by those who are. They say he himself is too modest to assume the position of a pastor and that he simply reads the Scriptures to small gatherings and distributes his meditations on them amongst the people.'

'But his presence must be an inspiration, nonetheless.'

'Indeed. He is so revered among our people – and I believe many have urged him to become a pastor, to be ordained.'

Samuel stretched and yawned. 'I am wearied by my travels, Lidie, but in truth my soul has not felt so light for many months. To think that more than two thousand of our brethren are hearing the word of God from the mouths of such brave men. It inspires me to think that there are those who risk all to serve our people, for truly we hunger to hear God's word preached with such conviction.'

'But how can they evade the King's troops,' asked Lidie. 'For there are informants everywhere, we know that from our experience here in Castillon. Why, your own father ...'

'Aye. And that is why the mountains of the Cevennes are so suited to such meetings. It is a region which is wild and cold and full of caves and recesses for hiding.'

'Are there not spies, even there?'

Samuel shook his head. 'It is a region where nearly all the inhabitants of the villages are Protestants. And these people know the land well, they know where to hide and how to melt away into the folds of the hills.'

'Brousson and his companions must suffer, though, going from place to place in this way, in such difficult terrain.'

'To be sure. I heard that they sleep in clefts of rock, on straw in barns, in attics and even behind false walls in Reformist homes.'

'And with winter coming on,' said Lidie. 'It will be harsh for them, indeed.'

Samuel smiled. 'These brave men trust in God to provide,' he said. 'I doubt they consider physical privations anything more than a sacrifice they make for Him.'

'Well let us thank God that you are spared such discomfort,' said Lidie dryly. 'You have a comfortable bed awaiting you and a wife who longs for your warmth beside her.'

Samuel drew her to him. 'Forgive me Lidie. I am so full of admiration for Brousson and his companions that I have hardly thought of aught else since I was on my way back to you.' He stroked her hair. 'I am, indeed, the luckiest of men.'

When, at length, Lidie broke free from his embrace, she took his hand. 'Come, you must greet Mama.'

'You will not say anything to her about Brousson?'

Lidie looked surprised. 'But she would be so heartened to hear that our people are gathering together in such numbers, and you know she is to be trusted. Surely you would not keep this news from her?'

Samuel hesitated. 'I … it is just that it was told to me in confidence, Lidie. I would much rather keep this between us.'

Lidie withdrew her hand. 'We cannot do that. She will sense that we are keeping something from her. And if we ask her to say nothing to others, she will certainly keep silent.' She frowned. 'No doubt you have every intention of telling your father about this?'

Samuel looked discomforted. 'Well, yes, I had intended …' he began.

'So you think, because he is a man, he is more to be trusted?'

Samuel shook his head. 'No, I …'

Lidie raised her eyes to the ceiling and walked out into the vestibule. She called up the stairs. 'Mama, Samuel has returned to us.'

A few moments later, Sara came down the stairs, a broad smile on her face.

'Samuel, how glad I am to see you safe returned,' she said. 'How was your journey and did the business fare well?'

He nodded. 'Aye, there is plenty of demand for Montauban textiles,' he said, 'And my brother in law is pleased with the orders I have secured for his business.'

'And your sister and the family?'

'All well, I thank you, Mama.'

'Samuel has some news to tell you, Mama,' said Lidie.

Samuel frowned. 'Lidie!'

Sara looked questioningly at Samuel and he sighed and looked about him but there was no one else in sight so he quickly told Sara about Brousson and his companions and what was happening in the Cevennes.

Sara clapped her hands. 'That is wonderful news, Samuel. How uplifted I am to hear that our faith is being kept alive by these brave people.'

'Please tell no one of this, Mama,' he said, looking at Lidie. 'As you know, there are spies everywhere. No whisper of this must

207

reach them otherwise Brousson and his friends will be in mortal danger.'

'Of course, I will keep this entirely to myself.'

'And not speak of it even to your sister?'

For a moment, Sara looked surprised. 'I warrant it is likely that she and Jacob will hear of it through their own contacts, but if you wish, I will say nothing to them.'

And then they could say no more, for the nurse came down from the upper chamber to join them, carrying little Esther and with the two boys following, clutching her skirts, for a joyous reunion with their papa.

Lidie looked on, smiling. How they adored him, and he they. He opened his travelling bag then and brought out presents for them, a game for Elias, a little carved wooden horse for Jean and a cloth doll for Esther, all of which were received with squeals of delight.

'You spoil them, Samuel,' said Lidie, but she could hardly be angry with him. She remembered so well how excited she had been when her own papa had returned from his long voyages and presented her and her mama with exotic gifts

Any anger that Lidie had felt towards Samuel soon dissipated and, though he was weary from his journey, Samuel made love to her with a fierce passion that night which surprised and delighted her. She fell almost immediately into a deep sleep but in the early hours of the morning, something wakened her and when she stretched her hand over to the other side of the bed, it was cold and empty. She frowned into the dim light and then made out Samuel's figure, standing at the high window in their bedchamber, his hands clasped together as if in prayer.

She sat up slowly. 'What ails you my love?' she whispered, but he didn't hear her so she got out of bed and went over to him.

'What ails you?' she repeated.

He started and whipped round, staring at her uncomprehendingly for a moment, then at last focusing on her.

'Lidie.'

'You were so far away,' she said. She put her head on his shoulder. 'Where were you Samuel?'

He shivered then. 'I was thinking of all those gallant souls in the Cevennes,' he said. 'And of the preachers, suffering such discomfort while I have a warm bed and every comfort I could wish for.'

'You cannot help them by worrying,' said Lidie gently. And then, when he didn't respond, she went on, her voice firm. 'Your responsibilities are here, Samuel, with your family.'

He looked away from her. 'Brousson left his family behind,' he said flatly. 'His wife begged him not to leave them, to stay in Switzerland, to continue with all the good work he was doing with helping our people to settle in a safe country.'

Lidie felt a sudden twinge of fear. 'And he refused to heed her pleas?'

Samuel nodded. 'He felt God calling him back to minister to all those left behind in such a spiritual wilderness.'

Lidie shivered. 'But he was doing God's work in Switzerland, was he not?'

He met her eyes then, but she could not see his expression well enough to discern his thoughts.

'You cannot ask a man to quarrel with his conscience, Lidie. They say that he felt overwhelmed with guilt that he was safely out of the country yet his fellow Protestants left behind were still suffering such persecution, and he knew that God was calling him to return to them.'

Suddenly Lidie felt an unreasonable anger towards Brousson, who had for so long been a hero for Samuel. His actions had affected Samuel deeply, she understood that, but she prayed that Samuel would not feel moved to put himself in danger in any way or that his own conscience would compel him to take risks.

She watched him as he stood there and a wild notion came into her head that he might go and seek out Brousson but then she dismissed it immediately. The Cevennes area was a long way distant, so distant that Lidie scarcely knew where it was.

As she crawled back into bed, she thanked God that winter was approaching and no sane man would try to travel to the Cevennes in winter. No doubt, when day broke, Samuel would have recovered his equilibrium and they could start to make plans to flee the country as soon as they could.

But his next remark chilled her heart. 'I feel so useless, Lidie. I am forbidden to defend my fellow Huguenots in the courts, I have become but a trader in cloth and I keep my family safe by doing nothing to upset the authorities. Where is the purity of conscience in that?'

When Lidie replied her voice was harsh with worry. 'Your duty is to keep us safe, Samuel and God knows, we shall need your strength and courage when we flee the realm. We must do nothing to upset the authorities, nothing to draw attention to ourselves, surely you must realize that?' Lidie drew the bed sheet up to her chin.

'They will soon be here again to question us about our plans to educate Elias,' she muttered. 'We shall need to flee very soon, Samuel.'

'It is true, Lidie, but it would be foolish to travel in the winter months, would it not?'

'I doubt that we shall be less troubled by the curé just because the cold weather is coming,' she said.

At last Samuel got back into bed and Lidie tensed as he put her arms around her.

'Are you angry with me, Lidie?'

Her voice softened then. 'I am only anxious that you cannot see where your duty lies,' she said.

'Ah Lidie,' he sighed, stroking her hair. 'My duty is to my family, to be sure, but it is also to my God.'

Long after Samuel was asleep, Lidie pondered these words.

Chapter Twenty

1690/91

As the winter of 1690 set in, the family, as most others in the region, stayed mostly in their home towns or villages, anxious whether the winter would be a harsh one.

There was always worry over whether next year's harvest would be fruitful and even though their future was so uncertain, Sara had talked earnestly with Jacob on plans for her land. He told her that they might consider planting the tuber recently brought from the New World, the potato, about which there had been much enthusiasm further North in the country.

The local curé had died from some winter ailment but Sara, Lidie and Samuel knew that they were living on borrowed time. Soon a new curé, possibly an even more diligent one, would be at their door, so they continued to plan for flight.

In the meantime, Lidie was well occupied in scribing Isaac's letters and making garments for the children. Their household still ran smoothly and Samuel did not make many trips away from home during the winter months. Lidie, Sara and Samuel continued to instruct Elias in his letters and to read the Bible to him in secret and whisper the well known psalms to him so that he became familiar with them. Lidie looked fondly at him as he frowned with concentration, serious looking like his father, and anxious to get things right and gain praise from his elders, unlike his siblings who were boisterous and noisy by comparison.

And then, as Spring came and the blossom was verdant against the pure blue Southern skies, Castillon awoke and once more there was movement among the people of the town, but with it came further anxiety about the family's future. It was as if they were holding their collective breath and waiting for a signal which would finally force them to leave.

One morning, Samuel announced that the following week he was to travel to Montauban once more, on business.

Lidie was busying herself with some domestic chore when he told her. She stopped what she was doing and turned to him.

'You will take care?'

Samuel put his arm around her. 'Of course. I shall simply go about my business and keep my opinions to myself. And when I return, Lidie, we shall make our arrangements to leave. Now that Spring is here, we shall flee. We cannot stay here and keep true to our faith. The new curé is by all accounts an idle fellow but even he will have to obey his masters and come to our door with abjuration papers before long.

Lidie nodded. She felt both fearful and relieved. 'How long will you be gone this time?'

He shrugged. 'It could be some time,' he said. 'I have not been there for a few months and there is much to discuss.'

He did not meet her eye when he said this.

When the carriage arrived at the front door, Lidie and Sara waved him off and watched until it had made its way along the cobbled street and then turned the corner out of sight.

'Do you worry when he is away from home?' asked Sara.

'A little,' said Lidie, 'But he has to travel and I suppose we are lucky that his brother-in-law is giving him work.'

'If only it was the work he's trained for,' said Sara.

Lidie sighed. 'Maybe, if we reach England…'

'The thought terrifies me,' whispered Sara, glancing round nervously. 'To leave all this behind?'

'We can no longer pretend that we can stay here and not abjure, Mama. Even Samuel is resigned to it.'

They wandered into the reception room and Lidie's glance automatically went to the portraits on the wall, different now, and replaced with those of Sara's long dead ancestors, taken down from the attic rooms. Sara followed her eyes.

'I hate not seeing him there,' she said. Then she put her hand against the wooden panelling. During the winter, they had employed a trusted carpenter to construct a sliding panel with a cavity behind it to make a hiding place.

'The carpentry here has been expertly done,' she said quietly. 'There is no join. Nothing to hint at what is behind.'

Lidie nodded. 'I pray to God that we shall never have to make use of it,' she said,

Later that day, Sara said. 'You have not seen Cécile for a long time, Lidie. Do you not think you should pay her a visit?'

Lidie frowned. 'I still find it difficult,' she said slowly.

'It saddens me that you have grown apart,' said Sara. 'You were so close when you were younger.'

'I know, I truly loved her and we had such happy times but …'

'If we are to flee, you may never see her again. You would not wish to leave without trying to make up your differences, surely?'

'I will think on it,' muttered Lidie. 'It was just that she gave so little thought to her actions. It was merely a convenience. Truly, I do not think she cares a whit about our faith.'

Sara sighed. 'But she is of your blood – our blood. Please, Lidie.'

And so, a few days later, Lidie set out with the nurse and the two younger children, to visit her cousin. She did not take Elias feeling it would not be prudent for him to be seen abroad.

Cécile greeted her warmly, embracing her at the door and then stooping to kiss the children.

'How they have grown, Lidie. And little Esther is so winsome. She is sure to break a few hearts one day!'

Having the children round their skirts made it easier to exchange pleasantries and the two of them talked of inconsequential matters and reminisced about the times they had spent together at the farms. They avoided mention of any serious topics and by the time Lidie left, she felt glad that their old friendship had been rekindled.

No one had told Cécile about the plans they were making for fleeing. It was felt better that she was kept in ignorance.

But at least she will remember me with fondness now.

The days stretched into weeks and still Samuel did not return. Lidie tried not to worry, for after all, he had said that he would be away for longer this time and that there was much to be done but when, day after day, there was no sound of a carriage at the door, no cheerful shout as he clattered through the house, she began to feel uneasy.

What was it he had said?

"It could be some time. I have not been there for a few months and there is much to discuss."

A simple enough statement, to be sure, but why should this visit be so much longer than any he had made the previous Spring?

Once these thoughts had lodged in Lidie's brain, she could not shift them and she began to think on the conversations they had had about Brousson and his work in the wild region of the Cevennes.

Surely Samuel would not contemplate a visit there?

She voiced her concerns to Sara one evening as they sat together sewing false pockets into their travelling dresses. Sara looked up from her work, startled.

'He would have told you, Lidie, if he had planned such a visit. He would not keep it from you. He has always been honest with you, has he not?'

Lidie frowned. 'He knows well that I would think it madness for him to make such a journey and I would have begged him not to consider it,' she said. 'I am not sure he would have risked confiding in me.'

Sara finished a hem and snipped the loose thread with her scissors. 'Surely the man has more sense than to endanger himself thus?'

Lidie stretched her arms over her head and then rubbed her aching eyes. 'Brousson is his hero, Mama. He has always looked up to him. And now that he has risked his life to return, he admires him even more.'

Sara sighed. 'I can understand that, but Samuel's responsibilities are for you and the children.'

'That is what I told him,' said Lidie. 'But he said that Brousson abandoned his family because God was calling him back here.'

'Samuel would *never* abandon you!'

'No, I truly do not believe he would, but I think the urge to meet Brousson is very great. This desire is not new; I think it has been brewing these last months and now, when everything is to change, when we shall be fleeing ourselves, perhaps he has seized the opportunity to seek him out and gain inspiration from him before it is too late.'

'I pray with all my heart that you are wrong in this, Lidie.'

'Not as fervently as I.'

But the more she thought about the matter, the more Lidie was convinced that Samuel had gone to seek out Brousson. After all, Montauban was a deal nearer the Cevennes region than Castillon, though still a long, wearisome and difficult journey. So, if he had gone, he would have gone in company surely? He would need a trusted guide, a member of their faith who knew Brousson's likely whereabouts in that wild territory.

When the household gathered for their evening prayers Lidie made her own silent prayer, calling upon God to protect Samuel.

Dear Lord, if my foolish husband has indeed embarked on such a dangerous journey, I pray you give him your protection and being him home safely to us.

Jacob arrived at the house the next evening. His face was drawn and his shoulders bowed.

'You look exhausted!' exclaimed Sara. 'Come and sit down and have some refreshment.'

Jacob took off his cloak and sank wearily into a chair, stretching his booted legs out in front of him.

'I came directly from the coast,' he said. Then he glanced towards the door and lowered his voice. 'If you want it,' he said quietly, 'I have secured a place for you on the boat of an English sea captain of my acquaintance.'

Sara gasped but Lidie looked at him steadily.

'Has something changed, Uncle, to make this more urgent?'

Jacob rubbed his brow. 'I fear it may have,' he said.

He had their attention then and both Sara and Lidie looked at him in alarm.

Jacob shifted in his seat. 'It may not signify,' he began, 'But I was speaking to a merchant of my acquaintance recently returned from Montauban.'

He cleared his throat. 'It is said that Samuel left the town some time ago in the company of two or three known Protestant radicals.'

Sara smiled. 'Then the Lord be praised,' she said, 'he will be home with us soon.'

215

Jacob shook his head. 'He was not on the road home. My acquaintance said that they were headed South.'

'I knew it,' cried Lidie. 'He has gone in search of Brousson.'

'What!'

Lidie turned to him. 'He heard that the lawyer Brousson has returned to the realm,' she said, 'and that he is hiding in the Cevennes region going about in the company of others preaching to those of our faith and giving them spiritual nourishment.'

Jacob rubbed his chin. 'I had not heard that,' he said. 'I know of Brousson's work, of course, but I did not know that he had re-entered the country.' He frowned. 'Then this is more serious than I had realised.'

'In what way, Uncle?'

'I do not wish to alarm you, Lidie, but if he was with those who are already marked out as radicals, he will be considered one of them.'

Lidie frowned. 'But if *you* did not know of Brousson's return, Uncle, would Catholic spies have had that intelligence? From what Samuel said, it was a closely guarded secret.'

'Then it may not be a secret for long,' said Jacob. 'These radicals are often followed by Catholic spies.'

'And you think that they may lead these spies to Brousson?'

Jacob shrugged. 'If the King's soldiers know that Brousson is there, they will make every effort to find him. He was a thorn in the side of the Catholics before he fled and they know in what high regard he is held. They will certainly want to capture him.'

They all looked at one another, each one thinking the same and not daring to voice their thoughts until Jacob put them into words.

'Brousson will have a price on his head,' said Jacob quietly. 'His life will be in danger for every hour he remains in the Kingdom. If he is captured, then he will certainly be put to death.'

Lidie swallowed. 'And if Samuel leads the way to him …?'

'Let us pray that he will not,' said Jacob, 'But once Samuel is seen to be conversing with known radicals, then he too will be watched. Even if he returns safely from the Cevennes, he will be marked out and he will be further hounded.'

Lidie shook her head. 'My foolish husband!'

Jacob heaved himself to his feet and came over to Lidie, putting an arm about her shoulders.

'Perhaps I am exaggerating the danger, but I still think you should prepare to leave just as soon as Samuel returns.'

Lidie said nothing for a few moments as she struggled to compose herself.

Has the time come at last? It hardly seems real.

Jacob squeezed her shoulders and then released her. 'Shall I tell you what I have arranged?'

Lidie nodded.

Jacob sighed. 'I fear you will have a long journey,' he said.

'To Bordeaux? That is not so far,' said Lidie.

Jacob shook his head. 'I could not risk trying to get you a passage from Bordeaux,' he said. 'Truly, Lidie, there is such danger of being captured there. The King's soldiers are rewarded for every Protestant they arrest and they and the sailors are on constant lookout for fleeing Huguenots, whether they have abjured or not, and you know the penalties if you are discovered. There are such dreadful accounts …'

Lidie remembered his tales of Protestants being gassed in the hold of ships, of being robbed and thrown overboard, or captured before they had had a chance to get on the water.

I will not think on it.

'So, from where shall we embark?' asked Sara, trying to keep her voice steady.

'From La Tremblade.'

Lidie frowned. 'I do not know this place, Uncle.'

'It is some days' journey North,' said Jacob. 'South of La Rochelle and close by to the town of Marennes.'

'And you think it really necessary to go all this way?'

Jacob bowed his head. 'I truly believe it is safer to avoid the main ports.' Then he continued, speaking in such a low voice that Lidie had to strain to hear him. 'I wish with all my heart that it was not necessary for you to leave, but I can no longer protect your family if the Catholic spies find out that Samuel has been associating with known radicals and particularly if it transpires that he has been conversing with Brousson.'

217

Lidie knew what Jacob meant. If this was discovered, Samuel would be pursued and he would be shown no mercy.

'What of you, Jacob?' asked Sara. 'Will they not suspect that you have helped us escape.'

Jacob sighed. 'They may. You are my family, after all. But even the magistrates have the sense to realize that my business is vital to this town, as is that of Cécile 's in-laws.'

'But you put yourself in danger,' said Sara. 'It will be on my conscience.'

Lidie frowned. 'What is the country like around La Tremblade?' she asked.

'There are forests and there is marshland,' said Jacob.

'So, there are places where we can hide?'

Jacob nodded. 'You will need to be resourceful. Travel at night and hide during the day. Take plentiful supplies of food with you. I have arranged for you to lodge with a citizen of La Tremblade while you await the arrival of the English ship but this fellow will put himself in great danger by harbouring you.'

'And how will we travel? And when?'

Jacob reached for his cloak. 'I have thought of everything, I can assure you. I will send a trusted man to drive you.' He didn't bother to put on his cloak but slung it over his arm. 'Now I must go to my house and embrace my wife. I have not seen her these past few days.'

They all walked with him to the main door.

'I do not know how we can repay you,' said Lidie.

His smile was grim. 'My repayment will be to hear that you have safely reached England. That is all the reward I need.'

At the door, Sara and Lidie watched him go.

Lidie sighed.'What of Annette? Are we to leave her here with the other servants?'

'If that's the case, we should tell her, should we not?' said Sara. 'We cannot desert her without a word, without saying goodbye.'

Lidie nodded. She could feel the tears coming to her eyes and she sniffed and wiped them away. 'And Isaac,' she said. 'We must tell him of our plans directly.'

THE KING'S COMMAND

That night Lidie could not sleep. She tossed and turned, all sorts of frightening images rushing through her mind.

Hurry home you foolish man. We need you here. We cannot embark on such a dangerous mission without you.

Chapter Twenty-One

The days dragged by. Neither Lidie nor Sara could settle and Lidie found herself being short tempered with the children, especially Elias who kept asking when his papa would be home.

Isaac visited frequently, as anxious as they about Samuel's whereabouts. He tried to reassure them.

'A journey into the Cevennes will take a good deal of time, Lidie. It is wild rough country. And then they will have to make enquiries to find out where Brousson is staying.'

'Samuel heard that he travelled from place to place all the time, sleeping in caves, in barns, all over the territory, to avoid detection.'

'Then there you have it,' said Isaac. 'Locating him will take time and no doubt Samuel and his companions won't leave the area until they have found him.'

'It is an absurd venture!'

Isaac nodded. 'I agree. I know how much he admires Brousson, but to put himself at such risk, and to give all of us such worry.'

When they told Isaac of the plans that Jacob was making for their departure, for a moment he looked shocked but then, on the instant, recovered himself.

'It is the right thing to do and especially now that Samuel has made this foolish journey. If you are determined on leaving the realm, then it is best you leave before Elias is any older and before any Catholic spies track Samuel down.'

Lidie came to him and put her arms round him. 'How we shall miss you,' she said. 'You are a father to me as well as a loving grandfather. It is a dagger to my heart to think that you may never see us again.'

Isaac turned his head. 'Do not say never. England is not so far away and maybe, one day …'

Sara looked at him fondly. 'You would not consider coming with us?'

'You are a good deal younger than I, Sara, and in better health. I would only be an encumbrance and, in any case, I still have responsibilities here. For as long as I can, I will tend the sick and, if I am arrested for breaking the law, then so be it.'

And it was then, as they sat solemnly together, contemplating the uncertainty which was to follow, that there was a sudden commotion outside and Lidie leapt to her feet and rushed to the outer door, closely followed by the others. She wrestled with the bolt in her hurry, her fingers trembling, but at last unfastened it and flung the door open.

And there he was, descending from a carriage, his hat askew and a broad smile on his face.

Lidie flung herself into his arms, weeping with relief and he held her tight.

'Lidie, I have such tales to tell you!'

She looked round nervously. There were people still walking the street.

'Quickly, come inside,' she said.

But Samuel seemed in no hurry, chatting with the coachman and waving him off then mounting the steps and scraping his filthy boots on the scraper at the door before greeting the others.

'Look at the state of you!' said Lidie.

Samuel laughed. 'I know, my love. I have been in such rough places, no opportunity to wash or change my apparel.'

Lidie was so relieved to see him unharmed that she could not bring herself to chide him, but Isaac felt no such constraints. He took him immediately to one side and spoke in a low and urgent voice.

'You have been to the Cevennes region? You have sought out Brousson?'

Samuel looked up, surprised. 'I … well, yes, but how did you know, Father?'

Isaac raised his eyes to the ceiling. 'You foolish, foolish boy,' he said. 'Did you not realize you would be observed? Did you not think that consorting with known radicals would bring you to the attention of Catholic spies?'

Samuel frowned. 'I … we were careful, Father. But it was such an opportunity. To meet with Brousson who has long been my hero.'

He turned to the others. 'I have returned so inspired,' he said.

'Be quiet, Samuel,' said Isaac, his voice harsh. 'Come away where we can speak freely.'

'But I am in our home Father. I can speak freely in every room here!'

'Walls have ears,' said Isaac, shortly. 'Do as I say.'

Samuel shrugged and marched into the panelled room, tugging off his cloak as he went and depositing it on the chair in the vestibule. The cloak was covered in mud and had thorns stuck in it and many small tears where it had been snagged by rough bushes.

They all crowded into the room after him and Sara closed the door. Samuel began speaking at once.

'It is so uplifting what he is doing there,' he said, 'Great crowds come to hear him speak and the pastors with him are taking services in these wild places. Our faith is rekindled there!'

Isaac still looked thunderous as Samuel continued to speak of Brousson and the groups of the faithful in the remote villages of the area. Indeed he was so carried away by his enthusiasm that he seemed not to notice his father's expression until Isaac suddenly intervened, slamming his hand down on the great oak table.

'Enough of this, Samuel,' he said. 'Can you not understand what you have done?'

Samuel looked puzzled. 'But Father ...'

Lidie and Sara stared at Isaac. In all the time they had known him, they had never seen him roused to anger in this way.

'Did you spare no thought for your family, hearing no news of you, worrying that some dreadful fate had befallen you? And going to seek out this man who is being sought by the King's soldiers, a man with a price on his head? Did you not consider that you might even have led his enemies to him?'

'No!' Samuel turned to Isaac. 'No! Of course not! I went in the company of true Protestants who already had some intelligence of his whereabouts.'

Isaac folded his arms. 'Then how, pray, do you account for the fact that Lidie's uncle knew you were headed South out of Montauban? If he knew, then it would not take long for Catholic spies to work out where you were heading, especially if you were in the company of known radicals.'

'I was following my heart, Father,' said Samuel quietly.

'Huh! It was a foolish and selfish action, Samuel. You have not only put yourself under grave suspicion but you have now put all of us in mortal danger.'

Samuel frowned. 'I did not think …' he began.

'No, you did not!'

Lidie moved towards Samuel and took his hand. 'But for now we must thank God that you are returned safely to us,' she said.

'Aye, we should do that,' said Isaac, his voice softer. 'But then you should immediately put into place the plans that Jacob has laid for you, for there is no doubt that your venture has been noted and you will be sought out and punished. You need to leave the realm at once.'

Samuel looked up, frowning. 'Jacob has made some plans?'

'For our departure,' said Lidie. 'He has made contact with a sea captain of his acquaintance.'

There was a heavy silence in the room, the only sound coming from the passing of traffic outside in the street, the snorting of horses and the cries of coachmen.

'Must we really leave?' said Samuel quietly.

Lidie took a deep breath. 'We discussed it, my love. You know that we decided, before you left, that we could no longer live here under such threat.'

'Aye, we did, I know that Lidie. But that was before I saw the bravery of all those faithful people in the Cevennes. They have no chance of flight. They are mostly poor peasants scratching a living from the soil in such hostile circumstances.'

Isaac was making an effort to control his anger. 'Can you not see how selfish you are being, Samuel? To stay now would be madness. Think of your family and how you have put them in danger.'

Samuel turned to Lidie and she saw the conflict in his face. 'Am I being selfish, Lidie?'

She did not answer his question directly. 'We need to leave, Samuel. For all the reasons we spoke of before you departed. And now, it is even more pressing.'

He stared at her for a moment and then his shoulders dropped.

'Then, tell me of these plans,' he said, but his voice was flat.

So Sara, Lidie and Isaac repeated to him all that Jacob had told them and how urgent it was to depart in time to be at the coast when the English ship was expected.

Samuel, who had entered the house so full of enthusiasm and fervour for the work of Brousson, at last fell silent. His face was no longer animated and he seemed suddenly diminished as he lowered himself into a chair and put his head in his hands.

Sara cleared her throat. 'Let us sing a psalm together,' she said, to thank God for Samuel's safe return and to ask His blessing on our forthcoming journey.

But the singing was muted as they repeated the familiar words, all of them dreading what lay ahead.

Jacob visited not long after daybreak the following day having heard of Samuel's safe return.

'You must delay no longer,' he told them. 'Leave as soon as you can. Today or tomorrow. That will give you plenty of time to reach La Tremblade before the English ship arrives. I have arranged for you to lodge with a Protestant merchant there who has recently abjured. The English captain will come to his house when the ship is at anchor and give you instructions for boarding.'

Then he told them the name and location of the man in La Tremblade.

'I will note it down,' said Lidie.

'No,' said Jacob. 'Commit it to memory. You must have nothing about your person to incriminate this good fellow. He will be putting his own life at risk on your behalf and if …'

Lidie finished his sentence. 'If we are caught,' she said.

'Aye,' said Jacob. 'I pray fervently that you will journey safely and reach England unharmed, but …'

'We understand,' said Sara softly.

Samuel looked at Lidie. 'Has it come to this,' he said. 'Are we now forced to flee like thieves, though we have done nothing but follow the Word of God?'

'It is for your safety, Samuel,' said Jacob, a flash of anger in his eyes. 'And I have done what I can for you.'

'We are for ever in your debt Uncle,' said Lidie quickly. 'Are we not, Samuel?'

Samuel looked up and then went forward and took Jacob's hand. 'Forgive me,' he said. 'We may owe our lives to you. Thank you for all you have done for us.'

'My thanks will be to see you gone,' said Jacob, 'though it breaks my heart.'

'Then we shall do as you say,' said Samuel. 'We shall leave tomorrow.'

'Why not today?' said Jacob. It is still early. You can leave at nightfall, travelling under cover of darkness.'

'I need to make some arrangements,' said Samuel.

'And we need to see Louise, and to speak to Annette. And to gather some provisions for the journey,' said Sara.

Jacob frowned. 'Leave as soon as you can,' he said. 'The longer you delay the more you are in danger.'

Lidie nodded. 'We shall leave tomorrow morning.' She looked at Samuel.

'Aye,' he said, sighing. 'Tomorrow.'

'Then I will send my man round before daybreak tomorrow,' said Jacob. 'He will drive you north before the town is stirring and he will find places for you to rest up in hiding during the day. Then he will drive you onward by night. He is utterly to be trusted and he will protect you as best he can.'

The rest of the day was spent gathering victuals together and collecting all the bundles that they had already prepared, of their clothes and those of the children, and the valuables and coin, carefully sewn into secret pockets in garments. As she was making final preparations in her bedchamber, Lidie looked sadly at the silks she had worn on her sixteenth anniversary. She had planned to pass these on to Esther when she was of age.

She took them from the armoire and held them up against her. She had put on a little weight since those times but the silks could always be altered. She laid them on the bed.

They do not weigh so much!

Carefully, she folded and rolled up the material, balancing it in her hand, then she ran down the stairs and fetched some twine and came back and tied the roll firmly and added it to her bundle.

Samuel left to go and seek out his father and make other arrangements and Lidie and Sara went across to see Louise.

The two sisters clung to one another. 'Shall we ever see each other again?' said Louise, holding Sara's face between her hands.

Sara could not hold back the tears and they ran unchecked down her cheeks.

There were no false promises, no assurances that perhaps their world would change in the not too distant future. They knew it would not.

'I pray that *you* will continue to be safe,' said Sara, stroking Louise's hair.

'Jacob is important in this town,' said Louise. 'but I cannot believe that even he is truly safe despite signing those vile abjuration papers.'

Sara searched Louise's face. 'Would you consider leaving?'

Louise shook her head. 'Having gone against his conscience to protect the livelihoods of others, I doubt Jacob will ever leave Castillon, but who knows what the future holds.'

When Sara and Lidie returned to their house, their spirits were very low.

'We must speak to Annette,' said Sara.

They found her in the kitchen, humming one of the tunes she often sang for the children.

This is the hardest of all.

Sara went to her, took the skillet she was holding from her hands and led her to the large scrubbed table.

'Sit down Annette,' she said gently. 'We would speak with you.'

Annette met Sara's eyes, alarmed. 'What is it? What has happened?'

But when they told her, swearing her to secrecy, she did not look surprised.

'You warned me that this day would come,' she said, dabbing her eyes with the corner of her apron.

'We plan to travel north and embark from La Tremblade. '

Annette frowned. 'Not Bordeaux?'

Sara shook her head. 'Jacob thinks it would be too dangerous now. The port is full of the King's troops. Truly Annette, we would take you with us but the journey …'

'I would only hinder you, Madame. My bones ache and I would not survive if I had to hide in the forest.'

'We would never ask you to put yourself in danger in that way, though we'd dearly love your company,' said Sara. 'We shall say to the others in the household that we are leaving to spend some days at the farm, but we wanted you to know the truth.'

'What will happen to us?'

Lidie took Annette's hands in hers. 'Uncle Jacob will look after you. It may be that his sons will come here to live. You will not need to leave here as long as he is able to protect you.'

'What about the little ones? Will the nurse go with you?'

Lidie shook her head. 'Mama and I will attend to the children.'

'Will you tell the nurse your plans?' asked Annette.

Lidie looked unsure but Sara answered strongly. 'No, the fewer people who know the better. But you, Annette, you have been a part of our family for so long. We owe it to you to be honest.'

'Then the nurse will no longer be needed here?'

'No,' said Sara, 'But no doubt Jacob and Louise will find her employment.'

Annette gave a weak smile. 'I cannot pretend that I shall miss her company,' she muttered.

All this time, Susanne had been listening. She had been at the back door taking delivery of a basket of vegetables and was carrying it back down the passage to the kitchen. When she heard the sound of low voices, she stood in the passage, just out of sight, knowing that she should not eavesdrop but horrified at what she was hearing.

And then, suddenly, there was a pounding on the front door of the house. In the kitchen, Sara, Lidie and Annette looked at each other and Annette made to move out of the kitchen to answer it.

'Wait!' said Lidie, and Annette frowned.

'It may be someone seeking Samuel,' whispered Lidie, looking across at Sara.

The pounding came again, more urgent now. For a moment no one moved, but then Sara spoke urgently to Annette.

'Quick, find Elias. If he is with the nurse, tell her that I wish his presence immediately. And then take him to the hiding place.'

'The secret panel?'

'Tell him it is a game,' said Lidie, finding her voice. 'Hurry Annette. At this rate they will break down the door.'

Annette raced up the stairs to the nursery, wheezing with effort, while the pounding at the door was now accompanied with shouts.

'Open up in the name of the King!'

'Patience!' shouted Lidie. 'I am on my way.'

While Annette was getting her breath back, Sara was reassuring Elias and helping him to step into the cavity behind the panel.

'It is a game we are all playing my darling,' she whispered. 'You must stay quiet as a mouse so no person shall find you.'

Elias started to protest but Sara dragged him further in while Annette slid the panel back into place.

Lidie moved towards the door just as Susanne appeared at her side.

'Who is it Madame? Who is making such a fearsome noise? Will I open the door?'

Lidie shook her head. 'Stay back Susanne. I will deal with them.'

Her hands were sweating and she wiped them down her skirts before sliding back the bolt.

Four soldiers stood before her on the doorstep, great rough men, and at the sight of them, that long ago attack on her person came back to her in terrifying clarity and she found herself stuttering over her words as she asked them their business.

But they just pushed past her. 'Where is your husband?'

'He is not here, sirs.' She could feel her heart thudding.

'Search the house,' said the oldest of the four men. 'She's lying. No doubt he's hiding, the Huguenot scum.'

'Sirs, I must protest!'

'Protest all you like, we're here on the King's business.'

As two of the men ran up the stairs and the other two searched the rooms downstairs, crashing through each door in turn and looking behind tapestries and overturning chairs, Susanne crept up to Lidie's side.

They heard cries from the children and from the nurse, which were met with rough oaths.

'Shall I go to them?' whispered Susanne.

'Best not, Susanne.'

Lidie could hear one of the soldiers banging his fists on the panels in the reception room. 'Inspect these panels well,' he shouted. 'These Huguenots are full of tricks.'

Do not cry out Elias. For pity's sake keep quiet.

Lidie could not tell how long the soldiers were there. Her whole being was overcome with terror and it seemed that every minute lasted an hour. At length, she realised that Susanne was asking her something.

'Should I go into the street in case the Master comes?'

Lidie took a moment to focus on the girl and understand what she meant. Her mouth was dry when she whispered a reply. 'Aye, that would be well, Susanne, and if you see him …'

The girl nodded. 'I'll tell him to flee.' Very quietly she let herself out of the door to keep watch.

Lidie did not move from her spot by the door. She tried to offer a prayer to God to keep Samuel safe, to keep all of them safe, but she was so keenly aware of the heavy footfalls, coarse language and shouts from the soldiers that she couldn't concentrate.

And then they were before her again and the older man was addressing her.

'I demand to know the whereabouts of your husband.'

'Truly sir, I do not know. He is about his business somewhere in the town no doubt.'

'His business, eh? And what business would that be? Business against the King's orders no doubt.'

One of the other soldiers spat on the floor.

It seemed then that they were preparing to leave but the older man suddenly turned back to Lidie. 'And where is your older son? We know you have a five year old boy. We are commanded to take him to the priest.'

Lidie did not reply.

'Speak up woman or it will go ill with you.'

Lidie could feel the tears coming and she was powerless to stop them.

'He is with his grandmother,' she sobbed.

For a moment, the man's face showed some compassion. 'Ah, he's dead is he? Well, one less Huguenot to hunt down I suppose.'

Lidie said nothing, stunned that the soldier had misinterpreted her words.

The soldiers left then but just before they slammed the door behind them, one said. 'We'll find your man. You can be sure we'll track him down.'

Lidie waited a good time behind the front door, leaning against it trying to calm herself then, at last, she crept into the panelled room and looked out of the window. She could see no sign of the soldiers so she went out into the street and looked both ways, into the alleyway across the way and up towards the town, but for now they had gone. She went back inside and directly to the false panel, feeling until she found the slight indentation, then she pressed it and slid the panel back.

'They are gone,' she whispered.

Elias tumbled out first, his eyes scanning the room. 'Who were those men, Mama? Why were they looking for Papa?'

For answer, Lidie put her arms round him and held him tight, looking over his head at Sara who was carefully smoothing out the creases in her dress as she stepped over the edge of the hole.

'We had a fine game hiding from them did we not?' said Sara.

Elias disentangled himself from Lidie's arms. 'It was all dark,' he mumbled.

When Elias had gone back upstairs, Sara and Lidie spoke in low voices.

'Pray God that Samuel will come back to us.'

'We must leave the moment he does,' said Sara. 'There is no time to lose.'

The mood in the house was sombre. Lidie and Sara had done everything to prepare for the next day's journey and they spoke softly to one another and repeated familiar psalms together. The children seemed to pick up on their anxiety and were fractious and demanding but Lidie was too distracted to pay them much attention. She told Elias and Jean that they were going to visit the farm the next day and this briefly excited them but then they resorted to quarrelling with one another and teasing little Esther until the nurse spanked them and sent them to their chamber.

And still Samuel did not return. As the afternoon drew on, Lidie started to pace up and down the reception room. Sara was trying to make some pretence at normality and was working on a piece of tapestry but most of the time the needle rested in her lap.

They sat in silence until Lidie suddenly cried out. 'Pray God the soldiers have not found him!'

The time ticked by and soon Annette came to close the shutters and light the candles. Still there was no sign of Samuel.

Nor yet of Susanne.

'What has happened to the girl? Surely she has not deserted us?'

Lidie shook her head. 'She would not do that Mama, she is loyal. We have been her only family these last years. I would swear on my life that she would not desert us.'

Annette served them a little supper but neither Sara nor Lidie could do more than toy with their food.

'Has Susanne returned?'

Annette frowned. 'No Madame. I cannot understand it. I am worried for her safety. Should I send one of the men to look for her?'

'It might be prudent,' said Lidie.

Several times, Lidie went to the great front door, opened it and looked out into the gathering darkness, but no one was abroad.

When she came back into the room, shaking her head again as Sara looked up questioningly, Lidie said. 'I feel such dread, Mama. I know in my bones that something has happened to Samuel. Those soldiers must have found him.'

Sara did not try to contradict her but threw down her tapestry and came over to Lidie, hugging her tightly.

'All we can do is wait, my darling,' she said. 'And pray.'

Chapter Twenty-Two

It was late when there was an urgent knocking on the front door. Sara and Lidie had long since lapsed into silence, sitting slumped in their chairs. Lidie was half dozing; she could not allow herself to sleep but the worry of the day had overwhelmed her and she had occasionally drifted off into a half-waking, half-sleeping state, but the noise instantly jerked her into wakefulness and she leapt up, stumbling in her haste to reach the door.

Unbolting it with fumbling fingers, she opened it a crack, her heart full of hope that Samuel would be standing there.

It was not Samuel. It was her Uncle Jacob, his head bowed, breathing heavily as if he had been running.

He said nothing but went past her, carefully closing the door behind him then he took her hands and drew her to him.

Lidie pushed herself free of him. 'What's happened? Where's Samuel?'

By this time, Sara was beside her and they both stared at Jacob. 'I'm so sorry.'

'For pity's sake, Jacob,' said Sara, keeping her voice low. 'What's happened?'

Jacob swallowed and then wiped his brow with his hand.

'They found him,' he said.

'The soldiers?'

'Aye, with the help of Catholic spies. They knew ... they knew where he had been.'

Lidie felt as though time was suspended. She knew in her heart what was coming but she could not bear to hear the words.

Jacob swallowed. 'They knew he'd been to find Brousson,' he said, 'And they ...'

He lowered his eyes. 'They questioned him.'

'Questioned him? Who? Who questioned him?'

'I don't know exactly,' said Jacob. 'All I know is that there were soldiers and others and that ...'

Lidie gripped the back of a chair for support. 'Are you saying he was tortured, Uncle?'

233

Jacob nodded and Lidie stared at him feeling the bile rising in her throat.

'How do you know this, Jacob,' asked Sara at last.

'One of my Catholic colleagues was privy to what happened,' he said. 'He was horrified to hear how Samuel was treated and he bravely came to inform me.'

All the colour had drained from Lidie's face. She sensed what was coming and she raised her head.

'Does he live?' she whispered.

Jacob shook his head.

Sara gasped and let out a cry but Lidie said nothing for a moment and then she met Jacob's eyes and he immediately understood the silent question she was asking.

Jacob nodded slowly. 'They say he abjured but only … only because his torturers told him what they would do to his family if he did not.'

And it was only then that Lidie gave way. She threw herself against her mother and howled like a wounded animal. Sara held her tightly and looked across at Jacob.

'We must leave before they seek us out,' she said quietly. 'The promises of torturers are meaningless.'

Jacob nodded. 'My man will be here by midnight. You cannot stay. They … they will be at your door directly, you can be sure of that. They will take Elias and they will punish you, too, Lidie.'

Sara gently prised herself away from Lidie. She held her shoulders and looked into her eyes. 'We have to go, my darling. We have to leave, just as we had planned. As Jacob says, before dawn, before people are stirring.'

'But Samuel!'

Jacob looked down. 'If he truly abjured, then he will be given a Catholic burial.'

Lidie shuddered. 'Can I not see him?'

Sara met Jacob's eyes and he gave a slight shake of his head.

'No Lidie,' said Sara. 'There is no time, my darling. We must flee to save ourselves. I have no doubt that Samuel is with God now and we live in the sure and certain hope that one day we shall be with him again.'

When at last Jacob left them, Sara turned to Lidie. 'You should try and get some sleep before Jacob's man comes. We shall have little time for sleep in the days to come.'

But Lidie whipped round. 'How can you speak of sleep! How can I sleep when my husband lies dead at the hands of torturers.' She broke off and started to shake but then immediately choked back the sobs and paced to and fro like a caged animal.

'I knew he should not seek out that man,' she muttered. 'He could not see the danger in it. I *knew* he would put himself at risk.'

She stopped pacing and stood in front of Sara, wringing her hands.

'Where is this God of ours now? How could He allow this to happen!'

'Please do not doubt God now, Lidie,' said Sara gently. 'Now, more than ever, we shall need our faith to be strong.'

'And if we are caught, Mama? What then? What shall we have achieved? My husband dead, you and I thrown into prison, my children taken from me.'

'Please, Lidie. You have always been so strong in your belief. And if we can reach England, then we shall be safe.' She took Lidie's face in her hands. 'Put your trust in God and let us pray to Him now that He will lead us there.'

Lidie twisted away. 'Do not ask me to pray, Mama. I cannot.'

She began her pacing again. 'What am I to tell Elias?'

Sara sighed. 'You must tell him the truth, Lidie. That Samuel is with God.'

'Do you truly believe that? Would that I could join him.'

'You cannot mean that. You must care for your children, we both must, it is what Samuel would have wanted.'

But Lidie just stared blankly at her mother.

Sara forced back her own tears and put her hands on Lidie's shoulders.

'Come, at least have some rest in your chamber. Jacob's man will not be here for an hour or two.'

Lide said nothing and allowed her mother to lead her up the stairs and into her chamber but when Sara started to help her out of her clothes, she pushed her away.

'I am not a child. Leave me alone.'

Sara hesitated, then she retreated and closed the door behind her.

Lidie continued to stand in the middle of the room. Eventually she forced herself to take off her clothes and lie on her bed. She knew she would never sleep, indeed she thought she would never sleep again. After a while, she got up and opened the shutters and then she stood at the window staring out at the darkness.

She had no idea how long she stood there, time had no meaning for her, and it was a while before she registered that someone was in the room with her. The lack of sleep had disoriented her and just for a moment …

Samuel?

But when she turned from the window, Annette was standing there and, even in the darkness, Lidie could tell she knew.

'Mistress Lidie,' she whispered.

'Did Mama tell you,' asked Lidie, her voice hoarse.

'Aye.' Annette sniffed. 'How has it come to this?'

Lidie went to her and Annette put her arms round her and feeling those comforting arms and smelling the familiar scent she had known all her life, Lidie broke down , sobbing against Annette's broad shoulders as Annette patted her back and tried to say some words of comfort. Lidie found her voice at last.

'Uncle Jacob will be at the burial.'

Annette nodded. 'A Catholic burial, then?'

'I'm not sure I can bear it, Annette. That he will be buried with the idolaters' rites he sought so hard to avoid. And to leave here without bidding him a final farewell.'

'Think of the children,' said Annette.

'I find it impossible to think.'

Annette sniffed again, set the candle down on a chest and wiped her eyes with the back of her hand.

'I have prepared something for you to eat, and for the little ones,' she said. 'And I have woken the children and told the nurse that you are leaving before dawn to go to the farm.'

'Did she question the hour of departure?'

'No,' said Annette. 'But after the soldiers' visit … she will know that something is amiss.'

Still, Lidie made no move to stir herself.

'Come Mistress Lidie,' she said, her voice firmer. 'Put on your travelling clothes and collect the bags you have prepared. The cart will be here for you within the hour and you must have something to eat before you leave.'

Lidie shook her head. 'I cannot face any victuals,' she said.

'You must eat,' said Annette firmly. 'You must keep strong.'

At midnight Jacob's man drew up in a cart by the main door and the sad little party loaded up their bags and set off along the street, passing through the faubourg and out by the ruined North gate, over the little bridge across the moat and onto the open road. The lantern which hung at the front where the driver sat, only gave enough light to show the way a few metres ahead.

Annette alone had seen them off, standing silently on the door step.

We shall never see her again. We shall never see our home again.

It was not comfortable, sitting on planks as the horse plodded on down the track, but at least they did not have to pass through a city gate as they left the faubourg. Esther, a toddler of two, squirmed on Lidie's lap and little Jean who had been the most reluctant to leave the house, was still crying and pulling away from Sara. Only Elias remained quiet, though he did question Lidie.

'This is not the way to the farm, Mama. We have to cross the river to reach the farm. And why are we not in the carriage'.

It was Sara who had answered him. 'It is an adventure, is it not, Elias?'

How could they explain that a cart would be less conspicuous on country tracks and able to travel more easily into the dark of the woods to hide up during the day.

Elias was the only one of the children who had not fussed when they left and Lidie was touched by his quiet acceptance, but as they left the town behind them he spoke again.

'Where is Papa?' he asked.

Lidie took a deep breath. She leant over and spoke quietly to him. 'Papa cannot be with us now, Elias,' she said, trying to keep her voice steady.

Elias frowned. 'But he was here yesterday. Has he gone away again?'

'Yes, Elias, he has gone away.'

Elias said nothing, absorbing the information carefully, as was his way.

No one spoke for a while and the two younger children finally slept.

Sara bent forward. 'Did Annette say that Susanne had returned,' she asked. 'I did not see her at the house.'

Lidie shrugged. 'I was wrong to think her loyal. It seems she has deserted us.'

Chapter Twenty-Three

But Susanne had not deserted them.

The soldiers had frightened her and she was thankful to leave the house and hide in a narrow alleyway across the way, but her thoughts were full of what she had overheard in the kitchen.

What will become of me? What will happen to Annette? Will she help me?

Her mind was in such turmoil that she was hardly conscious of the passing time but suddenly she felt a change in the air about her.

There was a presence, a breath, a filling of the space behind her. and the hairs on the back of her neck rose. Her whole body tensed and she whipped round.

Before she could cry out, she was roughly seized and held fast. She tried to scream but the scream was stifled before it began, a large rough hand clamping down over her mouth.

'Susanne!'

The voice of her nightmares.

She struggled, biting the hand that gagged her and kicking out at her assailant.

There was an oath and then she felt a stinging blow to her cheek. 'Vicious little she cat!'

Susanne twisted round, fighting free from her attacker and ran from the alley but he caught her and dragged her back.

'Back working for those Huguenots, are you?' he said, breathing hard. 'Well, I warrant that they'll not be here much longer. We know where your master has been. The King's troops are after him and when they catch him …'

Susanne was shaking. The man put his arms about her clamping her to him. 'You're still a comely wench,' he said, pushing close into her from behind.

The bile was rising in her throat but somehow she managed to speak. 'Haven't you tortured me enough?'

'Tortured you? How so, Susanne? Didn't I rescue you from your life in Bordeaux and we enjoyed each other's bodies, did we not.'

She could not see his face but she could imagine the lascivious grin on his face.

Please God, not again.

'And I nearly died giving birth to your child,' she blurted out.

He grabbed her shoulders and turned her roughly to face him.

'There was a child?'

She nodded. 'A girl.'

'Does the child live?'

She shook her head, her eyes filling with tears as she saw again that tiny, still body lying in her arms.

I would have loved her. Even though she was made through threats and force,

There was a beat of silence then he said. 'I did not know there was a child.' He cleared his throat, gesturing at the house opposite. 'I kept watching the house but you had gone. I thought you had been dismissed.'

'I was sent away to have the child.'

There was another silence and then he said. 'I'm sorry about the babe, Susanne.'

She looked at him properly then, perhaps for the first time. Their relationship had been one of fear and violence yet now, fleetingly, she saw a different expression on his face.

'Why did you treat me so?'

He shrugged. 'A man must eat. I'm paid well to inform on Huguenots.'

'I was but a child. I did not know … you used me. I was helping you to line your pockets. I did not understand …'

'I …' he began. But then there was a sudden commotion opposite and the soldiers were crashing out of the house. The older one came directly over to them.

'Ah, good man, you have the maid. We'll take her with us.'

'I have questioned her already, sir. She knows nothing. Best let her go back to her work.'

The soldier laughed. 'Let me be the judge of that.' He paused, looking Susanne up and down. 'Getting soft, are you? She's a pretty wench, I grant you.' He beckoned to the two younger soldiers. 'We'll take her with us. Servants hear much in a household. I warrant she knows more than she pretends.'

The two younger soldiers grabbed her and the man from Bordeaux came out of the alley and stood watching as they walked on up the hill, dragging Susanne between them.

They took her to a house in the town where they had been quartered. Although she had struggled all the way, they had held her fast, only laughing at her feeble attempts to free herself.

The questioning went on and on, always by the older soldier. He wanted to know about secret gatherings, about who the family saw and whether they still prayed together, who else was in the household and whether they held true to the Protestant faith.

Susanne wept and wailed, hoping she would be seen as a stupid wench, frightened out of her wits, who could tell him little, but all the time she was thinking what she could say that might satisfy him but not harm the family.

'I know nothing of their beliefs, sir. I'm only a lowly maid. They have been good to me and treated me well.'

'Who visits the household?'

'The dressmaker,' said Susanne. 'And those supplying goods for the household. Oh, and sometimes the Master silk weaver with his pattern book.'

'I have no interest in trades people. Who are their friends?'

Susanne frowned. 'Why, just their family. The Mistress's sister and my master's father.'

'And the children?' he asked. 'What ages are the children?'

It was on the tip of her tongue to reply truthfully when she remembered how Elias had been hidden from them.

'Two babes of three and two,' she said.

He went on and on, trying to trick her into saying more but always she answered with guilelessness, frowning as if trying to think. Every now and then she stole a glance at him and she could see he was becoming frustrated that he could get nothing from her.

Please God, let them think I am soft in the head and know nothing.

Then suddenly another soldier burst into the room.

'We've found him!' he shouted. 'We have found that so-called lawyer. We have him outside.'

'Excellent!'

The older man looked at Susanne. 'She's a fool. She knows nothing of import. Let her go. We have bigger fish to fry.'

And then she was thrown out onto the street but not before her man-handler had put his hands on her breasts and squeezed her rear, grinning at her discomfort.

She scrambled to her feet and saw that her master was being taken into the house. She gasped as she noted the state of him, his clothes torn and his face bruised and swollen. As he was being thrust through the door, he turned and saw her and for a moment their eyes met.

Then she ran. But not back to the house in the faubourg.

It will be too dangerous there. I dare not go back. They have my master - and the family are planning to flee. The soldiers will be there again, to be sure.

She was sweating profusely and her heart rate was so fast that she felt faint, but she kept going, arriving at last at the banks of the great river and it was only then that she stopped and sat down on the ground, her whole body shaking.

Then someone was standing over her, speaking to her.

'What ails you, Susanne?'

She looked up, recognising one of the fish sellers. She swallowed and tried to gather her wits.

'I …' she began.

'Are you looking to cross the river?' asked the woman.

The farm. I shall be safe at the farm.

Susanne nodded. 'I am sent to help at my mistress's farm,' she stuttered, the lie coming easily, 'but I was robbed by some fellow and he took my purse.'

'It is little wonder you look so upset, girl. Come, my husband is going over to the other side directly. He will take you for free.'

Susanne looked up at her. 'Thank you.' Then she started to cry.

The woman smiled. 'Do not take it so hard, child. It was not your fault. Your mistress will not chide you. What a villain to take the coin from you. You must tell her what occurred. Did you recognise the man who robbed you?'

Susanne shook her head.

The woman made a tutting noise with her tongue. 'Poor child. Now come, he is leaving directly.'

It was a sunny day with enough breeze to fill the sails and the crossing did not take long. As they headed for the far bank. Susanne looked back, half expecting to see soldiers coming for her but all was as usual with people going about their daily business and boats criss-crossing the river or going downstream towards Bordeaux.

When they reached the other side, the boatman lowered the sails and pulled the boat up on the bank. Susanne began to thank him but he asked her where she was going and when she told him, he rubbed his chin and frowned.

'It is a long walk, child. If you wait here there will be carts coming to the river's edge soon, filled with goods for me to ferry over. No doubt one of the drivers can take you close to your mistress's farm.'

Susanne felt tears coming again but wiped them away before the man noticed.

A word of kindness and I am undone.

She sat at the river's edge then, while the boatman arranged things in the craft and then lent against the bow to wait.

It wasn't long before they noticed a cart in the distance, the horse dragging a heavy load behind it. The boatman shaded his eyes and stared.

'I know the man,' he said. 'He's a good fellow. And if he can't take you there will be others following.'

He was right. There were other laden carts, now, coming into view, all heading their way and now there were other boats coming from across the river and landing nearby, Soon there was quite a crowd of folk unloading and loading, talking, laughing, heaving.

Susanne looked about it. It was all so normal, the cheerful exchanges, the day to day activities.

And yet everything has changed.

Soon she was seated in the cart of the boatman's acquaintance and they were heading towards the plains. The driver spoke little during the journey and Susanne was grateful for it. When they reached the track which led up to the farm, he reined in his horse.

'Can you walk from here?'

Susanne nodded and scrambled out of the cart. Then as she turned to thank him, he looked down at her.

'Take care, child,' he said.

Does he know about the family and their strong beliefs?

As she walked up the track, she looked up towards the village of Pujols on the high ground, with its magnificent Catholic church dominating the landscape. Her folk in Bordeaux had never given much thought to God but since living with the Castillon family she had come to admire their refusal to deny their faith though she found it hard to understand. She stopped for a moment and stared at the church.

Their God is not there. But where is he and why does he cause them to suffer so?

When Susanne knocked on the farmhouse door, she heard Martha approaching.

'Who is there?'

'Susanne.'

Then Martha flung the door wide and put her arms out to embrace her.

'Lord be praised, I had thought it was … never mind. What are you doing here, child? Has the mistress sent you? Surely not on your own?' She glanced around and then, seeing no one else, her expression changed.

'Something has happened?'

She ushered her inside, still talking and as Susanne looked around at the surroundings which were so familiar and so dear to her, she could not help the tears from flowing again. Martha held her tight and then drew her into the kitchen where, little by little, Susanne recounted all that had happened. Martha put her head in her hands.

'Oh Susanne, how could the soldiers treat them so harshly. What harm have they ever done to others?'

Then Abel joined them and Susanne had to recount the whole story again.

'And you say that the family plans to flee?'

Susanne nodded and Abel turned to Martha.

'Then they may come here if they plan to leave from Bordeaux.'

Susanne shook her head. 'No, they will not leave from Bordeaux but from somewhere to the North.'

'Are you sure of this?'

'It is what they told Annette.'

'But the soldiers will not know that. They may assume that the family will rest up here before going to Bordeaux.' He looked again at Martha. 'They may come here and question us.'

'Then we must be prepared,' she said, returning his gaze. She rose from her chair and began to busy herself at the stove.

'Meanwhile,' she said. 'This child needs our care.'

Abel did not answer but he was still frowning as he left the house to continue his work on the farm.

Chapter Twenty-Four

In the cart, the children were all awake and Lidie needed what strength and patience she could muster to keep them from quarrelling or crying.

'We are going on a great adventure, children,' she said. 'And I need you to be very good for we shall be travelling for a long time.'

The two younger children stopped their whining for a moment, looking towards the sound of her voice in the darkness but then snuggled back into the arms of their grandmama. Before long they were both asleep.

Elias was sitting beside Lidie. 'Papa would like an adventure,' he said. 'When is he coming?'

Lidie swallowed. 'He will not be coming, my love.'

'Why not?'

The seating in the cart was hard and uncomfortable and the family was already cramped, but Lidie moved still closer to Elias and put her arm round his narrow shoulders. She felt him tense up – of the three children he was the least spontaneous, awkward when hugged – but she ignored his resistance and held him tight.

'Papa is with God,' she said quietly.

In the darkness, she could sense that Elias was trying to process what she had said.

'Where is he with God?'

'In heaven, my darling.'

Elias said nothing and Lidie did not know whether he had understood.

'Papa is dead, Elias,' she said, still keeping her voice low. 'And we shall have to manage without him. You will have to be very brave.'

'Was he killed?' asked Elias.

Lidie tried to keep her voice steady.'Yes.'

'Is that why we are going on an adventure?'

'It is. We are going to get on a boat and go across the water to a place where we shall all be safe.'

'Shall you tell Jean and Esther?'

'Not yet. '

'So, it is our secret?'

'Yes. I have told you because you are the eldest and I know you will be my big boy and help me.'

Elias leant into her body then and this rare gesture of affection almost broke Lidie. She found it impossible to speak further as the cart trundled on down the track.

Sara, who was sitting opposite, cradling the other two children, had overheard the exchange and she reached over and put a reassuring hand on Lidie's knee.

At length, Elias, too, slept, but Lidie and Sara stayed wakeful and alert. There was no other traffic on the country road and the driver only had one lantern to guide him, giving just enough light to show the way so that he could direct the horse and keep him going at a steady trot.

They were all silent now and as they journeyed deeper into the countryside, the only sounds were the steady clopping of the horse's hooves on the ground, the squeals from small creatures, prey to a hunting owl, or the occasional bark of a fox.

We are truly travelling into the unknown.

Lidie could only see Sara's outline in the darkness but she could hear her whispering some familiar psalms.

Why can I not pray?

But she knew why. Her heart was too full of anger. Anger that Samuel should have gone to seek out Brousson, anger that he had put them all in mortal danger. Loathing for his torturers. And she had such overwhelming dread for the future which lay before them, full of danger and without Samuel, without friends or extended family or the familiarity of her home.

The night wore on and the horse's pace became slower and then, as the sky began to lighten with the first streaks of dawn, the driver turned off onto a much rougher track. He extinguished the lantern and they made their way forward bumping and lurching so that Lidie and Sara had to clutch onto the sides of the cart. The driver turned round.

'It will be rough for a while, ladies, but we need to reach the safety of the forest and find a hiding place.'

'Of course,' said Sara. 'Please do not concern yourself about us.'

At first the trees of the forest were sparse but as they continued on, they grew more and more closely packed. At length, the driver alighted from the cart and led the horse forward until he reached a point where it became impassable for the cart.

There was very little light penetrating through to the forest floor but the driver pointed to a clearing ahead where there was a small stream.

'We can rest here,' he said. 'We are well hidden from the road and the main track petered out some time ago. It is not likely that we shall be disturbed. And there is fresh water.'

Stiff and chilled, Lidie and Sara alighted. The children had woken when the cart stopped and were looking around them in confusion. Esther began to cry and Jean stood with his thumb in his mouth, staring at the trees. Elias said nothing but began to help his mother and grandmother unload some victuals and take them to the clearing. The driver took off the horse's harness and led him to the stream to drink and then tied him to a tree and fixed on his nosebag. Jean watched and then went over to the horse and stroked its nose. The driver smiled.

'We need to look after him well,' he said.

'Indeed we do,' said Lidie, taking Jean by the hand and leading him to where they had spread out the food. 'We are relying on his steadiness.'

Sara, meanwhile, was trying to change Esther's soiled napkin and clean her up with water from the stream but the little girl was struggling and protesting loudly. Quickly, Lidie grabbed some bread from their supply and spread it with Annette's preserve. She gave it to the child and Esther's yells subsided.

She looked across at the driver. 'I'm sorry,' she said. 'I know we need them to be quiet but with young children …'

He nodded. 'I am a father,' he said. Then he sat down and began to eat the food which Lidie passed to him.

'We are so grateful,' she said to him. 'You are risking much on our behalf.'

'It is scant repayment for what your uncle did for me,' he replied, breaking a piece of bread in half and cutting into one of the round cheeses which Lidie had put before him.'

'What did my uncle do for you?'

Let him recount a tale of goodness to distract me from the horror of all this.

The driver shrugged. 'I was an impetuous young man,' he began, 'And in my youth I did many foolish things and fell into bad company.'

He paused and chewed thoughtfully. 'I began to thieve.'

'You stole – from Uncle Jacob?'

He nodded. 'He caught me in the act,' he said. 'If he had reported me my punishment would have been severe – the galleys or even death – yet he did not. He spoke kindly to me and found out how I had been deserted by my family and then …'

'And then?'

'He gave me a chance. He entrusted me with a job and I have worked for him these ten years.'

They were silent then and Lidie looked across at the children, absorbed in eating and, for the moment, quiet. Elias was helping the younger two and her heart bled for him but she was glad she had told him the truth.

What a solemn child he is. Even at this young age he takes his responsibilities so seriously.

Sara came over to her. She was holding some rough blankets she had taken from the cart. 'We should all try and get some rest,' she said, spreading them out on the forest floor between the trees.

Lidie nodded. 'Let the children run free for a while Mama, until they tire themselves.'

The driver stood up and walked over to the horse. He removed its empty nosebag and undid the rope from its halter. Jean glanced over at him.

'Won't the horse run away?'

'No, son. He'll not wander far. There's a little grass over there by the stream and he'll graze on that and then, once he's had his fill, I'll wager he'll have a good long sleep.'

Jean frowned, looking at the closely packed trees. 'Is there room for him to lie down?' he asked.

'He'll sleep standing up. He doesn't need to lie down.'

Jean turned to Sara. 'The man says the horse can sleep standing up,' he said.

Sara ruffled his curls. 'Yes, indeed. And would it not be useful if we could, too?' Then she sat down next to Lidie. 'We can imagine we are on a family picnic,' she said softly, 'And not fleeing for our lives.' Then she stroked Lidie's face. 'Please try and sleep, my love. I will see to the little ones.'

'I feel I shall never sleep again, Mama.'

'You will be of no use to any of us if you do not rest,' said Sara, her voice sharp. 'Do you not think that I too am fraught with worry, that my head is full of the images of nightmares?'

For a moment, Lidie looked shocked and then she burst into tears and clung to her mother.

'Weep freely,' Sara whispered, stroking Lidie's hair. Then she gently laid her down and covered her with a blanket before shooing the children off towards the stream where she and the driver devised some games for them.

Chapter Twenty-Five

For the next few days, the small party led a twilight existence, hiding during the day and travelling only during the hours of darkness. Sleeping out in the open began to take its toll for the Spring air was cool in the woods, and little Jean developed a worrying cough which wracked his body. They nursed him as best they could and put the children to sleep under the cart so that they had protection from the weather, while the adults huddled on its perimeter, getting what shelter they could. Once they found a deserted barn and gratefully hid and slept there, away from the wind. And from time to time, the driver, having settled them in their hiding place, would walk back to the nearest village to buy some simple victuals.

'Do the folk in the village question you?' asked Sara, when he had returned from one of these forays.

He shrugged. 'If they do I say I'm travelling South with my family to find work on my cousin's farm.' He looked down at his stained clothes and scratched his untrimmed beard. 'They easily take me for a rough farm worker, I warrant.'

'And we can easily pass as your rough family, no doubt,' said Sara, smiling grimly as she observed her muddied dress and cloak and the children's filthy clothes.

Lidie was so low she hardly said a word and even when Sara spoke to her about Jean's cough she hardly rallied. She looked at her mother with dull eyes.

'But what can we do?' she asked, shrugging. 'As you say, Mama, our lives are in God's hands.'

Sara had no answer to that and she turned away.

After several days' travelling, they reached the great pine and oak forests which backed the long beaches of huge sand dunes which led to the sea near La Tremblade.

There were wider paths in the forests here, where hunters chased down deer and boar and the driver warned them that they might be disturbed and they did, indeed, once see through the trees, a roe deer being pursued by huntsmen. They huddled nervously together keeping as quiet as possible, only little Jean's cough breaking the silence, but the huntsmen passed by some way in the distance and they were unnoticed.

'We are close to the port of La Tremblade now,' said the driver, 'And we should lay our plans carefully for we must assume the good folk of the town will not allow us entry by night so we must go in during the day.'

Sara looked towards the cart. 'I believe you said you have some goods to sell?'

He nodded. 'Your brother in law gave me a supply of sundry goods. If we are questioned, I will say that I am to trade them with the townsfolk while we are here to visit your sick relative.'

'Jacob has, indeed, thought of everything,' said Sara. 'Let us pray that we do not have to resort to falsehoods.'

'Better to lie than to die.'

'Is it?' said Sara quietly. 'We are surely in this predicament for the very reason that we have refused to lie.'

The driver smiled. 'You are a woman of great courage and strong faith, Madame.'

They spent that night in the forest and set out early the next morning for the little port town of La Tremblade. They were a bedraggled party. Jean's cough had not improved and, though they tempted him with the best of the food they had procured, he refused it.

'You must eat,' urged Sara, but Jean shook his head. Sara put a hand to his brow and whispered to Lidie. 'He is burning up. Let us pray that this good citizen of the town is ready to help us.' She put her arms round Jean's frail body; he had set out on the journey a plump healthy lad and now he was but skin and bones, his eyes staring with fever.

'You remember the name of the man and where he lodges?' she asked Lidie.

Lidie nodded. 'It is burnt into my brain.'

As they left the protection of the trees and came out onto the track which led up to the road, they blinked in the bright sunlight. In the distance, on their left hand side, they had a glimpse of the ocean beyond sandy dunes. The driver pointed towards the sea.

'I believe you are to board from the sands,' he said.

'How so?' asked Sara. 'A large vessel could not come into shore.'

The man shrugged. 'No doubt your contact in the town will tell you more,' he said. 'But I imagine that the English vessel will anchor some way out and that you'll be conveyed to it in some small craft.'

'So we are not to leave from the port itself?'

Lidie stirred herself from her reverie. 'It would be too dangerous, Mama,' she said. 'Remember what Jacob told us. Even the smallest ports are patrolled and any soldiers will be paid several pistoles for finding a Huguenot boarding a vessel.'

They were silent for a while as the patient horse plodded along the road.

'I thank God the horse has not gone lame on this long journey,' said the driver. 'He has served us well.'

'Indeed,' said Sara. She looked down at Jean, the little boy who loved animals above all else, who was still cradled in her arms.'

'Did you hear that, Jean?' she asked softly. 'Our patient horse has not once let us down since we have been travelling.'

Jean moved his head listlessly to look up at the animal trotting ahead between the shafts of the cart.

It was late afternoon when at last they reached La Tremblade. Elias looked about him but said little, Jean was asleep in his grandmother's arms, a feverish, restless sleep, but Esther was fretful and crying.

Sara tried to hush her, drawing her attention to the activity on the road and in the fields beyond but she wouldn't be consoled until, at last, Lidie picked her up and found a scrap of silk material which she had secreted in one of her pockets. She handed it to Esther who ceased her crying and began to stroke it with her fingers.

Lidie smiled. It was a brief and tentative smile, but Sara saw it and rejoiced.

'Just like her Mama,' she said. 'She loves her silks.'

For a long moment, Lidie held her mother's gaze while they both remembered that time of innocence when Lidie had danced with Samuel on her sixteenth anniversary.

And then they rounded a bend and the town of Tremblade lay before them in the distance where the land was flat and marshy.

It was a small port town and they were soon absorbed into the traffic of the bustling streets. Furtively, Lidie looked around her and noted that their party did not look so different from many others. Being a port, albeit a small one, people of every sort thronged the streets.

Lidie had told the driver the name of the street. They found it quite easily and drew up outside what was obviously the house of a merchant. Although it looked reasonably well appointed, it was in no way grand and they were glad. They wanted to be able to rest somewhere simple and melt into the fabric of the town.

The driver dropped the reins, got down stiffly from his seat at the front of the cart, and climbed up the steps to the front door where he raised the knocker and let it fall heavily onto the solid wood.

Almost immediately, the door was opened, just a crack, and a man's face looked out. Before speaking, he glanced up and down the street and then addressed them in a low voice.

'Come in quickly,' he said.

'We have come from …' began the driver, but the man waved his hand impatiently.

'I know who you are,' he said. 'Quickly, unload your bags then take the horse and cart down the side street to the back. You'll find stabling there.'

He ushered Sara, Lidie and the children inside the house then started to help the driver unload their bundles from the cart. As soon as this was done he came inside the house himself, closing the front door firmly behind him, having glanced up and down the street once more.

All of them were dishevelled and stumbling in their fatigue, the children looking about them, wide eyed.

'Sir,' said Lidie, 'We thank you from the bottom of our hearts.'

'Indeed,' said Sara. 'You are generous to give us shelter.'

The merchant seemed to be alone in the vestibule and there was no sign of a servant to help them with their luggage. He nodded to them, his eyes darting from one to the other.

'Come with me and I will show you to your rooms.' He started to pick up some of their bundles and Sara and Lidie took the rest.

As he mounted the stairs, he turned to them. 'You may sleep in the attic rooms,' he said. 'It is cramped but it will be more discreet.'

They dragged themselves up the stairs behind him and even Elias had a bundle in his arms though he was weak with exhaustion.

'An attic room, sir, will be luxury indeed,' said Sara. 'We have been hiding in woods and farm buildings these last days.'

'It is shameful that you should have to hide like hunted animals,' he said.

When he had shown them to their quarters which were two small attic rooms with one bed in each, Lidie said to him.

'We would dearly love some water, sir, to clean ourselves and the children. Is that possible?'

He frowned. 'Yes, forgive me. I only have one servant here. There is none else in the house with me.' He hesitated and ran his hand through his thinning hair. 'Since I have been hiding those of our faith in the house … the risk.'

'We understand,' said Lidie. '

'I will ask my servant to bring water,' he said. And when you are ready we will have a simple meal.'

'You are doing God's work,' said Sara.

The man looked down at the floor. 'In my heart, Madame, I am a true to the Word of God but it became impossible …'

'You do not have to explain yourself to us, sir,' said Lidie.

The merchant nodded. 'I will go and arrange water,' he said. 'And show your driver where he can sleep. There is room above the stable.'

'Without him, we would have been lost,' said Sara. 'I hope you will invite him to eat with us?'

The man nodded again and then scuttled away.

'He is very nervous,' Lidie whispered to Sara as she began to strip off the children's filthy clothes.

'Who can blame the poor man,' said Sara.

In the days that followed, the little party gradually recovered from their travels, cleaning themselves up as best they could and having regular food and sleep.

All except Jean, whose fever continued. Lidie spoke to the merchant who sent out to the apothecary for the remedies that she requested, but nothing seemed to help the little boy and Lidie spent a good deal of her time sitting by him, wiping his brow with a cool cloth and trying to get him to take nourishment.

Sometimes he seemed to rally and she and Sara thanked God, but then he would slip back into a delirium, tossing in his bed, consumed by fever.

Meanwhile, their driver went down to the port most days to hear news of ships expected and while he was there, trading some of the goods he had brought with him, he got into conversation with some of the local fishermen. While they were eating together one evening, he asked the merchant about these men.

'They seem very friendly towards me,' he said. 'Do they sympathise with our cause?'

The merchant nodded. 'The curé here worries for their souls for they pay scant regard to religious belief of any kind though they pay lip service to the Catholic faith and attend Mass, but they are a rough bunch and our curé is a sensitive fellow and he is more interested in ministering to his own kind and rooting out Huguenots than preaching to the likes of the fisher folk.'

'Then might the fishermen help us?' asked Lidie.

The merchant nodded. 'When we have news that your ship has arrived, I can find a fisherman to take you to the vessel. The fishermen have no love for the curé and most of them have sympathy for those trying to flee from persecution. If you can pay them, they will probably help you.'

The days wore on and still there was no news of their ship. Each morning, their driver would set out for the port for news and come back shaking his head.

'I dare not ask for too much information for fear of raising suspicions,' he said.

Sara turned to the merchant. 'The longer we stay here, the more danger you are in, sir,' she said.

The merchant did not answer immediately, crumbling the bread in front of him and staring down at the table. Then he said something which took them all by surprise.

He cleared his throat. 'I fear I must ask you to leave,' he said, mumbling into his beard.

Lidie's head shot up. 'Leave sir? When?'

The merchant stroked his beard. Still he did not meet her eyes. 'I have heard rumours that I am under suspicion,' he said. 'I am fearful that my house may be searched.'

They all stared at him then and he continued. 'If they find that I have been harbouring Huguenots under my roof at the very least I shall be fined and my property confiscated.' He swallowed. 'For your own sakes, and mine, you should go as soon as possible.'

'But sir, where should we go? We have still heard nothing of the arrival of the vessel even though it has been expected for days.'

The man slammed his fist on the table, startling them all. 'I have already damned my own soul to save my property,' he shouted. 'I cannot now risk losing it to save yours.'

Sara, Lidie and the driver sat in shocked silence. The driver was the first to recover.

He stood up. 'I will go to the harbour immediately,' he said, 'And make discreet enquiries among the fishing folk. It may be that I can find someone to take us in.'

'Indeed,' said the merchant, plucking nervously at the lace collar at his neck. Then he said, more quietly, addressing Sara and Lidie, 'I am sorry, ladies, but if the soldiers come here and find you then we shall all be damned. You understand that do you not?'

Sara nodded. 'Of course,' she said, but her voice was weary. 'We shall leave as soon as we have gathered our belongings. We would not wish to put you in any danger.'

As Lidie and Sara set about repacking their clothes and few belongings into bundles, Lidie said. 'Do you believe him, Mama?'

Sara shrugged. 'We cannot blame him for wanting us away from his property if he has, indeed, heard these rumours.'

Lidie sniffed. 'In my opinion he finds having a family here a great trial, and would do even if there were no danger.'

They waited for the driver's return, the merchant pacing up and down and from time to time, opening the front door a crack and peering up and down the street.

'You should go immediately,' he said.

'Please sir,' said Sara. 'Just give us leave to wait until our driver returns. We will be less conspicuous if we are riding on the cart, do you not think, rather than walking the streets weighed down with our possessions?'

The merchant was in such a fright that he didn't answer but kept close to the front door listening out for any commotion outside.

At last their driver came back to the house. He was out of breath and it was clear that he had been running.

'Quick,' he said. 'Come round to the stables at the back. We should go immediately. I have found some kind fisher folk who will help us but they report that what the merchant has said is true. Even now, a magistrate and some soldiers are heading this way.'

The merchant wrung his hands. 'Go, go. Make haste I beg you.'

There was no time for thanks or farewells. Sara scooped up Jean, who was too weak to walk, and Lidie carried Esther in her arms. The driver harnessed the horse to the cart as quickly as he could and loaded them all on board.

'Do not come round to the front of the house again,' said the merchant, flapping his arms at them. 'Go down to the coast by the back way.'

'God bless you for your kindness sir,' said Sara, to his retreating figure. But he did not hear her and rushed through the back entrance, slamming the door behind him in his urgency to be rid of them.

As they set off once more, they heard a banging and a commotion coming from the front of the merchant's house and harsh commands from soldiers.

'Open up at once, in the name of the King. We have authority to search your property.'

258

They all looked back in terror and the driver hastily steered the cart down the nearest lane so that they were out of sight, then he twisted round.

'These lanes are very narrow,' he said. 'The cart may not get through them but we cannot use the main street.'

'God has preserved us thus far,' said Sara. 'We shall pray to Him to continue to protect us.'

Jean lay across her lap, still shuddering with fever, and she held him tightly and began to recite from the Bible and after a moment's hesitation, Lidie joined in. Esther was squirming and fretful beside her mother but Elias sat quietly with his head bowed.

Chapter Twenty-Six

They made some wrong turns and once they all had to dismount so that the driver could turn the cart round when one of the little streets became too narrow to get through, but at length they could see the harbour and hear the hustle and bustle and the shouts of those working there. The driver reined in the horse and pointed.

'The fishermen's cottages are further down the coast,' he said. 'Some way from the town. They tell me that their community is not much bothered by the magistrate or the curé.'

'Do the Catholics not consider their souls worth saving?' said Lidie.

The driver shrugged. 'They are a rough and independent lot,' he said. 'You do not get to wrestle with the tides and the winds without respecting your Maker, but they have no time for the fight between Catholics and Protestants. They are Catholic in name only but they have sympathy for those brave enough to stand up for their faith.'

For a while, they bumped along the road out of the little town, parallel with the coast, and then they dropped down a track and found themselves in the middle of a cluster of small, rough houses.

There were children running barefoot among the houses and men and women sitting outside, all busily employed, some mending nets, others putting tar on the bottom of an upturned boat and still others patching sails.

Further away, at the water's edge, there was a wooden jetty and it was clear that a catch had just been unloaded from a boat for there was a large group of women gutting the fish and then loading them into boxes.

As the cart approached, all the workers looked up briefly but then went back to their tasks. All except one woman, who tossed a gutted fish into a box, wiped her hands down her stained apron and climbed down the jetty onto the sand. She made her way over to them and she and the driver spoke together.

Then she turned to the others and her accent was so thick and guttural that they had the greatest difficulty in understanding her.

260

'Our cottage is that one there, at the end of the row,' she said, pointing. 'Unload quickly and put the cart round the back.'

Lidie nodded and Sara began to thank the woman but she held up her hand and smiled.

'You will find it simple, Madame,' she said, 'And you will be crowded together, but we are used to concealing Protestants. Not many set off these days. It is not like in '85 when all the ports were filled with those trying to flee.'

Then she turned to the driver. 'Make haste,' she said. 'Do not draw attention to yourselves. I'll be with you directly.'

She was right about the crowded conditions. The fisher family had several small children who regarded the visitors solemnly. Elias nodded to them but Esther just stared at them and Jean was too feverish to notice them. The fisherman's wife showed them a corner of the room downstairs where they could sleep and put some rough sacking down on the floor for them.

'I fear there's no room for you in the bedchamber,' she said. 'Our own family has but the one room.'

Lidie took her hand which was roughened with toil. 'Madame,' she said. 'We passed several days and nights sleeping in the forest. To have a roof over our head is a luxury. We cannot thank you enough for your kindness.' Then she looked around her at the sparse furniture and old cooking pans and cleared her throat. 'We have some coin and will pay for our lodging.'

The woman nodded. 'I will not refuse,' she said shortly. Then she looked at Jean.

'What ails him?' she asked.

Lidie shook her head. 'He suffered from being exposed to the elements when we were travelling,' she said. 'He still coughs and cannot throw off this fever.'

The woman looked at him for a moment longer and then turned her head away. Lidie felt a sudden stab of fear.

When the fisherman himself came in towards evening, he greeted them all warmly and asked if arrangements had been made to take them across the sea.

ROSEMARY HAYES

Sara mentioned the name of the vessel and of the English Captain who Jacob had told them of and the fisherman stroked his beard.

'I had heard that it was delayed,' he said. 'But I believe it is due to anchor outside the port tomorrow morning.'

'Praise God,' said Lidie.

'Aye Ma'am, but do not praise Him until you are safely away. This last part of your journey will be the most dangerous.'

'Will they search the vessel?' asked Sara.

Lidie remembered Jacob's tales of Huguenots smoked out from the holds of ships and shivered.

'Aye. The vessel will not be allowed to leave until the Customs Officers have inspected it and there will be a pilot on board who will not be put off until the vessel is out to sea. It is only after she has weighed anchor and is on her way that it will be safe to board her.'

'Then how ...' began Lidie.

The fisherman raised his hand. 'You will get your instructions,' he said. 'I shall seek out the Captain once the ship is arrived and he will inform us of where he will head and I'll warrant, with the prevailing winds at this season, that he will offload the customs officials and the pilot at the extreme point of the Isle of Oléron and then once the visitors are out of sight she will slacken her speed so that a small boat can catch up with her.'

They all looked at him questioningly then.

'A small boat?' said Sara.

He smiled. 'I will take you. It is a journey I have made before.'

'But it is such a risk for you sir,' said Lidie.

He said nothing for a moment, then he cleared his throat. 'I should also warn you that the King's frigates still patrol this coast. If they spy an English vessel leaving they will hail it and go on board and search every last inch of it.'

'So even if we board safely, we still may be discovered?'

He nodded. 'Until you are out of French waters you will be at risk.'

'Also,' he went on. 'If you are discovered on my boat you will be shown no mercy. It will be as well to lie low in the bottom, concealed.'

'Then they would show no mercy to the boatman, either?'

'No.' He shifted in his seat and there was an awkward silence. 'Are you armed?' he asked.

Their driver nodded. 'I have a firearm,' he said, 'but I am not to come on this journey. My task is to see this family safely away and then to return to our town in the South.'

'So, neither of the ladies will be armed?'

Sara sighed. 'Even if we had a firearm, we would not know how to use it.'

'Then,' said the fisherman, 'You must pray to God for protection.'

'Indeed,' said Sara. Then she asked. 'Do you know of others who may be seeking safe passage on this vessel?'

He nodded. 'There are other Protestants hiding amongst us but it is better you are not seen together until you are safely on board the vessel.'

Then passed several anxious days. Sara and Lidie tried to make themselves useful patching sails and minding the children though, in truth, the children in the village ran freely from family to family and were given small tasks to do as soon as they could walk. They largely minded themselves.

'How different it is from the life we lived in Castillon,' said Lidie, watching Elias hovering at the fringes of a crowd of village children, unsure and silent.

'I'd trust these families a deal more than that merchant in the town,' said Sara. 'They are generous and welcoming and only see a family in trouble.'

'The merchant was under great strain, too, Mama,' said Lidie. 'He was not obliged to take us in.'

Sara nodded. 'I know. And I have examined my conscience to consider whether we would have opened our doors in the way he did.'

They continued with their work for a while, then Lidie glanced over at Jean who was asleep, lying in the corner of the room, the

263

rattling in his thin chest audible even over the hubbub of noise outside the cottage.

'I pray constantly that he will survive.'

Sara stopped her work and knelt beside Lidie. 'We can do no more for him,' she said. 'His life is in God's hands.'

'Do you think that Samuel is looking down on him, Mama?'

'Of course. I am certain that the dear man is with God, there is no doubt of it, and if the worst happens and little Jean does not survive this fever, then you can be sure he will go straight to his papa.' She sighed. 'Samuel would be so proud of you, Lidie.'

Lidie swallowed. 'I keep thinking of the way of his death.'

'I, too. But we must care for the living, now.'

'What must Isaac be thinking. We have abandoned him to his grief and to face reprisals.'

'He is sure in his faith, Lidie. Whatever befalls him, it will sustain him, of that I have no doubt.'

'But to know that both his children abjured after all he has suffered because of it.'

'Who is to know what we would do if we were subject to …' Sara looked down at the bare earthen floor of the cottage and did not finish her sentence.'

Then she went on. 'Jacob may be a man of great wealth and influence but I know that his abjuration cost him dear. I was so angry with him when he signed those papers, but since then I have had to look deep into my own conscience and question my reaction. If he had not abjured, then how many livelihoods would have been put at risk? Our land would have been confiscated if he had not taken it over. In truth we have benefitted from that abjuration.''

'Poor Uncle Jacob,' said Lidie.

'And my beloved sister. She feels their abjuration even more keenly. It is a wretched business. We can only pray that we shall survive the journey ahead of us and be able to start afresh.'

'If we can but put to sea,' muttered Lidie.

That evening, the fisherman came back from the harbour with news for them.

THE KING'S COMMAND

'I have spoken with the Captain of the English vessel,' he said. 'And he has asked me to pass on his instructions.' He cleared his throat and looked directly at Lidie.

'He impressed on me the risk. He said again and again, that if there was any trouble he would be obliged to set sail without you, but that he plans to leave the day after tomorrow and will pass between the islands of Ré and Oléron and if you would put to sea in a small craft in the vicinity then he would take you on board after he had got rid of the pilot and the customs men, but that he cannot assist you in any other way.'

The fisherman rubbed his chin. 'It seems to me a sensible plan,' he said. 'You will be obliged to travel further down the coast under cover of darkness and wait the next day on the sands near the Forest of Arvert.'

'We became quite accustomed to travelling by night on our journey to La Tremblade, sir,' said Lidie. That will be of little matter.'

'It will be essential, Madame, for you will have to pass the pinnacles where guards are posted and the fort of Oléron, which is heavily guarded. If you travelled by day you might well arouse suspicion.' Then he went on, frowning. 'It would not be wise to take your cart down onto the sands there for it would hold you up should you be pursued and could become bogged in the dunes.'

Sara and Lidie exchanged a glance. If they were pursued, they would not evade capture, encumbered by their baggage and the children.

The fisherman stood up and stretched. 'I will sail down the coast in my boat early in the morning and set my nets not far from the sands. My presence should not arouse any suspicion and you will be able to conceal yourselves in the trees behind the dunes while you await my arrival.'

Then he stood up and headed out of the cottage, turning back at the door,

'The English Captain set a rate of ten pistoles per person,' he said. 'It is a high price but then he is risking much. Will that be acceptable?'

'Of course,' said Sara quickly. 'We are in no position to bargain and we have coin for just such an eventuality.'

When he had left them, Lidie spoke to the fisherman's wife. 'Your family has been so kind to us. We should have been captured and imprisoned already if you had not taken us in, and now, your husband is to put himself at risk for us.'

'We may live roughly, Madame, without airs and graces, but we do not like to see injustice. And you were wise to come this far. Not many Huguenots escape from this coast now, so the scrutiny is not so tight, though the King's frigates do pass by from time to time.'

As they huddled together on the floor of the cottage that night, the children curled around them and Jean's chest heaving with effort and his breath yet more shallow, Lidie touched Sara's arm and whispered. 'By the day after tomorrow, then, our fate will be sealed. Either we shall be taken aboard by the English Captain or we shall be captured.'

'Pray with me, Lidie,' Sara whispered back. 'Pray more earnestly than you have ever done.'

They prayed deep into the night until eventually they fell into an exhausted sleep.

When they woke, Lidie felt extraordinarily calm.

Whatever it is You have set out for my future path in life, Lord, I shall accept it even if be death.

This mood of acceptance of her fate continued with Lidie all day and was even upon her when they set off after dark, having bid farewell to the fisherman's wife, pressed more coin upon her and thanked her warmly for her hospitality.

'There is such goodness in this world,' said Sara, as they jogged along the coast road.

'Aye,' said the driver. 'And we must thank God for it.'

Lidie leaned forward. 'And we must thank God for your loyalty, too. Without you we should have been lost.'

He didn't answer but Lidie could tell that he was thinking what she was thinking. They were so near to their departure for England now and yet, this was where they could encounter the most danger. Here they could so easily fail at the last obstacle in their way.

Esther was whining and fretful and Sara and Lidie took turns to rock her and sing quietly to her until at last she slept. Elias, as always, was quiet and thoughtful and Jean's fever seemed to have left him for the moment and he lay quiet and still but Lidie could sense that he did not sleep. She felt his brow and it was cool and at first she rejoiced but then she turned to Sara.

'Can you feel his brow, Mama?'

'It is very cold,' said Sara, and she took off her shawl and tucked it round him, then she stretched out and grasped Lidie's hand strongly in her own.

'He may …' she began, but Lidie interrupted. 'I know. And if it is God's will, then so be it.'

And for a moment, her thoughts turned to the pastor Pierre Gabriac, and his troubled wife. How many babes had they lost?

'I rejoice that your faith has returned to you,' said Sara quietly.

'I admit that it wavered when Samuel was taken from me, but if I do not have faith now, then for what are we doing this?'

Sara squeezed Lidie's hand.

After that, they were all quiet, conscious that they were drawing close to the fort of Oléron on the coast opposite. By this time, the driver had extinguished the lantern and trusted to the surefootedness of the horse which had slowed down to a walk, his hooves were almost soundless on the turf beneath them.

Dawn was streaking the sky when at last they reached the cover of trees, part of the forest of Arvert which fringed the sand dunes, and they were soon hidden from view. They unloaded their baggage from the cart and took a little refreshment.

'It is as if we were again on the road travelling to La Tremblade,' said Lidie.

'Aye,' said the driver. 'And, again, we shall be waiting, I warrant, for most of the day here.'

'Were you given any idea of when the vessel might appear?' asked Sara.

The man shrugged. 'It will set sail once the Customs people and the pilot have disembarked, but there is no telling when that will be. I will go down to the sands and keep watch. The fisherman told me he would leave at first light to sail down the coast and he has agreed a signal with the English Captain.'

The driver walked off to take up a position where he could see when the fishing boat arrived, and the family settled down to wait in the forest. Elias sat down with his back against the wheels of the cart, twisting a stalk of grass in his hands and Esther ran hither and thither, a bundle of energy, and when either Lidie or Sara tried to restrain her joyful shouts, she ran away from them, shrieking even louder.

At length they quietened her and is was then that they heard something else. The snort of a horse.

It was not their own horse. Lidie and Sara locked eyes then Lidie picked up Esther and Sara gently moved Jean to beneath the cart and beckoned to Elias to crawl in beside him. They all huddled there and even Esther, sensing the fear in her mother, stopped resisting and fell silent.

Chapter Twenty-Seven

There was another snort, closer now, and the soft thud of hooves and the jingle of harness.

A party of three people on horseback were approaching slowly but steadily towards them on the same broad path they had followed which wound through the trees.

Lidie held Esther tightly to her breast and looked over her head towards Elias.

'Keep quiet my love,' she whispered.

They hardly dared to breathe as the horses approached. The riders were strangely silent. There was no exchange of remarks between them even though they were riding so closely together, but then the front horseman drew rein and pointed.

Lidie mouthed a silent prayer.

Then Esther started to whimper and the front horseman drew closer and leant down, peering beneath the cart. Lidie held the little girl even more tightly and met the man's eyes. He looked startled and sat back in his saddle, turning to the rider behind him and saying something in a low voice.

There was no noise in the forest except the birdsong and the distant murmur of the sea. Then, very slowly, one of the other riders dismounted, handed the reins of his horse to the man at the front, and approached the cart. He dropped to all fours.

He addressed Lidie. 'From whom do you hide Madame?' he said and as she heard the note of fear in his voice, she felt a tiny flicker of hope within her. She said nothing, not wishing to identify herself, wanting him to speak again first.

'Are you Protestants?' he asked.

'Are you?'

And then his face broke into a smile. 'Aye,' he said.

Lidie was shaking as she crawled out from under the cart and stood up, still clutching Esther. She put the child down and held out her hand.

'Then we are well met,' she said.

The man introduced himself as Louis Boisson, travelling with a guide and accompanied by his wife Elizabeth.

At first, conversation between the two parties was stilted, but after a while, trust was established and Louis told Sara and Lidie of their experiences.

'I am a Master Silk Weaver,' he said, 'And we hail from Lyon.'

'Lyon!' said Sara. 'Then you are indeed far from home!'

Elizabeth sighed. 'That is the truth,' she said. 'Our family managed to get to England some years ago but we stayed to try and continue in our work.'

'A foolish move, as it happened,' said Louis. 'My journeymen either fled or abjured and I could do no business with all the restrictions placed upon me. I could see that our lives would become impossible.'

'So, you did not abjure?'

'Never,' said Elizabeth. 'But we have been trying to leave this last year. We had hoped to escape from Geneva but we nearly perished in the mountain pass, then we were betrayed and pursued. Since then we have wandered far and near, staying with fellow Reformists and trying to find safe passage.'

'Lyon is so far from the sea,' said Lidie. 'You must have travelled far.'

'Aye. We were nearly captured at another port and then we heard through contacts that the coast near La Tremblade was less heavily guarded.'

'We, are only here through the good offices of others,' said Lidie. 'With the help of our relations and the kindness of the fishermen and their wives.'

'Thank God we had with us a supply of méreau coins,' said Louis. 'We had to show them to those brethren we did not know as proof that we were genuine Reformists.'

Lidie looked at her mother and knew that they were both remembering the moment when Pierre Gabriac had given them méreau coins before he had been forced to flee to England.

Sara nodded. 'We have some with us, too,' she said. 'But as yet we have had no need of them. We simply mentioned the name of my brother-in-law to the merchant in La Tremblade and he was satisfied.'

Louis nodded. 'We showed one to the fishing family who have been hiding us in their cottage these past few days but they laughed and waved it away, saying that it was clear who we were.'

He lowered his voice then and tugged at his beard. 'God willing, we are to board an English vessel later today.'

'Then we shall travel together,' said Sara.

'That is good news indeed, Madame.'

'If only we can manage to do so without detection,' said Lidie.

The four of them then prayed together for God's help and guidance in the dangerous hours ahead and it was when they were at prayer that their driver came back.

Louis immediately sought his weapon to challenge the man, but Sara reassured him.

'Sir, this is our driver. He has been our constant companion and saviour. He has been at lookout on the sands.'

When he had recovered his composure, the driver told them that there were now two fishing boats on the water, the boatman of one was their host but he did not recognize the other; however, they seemed to be acquainted.

'God be praised,' said Louis. 'Then that should be our boatman come, too.' He turned to their guide who had returned to their side having loosed the horses.

'I'd be obliged if you could ascertain that it is indeed he at the helm of the other fishing boat,' he said. The man nodded and set off.

While they were waiting for him to return, Louis told them that he had heard that the forest of Arvert was often the site of secret Huguenot meetings.

'Our fishermen friends told us of many arrests at the port over the years but also of escapes from these sands. We must pray that these closely packed trees can aid our own escape as they have helped others.'

'And given shelter to the faithful, meeting and praying together,' said Sara. 'What tales these trees could tell if they could speak!'

'Indeed,' said Elizabeth.

When the Boisson's guide returned he brought news that the other fishing boat did, indeed, belong to their contact and that he had urged the guide to get both parties down to the shore as soon as possible.

'There is no soul in sight on the beach. It is a good moment to get on board the fishing boats.'

'Will we take the horses?' asked Elizabeth.

The guide shook his head. 'The sand is very soft and there are many dunes. It would be quicker if we handle the luggage ourselves.'

'We shall set about it immediately,' said Louis.

It took several trips back and forth, through the dunes and shifting sand, from the edge of the forest to the water and even little Elias staggered to and fro with bundles to place in the boat. All of them kept a sharp lookout for any other folk on the beach but there was no sign of anyone except the men in the two fishing boats who had come into shore and were waiting for them.

At last Lidie and Sara and the children and all their baggage, were in the fishing shallop with their fisherman friend at the helm and Louis and Elizabeth were in the other. The guide and their driver helped to push the boats out into the waves and there was hardly time for the heartfelt thanks, farewells and blessings as the two men made their way swiftly back to the shelter of the trees. Lidie watched them until they disappeared from sight.

We shall never see our driver again, yet we owe him everything.

The fisherman hoisted the sail and they crested the gentle waves at the edge of the ocean before heading out further.

When he had set the sail, he turned to Sara. 'I fear, Madame, that you will not be comfortable while we wait, and if there are any other vessels about, or if we see any person on the sands, then I shall be obliged to ask you to lie still in the bottom of the boat and cover yourselves.'

'We shall do exactly as you say,' replied Sara. 'You are putting your life at risk on our behalf.' She grasped the edge of the boat as it lurched suddenly. 'But I beg you to save yourself if we are captured.'

272

'If that should happen, then it will be everyone for themselves, Madame.'

It was not long before they lost sight of the other boat and Lidie prayed that Elizabeth and Louis were safe and that they would in due course be reunited with them.

As they came in sight of the fort at the bottom of the Isle of Oléron, the fisherman obliged them to lie in the bottom of the little boat while he flung some nets over them until they had safely rounded the end of the island and were heading up its coast on the further side. And then at last they could see in the distance a large vessel anchored at the furthest point of the island.

'Is that the English vessel?' asked Lidie and when the fisherman nodded, she and Sara immediately began to recite a psalm of praise. Their joy was short-lived, however, as it was clear, even from a distance, that the pilot and the official visitors were still on board, for their boat was still alongside.

The fisherman lowered his sail and then immediately hoisted it again before dropping it once more.

'Is that the signal,' asked Sara.

He nodded. 'They should respond by lowering the mizzen sail twice.'

But there was no response from the English vessel.

'They will not risk giving us the signal while the visitors are still on board,' he said. He rubbed his chin nervously. 'But I'll wager they will soon be putting them off.'

He was proved right and shortly after this they saw the pilot and the customs men being put off the vessel and watched as they sailed off back towards La Rochelle. The fisherman waited until they were out of sight and when he saw the mizzen sail of the English vessel lowered and dropped, lowered and dropped, he immediately put up his sail and headed towards it.

Their progress towards the English ship in the open sea was slow and unpleasant as the swell of the ocean and the stink of fish made the children vomit, though Jean was too weak to spew anything up into the sea and Lidie gently wiped bile from his mouth.

Esther was the sickest of all of them. Mercifully, when she had emptied her stomach, she moaned and writhed in the bottom of the boat but eventually fell into an exhausted sleep.

They were very exposed now in their little fishing boat, far out to sea and away from any place where they could safely anchor. The swell was constant and they were frequently faced by a great wall of water which threatened to engulf them until, at the last moment, the boat climbed atop it and then slid down the other side.

Sea water constantly soaked them and Elias sat shivering in the bottom of the boat. He shifted closer to Lidie. 'Are we going to drown, Mama?' he asked.

Lidie didn't answer but Sara said. 'We will trust in God to preserve us.'

'Is God bigger than the sea,' asked Elias.

'He is greater than everything on the earth,' replied Sara, but Lidie could hear the terror in her voice.

The English vessel was still off the island and they were getting ever closer to it. They could even see sailors on board hauling up the anchor.

'Not much further,' shouted the fisherman, as the little boat was tossed about in the contrary winds.

Lidie saw how the man was struggling to keep the shallop on course and she thanked God for his bravery and constancy.

So many good people have risked themselves for us.

The afternoon was wearing on and the sun was already sinking down to the West when, for a moment, Lidie took her eyes off the English vessel ahead and looked towards the horizon.

It was just a smudge and at first she thought she had imagined it. Surely it was only a low cloud or the top of a distant wave? She rubbed her eyes.

I am overwrought and bone weary. My mind is so confused that I am imagining things.

But when she looked again, it was still there.

The fisherman was fully engaged in keeping the boat on course, fighting with the wind and the waves. Lidie moved over to him and tugged on his arm to get his attention, shouting a warning, but the wind snatched away her words, so she pointed.

Then, at last, he turned his head and looked in the direction of her finger.

'Merciful Christ,' he muttered and immediately began to alter course, going about so abruptly that the party was pitched from one side to the other.

Sara had not heard the man's words but she saw the look on Lidie's face and raised her eyes to scan the horizon. What had been a mere smudge only minutes ago was clearly defined now as a ship and it was heading in their direction.

'What vessel is it?'

The fisherman didn't answer so Lidie once again tugged on his arm.

He yelled over his shoulder. 'It is one of the King's frigates. Hide yourselves, for pity's sake. Cover yourselves with the old sails in the bulkhead. Hurry or we shall all be taken.'

Lidie cast her eyes back to the English vessel, still at the far point of the island, becoming smaller now as they sailed away from it.

We were so close to the promise of safe passage.

But now the fisherman was heading his craft in the direction of La Rochelle.

'Hide!' he shouted.

Sara and Lidie crawled around in the bottom of the boat, pulling some old sails out of the bulkhead. The children watched them; Esther was awake now and whimpering and little Jean was shaking with fever. Only Elias was still, his fists clenched.

'We shall all lie under the sails and see how quiet we can be,' said Lidie trying to keep her voice steady as she and Sara pulled the children down and started to cover them, but Esther immediately shrieked in protest and fought to free herself.

Then, as her screams grew in intensity, Elias grabbed her arm and shook her. 'Be quiet Esther,' he hissed. 'Stop your noise!'

The child was so taken aback by the fury in her brother's words that she ceased her screaming and sobbed quietly, her thumb wedged in her mouth.

When they were all covered by the sails, Lidie spread her arms so that each of her three children could feel her touch.

'Lie as still as stones, my darlings,' she said. 'Make no sound, I beg you. If you cry out we shall be discovered.'

There was no chance that they could outpace the oncoming frigate. The fisherman knew this and took no avoiding action, indeed he sailed deliberately towards it. For an age, while the frigate drew ever closer, the little party lay still at the bottom of the boat and then, as their teeth chattered with the cold and sea water swirled around their bodies, they heard the frigate hailing them.

'Whence are you bound?' came the shout over the water.

The fisherman glanced down at his firearm.

'Whence are you bound?'

'I got into difficulties Sir,' shouted the fisherman. 'I am from La Tremblade but the wind is contrary now and I will not get back before nightfall, so I am heading for La Rochelle.'

'A wise decision. The wind will be with you all the way. What have you on board?'

'Just ballast,' he replied. 'This little craft is tender in these waters. I need it well weighted.'

'God speed, then. We will go and board that English vessel at anchor by the island and search if for any accursed Huguenots.'

'It has just put off the pilot and the customs men,' said the fisherman. 'No doubt they will have searched it well. It is even now preparing to set sail again.'

'You saw the pilot and customs men leave?'

'Aye, just now. Did you not pass them?'

'We did see a boat heading across our bows.'

'It would have been them.'

'Thank you, my man. You have saved us a tedious job. If they have just left then we need not search the vessel. They will have made sure there are no traitors aboard.'

There was silence then and the party at the bottom of the boat heard the sails crack as the wind filled them and they were on the move again.

Eventually, after they had been moving through the water at a steady pace for some time, Lidie risked raising the sailcloth and crawling out. She peered over the edge of the boat and looked about her.

'Are they gone?' she asked the fisherman.

At first he did not hear her so she repeated the question, more loudly.

He turned back then. 'They are only just out of sight,' he said. 'In a few more minutes I will change course and head back towards the island.'

'Thank God for your presence of mind,' said Lidie.

The fisherman risked a glance in her direction. 'I just pray that the English vessel will not have already sailed away.' He gave her a quick smile. 'But we have come thus far and I shall not give up now.'

And at that, he went about and Lidie was thrown back onto the bottom of the boat.

Thereafter, their progress was slow as they had to make their way back towards the island, against the wind. It was getting late and it was already twilight as they approached the island.

The English vessel had rounded the far point and anchored once more and as they drew closer they saw another little shallop alongside it.

'That is the boat of my friend,' said the fisherman, 'with the weaver and his wife on board. It looks as though they are being taken up now.'

'Thank the Lord,' breathed Lidie.

It was nearly dark when at last they came alongside the vessel. A rope ladder was immediately lowered and the party, all stiff with cold, damp and fatigue, began to transfer their baggage, and themselves, on board.

They were greeted by the Captain, a large Englishman with a fiery red beard who frowned at them and spoke to them in his own tongue.

Lidie and Sara indicated their thanks but it was obvious, from the man's gestures, that he was demanding payment before he would let them further, so they handed it over at once, not wanting to antagonize him. As the fisherman brought up the last of their baggage, Sara asked him. 'Can you return home tonight?'

He shook his head. 'No. My friend and I will anchor in the lee of the island and set sail back to Tremblade at first light. And I imagine that you will be here until dawn, too.'

Sara pressed some coin into his hand. 'But you have already paid me,' he protested.

'I would that I could give you more,' said Sara. 'For you have saved us from certain imprisonment.'

He took her hands in his. 'God speed, Madame. I pray that you will have an untroubled voyage to England.'

Louis and Elizabeth joined them and they all watched as he climbed down the ladder and back into his boat, hoist the sail again and make his way to a safe anchorage on the island. Then they followed the Captain down to the hold where he showed them where they could stow away.

Chapter Twenty-Eight

London, Spring 1691

Pierre Gabriac came out of the great temple in Threadneedle Street. He paused before turning down the cobbled street towards his lodgings, marvelling, as he had so many times, at the industry which had led to the temple being rebuilt, by Huguenot hands, in only three years, after the great fire of London in 1666. The temple dominated the street with its great circular windows and he continued to stare at it, lost in thought, oblivious to the shouts around him from street hawkers selling all manner of goods - from mops to oysters - and the clatter of horses' hooves which were background to the hacking cough of a young street sweeper who stood beside him at the street crossing, bending over his broom.

He took his time, walking slowly towards home, observing the life around him, a jumble of tradesmen at work in their shops, making all kinds of goods. There were shoemakers, tailors, saddlers, glovers and nearer the river, chandlers with supplies for both the trading ships that docked at the wharves and the smaller vessels that crossed and re-crossed the great river, ferrying folk from side to side and up and down its waters. This part of London had been badly affected by the great fire and indeed Pierre's lodgings were only a few streets away from Pudding Lane, hard by the river, where the fire had started. Many of the original buildings had been destroyed, the fire spreading fast from one timber house to the next, and there had been much clearance and rebuilding since that time.

So many Protestant pastors had arrived in the city in 1685 when Louis had exiled them from France, and many had converged on this part of the city where they already had contacts among the established French population. Pierre had found lodgings near the river, hoping that this might ease Hannah's soul and remind her of Castillon but nothing calmed her and if it had not been for the kindness of his fellow Huguenots, he wondered if he, too, would not have lost his wits in an effort to help her.

However, he counted himself blest. He was free from persecution, he was doing God's work and, like many of his compatriots, he had taken on some tutoring. The English nobility had an appetite not only for French fashions but also for learning the French language, and now that he had acquired a good knowledge of English, there was much demand for his services.

Today, though, even Hannah's plight was not at the forefront of his mind. Rather it was concern for those left behind in Castillon and he was covered in guilt that he had not thought of them more often as his own life became busier.

Today he had been given a sharp reminder of their fate. He had received a letter from Jacob informing him of Samuel's death and that Lidie, Sara and the children had fled from Castillon. Jacob had also given him the name of the vessel on which he hoped they would sail across to England. Pierre noted with relief that the seal on the letter had not been broken so, by God's grace, the plan was not known to any Catholic spies in France.

He had received many communications from his native land and sometimes it was obvious that they had been intercepted and read, so his correspondents knew to write only in the most general terms and not to criticize the King or his Catholic enforcers. This letter, though, was different, and he guessed that Jacob had given it to a sea captain of his acquaintance, to be conveyed through other trusted hands.

He had nearly reached his lodgings but then he hesitated for a moment, changed direction and headed down to the river. He stood on its banks, his hands thrust into the pockets of his black coat, and stared out across the water.

The tide was out and there was a huge expanse of brown evil smelling mud before him. The river traffic was as busy as ever and the screeching of gulls quarrelling over the rotting detritus, as raucous, but his mind was too occupied to observe his surroundings in any detail. He felt in the pocket of his coat, drew out the letter and re-read it. Jacob had given only the barest details and though he had made no mention of it in the letter, Pierre knew that he was being asked to give what help he could to Lidie and Sara.

If, indeed, they reached England safely.

And if they did not? Pierre felt a clutch of fear in his gut, the sort of fear he had not experienced these past five years.

Jacob had said nothing of the details of Samuel's death but Pierre doubted it had been from natural causes and the fact that Lidie and Sara had fled immediately suggested that they, too, had feared for their lives.

Carefully, Pierre refolded the letter and replaced it in his pocket, his thoughts   returning to Castillon. How easy his own life had been in comparison to theirs these past six years. How his heart ached for Lidie and her family. How cruel to have Samuel taken from them and then be forced to flee, always in fear of being discovered and imprisoned. He sighed and took a deep breath of the briny air. Jacob had not mentioned the port of embarkation, only the name of the vessel, but it should be easy enough to find out when she was likely to arrive in England, and where. He would make enquiries directly. For all he knew, the family had already arrived and he would make it his business to welcome them.

Suddenly resolved, he turned left alongside the river and strode towards London Bridge. He would make enquiries at the docks on the West bank.

The evening was well advanced by the time Pierre mounted the stairs to his lodgings and opened the door into the rooms he shared with Hannah and a young servant. The window in the main room faced West and the setting sun blazed into it, silhouetting Hannah's figure in her chair in the centre of the room, but she didn't rise to greet him or make any acknowledgement of his presence. The young servant girl came to the door and Pierre spoke to her, his voice low.

'How has she been today?' he asked, in English.

The girl pouted and shrugged her shoulders and, for a moment, Pierre was filled with irritation at her casual response, but then he bit back an angry reply and remembered that the girl was, after all, loyal, and it must be a dull task to mind a woman like Hannah who hardly spoke and, when she did, it was not in the girl's native tongue.

Pierre went over to Hannah. He knelt beside her chair and took her hands in his. Seeing that there was a piece of embroidery on the stool alongside the chair he picked it up.

'Have you been working on this?' he asked, his spirits rising at the thought of her taking an interest in anything, however trivial.

Hannah blinked and looked up at him. She shook her head slowly but she said nothing in reply and the brief flare of hope that Pierre had experienced immediately died.

Later, after they had eaten a simple potage and Hannah was settled in their chamber and the servant had gone to her little room above, Pierre took out the rough map that he'd been given. It had taken him some while to find the information he sought about the vessel carrying Lidie and Sara, and he was in a quandary. He had assumed that they would be on a ship which had left from Bordeaux and that it would dock at the port of London or if not here, then in Rochester or Dover, but he had learned that this vessel left from near La Tremblade and was likely to make landfall in the West of the country, at Appledore in the Bristol Channel, near Barnstaple.

Since his time in London, Pierre had only ventured out of the city to help oversee some of the work in building more French Protestant churches on the outskirts and, once or twice, he had travelled to Rochester to greet French refugees, so he had little knowledge of the geography of the rest of the country but he realised that for him to travel to Appledore would take many days - even weeks. And there was no knowing when the vessel would arrive or, indeed, if it had already arrived.

He had fully hoped to meet it and, if Lidie and Sara were on board, to greet them and escort them safely to London, but this would be a fool's errand.

Hannah was already asleep when he went into their bedchamber, hunched on one side of the bed so that she would not have to touch him. He watched her steady breathing for a while, hoping that at least her dreams were peaceful, and trying to remember how she was when they were first married though, in truth, that memory was fast slipping from his grasp. And then he thought of Lidie and Sara and of the occasion of Lidie's sixteenth anniversary when

Lidie was so full of joy and wonder and trying hard not to show vanity at how well she looked in her new silks.

He smiled as he blew out the candle and slipped into bed. No doubt that joy was but a faraway dream for her now, a terrified mother trying to get her family to safety.

God bless you Lidie and, in His great mercy, keep you and your family safe from harm until we meet again.

ROSEMARY HAYES

Chapter Twenty-Nine

Journeying

Had it not been for the companionship and comfort afforded to them by Louis and Elizabeth, Lidie and Sara wondered whether they would have survived the journey. There was precious little food on board for them, much of which was stale or putrid, but the Captain would not put into any French port for provisions as they sailed up the coast, for fear his fugitives would be discovered. Louis and Elizabeth shared their food with Lidie and Sara and the children and, as Louis had a good knowledge of the English tongue, they were able to communicate freely with their Captain, though his remarks were hardly informative.

He has little interest in our plight,' said Louis. 'Now that he has received our payment, we are just so much cargo to be conveyed to England like any other goods.'

'But he risked much,' said Sara. 'And if he can deliver us safely, that is all we can ask of him.'

Meanwhile, little Jean's condition had not improved. Either Lidie or Sara were constantly at his side trying to persuade him to swallow a little gruel but much of the time he was too weak to respond.

On the third evening, Sara put her arms round Lidie.

'He is slipping away,' she whispered. 'I have prayed so earnestly for a miracle but I fear we shall lose him.'

Lidie leant forward to stroke his forehead. 'To think, he was so lively only a few weeks' ago.'

'Perhaps, even now ..' began Sara, but Lidie cut her short.

'No, Mama. We both know that he is near the end.'

Sara bit her lip and held Lidie tightly to her. 'We shall not let him die alone.'

Both women were hollow eyed with exhaustion when, in the middle of the next day, little Jean finally gave up the fight. Lidie held his lifeless body to her, rocking it gently.

'No more pain and struggle, my darling,' she whispered.

284

THE KING'S COMMAND

Louis and Elizabeth took it upon themselves to occupy Esther while Sara and Lidie made a makeshift shroud from some sailcloth, weighted down with ballast that the Captain allowed them to take from the hold.

Elias stood between them as they recited psalms, their voices weak against the wind, as they hefted the little body over the side of the vessel and consigned it to the deep. As it disappeared from view, Lidie let out a great cry of anguish and crushed Elias to her breast.

'Where has he gone, Mama?' asked Elias.

Lidie could not speak but Sara answered him calmly. 'He has gone to join your papa, my darling,' she said.

'In heaven?'

'Most assuredly, in heaven.'

'Would that I could join them,' muttered Lidie, stumbling as she made her way down into the hold.

They all suffered from sea sickness and from lack of food and water and although the adults assumed that their suffering would come to an end, Esther cried constantly and would not be comforted. Elias withdrew into himself but the weight was falling off him and his eyes were unnaturally large in his face.

Louis kept them all informed of progress, speaking every day with the Captain.

After a few days, he told them that they were now in the open sea and heading to the English coast but shortly after this they encountered contrary winds and the Captain informed them that their arrival in Appledore would be further delayed.

'Did he say how much longer?' enquired Sara.

'Have courage, dear Madame,' replied Louis. 'We will make landfall in a few days' time. We have to round the very Western tip of England and then turn to go up the coast.'

'I wonder if we can hold fast for even that time,' Lidie whispered to Sara, looking at the gaunt faces of the children.

It was a further four days before they finally sailed into the wide river mouth on the morning tide and dropped anchor just outside the village of Appledore to which they were conveyed from the vessel by a small rowing boat, the crew going back and forth, making several journeys to get them safely on dry land. They were all so weak that they could hardly stand when they stepped out at the little harbour and were surrounded by a crowd of villagers.

Lidie was willing herself not to faint as the noise of chattering in an unfamiliar tongue came at her in unintelligible waves, but even without Louis' attempts to convey their needs, the good folk of Appledore were immediately offering them sustenance. Lidie did her best to convey her thanks through gestures and smiles.

The Captain was anxious to leave as soon as he had bought a few provisions, as he had business in Ireland and had already lost time on the journey, but he did indicate where they could stay and in due course, they were accommodated among the villagers and being shown such kindness that Lidie and Sara began to revive somewhat.

'Are we truly safe?' asked Sara, as the group huddled together on the stony beach.

'Aye,' said Elizabeth, 'It is hard to believe. How good it will be to be settled with our family in Spitalfields and to be able to rest and wear clean clothes.'

'Even in your plainest garb, you are elegant.'

Elizabeth sighed. 'One should not put value on such things but I confess that I long to wear silks again.'

Louis smiled. 'We still have another long journey ahead of us before you can think on that, my love!'

Sara and Lidie had discussed what they should do. At first, the thought of forcing themselves and the children to undertake yet another long journey had appalled Lidie and she had mooted the idea of settling somewhere nearby, but finally Sara and the others had dissuaded her.

'We know no-one here, Lidie,' said Sara. 'We need the support of our fellow Protestants in London. She put out her hand and stroked Lidie's cheek. 'For sure, the onward journey will be long, but we should not be in danger and then, when we reach London, we have many contacts there, including Pierre Gabriac. Pierre will help us settle, you can be sure of that.'

It took some time to persuade her but at length she was convinced that they should all journey on to London together.

THE KING'S COMMAND

It was agreed that they should first recover their strength after the ordeal of the last few weeks and, with the help of the folk of Appledore, they were gradually restored. Lidie watched Elias and Esther as their bodies filled out once more and they played among the children of the village. Sometimes, Esther would ask where Jean was and Lidie's answer was always the same.

'He is with Papa, my darling.'

Elias never asked, and Lidie knew that he understood. He had always been a solemn, thoughtful little boy and although he joined in with games and had striven to make himself understood to the village children, there were times when she saw him walk away from the noisy throng and find a quiet place.

It is too much for him, poor lamb. He idolized his papa.

Lidie voiced her fears about Elias one evening when they were all together, huddled in the downstairs room of one of the cottages.

'He is very young, Lidie,' said Elizabeth. 'And he has had such confusion in the past weeks, but the memories will fade.'

'I would not have him forget his papa or his brother,' said Lidie. 'We remember them every day in our morning and evening prayers and he repeats the prayers carefully.'

'Aye,' said Sara. 'Whatever befalls us, we shall continue to pray for their souls.' She smiled and straightened her coif. 'But little Esther …'

'Esther is at heart a cheerful soul,' said Lidie. 'She may mouth the prayers after me, but she has little understanding of what has happened.'

'And she loves her silks,' said Elizabeth, smiling. 'Every time I show her some of our samples, she strokes them and remarks on how pretty they are.' She leant across to Lidie and patted her arm. 'When we arrive in Spitalfields, we shall have plenty to show you, Lidie. You will see the new season's patterns and marvel at the skill of our silk weavers there.'

Just for a moment, Lidie allowed herself to imagine seeing such sights, poring over new patterns and feasting her eyes on beautiful garments, then she sighed and put such thoughts to the back of her mind.

They were all well rested now and Louis began to make enquiries about their mode of travel to London.

'We could take to the water again and sail along the South coast then turn North and then from there sail up the River Thames and into London,' he said.

Lidie looked up sharply. 'Oh no, I beg you, not another sea voyage, Louis. Please say there is another way.'

Sara and Elizabeth nodded their agreement and Louis sighed. 'It would be quickest and smoothest by water,' he said, 'But if you are all so reluctant to undertake another sea voyage, then we can make our way overland, but it will take a deal of time and you will be less comfortable than on board a vessel.'

'I would rather endure any discomfort as long as I know that there is solid ground beneath me.' Said Lidie.

Sara and Elizabeth both nodded their agreement.

Louis frowned. 'Well ladies,' he said, at length, 'If that is really your preference, then I will see what can be done, but it is a long way and I fear that the country roads will be rough.'

'We are beholden to you,' said Sara. 'Without your knowledge of the language, Lidie and I would have been at the mercy of …' She swallowed. 'I dread to think how we would have fared.

Louis was as good as his word and found a driver with a cart to take them as far as Barnstaple, a large and prosperous river port some six miles from Appledore. So a few days later, they packed up once more, and Lidie took out more of the coin she had sewn into the hem of her dress. She and Sara still had a little left for expenses and there were also pieces of silver and jewellery tucked away safely in their baggage.

'We were wise to bring these valuables with us,' said Lidie.

Sara frowned. 'Indeed, though we shall need the support of fellow countrymen once we reach London.' She paused in her packing. 'We have never been short of money but now the future is so uncertain.'

'It is a deal more certain than it was, Mama. We are safe and surely that is more important than any riches. And Uncle Jacob promises to send money for us once he knows we have arrived.'

Sara straightened up and smiled. 'You are right my love.' She hesitated. 'But you are young and strong.'

Lidie looked up, surprised. 'Does something ail you Mama?'

Sara shrugged. 'I am not as young as I was, Lidie, and I worry …'

Lidie laughed. 'You will always be strong to me.'

But as Sara continued with her packing, Lidie observed her.

I have been so concerned about the children that I have not given enough thought to how Mama has been affected. She is so much thinner than she was and she does not bend so easily.

On the morning of their departure, they all mounted the rough cart which was to take them to Barnstaple, at the mouth of the estuary. Many of the kind folk who had befriended them came to bid them farewell and wish them God speed, and Lidie's eyes filled with tears as she waved to them and mouthed a blessing on them for their kindness and hospitality. Esther was fretting at leaving her newfound friends and cried loudly until they turned the corner and the fishing village was lost to view. Lidie put an arm round her and tried to comfort her. She reached for Elias, too, but he frowned and wriggled from her grasp, his eyes fixed firmly ahead.

Although it was only six miles distant, their pace was slow and they didn't arrive in the town until well into the afternoon. As they made their way through the streets, Lidie, Sara and Elizabeth all remarked on the impressive town houses.

'It is a bigger and more prosperous place than I had envisaged,' said Elizabeth.

Louis nodded. 'They tell me that there is a good deal of wealth in the town,' he said. 'Much of it as a result of the shipbuilding industry here and the trade with America, and I believe that there is a community of our own people here, too, with their own pastor and church.'

They drove into the centre of the town and found an inn where they could put up for the night. They unloaded their luggage, thanked the driver of the cart and paid him for his trouble, and then Louis went out again to make enquiries about travelling on to Exeter from where they could board the public stage coach to

London. It was evening by the time he came back and he looked exhausted.

'Would that my knowledge of the English language was more fluent,' he said, wiping his brow. 'Doing business with a coach driver whose local accent is strong has tested my skills to the limit.' He took a long draught of ale and winced at the taste.

'But I tell you, ladies, there are more things to become accustomed to than the language. I doubt I shall ever understand the Englishman's love of ale.'

The women urged him to sit and take some refreshment and as he ate he told them that he had managed to procure the services of a private carriage and driver which would leave the day after next to take them as far as Exeter.

'Exeter is some forty miles distant,' he said, 'But we shall travel at a good pace, God willing, and the driver assures me that he can find us accommodation along the way, though I fear it will be somewhat crude.'

Sara smiled. 'My dear Louis, you must know by now that Lidie and I are well used to crude shelter!'

The children were fretful and ill-tempered and it took all of Lidie's patience to settle them but when they were finally asleep, she and Sara spoke together in low voices.

'Mama, we must pay our share of these expenses. We cannot let Louis and Elizabeth bear all the cost for the hire of the coach.'

'I have been thinking the same,' said Sara, frowning into the darkness of their stuffy attic room. 'But we are running short of coin so perhaps we should spend tomorrow finding a place to sell some of our silver and jewellery.'

'I would not like to be parted from the pieces Samuel gave me and I feel I must retain the family seal, too.'

Sara nodded. 'No indeed, those hold too many precious memories. But there are good small silver pieces we can dispose of which are not too meaningful, though we shall need Louis' help to do so.'

'Lidie smiled. 'The poor man has been much used by us all. We must learn the language ourselves.'

'Aye, said Sara. 'When we reach London, then it shall be our first priority. Pierre Gabriac must speak it fluently by now. He could, no doubt, help us in that regard.'

It was hot and uncomfortable in their little chamber and the children were restless beside them. Sara finally fell into a shallow slumber but Lidie lay awake for a long time, trying to envisage what lay ahead. Until now, the future had been so uncertain that she had not let herself think of it but they were on English soil now and God willing, in a few days time they would be boarding the stage coach which would convey them to London.

How does Pierre fare? Has Hannah recovered her wits? Will he welcome us? And what of those we left behind in Castillon, my beloved father in law and dear Aunt Louise and Uncle Jacob and the boys? And Cécile and her family?

Lidie and Sara both felt poorly slept in the morning and Esther was whining and fretful, but once she had breakfasted on some wholesome fare set out for them by the innkeeper, her temper improved and Lidie was able to find time to ask Louis to help them dispose of their silver trinkets. He protested that they need not repay him, or at least not until they were settled in London, but she and Sara insisted and through his good offices, once again, they had coin at their disposal. This they insisted on sharing with Louis to cover the expenses he had already incurred on their behalf and they also bought some victuals for their journey to Exeter.

'I cannot believe how cheap the bread is here,' said Lidie. 'I handed Louis four pence for these two large biscuits and he informed me that they only cost a halfpenny each. At home in Castillon they would have cost at least two pence each.'

When the hired carriage arrived at the door of the inn early the next morning, Sara and Lidie both congratulated Louis on finding such an excellent vehicle.

Louis looked pleased, rubbing his hands together and smiling.

'Aye. It was a lucky find,' he said 'It is a berlin carriage and we should cover fifteen miles or more each day in it. It should only take four passengers but I managed to persuade the driver that none of you ladies were heavy and that the children could sit on your laps.'

Their baggage was put on top of the carriage and they all climbed into the small compartment inside. They were somewhat crammed together since it was, indeed, designed to seat only four people, facing each other, but no one complained and even the children seemed delighted.

'Look, Mama,' said Elias. 'There is glass in the windows!'

He had spoken so little in the last days that Lidie was delighted that he was showing an interest. She hugged him close.

'It is good, is it not, my love. The rain may pour down from the heavens but we shall not get wet.'

Even though they were wearing rough travel stained clothes, their bodies stank and their limbs were weary, all the adults had a lightness of heart as the driver, sitting in front above the front wheels, cracked his whip and the pair of horses sprang forward at a sprightly pace and even the bumps in the rough road, once they were out of the town, were less hard on their bodies on account of the curved metal springs which absorbed the worst of the shock.

During the next two days, their good humour was dented somewhat by their close proximity in the carriage, by the children's dislike of being confined and their rough overnight accommodation, but they finally reached Exeter and were settled there in a coaching inn to await the arrival of the public stage coach which came by once a week and which would convey them to London.

When the morning of their departure arrived, the innkeeper and one of the stable boys helped to heave their baggage onto the cobbled street outside and their party stood, bleary eyed in the Spring morning, to await the coach. They were soon joined by others and Lidie became quite alarmed by the growing crowd, all with their luggage.

She turned to Elizabeth. 'I have counted upwards of twenty bodies here,' she whispered. 'I cannot believe that they can all fit into one coach.'

Louis overheard her remark. 'They will,' he assured her. 'By all accounts these coaches are great cumbersome vehicles. But I have secured seats for our party inside, Lidie. There is room inside for eight persons.'

292

Lidie still found it hard to imagine where all the other passengers might be accommodated, but she kept her silence and a little later they heard the rumble of the stage coach approaching along the road.

It was indeed a great cumbersome thing. Drawn by six horses, in addition to room inside the carriage, seats were available in a large open basket attached to the back and as they watched their bags being slung onto the roof of the carriage, Lidie was amazed to see more travellers climbing up with it and settling down amongst it, clasping the handrail to prevent themselves slithering off.

Sara touched Lidie's arm. 'Do you see that man sitting beside the driver?' she whispered. 'He is armed.'

'Aye, Madame,' said Louis, 'That will be the shotgun messenger. He will be travelling with us as a guard.'

Elizabeth looked up, frowning. 'Surely, Louis, there will be no need ...' she began.

Louis interrupted her. 'Let us pray that a guard will not be necessary,' he said. 'But we shall be travelling on rough roads and we shall no doubt pass through many isolated areas.' He took off his hat and scratched his hair. 'Our journey will be very long my love, and it is necessary to be prepared for any ... any eventuality.'

He did not think it prudent to alarm them further by mentioning the stories he had heard of armed highwaymen who attacked coaches on country roads far from towns, demanding money and valuables from travellers at gunpoint.

'When you say that our journey will be very long,' said Sara. 'Have you any notion of how many days it will take us?'

'I am told that eight days is the least time it will take Madame,' said Louis. 'This great lumbering vehicle can only travel at a few miles an hour, the roads are rough and the city of London is more than one hundred and fifty miles distant. I fear it will be a long and uncomfortable journey with many stops, but,' and here he smiled at her, 'at least you will have solid ground beneath you!'

Sara grimaced at the jibe. 'Then we shall endure it with fortitude,' she said.

But as they scrambled inside the coach and settled themselves down, they all wondered whether they had, indeed, made the right decision and as it finally moved off, lurching over the cobbles, Lidie could not help comparing the heavy un-sprung vehicle with the speedy carriage they had hired. This was a very different beast, jolting them from side to side as the coachman cracked his whip and the horses moved forward, labouring to pull the great weight which lay behind them.

'The last part of our great adventure,' said Sara. 'To think that we should be in London and among friends again before the month is out.'

'Amen to that,' said Elizabeth.

THE KING'S COMMAND

Chapter Thirty

Castillon, Spring 1691

It was a beautiful Spring morning in Castillon and the sight of the trees in leaf and the sound of the birdsong calmed Isaac Verdier's soul as he rode slowly into the town to call on Jacob and Louise and find out if they had received any news.

The years since the Revocation had aged them all and since Jacob had abjured, Isaac's intimacy with him and Louise was not as before. There was always that distance between them now, with Isaac's unbending resolve holding a mirror to Jacob's conscience. But that said, they were bound together by their love of Sara and Lidie and they still took comfort in one another's company.

As he rode around the market square at the top of the town, Isaac glanced down the street where Pierre Gabriac used to live, and he wondered how the pastor fared in London. Last time there was news of him he had sounded content and settled and well occupied, though there was scant mention of Hannah.

He dismounted at Jacob's house and handed his horse to the stable boy then he banged on the great door which was opened by a servant girl. Isaac handed her his hat and cloak and walked towards the main reception room but before he reached it, he was met by Louise who ran to embrace him, her face wet with tears.

At the sight of her, Isaac's step faltered.

Merciful God, it has happened. Lidie and Sara have been captured.

But then he saw that Louise was smiling through her tears.

'They have boarded the vessel,' she managed to whisper. 'Our man who conveyed them to La Tremblade arrived back just this morning and has told us that they boarded an English vessel off the Isle of Oléron.'

Isaac could not control his emotion. Still grasping Louise by the shoulders, he bent his head, tears coursing freely down his cheeks and into his beard.

'Thank God! Oh thank the good Lord for preserving them. Is he sure, your man? Did he see the vessel leave?'

Louise nodded. 'He waited overnight until the fishermen who had conveyed them over returned at first light and reported that the vessel had departed for England and that Lidie and Sara were on board.'

Isaac sat down on the nearest chair and tried to compose himself. Louise knelt beside him, her hands in his.

Isaac cleared his throat. 'Does Jacob know?' he asked.

She shook her head. 'He left the house early and I have sent a trusted servant to go and seek him out and ask him to come back here with all speed.' She gestured with her head towards the kitchen. Our man is here now, having some refreshment.'

Isaac rose slowly to his feet. 'Then I shall go immediately to offer him my thanks and if there is anything ...'

Louise interrupted him. 'He will be well rewarded, Isaac, you can be sure of that. The safety of my sister and her family is beyond price and his loyalty to us and to them, well ...' She sniffed and took a linen kerchief from her sleeve to wipe her eyes. 'We shall see to it that he and his kin will have every comfort we can give them.'

Isaac spent some time with the driver. First he sent the servants from the kitchen, wanting to question him privately. He asked anxiously about the condition of Lidie, Sara and the children and was very concerned to hear that little Jean had been so sick when the driver left them. To satisfy himself he felt bound to question the driver more closely as to the boy's condition but then he noticed how the man's head was drooping.

'Forgive me,' he said, rising to his feet and clapping the driver on the shoulder. 'You are so fatigued. There will be plenty of time for questions later. Please eat and then go to your own family and rest.'

At the door, Isaac hesitated. 'There are no words to express our thanks to you. To risk so much on our behalf ...'

The man looked up wearily and smiled. 'I thank God that I could see them safely to the vessel,' he said. 'And I pray that their journey to England will be uneventful.'

'Amen to that,' said Isaac.

A few moments later, Jacob arrived at the house, crashing through the front door, his boots clattering on the stone flags. 'What is it? What has happened? Why did you send for me?'

But when he heard the news he, too, was brought to tears of relief and having thanked the driver and seen him conveyed to his home, he returned to be with Louise and Isaac.

Isaac stayed and ate with them and after the first wave of euphoria had receded, Isaac voiced his fears about little Jean and their joy turned once more to concern, both for the boy and, indeed, for their own situation.

'Sara's household is becoming ever more anxious at the continued absence of the family,' said Jacob. 'I have reassured them as much as I can but they know something is amiss.'

'Annette knew the truth of course,' said Louise. 'But I would trust her with my life. Though it must be very difficult for her to keep her counsel. The rest of the household must suspect …'

'Aye,' said Jacob, tugging at his beard. 'And the new curé has visited several times, I'm told, and some soldiers, but they were told that the family were at their farm.'

'Have soldiers been to the farm?'

Louise nodded. 'I heard from our man bringing supplies across the river. He said that there had been some commotion at the farm but of course, they did not find the family.'

'Then they will suspect that they are fled abroad, will they not.'

'Of course,' said Jacob, 'But we can only hope that they would assume they left from Bordeaux and by now the trail will have gone cold.'

'And they will suspect that you have had a hand in helping Lidie and Sara escape, will they not?'

Jacob shrugged. 'Of course they will have their suspicions, but since I have abjured and Samuel, too, before he died, I doubt they will bother us now '

'So the Catholics have achieved their purpose,' said Isaac bitterly.

There was an awkward silence and then Isaac continued.

'First Cécile and then you, Jacob and the rest of your family.'

'And even poor Samuel,' said Louise.

Isaac's head whipped round, his eyes hard. 'You cannot speak of Samuel in the same breath as the rest of you, Louise. He abjured under torture.' He flinched as he said the word.

Louise's bowed her head. 'Forgive me, Isaac. I spoke thoughtlessly.'

Jacob cleared his throat. 'I fear that my sons and Cécile and her husband's family see converting to the Catholic faith as a necessary evil,' he said. 'Their consciences do not seem troubled in the way that ours are.' He looked across at Louise and she gave a brief nod as Jacob moved over to Isaac and put a hand on his shoulder.

'How we admire your steadfastness, Isaac. You are an example to us all.'

'I know the struggle you had with your conscience my friend,' said Isaac quietly. 'I know what it cost you and I know that Sara and Lidie and the children would not be free now if it were not for your good offices and connections.' There was a brief silence then Isaac continued. 'In truth, we have all benefitted from your decision but I cannot do it. I cannot desert my faith; I am answerable only to God and my conscience.'

The two men looked at each other for a long moment and then Isaac got to his feet and started pacing the room.

'Why can this foolish King not see beyond his nose?'' he asked.

Louise's eyes darted to the door. Jacob saw her look and he strode over and closed it softly.

Isaac seemed not to notice their nervousness and he continued to pace and gesture.

'By forcing us out, Louis is killing this country,' said Isaac. 'What was a rich and diverse realm has lost so much. Its weavers, its silversmiths and watchmakers, its doctors and lawyers, all those diligent Huguenots who have made the country prosper have fled to other countries and it is foreigners who benefit.'

'You have no need to convince us, Isaac,' said Jacob. 'The evidence is everywhere, even in our little town. Empty workshops, looms untended, a dearth of skilled professionals.'

Isaac stopped his pacing and stood by the window, his hands clasped behind his back, looking out into the street and beyond to the gleam of the River Dordogne.

'I had so many plans,' he said softly. 'I have learnt much from my correspondence with colleagues in other countries. There are advances in my profession all the time but ...'

'You still help others Isaac,' said Louise gently. 'You came when our maid was sick last week and without your skill ...'

'I do what I can, Louise, but the infirmary is closed to me and no Protestant apothecaries can practice and no Catholic one will serve me so I cannot administer any drugs.'

'Do you have any news from the infirmary? Do you know how it fares?'

Isaac gave a wry smile. 'From time to time I am visited by the colleague who runs it now, a new convert who urges me to abjure. He has recruited new Catholic staff and my two nurses have abjured in order to keep working and caring for the sick.' He turned away from the window and came to sit down beside Jacob and Louise.

'I hate what they have done but I cannot find it in my heart to blame them,' he said. 'They have confessed to me that they are wracked with guilt but they see it as the only way they can continue to give succour to the sick.'

They were silent for a while, then Isaac spoke again.

'As a young doctor,' he said. 'I swore an oath to help cure the sick and I will continue to do so in any way I am able, whatever the consequences.'

'We had such hope,' said Louise. 'We were raised in a time of peace and tolerance after the Edict of Nantes was made law.'

'A brief respite, as it turned out,' said Jacob wearily. 'Our ancestors fought so bravely for religious freedom and now we are impotent, unable to retaliate in any meaningful way.' He rubbed his chin. 'Though I have heard some talk of resistance in the region of the Cevennes, but how can rough peasants prevail against Louis's army?'

At the mention of the Cevennes region, Isaac gave an involuntary shudder. That region would for ever be associated, in his mind, with Claude Brousson, the lawyer and preacher with whom Samuel had become so obsessed.

Foolish, foolish boy. If only he had not sought out the man he might yet be alive.

He pushed the thought from his mind and answered Jacob. 'I abhor violence,' he said. 'And we Protestants were also guilty of gross acts against our fellow men in the past wars.'

'Aye, and those of the Catholic faith have been persecuted in other countries,' said Jacob. 'In England, for years they were hounded and now that King James has been replaced by his Protestant daughter, no doubt they will suffer again.'

Louise got up from her chair and made to leave the room. 'Well at least Sara and Lidie will not be at risk if Protestants rule the country. I suppose that is of some comfort.' As she reached the door, she turned. 'All this bloodshed over the manner in which we worship our loving God,' she said. 'Do you ever wonder how He must despair of His people on earth?'

Isaac nodded. 'You put us to shame, Louise. We should be thinking on a higher plane, not about how we poor imperfect souls are suffering in this life.

'Aye,' said Louise, glancing across at Jacob. 'But when we leave this world will we be accepted into God's presence now we have abjured?'

The men watched her as she went out of the door to deal with some domestic matter.

'She bears her sorrow with such fortitude,' said Isaac. 'For it is certain she will never see her sister again, nor yet her niece and her children.'

'And you, too, Isaac,' said Jacob quietly. 'And your sorrow is the greater. The loss of your beloved son …'

'I have to accept what God has planned for me,' replied Isaac quietly. 'I know that I shall be visited again by agents of the King with the abjuration papers and no doubt they will bring soldiers with them. Meanwhile, I can only do my best to live out my life here boldly, be true to my faith and trust that one day I shall be reunited with Samuel and my beloved wife.'

Jacob looked at him. 'How I wish that my conscience was as pure as yours, my friend.'

Chapter Thirty-One

London, early Summer 1691

The warmer weather brought a stench from the rotting detritus on the banks of the River Thames and the streets were more often than not jammed with carriages trying to pass one another. The air was noisy with the shouts from drivers and passengers while the horses neighed and pawed the ground and an acrid smell rose from the urine and the steaming heaps of manure they deposited.

Pierre Gabriac's eyes were streaming and he was sweating in the dark coat he wore. He knew that before the great fire of London, conditions were much worse in this part of the town. To be sure the streets had been widened and there were now more squares and gardens laid out and planted prettily where folk could walk at their leisure, but he had a sudden longing for the little town of Castillon where there was easier access to green fields and the river was not so crowded and polluted.

If we were still there, maybe Hannah could have recovered. Isaac might have found a way to ease the distress in her mind.

But he dismissed these thoughts angrily. He knew he and Hannah could never return and he chastised himself for such foolish dreams.

He was able to leave the city from time to time to visit some of the new French Protestant churches built outside and he treasured these trips. At first he had tried to persuade Hannah to accompany him, but she was frightened of venturing far from their lodgings and would become so distressed that he eventually stopped suggesting it.

There was, however, one place where she did feel at ease. Early on, he had taken her by carriage to King's Square which had been built some nine years ago with a garden at its centre. Her eyes had lit up on seeing this pleasure ground, laid out with ornamental flowers, shrubs and trees, with a great statue of King Charles II at its midst and surrounded by elegant houses. It was too far for her to walk from their lodgings but, every year since their first visit, he had taken her there in the early summer and it was the one time that she would consent to travel in a carriage, though all the time tense and anxious until they arrived. But she had deteriorated so much during the past year that he wondered whether she would be able to make the journey or whether the prospect would fill her with so much anxiety that it would not be worth trying to persuade her to come.

He was due to visit the square that afternoon, to tutor the son of a wealthy English family who lived in one of the grand houses, so he decided to ask Hannah if she would like to come with him. Filled with sudden resolve, he quickened his stride and headed for his lodgings.

As he climbed the stairs to their rooms, he tried to fight back the feeling of dread as he stood at the door. He always prayed that one day something would change, that he would find her more communicative, that he would be able to raise a smile from her, that the servant girl would be less sullen, but his optimism was always dashed and today was no exception. As he squared his shoulders, opened the door and fixed a smile on his face, he was met by the stuffy, stale smell of the place with which he'd become drearily familiar, for Hannah would not allow the servant to open the windows such was her suspicion of the outside world.

His eyes adjusting to the gloom, he entered the room and immediately saw that Hannah, instead of sitting mutely in her chair, was standing, looking out of the window.

He went over to her and she turned her head slowly towards him but her eyes were dead. He smiled at her and cleared his throat.

'I have to go to King's Square this afternoon, Hannah. The flowers will be in bloom so I thought you might care to accompany me.'

She continued to stare at him.

'You love it there,' he persisted. 'It is the best time of year to visit. We'll take a carriage ' He faltered, all his enthusiasm drying up as he saw that there was not even a flicker of interest in her face.

How much worse she has become during this past year. Only last summer she consented to come with me but now…

He turned away, defeated. 'Perhaps I should wait until Lidie and her family arrive,' he muttered, more to himself than to Hannah. 'Then we can go with them.'

He had not mentioned Lidie's imminent arrival to Hannah before now as he did not want to raise her hopes of seeing an intimate from her old life. However, having heard that the family had reached the West of the country, he assumed that they were now travelling overland to London since they had not arrived by vessel.

He was not unduly concerned as he knew how slow the journey by stage coach could be, but he had recently received a substantial sum of money through Jacob's contacts, to be kept for Lidie and Sara to help them settle, and he was uneasy being its guardian.

He was absorbed in these thoughts, so at first he failed to hear Hannah's whisper, but then he felt her pulling at his coat sleeve.

'Lidie?' she said. And for once there was a tiny gleam of interest in her eyes.

'Yes, my love,' he said gently. 'Lidie has escaped from Castillon and is travelling to London with her family.'

'I shall see Lidie?' she repeated.

It has been five years but she still remembers Lidie! Yet she never speaks of the friends here who have shown her so much kindness.

Pierre patted her arm. 'Aye, with God's grace you will see Lidie again,' he said.

And then, suddenly, Hannah smiled. A weak smile, to be sure, but so very rare that his heart contracted for love of her.

Pray God you are well, Lidie, and that you will reach us in safety. And maybe your presence among us will help my Hannah.

Chapter Thirty-Two

Journeying

The party tried to keep up their spirits but every time they left an inn along the way, Esther screamed when she was bundled, yet again, inside the great lumbering stage coach and Elias asked repeatedly when they would arrive.

The adults were hardly less anxious for the journey to end. The conditions in some of the inns were rough and the bedding full of bugs. Their clothes were stinking and Lidie thought back to her mother's elegance when they lived in Castillon. Observing her now she saw how the rigours of their journey had taken their toll, to say nothing of the grief that sometimes threatened to overwhelm them both. Sara's face was pale and drawn and she had lost a deal of weight so that her clothes swamped her.

She has suffered so much and I have been too taken up with my own grief to concern myself with her troubles.

Most of the time, Louis had managed to secure seats inside the coach for them but on occasion they were obliged to sit in the great basket behind, open to the weather and a deal less comfortable.

There was an enforced delay, too, when a wheel had to be mended and another when one of the horses went lame, but once on the Great West Road, the conditions improved a little and their progress improved.

When, finally, they reached the last coaching inn of their journey, on the West side of London, it was early evening. Louis arranged the hire of a hackney carriage the next day to take them East to Spitalfields and also sent word to his family of their arrival and to Pierre Gabriac, on behalf of Lidie and Sara.

The inn was bursting with customers and the noise and smell within overwhelming, but they managed to secure rooms in the top of the three-storey building, close under the eaves and stiflingly hot. By this time Esther was in a rage and Elias was weeping with fatigue.

Lidie held them close though, in truth, she was near breaking point herself.

'Only one more journey, Elias,' she said. 'And it will be in a small carriage which will take us to our destination.'

'And then we shall stop?'

'Yes, my love. Our kind friends have invited us to stay with their family until we can find our own lodgings.'

Esther continued to rage and Lidie found it impossible to comfort her.

Sara spoke over her noise. 'It is very kind of Louis and Elizabeth to offer us accommodation. They have already extended so much generosity towards us and I do not like to take further advantage.'

'No doubt Pierre will make arrangements for us directly, Mama.'

And as she said his name she allowed herself a brief smile. It would be good to be reacquainted with him.

Esther seemed to sense the release of tension and she stopped crying at last and held fast to her mother, gripping her around her waist with a fierceness that took Lidie's breath away.

The journey across the city from West to East the next morning had them all exclaiming and pointing.

'So many people!' remarked Elizabeth.

'And such contrasts in housing,' said Louis as they passed down a narrow street with timber framed houses almost meeting one another at their top storeys, shops beneath them and an open sewer running down the street's centre, before emerging further on into a tree fringed square with large quality houses surrounding it.

'I heard it said that a deal of rebuilding took place after the great fire in 1666 ravaged this part of the city,' said Elizabeth.

'And coming after the great plague, too,' said Louis. 'The people of London suffered much.'

Lidie turned back from looking out of the carriage window. 'In one of his letters to Jacob, Pierre told us that it was the North East part of London which suffered so badly and that the French temple there was burnt to the ground.'

'And the great cathedral of St Paul's,' said Elizabeth.

'Aye,' said Louis. 'My family say there has been much rebuilding in Spitalfields, too and that many of our faith have settled there.'

'But the fire and the plague all happened over twenty years ago,' said Elizabeth. 'Long before our family arrived.

'You must yearn to see them again,' said Sara.

Elizabeth looked down at her hands. 'You cannot imagine how much,' she said quietly. 'There have been times when we almost lost hope that we would see them again. So often we made attempts to escape only to fail at the last moment.'

'And now you are so near,' said Sara. 'But truly, Elizabeth, we should not disturb your reunion. It will be such a precious time. I'm sure that Pierre Gabriac can accommodate us.'

Elizabeth put out her hand and took Sara's. 'Louis sent word last night. They will have prepared a room for you and are waiting to welcome you. There will be time enough to find your own place and meanwhile you can rest and gather your wits surrounded by peace and harmony.'

'Peace and harmony,' repeated Sara. 'How wonderful those words are to my ears.'

'We have gone through too much together to abandon you now,' continued Elizabeth, 'So we will have no more talk of disturbing our reunion.'

They were approaching a river and the driver slowed down to wait his turn to cross the bridge over it. Louis leaned out of the window and spoke to the man in English.

'Surely this is not the famous river Thames?'

The driver twisted round, grinning.

'Oh no sir, this is the River Fleet, though it flows into the Thames for sure.' He slapped the reins on the horse's back and urged it forward. 'We are not far from Spitalfields now.'

Louis withdrew into the carriage. 'Not the Thames,' he said to the others. 'I had thought it a bit small!'

He took Elizabeth's hand in his. 'The driver says we shall be there directly.'

For the rest of the journey, they were quiet, and the only sounds came from the wheels of the hackney carriage and its creaking and bumping and the noise of folk outside going about their business as the driver negotiated his way through the narrow streets of the East end of the city.

'Spitalfields!' he cried at last and Louis woke from his reverie.

'My family live in Spital Square,' he said and repeated the address that had been engraved on his heart for so long.

They then passed through some streets of recently built modest houses on wider plots of land.

'I believe that this was developed only ten years ago,' said Louis, 'On the site of the old Artillery Ground.'

'Then we must be on the edge of the city here,' said Sara.

'Yes, I believe that is so,' said Louis. 'My son told me that the fields to the south are still reserved as tenter land, where fabric is stretched to dry on tenterhook frames to keep its shape.'

'So, there are many from the weaving trade in this area?'

Louis nodded. 'Aye. And most of them of our faith.'

As they drove slowly on, they caught sight of a bustling market a few streets away and then entered a street where there were some newly built houses a deal larger than others they had seen in the area. Finally the carriage drew up outside one of these houses and they all climbed stiffly down. Louis banged on the front door of the house and there were shouts of joy as it was immediately flung open and a handsome couple rushed into the arms of Elizabeth and Louis. Standing behind them, in the doorway, were three children, The youngest a girl of about Esther's age and she stared at them, frowning. Behind her were two older boys.

There was such joyous confusion then. Hugs and tears and questions, Lidie and Sara stood back, rejoicing for their friends but a little jealous, too, of this reunited family. It was a while before Elizabeth and Louis remembered themselves and set about introducing their travelling companions to their son, Etienne, his wife Isabella and their children.

When, finally, their luggage was all unloaded and the party were inside, Sara

whispered to Lidie, 'It is just like home!'

And, indeed, there was much that was familiar to them. Though the house was not as large as their home in Castillon, there were

308

touches of French elegance within it, chairs covered in tapestry, the delicate side tables, the silver candle holders on the wall, the family portraits.

'It seems that their son has done well in the silk weaving trade,' said Lidie

Meanwhile, Etienne was firing questions at his parents. 'Tell us about your escape? Was the crossing perilous? Are you in good health?'

Isabella put up her hand. 'Hush, Etienne, there will be plenty of time for questions later. Can you not see that your parents and their friends are exhausted? What they need now is a change of clothes and some refreshment.'

'And to wash,' said Elizabeth. 'Above all else, to wash.'

All the travellers concurred and Isabella had begun to mount the stairs to show them to their chambers when there came another knock on the front door.

'Ah,' said Etienne, striding forward, 'I think I know who that is. I sent him word.'

Sara and Lidie had not expected that it would be anyone of their acquaintance and they did not turn to look at the new arrival, but continued up the stairs.

But then they heard Etienne's greeting. 'Pierre Gabriac, my friend. Welcome, welcome.'

Lidie stopped in her tracks and spun round. It took a moment for her to recognize the sober clad man standing beneath them, his arms wide in welcome but then, when she did, something inside her broke and all the emotions which she had held in so tightly ever since their flight from Castillon, came rushing to the fore, completely overwhelming her and she rushed headlong down the stairs across the floor and flung herself into those welcoming arms, sobbing uncontrollably.

Pierre hesitated for only a moment before wrapping his arms around her

'Lidie, my poor child,' he murmured, looking over her head at the others, frozen in a tableau at the foot of the stairs.

At last, her sobs subsided and she broke away from him. 'I'm sorry. Forgive me. But seeing you…' She sniffed and rubbed her eyes. 'So many memories,' she muttered, looking down at the floor.

'Indeed. Indeed.' For a moment no one spoke and then Pierre cleared his throat.

'How you must have suffered,' he said gently, including Sara and the children in his gaze. 'I have been praying for you all constantly.'

Lidie looked up at him then, her face ingrained with dirt and wet with tears.

'Every day,' he went on. 'Since I heard of your flight and of Samuel's death.'

Lidie managed a weak smile. 'Then God answered your prayers,' she said. 'For we are here and we are safe. Though I fear we are all much changed.'

He held her away from him and smiled. 'Maybe changed a little through sorrow, Lidie, but you are still that brave young woman I knew in Castillon and now that you are safe, you will find joy again, of that I am certain.'

She didn't answer but shook her head sadly. By this time, Sara had joined them and she embraced Pierre warmly. 'How good it is to see you Pierre. When we are rested we must hear all your news.'

Pierre nodded, but there was shock on his face as he took in Sara's ravaged appearance. 'Pray take time to rest, Madame, and then we shall speak again. I have money for you sent from France and I will seek lodgings for you all directly.'

He turned back to Lidie. 'I will do all in my power to help you settle,' he said.

Etienne interrupted. 'Come and dine with us tomorrow night, sir,' he said. 'And then we can all talk further; there is no need to secure lodgings for them directly. They can stay here for as long as they wish. We have plenty of room and all of us in this community will welcome them as we have welcomed so many who have fled from the King's persecution.'

Pierre nodded. 'Indeed. It has been a privilege to help them.'

'But you also left in difficult circumstances Pierre,' said Lidie. 'You were forced to abandon your flock and your home.'

'But no soldiers stood in my way; the King was delighted to be rid of us pastors. I was not one of the brave ones, Lidie. Those were the pastors who stayed and did not abjure and suffered so terribly – and families like your own who were in constant fear of their lives. The least we can do now is to help those brave souls who have risked so much to reach these shores.'

'Come now,' said Isabella, addressing Lidie and Sara. 'I must insist you go to your chamber. I have laid out some clothes for you in case you have need of them. All is prepared.'

'My pardon, Madame. I must not delay them further,' said Pierre, making for the door.' I only called to reassure myself of their safe arrival.'

Sara turned to go back up the stairs but then hesitated. 'How is dear Hannah, Pierre?'

Pierre did not answer at once, then he cleared his throat. 'We will speak of Hannah when we meet tomorrow evening,' he said.

Chapter Thirty-Three

Isabella took Lidie, Sara and the children to a large well appointed chamber where they were all to sleep.

Isabella pointed to the garments laid out on the large four poster bed.

'These are yours if you can make use of them.'

Lidie picked up some of the clothes, not only garments for women but also a plentiful supply for the children. Isabella watched her anxiously.

'They are given by many members of our community,' she said, 'so they may not necessarily be of high quality.'

'They are clean and generously given,' said Lidie.

'Before long, I warrant you will be able to dress in silks again,' said Isabella, gently.

Lidie picked up one of the plain dresses and held it to her, smiling. 'For now, this will be luxury indeed.' Then she gestured at Isabella's elegant attire. 'Though I must confess to being a little envious …'

Isabella laughed. 'When you are well rested, Etienne will show you the books of patterns for next season's silks,' she said.

'That would indeed be a feast for our eyes, would it not Mama?'

Sara nodded but she stumbled a little as she made to sit down on one of the chairs.

Isabella was all concern. 'Madame, you are exhausted,' she said. 'I shall have hot water sent up for you and a light repast and then you should all rest.'

Elias was sitting on the floor staring at Isabella with his big solemn eyes but Esther, who had been clutching Lidie's hand all the while, suddenly freed herself and crept quietly over to Isabella and began to stroke the material of her dress with her grubby hands.

'Esther!' said Lidie.

But Isabella stooped down and spoke to Esther. 'Etienne's mama has told me how you loved to stroke their silk samples,' she said. 'I will find you one or two of your own. Would you like that?'

THE KING'S COMMAND

Esther nodded vigorously.

'She has always loved pretty things,' said Lidie.

When Isabella had left them, Lidie sat down on the edge of the bed and looked about her. She could tell at once that most of the furniture was made by French craftsmen; the washstand in the corner of the room, the finely wrought mirror above a bow legged table. Although there were shutters at the window which overlooked the street, there were also heavy drapes. Sara followed her gaze. 'No doubt it is colder in England,' she said, 'and they have need of such fabric to keep out the draughts.'

Soon a maid appeared with a jug of hot water for the washstand followed, some time later, by a kitchen servant with bowls of hot chocolate and bread for them.

When, finally, they were washed and fed and had peeled off their travel stained garments, they all lay down to rest in the large bed. The bed linen was freshly washed and smelled of lavender and the goose feather pillows were soft. Although a truckle bed had been rolled out for the children, they snuggled either side of Lidie and Sara in the big bed and Lidie was in no mood to chide them.

As she drifted off to sleep, with the smell of lavender in her nostrils, she dreamt of their farm in Gascony and her childhood room there.

She slept like the dead for several hours but she was the first to stir and she managed to creep from the bed without disturbing the others. It was still light but when she looked out of the window she could see that the sun was already well down in the sky.

She glanced back at the bed, at Sara, her arms round Elias, both profoundly asleep, and at little Esther on the other side, her fist firmly clutching the silk sample. Lidie dressed quietly in the garments left for them and splashed some water on her face. She rummaged in her luggage for a comb and dragged it through her tangled hair, then she found a crumpled coif in her bag but eventually gave up the struggle to put it on and left her hair loose. She crept out of the chamber and made her way down the stairs.

She found Isabella and her children in the kitchen. The children were having their evening meal and Isabella was overseeing it, with the help of a nurse.

Isabella immediately welcomed her. 'You look somewhat refreshed, Madame. Did you sleep?'

'I slept more deeply than I have for this past month.'

'The others still sleep?' asked Isabella.

'Yes, but I can rouse them.'

'No, please do not. Let them sleep as long as they need.'

The children were looking at Lidie with curiosity and one of the boys asked her a question in English. Lidie frowned and looked at Isabella.

'I fear that I speak no English,' she said.

Isabella addressed her son. 'Speak in French,' she said.

He repeated it in fluent French. 'Did you come in a big boat?'

Lidie smiled. 'We came first in a cart to the edge of the ocean, and then in a boat over to England and then we had a long journey over land in the stage coach.'

'Was it exciting?'

Lidie paused. 'Not exactly exciting.' she replied.

'Was it frightening?'

'A little.'

'Come on children, eat up,' said Isabella briskly. 'Madame Verdier and I have much to talk about.'

The girl of Esther's age stopped chewing and looked directly at Lidie. 'Can I play with your little girl?' she asked.

Even this little one can converse in both languages!

'When she is rested,' said Isabella firmly.

Later, Lidie and Isabella settled themselves in the reception room. It was not of any great size but it was homely and comfortable and Lidie noticed several pieces of quality furniture and ornament around the room.

'Surely, you did not bring all this with you from France?'

'No. Though we left well before the Edict was revoked, so we were able to bring a good deal with us. But there are so many skilled French artisans living in London now. She counted them off on her fingers; clockmakers, silversmiths, lace makers, shoe makers, jewellers, glove makers, book binders, perfumers. There is plenty of quality to buy here.'

'And are all these skilled craftsmen of our faith?'

'Mostly,' said Isabella. 'Some have been here for years so they are well established. The work of the French silversmiths is particularly admired here. Many of them arrived long before the Revocation. Their trade was badly affected when King Louis ordered silver objects melted down to pay for his wars and then banned the creation of new pieces.'

'Your husband's business, too, must be well established, said Lidie.

Isabella nodded. 'We were lucky. Etienne's father was anxious that we left as soon as possible so that we could set ourselves up here.' She sighed. 'The intention was that he and my mother in law would leave once he had settled his business matters and come and join us but by then, of course, it was too late.'

'What a time they had,' agreed Lidie. 'And it was our good fortune that we met up with them when we did. In truth, I am not sure that Mama and I would have succeeded in getting here without them. We owe them a great debt.'

Isabella sighed. 'I thank God that they have come to us at last. We have worried so much about them these past years and in truth, Etienne began to believe that he would never see his parents again. They are no longer young and ..'

Lidie nodded. 'I worry about Mama. She has always been so strong but now …'

'With rest and nourishment, she will regain her strength.'

'I pray that is true,' said Lidie. 'But that is what we said about my little Jean.'

Isabella nodded. 'Elizabeth told me how you had lost him,' she said. 'I am so very sorry.'

Lidie turned away. 'First my father, then my husband and then my beloved little Jean.'

'God has surely tested you,' said Isabella quietly.

They said nothing for a while and then Isabella spoke again. 'Pierre Gabriac has done much for our community,' she said. 'He is a good man.'

'I did not realize that you were acquainted until he came earlier.'

315

'Oh, all we Huguenots know each other. It is a close-knit community and many of us worship in the Temple in Threadneedle Street.'

'How good it will be to be able to worship freely again,' said Lidie.

'Inded.' Isabella frowned. 'You know, of course, that Pierre's wife is not herself?'

'Is Hannah still unwell?'

Isabella nodded. 'It is very sad to see; she is sick in her mind. Many goodhearted people have tried to help her but it is difficult. She is nervous of any stranger and she hardly leaves their lodgings.'

'We had hoped that when she was safe she would be more settled in her mind,' said Lidie.

Isabella shook her head.

The rest of the day was spent quietly. When Elizabeth and Louis and Sara and the children awoke the whole party gathered for a simple meal of spiced veal pie and a few vegetables followed by custard.

'How delicious this is,' remarked Sara.

'We have a good supply of spices from the East,' said Isabella, 'And now that the price of peppercorns has dropped a little, we make freer use of them to flavour our food.'

Etienne and his father spoke about the cost of importing spices and other goods and then, before long, they were deeply engrossed in a conversation of the state of the silk weaving trade. Lidie tried to follow their talk but the children kept wanting her attention and eventually she gave up, but a little later, Louis turned to her.

'When you are settled, Lidie, I am sure that Etienne would be happy to show you and Sara some of next year's patterns.'

'I would dearly like to see them,' she said.

Louis smiled. 'Even in those cast off clothes, you look well, Lidie.'

Lidie coloured and laughed. 'To me these simple clothes are the height of fashion, sir.'

Louis sighed. 'Well said. We are indeed fortunate to have come to a community where we are welcomed and where charity is in bountiful supply.'

Sara looked up. 'To think,' she said. 'When we were in Castillon, we were the ones dispensing charity to those less fortunate than ourselves and now it is we who are receiving it.'

'But we cannot impose upon your family for too long,' said Lidie. 'I still have some of Samuel's coin and some jewels to sell and Pierre has received money from France for us.'

Louis, Elizabeth, Etienne and Isabella all protested that they must stay as long as they wished but Sara joined Lidie in insisting that they must set up their own home forthwith.

Esther kept peeping at Isabella's children and at length she and their little girl began to play together. Lidie watched, delighted that they were taking such pleasure in each other's company and she and Isabella laughed at the mixture of French and English language which was going on between them. Elias was less ready to make friends and he stood shyly to one side.

'I must take lessons in the English language,' said Lidie. 'I feel so ignorant around you who switch with so little effort between the two tongues.'

'It will come, Lidie,' said Isabella. 'Remember, we have lived here for some years. It would be shameful if we did not speak English and, to be truthful, the children are more at ease speaking English now, though we all speak French in the house.'

Before they all retired, Isabella insisted in taking all their soiled under clothing to be laundered. As Sara and Lidie bundled it up and handed it to Isabella, Sara said. 'I would not weep if I never saw any of these filthy garments again. I am ashamed to give them to you in this state.'

Isabella laughed. 'The English scarcely wash their clothes from one year to the next, but we have an excellent French laundress nearby and it is time we took some of our own undergarments to her; it has been many weeks since I did so. They will return as good as new, and our man servant will brush down all your outer garments for you.'

Chapter Thirty-Four

The next morning, Lidie asked if she could accompany Isabella to the laundress. In Castillon there were several wash houses to which households sent their clothes and she was curious to see how clothes were laundered in London.

When they arrived at the cottage which was situated some streets away, well behind the bigger houses, her eyes started to smart from the smell of ammonia even before they went inside. The heat in the cottage was stifling and they were greeted by a woman wearing a simple blouse and skirt covered by a large apron. She was sweating profusely and her hair was tucked into a closefitting cap.

Lidie asked the woman about the process of washing their garments and was treated to a full explanation.

'First I soak them in urine overnight and rub all the stains out the next day and then, Madame, they are put to soak in a buck tub,' she said, pointing at a huge barrel which was raised from the floor and sat on wooden legs giving room for the water to be drained into buckets when the holes underneath were unplugged. 'Then,' she continued, 'I cover the tub with buck cloth and pass potash through it. Then the linen is soaped and paddled with a stick.' She pointed to a dolly stick standing close by the tub. 'Then it is rinsed again and again and then hung out to dry.'

Isabella smiled at her. 'It is a great labour,' she said, 'but the results are wonderful.'

Lidie's eyes were weeping freely now and she had started to cough.

'We will leave you to your labours,' said Isabella to the woman, and she and Lidie left the cottage and began their walk back to the house.

'She uses the English soap,' said Isabella. 'It is made from goat's fat and not scented like the French soap.'

'But effective, nonetheless?'

Isabella nodded. 'And expensive.'

They walked along slowly in the summer sunshine and Lidie asked how the poorer folk washed their clothes.

Isabella shrugged. 'They do not wash themselves or their clothes with any frequency, but most folk take their linen in tubs to the river Thames and wash them in the river water. And the grand houses, of course, have their own laundry rooms.'

Lidie's eyes were still streaming and she stopped and wiped at them with a kerchief.

That evening, the whole company joined together to eat and give thanks. When Louis and Elizabeth came down from their chamber, Lidie rose to her feet and embraced Elizabeth.

'Oh how elegant you look!' she exclaimed.

Elizabeth smiled. 'We brought a few of our finer garments with us,' she said. 'It does the heart good to dress in them again and tonight we have much to celebrate.'

Lidie stared at the flowered silk dress that Elizabeth was wearing and she found herself fingering the fabric which was soft to the touch. 'I don't think I have ever seen such beautifully woven silk.' Then she turned to Louis. 'And your waistcoat, sir. It is very fine, with the silver thread woven through it.'

'And you, Lidie. It is so good to see you in silks,' replied Louis.

Lidie had dressed in her anniversary silks, the only elegant wear she had brought with her. She had lost so much weight on their journey that they fitted her perfectly.

A little later they were joined by Pierre Gabriac and when he saw Lidie he was momentarily taken aback.

'Your anniversary silks,' he said. 'And in them you danced so skillfully on that splendid evening.'

'It was so long ago, I am flattered you remember,' said Lidie.

'How could I forget,' he said quietly.

After they had eaten, Pierre led them all in praying and singing psalms and afterwards, Lidie said to him. 'It is wonderful to be able to pray and to sing our psalms with a full voice and not to fear being overheard.'

Pierre smiled. 'Wait until you join us all at the Temple,' he said. 'There is such a joyful crowd there and the singing rings around the rafters.'

'Will Hannah join us at the Temple?'

'No, I fear not. She …' he hesitated and then looked directly at Lidie. 'Would you come and visit her, Lidie. She would dearly love to see you.'

'Of course.' She was about to say more but something in Pierre's demeanour stopped her and then she became caught up in what Etienne was saying.

'….it was such a splendid show,' he was telling his parents. 'I can remember every detail to this day.'

'Oh indeed, you should have seen it,' remarked Isabella. Then she saw Lidie looking puzzled. 'We are talking of King James' coronation,' she said. 'It was in '85 and we all joined the throng to see the spectacle, for the silk weavers had been employed night and day in preparation.'

'Indeed,' said Isabella, 'The coronation did more than any other event to boost the fashion for luxury silks.'

'Etienne nodded. The King and his entourage walked from Westminster Hall to the Abbey and the whole route was covered in broadcloth, with women strewing their path with flowers and sweet herbs. It seemed that the whole of London was watching. Folk were leaning over balconies and crowding into doorways and side streets. The crush was frightful but the spectacle was unlike anything I have witnessed.'

'It all sounds very splendid,' said Louis dryly.

'Oh, indeed it was,' continued Etienne. 'The King had a cloak of crimson velvet and underneath he wore more silks, satins and velvets, and the Queen was splendid in purple velvet. They walked under a canopy of cloth of gold held up by barons and the aristocracy also wore velvets fringed with gold and silver and even the soldiers guarding the routes were gaily dressed in greens and yellows and crimsons.'

'An excellent way to show off the skill of the silk weavers,' said Louis. 'So you are saying that the Catholic King James helped our trade?'

Etienne caught the note of sarcasm in his father's remark.

'King James was not intolerant to us Huguenots, Father, but he was not a popular monarch here and, in truth, since he was ousted by his Protestant daughter and her husband, I cannot deny that we all feel more secure.'

'But the enthusiasm for our silks has continued, you say?'

'Oh indeed,' said Etienne. 'The English aristocracy cannot get enough of the French silks.' He paused for a moment and frowned. 'But to keep up with demand we need to make some changes.'

'What sort of changes?' asked Sara.

Louis passed his hand over his brow. 'Etienne has so many plans that I confess I feel quite fatigued to think on them,' he said. 'Explain to the ladies, my son. But please take care not to bore them senseless.'

Etienne laughed. 'Father pretends he is too old to embrace my ideas,' he said, 'but I do not believe this for one minute!'

Then he lent forward and eagerly addressed the others.

'Several of us master silk weavers have ideas to make the trade run more smoothly,' he said. 'We are making presentations to the city planners for streets of purpose-built houses. Solid, roomy three storey houses built of brick and with an attic garret with windows the length it, where weavers can work with good light.'

Isabella broke in. 'At present, most of the journeymen weavers do their work in their own homes, often in poor light and in cramped and dirty conditions. Etienne and his colleagues want to bring them into the masters' houses and give them space and light.'

'It would mean much time would be saved, too,' said Etienne. 'At present we have to take silks and patterns to them.'

'It sounds a very ambitious plan,' said Sara.

Louis laughed. 'Indeed it is and I applaud you for your vision, Etienne. I sincerely hope that it will become a reality.'

'I am sure of it, Father,' said Etienne.

'I am curious about the English weavers,' said Sara. 'Has there been no jealousy at your success? At the influx of the French bringing all these new skills?'

Etienne stroked his chin. 'Aye, at first there were riots and jealousies, Madame, but as you know, we Huguenots are generous in sharing our knowledge. We do not guard our trade secrets and it is not only the weavers who have benefitted from our success.'

Isabella nodded. 'There are many that depend on the trade such as dyers and the throwers who twist the silk onto spindles and the drawboys who work on the loom alongside the weavers.'

'I see I have much to learn,' said Lidie. 'Samuel,' she began, faltering a little over his name. 'Samuel used to tell me a little of his brother-in-law's business in Montauban but those textiles were very different, I believe.'

Etienne nodded. 'Here our weavers specialize in damasks and other flowered silks and in taffetas and satins as well as brocades.'

'We really only supply to the rich,' said Isabella. 'To those who can afford to pay for such luxuries.'

Etienne nodded. 'My job is to procure orders, to show patterns to my clients for next year's fashions.'

Lidie said nothing but her thoughts flew back to all the people who had helped them in these last turbulent months. To the simple fishermen who had taken them into their homes, to the driver who had risked his life to take them to the coast, and she was overwhelmed by a fierce sense of injustice.

Why should these rich clients be so entitled? Do these wealthy folk give any thought to those who serve them?

It was as if Isabella had read her thoughts. 'We have a comfortable life here, Lidie,' she said, 'But we offer a living to many others.'

Pierre cleared his throat. 'We look after our own, too, Lidie. There are many French Protestants who have come to this country with nothing. They have escaped with their lives but they have only the clothes on their backs and they rely on us to feed and clothe them and help them to find employment.'

There was a sudden quiet in the room. Lidie looked up at Pierre who had moved closer to her and she observed the deep lines in his face.

'I would like to hear more about this charity to poor refugees,' she said quietly. 'Perhaps I can do some small thing to help them, too.'

Sara looked up sharply. 'Do not think on that now Lidie. There is much to do before you can think of involving yourself in other work.'

Lidie heard the fear in Sara's voice and she glanced over at her. She was stooped and her face was pale and lined with fatigue. As she stretched up to tuck a stray lock of hair under her coif, Lidie noticed a tremor in her hand.

'Of course, Mama,' said Lidie, smiling. 'First we must settle. Pierre has said he will find us lodgings and we shall make a cosy household together, shall we not?'

Sara's face lost some of its tension then and she nodded.

'We shall find a nurse for the children,' Lidie continued, 'and we shall all learn the language.'

'We can recommend a good teacher,' said Isabella quickly. 'And a tutor for Elias, too.'

'Well, there you are, Mama. We are surrounded by those who will help us and we shall be settled in no time.'

Just before Pierre left them to go back to his own lodgings, he said quietly to Lidie. 'You will come soon to see Hannah?'

'I will come tomorrow,' she said.

He smiled broadly at her and looked, for a moment, a little more like his old self.

Chapter Thirty-Five

The next morning, Lidie set off with Elias to go to Pierre's lodgings. Sara had announced that she would stay to help mind Esther, but Lidie knew that she was still exhausted and welcomed an excuse to stay at the house.

It had surprised Lidie that Elias had wanted to go with her. At first she had refused him but then, seeing the disappointment in his eyes, she had relented.

Isabella had insisted that Lidie take a servant with them to guide them to Pierre's lodgings and Lidie was glad of it. If she missed the way she would not be able to make herself understood.

Since Lidie had no English and the manservant only a smattering of French, they did not converse, though Lidie smiled at him and made it clear that she was grateful for his presence.

Elias clung to her hand as they walked through the crowded streets, alarmed by the jostling throng and the shouts of hawkers and wheels of hackney cabs as they bowled along, jerking the occupants within and forcing all on foot to make way for them. Lidie kept her eyes on the ground as they walked, lifting up her skirts and carefully stepping over the horse droppings and other filth.

Elias stared at everything, taking it all in. Lidie squeezed his hand. 'Monsieur Gabriac lives near the great river Thames,' she said. 'I wonder if it will be like our river in Castillon.'

Elias didn't answer.

'You were a little babe when Monsieur Gabriac had to leave Castillon,' said Lidie, 'But he baptized you and held you in his arms and gave you his blessing.'

Elias looked up at her. 'I like him,' he said.

Lidie smiled. 'Aye, he is a good and kind man.'

The manservant had picked up on Lidie's remark about the river and he stopped suddenly and pointed. 'The River Thames, Madame,' he said.

Lidie shaded her eyes and stared ahead, but she only caught a glimpse of it in the distance, the morning sun reflecting off the silver gleam of water, and then they turned left down a side street and it was lost to their sight.

'Can we go down to the river?' asked Elias.

'We shall see, Elias. Perhaps on our way back.'

All about them as they walked there was still evidence of the fire of more than twenty years ago. New houses beside old and gaps where there had been dwellings. Lidie pointed this out to Elias.

'A long time ago, before you were born, there was a great fire in the city, Elias, and many houses were burned down around here.'

Elias nodded and asked how much further it was, but almost before he had finished speaking, his question was answered, for the manservant stopped outside a small two storey house squeezed in between two more recent buildings. He knocked on the door and they heard light footsteps crossing the room.

A sullen looking maidservant came to the door and the man with Lidie and Elias spoke to her in English. She nodded then and let them in, indicating that they should walk up the wooden stairs to the next floor.

'It is a sad house,' whispered Elias, and Lidie looked at him and frowned.

How perceptive children are!

She could not but agree with him. There was, indeed an atmosphere of gloom here, not helped by the maidservant's resigned expression as she led the way up the stairs.

Pierre had heard them coming and was at the top to greet them.

'Welcome Lidie,' he said, stretching out his arms, 'And young Elias. How glad I am to see you again. Come in, come in.'

Their manservant hovered uncertainly but Pierre spoke to him in English and he nodded and went back down the stairs. Lidie looked a little alarmed but Pierre smiled at her.

'I have told him that I shall accompany you back to Etienne's house,' he said. 'When you have seen Hannah, I want to take you to some lodgings I think might be suitable for you.'

'Are they near the river?' Elias piped up.

Pierre smiled. 'Quite near,' he said. 'And not far from here.' Then he looked uncertain. 'They may not suit you, Lidie. Your house in Castillon was so large and well appointed, I fear you may be disappointed.'

Lidie laughed. 'If you could have seen some of the places in which we have stayed over these past weeks, Pierre, you would not say that. A roof over our heads is all that we ask.'

Pierre looked relieved. 'Come in,' he said. 'Come and speak to Hannah.'

As soon as Lidie walked into the chamber she could feel the change in the atmosphere. The room was stifling and the only slight movement of air came from their entrance which caused the dust motes to drift down a shaft of sunlight that came through the closed window. Despair seemed to seep into the very walls of the place.

She made herself smile as she walked across the room towards a chair in which Hannah was seated, her face turned away, looking at the wall.

Lidie knelt beside the chair and took her hand. 'Hannah,' she said gently. 'Hannah, it is Lidie.'

At first, Hannah seemed not to recognize her and she made to pull her hand away but Lidie continued to grasp it.

'It is Lidie. From Castillon.'

As Hannah finally turned her head Lidie had to force herself not to recoil. The woman before her was ravaged, all skin and bones, her eyes deep set and staring, and with such an expression of rage and misery.

Lidie could not help herself. 'Hannah, what has happened to you?'

Pierre stepped forward as if to shield Lidie from a violent outburst but instead, Hannah's fierce expression softened and tears squeezed out of her eyes and rolled down her cheeks.

'Lidie,' she whispered. 'Is it you Lidie?'

For answer, Lidie moved closer to her and put her arms round Hannah's frail body, holding her and stroking her back. Beneath her hands every bone was prominent.

Lidie looked over the top of Hannah's head and caught Pierre's eye, seeing in his expression all the strain with which he must live every day.

Lidie stayed beside Hannah, talking to her of things she might remember of her life in Castillon, of the river, the meetings in their old Temple, the market, her house; anything that she felt might stimulate her interest. Occasionally Hannah would respond with a whispered word but mostly she just watched Lidie, her face slack.

Meanwhile, Pierre took Elias to one side and showed him some books and told him a few simple words in the English language. The little boy frowned with concentration copying Pierre and mouthing the unfamiliar words. As Lidie continued to speak softly to Hannah, she could hear them murmuring together.

After some time, Hannah's eyes closed and her head slumped forward. Pierre noticed and broke off from talking to Elias. He came forward and stroked Hannah's head.

'She tires so easily these days,' he said. 'I will call the girl and we will get her into the bedchamber.'

While Pierre and the maidservant were dealing with Hannah, Lidie watched Elias, still absorbed in one of Pierre's books, and smiled.

What a studious little fellow he is. He will be speaking the language long before I have even the smallest grasp of it.

When Hannah was settled, Pierre came back into the room.

'Now Elias,' he said cheerfully, 'Shall I show you and Mama the great river Thames?'

Lidie felt great relief when they left the house and Pierre's expression, too, was lighter. They spoke of inconsequential things as they walked and when they reached the river, Pierre pointed out landmarks to them both.

'See Elias,' there is the great London Bridge down there to the left of us which takes traffic over to the South bank.'

They stared at it and even at a distance, they could see the crowds of carts and carriages and folk on foot, making their way across. There were shops on either side of the bridge and knots of people were making purchases from these, too.

'Did the bridge suffer in the great fire?' asked Lidie.

'Oh yes, indeed. Much of it was destroyed.'

The river was at high tide so a deal of the usual debris and stinking rubbish was under water and with the summer sun shining on it, it seemed very fine.

'So much river traffic,' said Lidie as they stared at the variety of boats going to and fro.

'It is a great thoroughfare,' said Pierre. He put a hand on Elias's shoulders and pointed. A little way away were some steps leading down to the river and a crowd of watermen were gathered there, all jostling for custom. Faintly they could hear the cries of 'oars, oars!' as people walked by.

'See Elias, it is by water that most folk travel through this city. You can hire a waterman to take you across the river or up and down to your destination and there are great ferries and barges taking heavier loads – grain and other goods and even horses and carts. And look over there,' he said, 'Do you see that grand barge going down river? That, I warrant, will belong to one of the Livery Companies or to some wealthy person with a palace on the South side.'

'I thought that our river at Castillon was busy,' said Lidie, 'But this great river is full of every sort of transport imaginable. It is strange that the city authorities do not build more bridges.'

'Ah,' said Pierre, 'That is the opinion of many people, Lidie, but the livery companies are set against it as are the ferrymen and the owners of the great wherries, for they see more bridges as a threat to their business.'

Elias was staring at the great bridge. 'Why are the watermen not going under the bridge?' he asked.

'You are an observant young man,' said Pierre. 'See those narrow arches and piers under the bridge?' Elias nodded solemnly. 'They hold the river back and act as a weir so it is dangerous to take a boat under the bridge when the tide is turning, as it is now, so people disembark at stairs one side of the bridge and take another barge on the other.'

They walked along beside the river for a while and then turned up another street and continued their journey.

'This is some distance from Spitalfields, is it not?' asked Lidie.

Pierre smiled. 'It is confusing, I grant you, Lidie, but no, we are heading North again going towards Spitalfields. And in this next street, we will inspect the lodgings I have found.' He paused. 'Though please do not take them if they are not to your liking. The house is owned by a fellow Huguenot, an honest man, so I can guarantee you will not be cheated, but if they do not suit, there will be others.'

The street they turned into was wider than most they had walked through and made up almost entirely of brick-built houses. They went down the street until they came to a house near to the far end where Pierre stopped and looked at Lidie.

'The whole house is for rent,' he said. 'But it is modest.'

Lidie looked up and down the street. 'It seems different here.'

'It is hard by the street where the great fire started,' said Pierre, taking a large key from his pocket, 'Many of the houses have been rebuilt.'

'And it is close to the river, Mama,' said Elias.

Lidie took Elias's hand. 'Then I am sure it will suit us admirably,' she said.

Although the house was of modest size, the rooms were of pleasing proportions and the place felt light and airy. It was sparsely furnished but there was everything necessary within it and the furniture was solid and well made. Downstairs there was a small reception room and a vestibule with a kitchen off it. A door from the kitchen led onto a small enclosed yard. When they climbed the stairs to the next floor, Elias immediately ran to the window and looked out.

'We can see the river,' he exclaimed, and when he turned back to Lidie and Pierre, there was an animation in his eyes which Lidie had not seen for many weeks.

'There are three bedchambers on this floor,' said Pierre, 'Then two small attic rooms above for servants.'

Elias was already climbing up to the attic and had rushed to a small window in one of the little rooms.

'You can see the river even better here, Mama.'

They followed him up the stairway and squeezed into the chamber under the eaves. Lidie stood at the little window looking

329

over Elias's head and beyond to the river. He was right; there was a splendid view of the Thames from here and she could see both up and downriver for some way.

I can make a home here.

Pierre stood anxiously behind them, stooping somewhat under the sloping roof. 'How do you find this, Lidie? If it does not suit I …'

She turned round and smiled broadly at him. 'My dear man,' she said softly. 'I cannot express my gratitude enough. This is perfect for us and we shall be very happy here.'

'Shall we stay here?' asked Elias, his small face puckered. 'Shall we stay and not go away again?'

'Yes, my darling. We shall stay here and not move. We shall be safe here.'

As she spoke, Pierre was forced to look away and compose himself.

Chapter Thirty-Six

On their way back to Spitalfields, Lidie was already thinking of what was needed for the house and she questioned Pierre relentlessly about where she might obtain the goods she needed.

'Enough,' he said at last. 'I have little knowledge of such things. It was always Hannah who made our home …'

A pained look crossed his face and Lidie immediately ceased her chatter.

'Oh Pierre,' she said. 'How thoughtless I am. And how I remember your cheerful home in Castillon before … before dear Hannah became unwell.'

Pierre stopped and turned to stare back in the direction of his lodgings.

'I cannot reach her,' he said quietly. Then he looked at Lidie. 'Today was the first time I have seen any response from her for a long time.'

Lidie took his arm. 'You have suffered so, Pierre.'

'Not as much as she. But I am at a loss to know what to do for her.'

'When we are in our new lodgings, Mama and I shall visit her often. Perhaps we can cheer her with talk of our common life. Remind her of the Gascon sunshine.'

He nodded. 'I am sure she misses the warmth, as we all do, but I fear she is too damaged. I fear she is beyond help.'

Pierre did not loose Lidie's arm and they walked on together, arm in arm.

'You talk of my suffering, Lidie, but it is of little significance beside your loss.'

She shook her head and looked down at Elias who trotted along beside her 'I have had little time to grieve,' she said quietly. 'These past weeks have been so taken up with fear. My mind is still numb and … and I find I cannot pray in the way I used to do.'

'Many refugees tell me that. But others say that their faith is the only thing that has kept them going.'

'I fear that is true of Mama. She has been so strong since Papa died. But now ...'

'Now she is diminished? I could see that at once.'

'Exactly. Diminished is an appropriate word. It is as if the fight has left her.'

'Perhaps Sara merely needs time to recover from your travails.'

Lidie nodded. There was a moment of silence then she continued. 'I hope we shall be accepted here. It is so different and I know I shall struggle to learn the language.'

Pierre smiled. 'You will have no difficulty making friends, Lidie. You and Sara and the children must come tomorrow to the temple in Threadneedle Street. There will be a great crowd of your countrymen and women there to welcome you and offer advice.'

'Is it far from Spitalfields?'

'Not far at all. An easy walk; and Etienne and Isabella and their family all worship there.'

'I shall much look forward to it.'

Pierre hesitated. 'We could go back that way, if you would like to see it? It is hardly out of our way.'

Lidie glanced down at Elias but he was still walking stoutly beside her.

'I would dearly like that, Pierre, but I do not wish to detain you.' she said.

A little further on they turned into Threadneedle Street. The temple dominated the street and Lidie gasped.

'It is vast, Pierre! What a fine building.'

'Indeed. It is a testament to the faith of its congregation, too. When the original temple was destroyed in the great fire, the temple was entirely rebuilt, funded by those who worshipped here.'

'How unlike our temples in Gascony,' said Lidie. 'All destroyed and with no chance of rising again from the ashes.'

They stood gazing up at the building with its great circular windows set in the top.

'As many as a thousand worshippers can be accommodated within it,' said Pierre.

'I can imagine,' said Lidie.

'And I will be your witness so that you can freely attend our worship.'

Lidie frowned. 'Do Mama and I need a witness?'

Pierre smiled. 'You never abjured, so it is only a formality, but many of our brethren did so and for them we hold a Reconnaissance where they are readmitted into our faith.' He stared up at the temple. 'It can be a very moving event.'

When Lidie and Elias were safely back at the Spitalfields, Lidie questioned Isabella more about the temple.

'Our worship there gives such great comfort to those who have fled from the French king's persecution,' she said. 'We ourselves immediately made many friends there when we first arrived. And you will, too, Lidie.'

'Is the worship conducted in the French language?'

Isabella smiled. 'Indeed it is. You will feel completely at home.'

When the family arrived at the temple the next day, Lidie, Sara, Louis and Elizabeth were quite overwhelmed by the crush of people. Some were simply dressed but there were many others whose attire was very fine.

Lidie took Sara's arm. 'So many beautiful silks, Mama,' she said, as her gaze swept over the congregation, the women dressed in their best to worship, in fashionable dresses, and the menfolk in their embroidered coats, silk waistcoats and fine breeches.

'It is a feast for the eyes, is it not?' she added, looking down at her own attire, that faithful anniversary dress which now seemed dowdy beside this display.

'Indeed,' said Sara, 'Though it is a little overwhelming, this opulence.'

'But the wealth has been earned through hard toil, Mama. Our faith allows us to enjoy it, does it not, when it is so honestly acquired.' Then, when Sara still looked doubtful, she continued. 'Think of all we had in Castillon. Think of your silks and the fine tapestries and the silver and ornaments.'

Sara sighed. 'You are right, Lidie. It is just that these past weeks have made me realize how fleeting are the riches of this world; passing pleasures, that is all.'

Lidie said no more but squeezed her mother's arm, noting how thin and frail it felt and then they both sat to pray and give thanks that they had been safely delivered from danger.

After the service had ended, they could not see Pierre in the crush, but she and Sara were soon swept up by Isabella to be introduced to some of their acquaintances.

They were received with such kindness and questioned with such concern as to their escape, that Lidie feared she would weep in the face of all this goodwill extended to them. She excused herself and turned from the knot of people, chattering in so animated a fashion, and made her way to the front of the temple. As she stood there, trying to compose herself, she felt a touch on her arm.

'You are only recently arrived, Madame?'

Lidie swallowed and turned around. There was an elderly man in front of her, smiling.

'It can be overwhelming, can it not?'

She nodded, not trusting herself to speak and she thought he would move away, but he continued to stand beside her and at length introduced himself as Doctor George Benneville.

'It will pass,' he said quietly, and Lidie looked up at him then.

'All that you are feeling now, Madame. The grief and the guilt at those left behind. It is very common.'

It is as though he has read my mind.

'But you will find new friends here,' he said. 'And you will, in due course, become used to the weather and the city and the habits of the English.'

She smiled. 'I apologise for my weakness, Sir. Everything is so new.'

They spoke for a little while after that and when Lidie told him where she was from, he was immediately alert.

'Castillon,' he cried. 'Then are you acquainted with my colleague, Dr Isaac Verdier?'

'He is my father-in-law!'

Dr Benneville clapped his hands together. 'Then we are well met, Madame Verdier. Tell me news of him for we have often exchanged letters and compared our experiences of treating the sick.'

Lidie was about to speak when she saw Sara advancing, holding Elias by the hand.

'Lidie, we lost sight of you.'

Lidie introduced Sara to Doctor Benneville and they exchanged pleasantries.

'And is Isaac in good health?'

Sara paused. 'As far as we know, Sir, but there has been so much to grieve him and, of course, he can no longer practise his profession since he stoutly refuses to abjure.' She hesitated, then added 'I fear he is in much danger.'

'Aye. It is so cruel. I brought my family out in '81. I could see the way things were going.'

'Are you well established here in London, Sir?' asked Sara.

'Oh yes. There is a large population of French here and I minister to them – and I am much involved with the medical institutions in doing research. It is on that research that Isaac and I corresponded.'

'Would that Isaac had such freedom,' said Sara.

Doctor Benneville frowned. 'Would he not consider coming to this country?'

'I doubt he would ever leave Castillon,' said Sara. 'Though we all fear for him. He is constantly harassed by the Catholics.'

'I admire his constancy,' said the doctor. 'But his life would be made so much easier if he would just …'

He didn't finish his sentence but looked thoughtfully at Sara. 'I wonder if I could call on you and your daughter so that we can speak more of Isaac?'

Sara looked doubtful but Lidie replied. 'With pleasure, sir, but we are not yet settled in our lodgings. We are at present staying with friends.'

The doctor pressed her to inform him further and when he found out where they were staying, he smiled. 'I know the family,' he said. 'I shall make it my business to call on you very soon.'

'I did not like the way in which he pressed his attentions on us,' said Sara, as they made their way through the crowd to re-join Etienne and Isabella.

Lidie frowned. 'He was kind, Mama. He could see how I am overcome with all that has happened and all that is new to me. And he speaks highly of Isaac.'

'But to imply that Isaac might abjure just to make life easier for himself. Did you not find that insulting?'

Lidie looked around her. 'I wonder how many of these good people abjured?'

Sara straightened up and there was something in her carriage and the defiant tilt of her chin that gave a hint of the woman she had been. 'I thank God, Lidie, that we were able to escape to these shores still true to our faith.'

'Aye, and how fortunate that we were to be able to do so, Mama,' said Lidie and there was a sharpness to her tone as she continued. 'Like Uncle Jacob and his family, many here would have faced ruin had they not abjured.' She looked around at the great crowd of people, all chattering in French and enjoying each other's company.

'Pierre told me that the folk who have abjured seek forgiveness from the Elders of the church and return to the true faith as soon as they reached safety.'

'How convenient that they can be so readily forgiven.'

'Well Mama,' said Lidie, sighing. 'You can be happy at least that your own conscience is clear, can you not.'

Sara frowned, hearing the edge in Lidie's voice, and kept silent.

For the next days, Lidie was busy arranging all manner of deliveries to their new lodgings. She consulted Sara in all matters, hoping to keep her mind occupied and, in truth, it did distract her and she seemed to rally somewhat and take an interest.

The day before they were due to move into their new lodgings, Dr Benneville came to call on them.

When he was announced, Sara looked alarmed. 'He is here to obtain news of Isaac, Lidie. To find out his situation and whether he might be tempted to abjure.'

Lidie closed her eyes. All the activity of the last days and the lack of sleep she had experienced with bad dreams about their journey and in comforting Esther who still woke, screaming, at night, had sorely tried her patience.

'Or, Mama, he could merely be coming to pay his respects and to welcome us.'

Sara turned away as George Benneville entered the room.

He was not so finely dressed as when they had met in the temple, but he still cut a prosperous figure as he swept off his hat and bowed to them, revealing a lustrous wig which curled down onto his shoulders.

After he had greeted them and enquired after their new lodgings and their plans for the future, he began to talk of Isaac.

'It saddens me that such a skilled doctor is unable to practise his profession,' he said. 'If only he were here, he could do so much good among our community – and beyond.'

Sara sniffed. 'Isaac has always been more concerned with those who live in poverty. He would be less interested in serving those who are prosperous and well settled.'

There was a brief pause as Lidie looked at her mother, embarrassed by the tone of her voice.

'Madame,' said George. 'As doctors we all took an oath to treat the sick and I assure you that we do much work among those less fortunate than ourselves.'

When Sara did not answer, he went on. 'I very much admire your bravery, Madame, and that you have managed to escape with your faith intact and your reputation as a true Protestant unsullied, but there are many of our compatriots who have come here with nothing – literally, with nothing – and they live here in poverty and loneliness, grieving their lost families and their homeland.'

Lidie broke in. 'Pierre has told me of how the congregation from the temple is helping such folk,' she said.

'Indeed,' said George. 'We try to look after our own, to be sure, but we do not keep to ourselves. It is important that we look outward and serve our new country where we have found shelter and been welcomed.'

'I would not argue with that, sir,' said Lidie.

There was a brief silence and then George said. 'Has Isaac still family in Castillon?'

Lidie looked down. 'His son – my husband - died just before we fled,' she said, quietly, 'And his daughter and her family live in Montauban.'

'Ah, Montauban. That town suffered greatly at the hands of the dragoons. I imagine that his daughter and her family were unable to stay true to their faith?'

Lidie swallowed. 'No, I fear they could not' she said, 'Their household abjured. It was a great sadness to him.'

'Difficult to stay strong in your faith when being so sorely treated,' said the doctor. 'When next I write, I shall earnestly entreat him to consider abjuring himself. His life will become impossible if he does not.'

Lidie did not reply.

'Isaac has a fine mind,' said George. 'We exchanged letters over the years about ways forward in medicine.'

'Indeed, I used to scribe some of them for him,' said Lidie.

'Ah, so yours was the elegant hand who wrote up notes for him?'

Lidie smiled at last and nodded. 'Yes, it was I. Though I confess I could not always follow the meaning.'

The doctor spoke of other things then, promising to help them in any way he could to settle in their new surroundings and to introduce them to his family and others.

When he left, Sara watched his departing back. 'He is worried that Isaac's ability to correspond with him will be curtailed. That is why he is so anxious to persuade him to abjure.'

'I suppose it is possible,' said Lidie.

'Well, if he does so, he will not succeed. There is no circumstance under which Isaac would deny his faith, Lidie, you can be certain of that.'

Lidie frowned and was about to say more in |George Benneville's favour but then, seeing the fury in her Mama's face, forced herself to swallow her comment.

She will always fly to Isaac's defence. She sees him as a model of constancy among those who have abjured. Pray God that he will not become a martyr for his faith.

Chapter Thirty-Seven

London, Spring 1694

Much had changed in Lidie's life since her arrival in London three years' ago. She had formed some friendships among the temple congregation, had established her lodgings to her satisfaction and employed a nurse to help with the children and a maid and a cook. The cook was a fellow French Protestant but both the nurse and the maid were English and spoke no French and it was mostly through them that Lidie learnt the language. Both Elias and Esther were soon chattering in a mixture of both languages, though Lidie always spoke with them in French at home.

Then, in the harsh winter of '93 a double tragedy had struck.

As the winter dragged on, Hannah had developed a persistent cough and lost even more weight and then began spitting blood. Lidie spent much time with her when Pierre's work forced him to be away. She was the only person who Hannah could abide to nurse her and in the last weeks of her life, Lidie hardly left her side, glad that she could give the poor woman some comfort at the end.

Meanwhile, Sara had developed a fever but it was only after Hannah finally slipped away that Lidie realised that her own mama was gravely ill.

She would never forgive herself for this carelessness and though she was there at the end, by this time Sara was delirious and hardly knew her. Doctor Benneville attended Sara and assured Lidie that, even if she had been at her mother's bedside for every moment of her illness, once the fever had taken hold, there was nothing to be done except to wait for it to reach its climax and then it would either begin to abate or the sufferer would die.

In the end, Sara died in Lidie's arms and Pierre was beside them praying for the deliverance of Sara's soul.

It was a solemn time for both Pierre and Lidie and they tried to console one another in their shared grief. Lidie was tortured by guilt that she had not done more for her mama.

If only Isaac had been here, he would have noticed. He was close to Mama, he knew her so well, and he may have prevented it.

Sara had been right about Isaac. Despite George Benneville's letters entreating him to abjure, he had remained steadfast in his decision. He had replied to the good doctor saying that he wished to die in Castillon and he wished to die true to his faith, and though Lidie had news of him thereafter, from letters he sent to George, she knew that she would never see her father-in-law again.

Hannah and Sara had both died in December and, as the winter dragged on, icy cold in December and January, then foggy and wet, Lidie's mood matched the weather.

'God forgive me,' she had said to Pierre when he was visiting one evening, 'I feel so down, so abandoned.'

'Abandoned? By whom?'

'By all those I love, by Mama, by Samuel, by Isaac. Even by God.'

'He will never abandon us, Lidie.'

'Will He not? Oh Pierre, I so envy your strength.'

'My strength! It is you who are strong, Lidie, not I.'

She was sitting in a chair by the fire and he'd come and knelt by her side and taken her hands in his. 'You do not appreciate your strength, Lidie. You have endured so much.'

'Not more than so many others,' said Lidie. 'I know that I should be grateful to be alive, to have two healthy children, but …'

'But it is not enough?'

'It is wicked of me to think like that, is it not? But when I remember the gaiety and the sunshine and warmth of my years growing up in Castillon. The gatherings and the times at our farm with my cousins.'

Pierre had not loosed her hands. 'There will be gaiety in your life again, Lidie. You are still a lovely young woman. The Spring will come and your mood will lift.'

Gently, he'd taken his hands from hers and got to his feet. 'Ask Isabella to take you to inspect the new patterns for next season's silks,' he said. 'And maybe order something new for yourself. Then in the Spring I will take you to visit the family whose children I tutor in King's Square. You will see how lovely it is there and you shall show off your new silks.'

Lidie had laughed. 'For a pastor, you are a persuasive tempter, Pierre, but thank you my friend. You have cheered me.'

She'd risen then and followed him to the door to see him out.

And at the door he'd surprised her by taking her hand up to his lips and kissing it, not briefly, as was usual between them, but at length, turning it palm upwards and kissing it again and then, ramming his hat on his head and wrapping his coat closely round him, he had walked off into the freezing night back towards his lodgings.

***

Now the Spring was here and of a sudden London had shaken off its winter gloom. Pierre had been right. Lidie's mood had lifted and she was pleased that she had, against what she felt was her better judgement, taken his advice and ordered some new silks. As soon as she and Isabella had been to the artist's workshop in Wilkes Street, only a step from Spital Square, Lidie had felt a surge of excitement.

The artist was English and her French was limited, but Isabella was there to help ease the conversation between them. Isabella explained which of the patterns Etienne had commissioned and how long they would take to make up and Lidie spent a truly happy hour poring over what, to her eyes, were truly innovative designs, many of them in floral patterns, in a riot of colours.

Between them they had chosen a charming floral design of pastel colours which, Isabella assured Lidie, would be worked in the softest silk and when Lidie had come to inspect the piece, some weeks later, it was, indeed, perfectly soft and with a glorious sheen, more beautiful than she could have imagined. Isabella had then taken Lidie to her own seamstress and after several fittings, she had finally taken delivery of what she thought the prettiest dress and underskirt she had ever seen.

Oh Mama, if only you could see this. It would give you such pleasure.

341

Lidie had not seen so much of Pierre in recent weeks. His work had kept him busy, much of it outside the city, but he had promised to take her to visit the family in King's Square and he did not renege on that promise. He called in to see her one day to tell her of the time and to ask if it was convenient.

She'd happily agreed and he'd stayed a little while and taken a glass of wine with her. As he left, he said. 'We shall take a hackney carriage.' Then he hesitated. 'Before Hannah became so unwell, a Spring visit to King's Square was one of her few pleasures.'

'Then I hope it will not bring back unhappy memories.'

Pierre had smiled. 'No, indeed, Lidie, I hope it will engender new and happy ones.'

When the day came for their visit, Lidie put on her new silks and both the nurse and the maid exclaimed at their quality. Elias said. 'You look lovely Mama,' and six year old Esther couldn't stop stroking the material so that Lidie was forced at last to reprimand her.

'Stop, Esther! You will mark the fabric!'

'Can I have silks like this?' she asked.

'One day, my darling, one day.'

When Pierre came to collect her, he was momentarily speechless.

'Lidie,' he said. 'You look so lovely. What beautiful silks.'

She frowned. 'I am not overdressed?'

'No, indeed. The English family in King's Square have great admiration for the work of the French silk weavers. They will be enchanted.'

As they settled into the hackney carriage, Lidie put her hand on Pierre's arm. 'I took your advice,' she said. 'It was you who persuaded me to buy new silks.'

'I am so glad you did, Lidie. I ...' He seemed at a loss for words and Lidie, even in the gloom of the carriage interior, could sense that the colour had risen to his cheeks.

And in that moment, Lidie thought back to the winter evening when Pierre had kissed the inside of her hand and she, in turn, blushed a little. She looked across at him and then quickly looked away.

When they arrived at the house in King's Square, the family greeted them warmly. Pierre introduced Lidie as an old friend from France and they spoke among each other in a mixture of French and English. The wife exclaimed at the quality of Lidie's silks and they spoke, too, about the new fashions.

They spent a happy hour or so with the family and then, just as they were leaving, a younger child ran into the room, released from her nurse and flung her arms round Pierre's legs. Laughing, he picked her up and kissed her cheeks.

The little girl pointed at Lidie. 'Your wife is very pretty,' she said.

'Non, ma cherie,'said Pierre, releasing her gently. 'This is not my wife. But she is a very good friend.'

When they left the house Pierre suggested that they take a stroll around the square before returning.

It was a beautiful day, the sky was a cloudless blue and the trees surrounding the large garden were all in Spring leaf, still new and fresh. The air had a chill to it but not enough to prevent them walking through the gardens and breathing in the untainted air.

After a while, they sat down on a bench. 'I do not wonder that Hannah loved coming here,' said Lidie, smoothing down her dress. 'The Spring weather and the fresh air are enough to lift anyone's spirits.'

Pierre was silent for a while and his next words took her by surprise.

'Do I seem very old to you, Lidie?'

She frowned. 'Why no, of course not! You cannot be more than ten years my senior, Pierre. You were still a young man when you fled Castillon.'

He looked up and smiled. 'I fear that life has made an old man of me.'

'Nonsense!' replied Lidie. 'You have many years ahead of you. You speak with such enthusiasm of your work here.'

He nodded. 'Aye. We must both learn to look forward, must we not?'

Lidie sighed. 'I fear I have been bowed down with sorrow and guilt at Mama's death.'

'Your mama would not wish you to feel guilty. He stretched and made to get up from the bench but Lidie put her hand on his arm to stay him.

'Why did you ask me if I found you old,' she asked, smiling up at him.

The silence that followed seemed to quiver with thoughts unexpressed, thoughts that once voiced, could never be unsaid.

Pierre sat down again. 'I feel that I cannot say what is in my heart,' he mumbled, looking down at the ground.

'Come now,' said Lidie gently. 'We have both been through too much to be dishonest with one another.'

Pierre continued to look at his feet.

Lidie put her hands either side of his face, turning his head so that he had to meet her eyes and in that moment she knew, as he put his hands over hers, that what she had felt in her heart for some time was true.

'You are so lovely, Lidie,' he whispered. 'But I am far too old for you.'

'You still feel passion, Pierre,' she said softly. 'I know you do. I can sense it.'

He swallowed. 'Too much, Lidie. Each time I see you I am overcome with it, but it is not right.'

'What? What is not right? Is it not right that because of what has gone before we should not find happiness again? With one another.'

There was genuine shock on his face and he stuttered as he replied. 'But you could not find happiness with me, Lidie. I am a poor pastor and can offer you nothing but my devotion.'

Lidie laughed then. 'What a foolish man you are Pierre! Your devotion is all that I could possibly ask for! Do you think I care for all the trappings of wealth? I know what is important to me and it is your steadfastness that attracts me.'

She could feel that he was trembling. 'Only my steadfastness?'

'No,' she said. 'Surely you know that I find you very attractive in … in other ways.'

344

She was blushing and Pierre laughed out loud with delight. 'You are even more lovely when you blush,' he said.

She continued to look a little discomforted but then she rallied and said briskly. 'Are you asking me to become your wife, Pierre?'

Immediately he leapt to his feet and drew her to him. 'Of course I am. If you will really have me, Lidie.'

For answer she put her lips to his and kissed him, caring not one whit that they were in a public place.

'It has been so long,' he whispered.

'And for me, too,' she said, withdrawing slightly. Adding, with a smile that reminded him suddenly of that young girl in Castillon with all before her, 'Then we shall have to practise a great deal, will we not?!'

'Amen to that,' he said, tucking her hand into his arm.

No-one who knew Pierre well could fail to notice the spring in his step and the constant smile on his face but Lidie had wanted to send word to Isaac, Louise and Jacob before saying anything to her new friends in London, so they had waited a while to announce their plans, even though some had already guessed them.

Isabella was one. 'Forgive my indiscretion, Lidie, she said one day, when she and the children were visiting, 'but do you and Pierre have an understanding?'

Lidie smiled broadly. 'Is it so obvious?'

'A little,' said Isabella. 'At least to me.'

'Then yes, you are right,' said Lidie. 'We wanted our Castillon relations and friends to know of it first, but we intend to marry as soon as possible.'

Isabella embraced her then. 'I am so very happy for you,' she said. 'May I tell my parents in law?'

'Yes, but no one else just yet, I beg you.'

As soon and Elizabeth and Louis heard the news Lidie and Pierre wore bidden to a celebratory meal at Etienne's house and there was such happiness for them around the table.

A few weeks' later, they were married in the Temple in Threadneedle Street in a simple ceremony and many people from the congregation flocked to it to wish them well.

Then, at last, they were alone together. The children were with Isabella, the nurse and maid had gone with the children and the cook had left them a meal to enjoy.

But the meal remained untouched for some hours. As soon as they were over the threshold, Pierre began to unloose Lidie's silks, his fingers trembling, and she was no less eager. She was surprised and delighted at his passion and, indeed, they were both so eager that their first coupling was a little clumsy but later, when their passions were roused again, they explored one another's bodies more slowly, taking their time.

Afterwards, they lay back exhausted, and Lidie stroked Pierre's hair.

'I am so glad you take pleasure in my body, Pierre,' she said softly.

He pulled her to him and kissed her forehead. 'For as long as I live,' he whispered, 'I shall never cease to take pleasure in it.'

Chapter Thirty-Eight

Thereafter

In her renewed state of happiness, Lidie became more aware of the plight of the less fortunate refugees. In the year after her marriage she had helped to set up a soup kitchen at the sign of the Pelican in the Artillery Lane area of Spitalfields and a chambres des hardes, a store of clothing and shoes for refugee families in need.

She was expecting a child, too, and Pierre entreated her to take care of herself.

'Please, my love, do not work so hard. You will become exhausted.'

She understood his mounting anxiety. Hannah's babes had either been stillborn or died soon after birth, so she did, indeed, try to do less but there was always much to be seen to and she had a deal of energy now.

She was brought to term in the Autumn of '95 and delivered of a healthy boy who she and Pierre named after Etienne to thank the silk weaver's family for all their help and friendship.

Elias, at ten years old, was delighted to have a brother, and Esther, at eight, enjoyed being the little nursemaid to him. For several weeks after the birth, Pierre's anxiety was palpable and he fussed constantly until Lidie was forced to reprimand him.

'See what a robust babe he is, Pierre! He is the very picture of health, as am I. If you fret so at his every cry he will become anxious, too.'

Pierre smiled and picked up his son, holding him gently to his chest. 'Forgive me, but I cannot but worry.'

'I know, my love, but you should rejoice. Do not look back on tragedies of the past but rather think of his future – and of ours.'

Pierre began to relax and enjoy being with his little son and during these happy domestic times, he and Lidie discussed what more could be done to help those refugees who were struggling in poverty and ill health.

'There's a pressing need for a school for their children,' said Pierre, looking at Elias who was bent over his books in the corner of the room.

'And an infirmary, too,' suggested Lidie.

Her thoughts turned then to Isaac. She had, that very day, received a letter from him congratulating her on the birth of the baby and asking for news of Elias and Esther. His hand had not improved over the years and she smiled as she pored over the indecipherable scrawl.

I must be one of the few who can make any sense of it!

Other news of Isaac had mostly been received through George Benneville with whom he corresponded regularly on the matter of their common research interests and George told Lidie that he was amazed that Isaac had not been more harassed. Lidie, however, suspected that Isaac did not care to speak of his personal plight.

However, his letter to Lidie was different. A deeply personal letter. It spoke of the sad little Huguenot community left in Castillon which had, through necessity, largely become New Converts. Most of these were now too fearful to gather together in secret to worship in the way they wished and trooped regularly to Mass where they were constantly under surveillance by the priests to make sure they worshipped in a seemly manner.

Isaac also touched on his own growing infirmities. Lidie was surprised that he made no mention of Louise and Jacob and this set her to worrying whether something had befallen them. She resolved to write to them directly, since she'd heard nothing from them since the birth of her baby.

Lidie could sense Isaac's loneliness and how much he missed his family and how he grieved at the news of Sara's death. He spoke also, in guarded terms, of new waves of persecution in Gascony where the Protestant faith had been showing signs of resurgence, of informers and arrests, of houses razed to the ground and children torn from their parents, but also of the growing congregation of Huguenots in the Cevennes area, 'The Church of the Desert'.

The seal on the letter had not been broken but Lidie knew that he would have written more of this if he had been secure in the knowledge that if would not be read by Catholic spies. Though his name brought back painful memories, she wondered at the bravery of the pastor and lawyer, Claude Brousson, who it seemed, continued to celebrate the Lord's Supper to the faithful in the wild terrain of the Cevennes, often attracting huge crowds.

Before she had time to write to her aunt and uncle in Castillon, she received communication from her cousin Cécile, giving news of her own growing family and telling her that her brothers were now fully in charge of Jacob's business interests, but, again, there was no mention of Jacob and Louise.

Lidie shared this information with Pierre.

'It is strange that she doesn't say whether they are in good health.'

Pierre frowned. 'Surely she would have told you if something was amiss? I beg you not to worry.'

'But to have no mention of my aunt and uncle,' she said. 'And Isaac's life sounds so closed up and dreary now. He must be one of the very few who has not succumbed and converted.' She sighed. 'Whatever happens, he will remain steadfast but I am fearful for him.'

It was not many weeks later that Lidie discovered the reason why Cécile had said nothing of her parents when she wrote.

It was because they were no longer in Castillon.

ROSEMARY HAYES

Castillon

For months, Jacob had gradually been withdrawing from his business, saying to anyone who expressed surprise, that he was getting old and tired and wished to hand over to the next generation. That was the story which he put out to anyone who asked, particularly the Catholic priests who kept a close eye on his movements. And it was true, as far as it went; he had been making meticulous arrangements for the management of his assets but there was another reason that he and Louise were retiring and no one, except their close family, knew of it.

He did not confide in his family until he had made all the arrangements. Arrangements fraught with danger.

'Papa!' said Cécile, when she heard. 'How can you go? How can you bear to leave us?'

Jacob could not meet her eyes. 'It is a huge sacrifice, my darling girl,' he said. 'And your mama and I have not taken this decision lightly, believe me.'

'I know your faith means much to you both,' said Cécile. 'But you abjured so that you could continue your business and continue to live in comfort. Why change everything now? Why take such a risk when you are no longer young?'

Louise had interrupted, moving closer to Jacob. 'It is precisely *because* we are no longer young,' she said quietly.

'What do you mean?'

'We want to return to the true faith before we die,' said Jacob.

'Does your faith really mean so much to you, Papa? More than your own flesh and blood?'

Louise got to her feet then and when she spoke there was an anger in her voice that astonished Cécile.

'Your generation may have thought little of turning to the Catholics,' she said, her eyes hard, 'But believe me, Cécile, the day that your papa signed those abjuration papers was the unhappiest day of our lives and we have wrestled daily with our consciences ever since. It is our dearest wish to be able to return to our own true faith.'

350

'And to do that you will have to flee the country.'

'There is no alternative.'

'And face capture?'

'Aye. And to face possible capture.'

'It is madness! What if you should die?'

'If we die,' said Jacob, 'Then so be it. And we shall pray that the Good Lord, in His mercy, will see into our hearts and know that we died in an attempt to return to His true Word.'

Cécile raised her eyes to the ceiling. She swallowed and her voice faltered. 'When do you plan to leave,' she said.

'As soon as we deem it safe,' said Jacob quietly. 'There are rumours that there will soon be a new declaration and that the ban on emigration by New Converts will be more strictly enforced. We hope to leave the realm before then.'

'Will you tell me …?'

Louise shook her head. 'We shall tell no one,' she said and then, seeing the shock on Cécile's face, added. 'It will be better that way.'

For a long moment they looked at each other. Then Cécile stumbled out of the room, her shoulders shaking. Louise ran after her and put her arms round her.

'I am sorry, my darling. But I must ask you to keep this to yourself. Promise me you will say nothing to anyone of our plans?'

'Not even my husband?'

'Not even your husband.'

Louise and Jacob did, however, confide in one person outside their close family, about their intentions.

They went to visit Isaac one summer's evening. It was some months since they had seen him as he tried not to draw attention to himself in such difficult times. Their carriage drew up outside his house and they alighted but could see no sign of life and when they raised the knocker and banged loudly on the front door, no one came to greet them.

Louise looked around at the tangle of weeds and overgrown shrubs in the garden.

'He has let the place go wild,' she said.

Jacob shrugged. 'Folk will be afraid to work for him no doubt,' he said.

As they stood there, uncertain whether to go and explore the back of the house, an old man came limping round from the stables. Seeing them, he drew back fearfully and seemed about to scuttle back from whence he came, but Louise recognised him.

'Adam!' she said, going forward to greet him.

He hesitated then, frowning. 'Madame?'

Louise was closer to him now and his face broke into a smile. 'Forgive me Madame,' he said. 'My eyes … I did not realise …'

'Is Dr Verdier at home?' she asked.

Adam nodded. 'I am sure he will see you, Madame, but you understand, he has to be so careful. The priests … he lives the life of a hermit these days, hiding from the Catholics, alone with his books. He hardly ventures out.'

'But you are still faithful to him, Adam.'

'I owe him my life Madame. I could never desert him.'

'How can it have come to this?' said Louise. 'And what of your son and daughter?'

'They both abjured, Madame,' said Adam. 'And the doctor found work for them with some New Converts.'

When, finally, they found Isaac, at work in his herb garden, they were shocked at the change in him. He was stooped and very thin and his hair was grey and wispy, but he stopped what he was doing and invited them into the house.

'I fear we live in much reduced circumstances,' he said, gesturing to some chairs clustered round the fireplace in the reception room. 'Please take a seat and I will find you some refreshment.'

'No, old friend, please don't inconvenience yourself,' said Jacob. 'We have only come to say farewell.'

Isaac looked up. 'Farewell? You are leaving?'

'With God's help, we shall sail to England very soon,' said Jacob quietly. Only our close family knows of our intention, but we wanted you to know. You who have been so steadfast in your faith.'

Isaac took his hand. 'Then I shall wish you God speed,' he said. 'And I will pray daily for your safe passage.'

'We need not ask that you say nothing to a living soul about our plans?'

Isaac smiled. 'I hardly see a living soul,' he said.

'Then the priests are not hounding you in the way they did?'

'For the moment they seem to have stopped.' He put a hand through his thinning hair. 'I think that even they don't see me as much of a threat these days. Mercifully they seem to have forgotten me for the time being. But they may return with their threats and enticements at any time.'

'Oh Isaac,' said Louise. 'Beside you we feel so weak.'

'I cannot blame you for abjuring, my dear Louise. It is just that I could not bring myself to do so.'

'Say that you forgive us, Isaac.'

Isaac took her hand. 'Of course. But forgiveness is in the Lord's hands, not mine, and He will look kindly on your courage. For it is courageous to try and flee at any time. And especially now and when you are no longer young.'

Jacob nodded. 'Indeed, it is a great risk but we have laid our plans carefully and fortunately I still have many friends among the sea going community. We shall have to trust that none of these will give us away.'

Not long after this, they parted. Isaac clasped Louise to him, and she felt the frailty in him. Then he kissed Jacob on both cheeks.

'We shall not meet again in this world, my dear friends,' he said, 'But with God's grace we shall be reunited in the next.'

When they were in the carriage Louise and Jacob looked back at Isaac, old and frail now, standing at his door, hand raised in farewell.

When he was lost to sight, Louise said. 'I fear so for him.'

'Aye,' said Jacob. 'Pray God that he will die unmolested and be buried with dignity.'

Louise nodded. 'There are such fearful stories of the bodies of the unconverted being dragged through the streets and flung to rot on the town dung heap.' She shuddered and Jacob reached over and took her hand.

Once their carriage was out of sight, Isaac walked slowly back into his house and stood for a long time gazing at the portrait of his wife.

THE KING'S COMMAND

London

Jacob and Louise sought out Lidie and Pierre immediately they arrived in London and although their reunion was initially joyous, Lidie was shocked by their appearance. They were old before their time and it was as if the life had been sucked from them by all they had endured during the intervening years.

Their passage had passed almost without incident. Jacob was a well known figure at the port of Bordeaux and he was often to be seen, in the company of his sons, introducing them to the intricacies of his business, inspecting shipments, speaking with sea captains and overseeing loading. In the weeks before their flight, Louise had often joined him there, so the King's soldiers were used to their presence at the docks and it was not registered that, one day, he and Louise failed to disembark from one of the ships when it set sail.

Almost their first action was to seek to rejoin the Protestant faith and Pierre arranged a Reconnaissance for them, though, in Louise particularly, Lidie could feel the sense of guilt and shame which hung over them.

They settled in Hammersmith, a rural settlement outside the city where there was a community of French Protestants and a small church at which Pierre, on occasion, ministered. When she could, Lidie visited them and they reminisced of happier times in Castillon.

'Oh Lidie,' said Louise one day, soon after they had arrived. 'I still feel guilt about our abjuration. Sara was stronger and braver.

'She was not put to the test, Aunt Louise, and nor was I. For sure, we were in danger when we fled, but so were you.'

Louise nodded and Lidie noticed how she constantly fiddled with her hands, stroking the fabric of her dress or feeling at her neck.

She is so restless. So unlike the old Aunt Louise who was so confident and capable.

Lidie asked after Cécile and the boys and their families, and she saw that Louise could hardly hold back the tears.

'It was such a harsh decision, Lidie, to leave our family, but in truth I understand now that their faith has never meant as much to them as it means to me and Jacob and we both found it so hard to watch them attending Mass without a care.'

She raised her eyes to Lidie. 'I am still burdened with guilt at our actions. Each time we attended mass or bent the knee, I was sick at heart, as was Jacob. During these past years our consciences have been deeply troubled and I thank God that we are able to worship according to His Word again.'

'It must have been veryhard to leave.'

'Harder than you can know, Lidie, and I miss my family every hour of every day. But I do not miss the place that Castillon has become – the fear of discovery if one but prays in one's own home, the spying, the unease. Our little Reformed community had shrunk to nothing and there was such suspicion everywhere.'

She put her hands to her throat again and then up to fiddle with her coif.

Lidie went to her and put her aunt's hands in her own to still them.

'You have only just arrived here,' she said. 'You will find so many with whom you have much in common. We have such joyful worship at the temple and there are many folk who are true Calvinists but who abjured through fearful necessity, as did you and Uncle Jacob. Do not distress yourself.'

Louise nodded. 'Aye. This small church here in Hammersmith has been very welcoming to us already and not judged us. Oh Lidie …'

She began to weep then, her shoulders shaking, and Lidie held her close until her crying ceased. She sniffed and unloosed herself.

'I must learn to look forward and not constantly think on what we have left behind,' she said, wiping her eyes. Then she sat a little straighter. 'You and Pierre are such a comfort to me. I would not have had the courage to come here had I not known you would be here to welcome us. And it is a joy to see your children, too. Elias growing so fast and little Esther becoming so pretty and such a chatterbox. And as for that babe, Etienne …'

Lidie smiled. 'It was indeed a blessing that I was able to give Pierre the child he had wanted for so long.

'I miss my grandchildren above all others,' said Louise. 'They will grow up without knowing us.'

Lidie patted her hand. 'Perhaps the time will come when Cécile and the boys and their families are free to travel. And for now they will rejoice for you and Jacob. Surely they will be glad that you have found peace in your souls at last?'

'I hope so,' said Louise softly. 'Although they were not happy with our decision, I think they understand.'

'And Isaac?' asked Lidie.

'He has a generous spirit. When we bade him farewell he never condemned us for our actions. He is sick and frail now, Lidie, and deserting him was almost worse than deserting our own flesh and blood.'

It was not long after this that Cécile wrote to tell them of Isaac's death.

He had died of natural causes. And he had been, to the end of his life, constant and true to his faith. Not being permitted burial by the authorities, he was laid to rest in secret in a corner of his orchard, with no marker for his grave, to ensure his corpse would remain undisturbed.

During the next few years, Louise and Jacob settled well into their new life and Pierre and Lidie did all they could to help them, drawing them close into their family circle. The children thrived and, under Pierre's tuition, Elias became quite the scholar.

'He has a real interest in the bible, Lidie,' said Pierre, one day. 'And an aptitude for learning.'

'Nurtured by you,' she replied.

'Aye, perhaps. But it is within him and that cannot be taught.'

Towards the end of 1698, Pierre received news of the death of the Pastor and Lawyer, Claude Brousson. He had been pursued by Catholic soldiers for years under the instruction of the Intendant of the Langedoc, Baville, but had always managed to evade capture, hiding out in caves and rough huts in the wild country of the Cevenne. However, he was eventually hunted down and tried in Montpellier.

Pierre held up the letter he had received. 'It makes my heart bleed to hear of it,' he said. 'The trial was a mockery, presided over by Baville, yet from what they say, Brousson spoke calmly and clearly, upholding his faith and saying that he feared only God who had called him to return to France to console his unhappy brethren.'

'But yet he was condemned?' said Lidie.

Pierre nodded. 'Yet, through his courage and calmness, it seems he influenced even the most hard hearted.'

'How so?'

Pierre consulted the letter once more. 'He was sentenced to be tortured upon the rack, then to be broken upon the wheel, and then to be hanged.'

Lidie shuddered. 'Such cruelty.'

'But it seems,' said Pierre, 'That Baville's conscience was smitten at the last moment and he changed the sentence and ordered that Brousson should be made to see the rack only, and then should be hanged and that afterwards his lifeless body should be broken on the wheel.'

'Some form of mercy, I suppose.'

Pierre went on reading. 'Apparently, Brousson tried to speak to the people from the scaffold but a roll of drums silenced him so he prayed fervently, then rose from his knees and presented himself, smiling, to the executioner, who was so unnerved that he could hardly perform his work.'

'Then Brousson truly was the bravest of men,' said Lidie. 'Perhaps I can understand now why Samuel so admired him.'

'Indeed. And here my correspondent quotes words from the executioner and one of the judges. The executioner said "I have executed above two hundred condemned persons, but none ever made me tremble as did Monsieur de Brousson."'

Pierre consulted the letter once more. 'And from the judge: "I should have fled away rather than have put to death such an honest man. I could, if I dared, speak much about him – certainly he died like a saint."'

THE KING'S COMMAND

Many of the Protestant company in London were greatly saddened by the news of Brousson's death and prayers were said in the French churches for the repose of his soul.

As Lidie's children grew, they spoke English as easily as French which helped her to become integrated into the English way of life. Also, many of her Huguenot friends were engaged in trade in the city where French-made goods were much admired for their workmanship. Through these friends, Lidie became acquainted with English families and she soon spoke the language fluently.

She noted, too, how the Huguenot artisans were generous in passing on their skills to their English colleagues, thus forestalling any resentment. For this they were both admired and made welcome, soon becoming absorbed into their adopted country.

As the years went by, Elias, to no one's surprise, became a pastor. To Lidie's dismay, he accepted a living at a Church of England parish in Lincolnshire, so that she seldom saw him but she rejoiced that he was happy there. In due course he wrote to say that he had met a fellow French refugee, from Normandy, and that they were to be married.

Esther, meanwhile, much to Lidie's amusement, became quite the lady of fashion, and married into the English aristocracy. She and her husband lived in London and Lidie was able to indulge her own passion for silks, encouraged by Esther, as they both embraced the changing fashions, particularly for the new Bizarre silks which were so different from designs which had gone before.

Young Etienne was a joy to his parents with his easy, loving nature and his happy demeanour. And nobody could have guessed that he would grow up to become a famous portrait painter.

After Pierre died, Lidie was supported by both Esther and Etienne and, in her last days, Elias, too, made the journey from Lincolnshire to be at her side.

Just before she took her final breath, she raised her eyes to gaze at the portraits of Samuel and of her father, hanging on the opposite wall.

Leaning in close, her children caught her whispered words. 'Grant me a place with them Lord.'

And at that very moment, Susanne, in a far away country, awoke suddenly from a vivid dream. She heaved herself from her bed and walked slowly to the window where the dawn was breaking over a landscape very different from that of her native Gascony.

Why should you come into my dreams now, Mistress Lidie, when so many years have passed?

She reached for a blanket and put it round her shoulders then lowered herself stiffly into a chair. She touched the scar which ran down the side of her face.

Did you ever think of me, Mistress, after we parted, and wonder what befell me?

THE KING'S COMMAND

Historical Note

The Edict of Nantes was signed in April 1598 by King Henry IV of France and granted the Calvinist Protestants of France, also known as Reformists or Huguenots, substantial rights in the nation, which was predominantly Catholic. The Edict opened a way forward for secularism and tolerance and brought to an end the French Wars of Religion which had been raging in France during the second half of the 16th century.

However, this new tolerance and freedom came at a price. Huguenots could no longer bear arms and Cardinal Richelieu, the most powerful minister during the reign of Henry's successor, Louis XIII, ordered that the walls of Huguenot strongholds be destroyed.

Then, in the reign of Louis XIV, Huguenots' rights were systematically eroded. The King had declared his intention to make of France 'One country, One religion, One King' and in 1685 the Edict of Nantes was revoked. Huguenots could no longer practise their professions or trades, own land, travel abroad or hold any kind of religious service. Pastors were commanded to leave the country within two weeks of the Revocation or face death. The consequences for flouting these rules were dire; Huguenot men were either executed or sent to row in the galleys in the Mediterranean (a death sentence) women were imprisoned, girls sent to nunneries and boys to Catholic schools.

Anticipating what was to come, many Huguenots had already left France. Many others converted to Catholicism at the time of the Revocation, but some held out or fled the country, risking severe punishment if they were caught.

The persecution of the Huguenots meant that France lost many of its most talented citizens, including doctors and lawyers, minor nobles and skilled artisans, all of whom enriched the Protestant countries to which they fled.

'The King's Command' follows, very loosely, the experiences of my own ancestors, doctors and lawyers, who lived in and around

361

the small Gascon town of Castillon sur Dordogne (now called Castillon- la- Bataille) and arrived in London in 1692.

THE KING'S COMMAND

Acknowledgements

Heartfelt thanks to Elizabeth Randall and Sandra Robinson, the two Huguenot scholars who have advised me on the historical background to 'The King's Command'. Any historical inaccuracies in the book are entirely of my own making.

Rosemary Hayes www.rosemaryhayes.co.uk
Cambridge 2023

Printed in Great Britain
by Amazon

28499144R00209